THIS *IS* YOUR CAPTAIN *SPEAKING*

JON METHVEN

SIMON & SCHUSTER PAPERBACKS

New York   London   Toronto   Sydney   New Delhi

Simon & Schuster Paperbacks
A Division of Simon & Schuster, Inc.
1230 Avenue of the Americas
New York, NY 10020

First Simon & Schuster trade paperback edition June 2012

SIMON & SCHUSTER PAPERBACKS and colophon
are registered trademarks of Simon & Schuster, Inc.

For information about special discounts for bulk purchases,
please contact Simon & Schuster Special Sales at 1-866-506-1949
or business@simonandschuster.com.

The Simon & Schuster Speakers Bureau can bring authors
to your live event. For more information or to book an event
contact the Simon & Schuster Speakers Bureau at 1-866-248-3049
or visit our web site at www.simonspeakers.com.

Design by Esther Paradelo

Manufactured in the United States of America

10 9 8 7 6 5 4 3 2 1

Library of Congress Cataloging-in-Publication Data
  Methven, Jon.
  This is your captain speaking / Jon Methven. — 1st Simon & Schuster
trade paperback ed.
   p.   cm.
  1. Aircraft accidents—Fiction. 2. Airlines—Fiction.
3. Public relations—Fiction. I. Title.
  PS3613.E885T48   2012
  813'.6—dc22   2011029185

ISBN 978-1-4516-4215-5
ISBN 978-1-4516-4217-9 (ebook)

For my family

The postman wants an autograph.
The cab driver wants a picture.
The waitress wants a handshake.
Everyone wants a piece of you.

—JOHN LENNON

TAKE THESE BROKEN WINGS
AND LEARN TO FLY

Air Wanderlust Flight 2921 crested the skyline that separated New York City from the heavens then banked a soft right into a raspberry sun. It climbed against an insatiable gravity and skipped toward an archipelago of pinkish clouds, a flat stone across a blessed sea. The captain tipped a left wing to the drifting metropolis. The passengers on that side, first class and coach and the man who had snuck on standby, lifted their chins toward the city, apex of human ingenuity, and snapped pictures on their cellular phones despite having been told to holster them until landing. Passengers blind to the city squinted in the other direction at the almighty orb, celestial and stunning off the eastern wing, and they pointed devices at the wistful sun warming and lighting the earth, and tugging it about the universe.

They were a gorgeous cargo, more attractive than the average flight, which made the morning ascent pleasant. Peaceful, syrupy, with the passengers content to know they would have their breakfast once the plane reached 30,000 feet. They would sip coffee and watch television monitors attached to the seats in front of them, and bask in the understanding that they were part of a connected and well-informed citizenry, everything as it should be, healthy plumes erupting from the plane's gills.

Then a startling explosion. It stuttered the plane; several passengers gasped and the man in Seat 26F hid his cell phone beneath his leg—as if his attempt at sending a sunrise photograph back to earthlings had somehow interfered with the mechanics. The captain overhead, "Ladies and gent—", but that was all he got out before a second explosion choked the other engine.

Silence; 160,000 pounds of metal and fuel floating on a cool breeze; everyone waiting for the conclusive boom. In the cockpit a mad dash of knobs as some knucklehead at LaGuardia inquired what sort of mess they found themselves in that Monday morning.

"Twenty-nine-twenty-one this is control trouble reading."

"Bird strike bird brain," the captain said. "Lost thrust in both engines. Turning back home, hoss."

"Copy that." A long pause, copilots shuffling through the engine restart manual. "Twenty-nine-twenty-one take runway one-six. That's one-six."

"One-six. Copy." And then, "Can't do it. We'll be in . . ."

"Say again."

"We'll be in the Hudson." He picked up the cabin radio. "This is Captain Hank Swagger." It had been only seventeen seconds since his last dispatch, but to the flock behind him the silence seemed eternal. "Brace for impact, folks."

They did their best bracing, which mostly involved squealing, fervent prayer, eyes hidden so they would not catch the gory parts. They spoke to God, to their fellow passengers, remnants of internal dialogue that were shouted tenderly:

Woman, Seat 17C: "HailMaryfullofgracetheLordiswiththee-blessed . . ."

Elderly man, Seat 19D: "Terrorists! What'd I tell you? Terrorists!"

"Just my luck," came a man with a FRANK RIP tattoo on his forearm, Seat 50B, forehead against Seat 49B: "Just my fucking luck."

Second Officer, cockpit: "I'm feeling odd."

Flight attendant: "Just like we practiced, just like we practiced."

Man, Seat 22E: "I see smoke! Everyone, smoke!"

Teenager, Seat 23A: "Of course there's smoke. We're crashing, dipshit."

Undercover sky marshal, Seat 9A, a giant man filling in a Sudoku puzzle.

"Screw it," said a woman with a burlap sack covering her left arm past the elbow, Seat 3B. "Might as well bury me with it."

And then an epic plummet as the plane's innards responded to the massive nothingness emanating from the engines. Captain Swagger banked the metal lug a hard left until it hung 7,000 feet over the Bronx, a patchwork of green and mostly brown twisting there in the basement for anyone with the mettle to glance. The trick was not in the landing. With gravity's counsel, planes always landed, just not in ideal locations. No, the trick was to steer an un-powered Airbus into the water without striking bridges or toppling buildings.

"What do we got?" Swagger asked the copilots. Over the bridge, the water coming to meet them, the copilots remained intrigued with the restart manual, not quite set on the captain's decision to baptize them in the Hudson and hoping for miraculous elevation. They shrugged collectively. "Come on, fellas, just say anything."

First Officer David Miles turned to Second Officer Peter Wrinkles; Wrinkles seized violently, slumping sideways in his seat.

"Uh, Captain?"

"Quickly Miles!"

"Wrinkles, sir. I think he's dead."

Captain Swagger glanced sideways. "Wrinkles, knock that off!"

First Officer Miles shoved into the unconscious man's shoulder. "He's not waking up, sir."

"Stay with me, Wrinkles!" Swagger glared into the control panel. "All right, you sonofabitch, one more time."

The aircraft cleared the George Washington Bridge at 4,400 feet and Swagger steered it toward the center of the river, narrower and rougher than he had anticipated. The white folds suggested one- to two-foot swells; he had been counting on a slick, black mirror, and was impatient with the wind for being such a bastard on a Monday morning. There was little congestion in the way of ferries and tugboats, no cruise ships, floating cities that would have pro-vided a wily game of chicken. He guided the avalanche gently. The center was where he wanted to be and he opened up a smooth path as he dropped elevation, the metropolis gliding past his left. There were no boats in his eye line as he settled on a patch a quarter-mile ahead. The sun had crested the city skyline, and the bright shaft of light across the dark water shone like a satin carpet. Second Officer Wrinkles groaned.

"Attaboy!" the captain encouraged.

It occurred to the passengers just before they ditched—a

simultaneous occurrence, one they failed to discuss aloud, the colossal trepidation of all congealing into a single, phantom thought—and it went something like this: That in all those buildings tearing past, in all those square windows and lofty verandas where the smokers of the world had been segregated, how many dozens of hundreds of people at that very instant were pulling out cameras and cell phones and e-mailing and texting and tweeting and abusing other communication technologies that may have been invented in the three minutes since Flight AW2921 departed LaGuardia—and were homing in on the steel thunder just outside their dwelling? How many would enjoy their morning cup while gathered around the office television, watching police boats pull fuselage and severed limbs from the tainted drink, whispering *awful, just awful* to one another, unable to look away from the morning intrigue? They would be the evening news, the YouTube sensation of the week, and somewhere on dry land someone would get the clever idea of building a memorial and stocking it with fresh flowers on the anniversary two, three, twelve years in a row before that got tiresome and the city parks department would argue with the city highway department as to whose responsibility it was to weedwhack around it. How sad that their last thoughts, as they drifted adjacent to the morning sunrise, were not of family, love, better days spent, but of infamy, a complex and surreal infamy?

Three hundred feet and Captain Swagger lifted his chin now, cracking the bones in his hot neck. When the plane hit water it bounced for an instant before transforming into a pillowy plow, displacing thousands of gallons that resulted in a dwarfed and nearly touchable rainbow just outside the cabin windshield. There were shrieks from the rear followed by a marvelous *whoooaaaahhhhh* as the plane caught mysterious elevation then more water then more air then *sploosh!* It sank instantly, emerged, sank some more, an indecisive buoyancy. A moment later it popped like a fishing bobber to a roaring applause. Then Flight AW2921 floated to the surface, reflecting a gleaming city off its wet bow.

And so erupts our story, passengers, a piece of Americana— a bona fide miracle, a state-of-the-art, one-of-a-kind halle-fuckinglujah. As the plane sinks and the helicopters scurry; as the rescue boats embark and those with the wherewithal grope for the exits— we pause momentarily and call your attention to the puffy white contrails, forgotten and distant across the morning descent, where the jet exhaust and humidity combine into violent bursts blossoming in the morning blue. From the ground we have always admired those tortured tails as another anxious tribe sets sail on a new adventure. We like to believe they are the exhaust of the passengers' dreams and heroes and hopes and miracles and faiths and secrets, all distilled through gravity's filter, pushed back where they belong toward this Earth of ours, happily littering our heavens. We could stare at those fresh crests of fuel excrement all day, wondering reverently on their meaning. But some lady in 19 busted her ankle. And Second Officer Wrinkles's heart is attacking him on the cockpit floor. And Captain Swagger must rescue 162 people in the next seventeen minutes to clinch this miracle.

Cue Monday morning.

MONDAY

GOOD DAY SUNSHINE

SEAT: Cockpit
PASSENGER: Captain Henry Theodore Swagger
REASON FOR FLIGHT: Pilot
LAST THOUGHTS BEFORE IMPACT: *I think we killed Wrinkles.*

An elderly woman with a busted ankle lay abandoned in the aisle between Rows 19 and 20, philosophically puffing away on a cigarette, leering at the commotion. She complained she would not be able to swim ashore, which made the other passengers shake their sweaty heads. It was rude, frankly, to split hairs over trivial grievances so soon after the gods had delivered them from their hellish plummet. Not to mention the cigarette, the secondhand smoke, and in the middle of a catastrophe no less. This was a nonsmoking flight, a nonsmoking world really, how could she be so brazen as to request assistance? Many pretended not to hear, stumbling over her to keep up with the orderly assembly exiting the plane. Someone toward the front kept calling for efficiency; to stop and assist a complaining passenger would upset the evacuation's feng shui.

A rumor spread that they were collecting cellular devices at the front, which caused a panicked reshuffling of priorities, survival or cell phone? Who was this *they* collecting them? What was the reason? It did not make any damned sense, especially at such a time. The windows perspired and water leaked in through the exits until it reached ankles and made escape all the more pressing. Flight attendants moved in synchronicity, as though they had just touched down in their actual destination of Los Angeles and at any moment passengers would start thanking them for the lovely in-flight service.

Many passengers were bruised and several seemed not yet to understand that they were survivors. Instead it seemed death had transported them into a similar dimension where they still existed but would be expected to find dry shoes and new jobs and fresh identities and apparently new cellular devices, an inconvenient rebirth of sorts.

"Calm and steady," the captain called out over the mess as he exited the cockpit. No one was calm or steady, everyone breathing heavy and hugging strangers and searching the ground for wet luggage. "That's right, folks. Everyone calm and steady so I can count heads."

"Captain!" cried the woman with the bruised ankle. The two strangers hoisting her had become do-gooders when the momentum of the line stalled just as they reached her, the still-lit cigarette aglow. They were disgusted with their predicament since everyone else had an evolutionary advantage of reaching safety without a broken old woman to cart around. The woman with the burlap sack covering her left arm was helping the complainer with her jacket. She seemed to be frisking the needy smoker with her good hand, ensuring she was not lying about the damaged ankle. "My ankle, Captain, I need help."

"You're okay, ma'am. These men will get you to the wing."

"But my leg," she complained.

"You're alive," the woman with the sack reminded her.

"That's right," the captain said. "We're all alive. So far."

"A puppy, Captain." She took a drag, blew it into the chin of one of her rescuers. "I snuck little Jeters on board. I knew I shouldn't have, but it was a gift for my granddaughter."

"It's okay," the captain said. "I'll get the pup."

"What about me? How will I swim with my leg?"

"We could leave you," one of the men suggested. "Send a boat when we get to shore."

"Onward gentlemen," the captain said sternly. Then he rubbed a hand through the woman's silver hair as though practicing how he planned to greet the contraband puppy. A moment later he retreated into the cockpit, whispering to the undercover sky marshal, and popping a young woman on the bottom before slamming the door.

The young woman he popped was not dressed as an airline employee. She was stationed at the exit collecting cell phones. If passengers wanted out, they had to place their phones into a black bag. The undercover sky marshal, a gargantuan man, enforced the edict, issuing glares to anyone who seemed on the verge of disobeying.

"I'm sorry," the girl said every time someone dropped a phone into her bag. In her early thirties with rectangular glasses too big for her Mediterranean face, she was anxious from the circumstances. "Federal regulations. During a crash landing, we have to confiscate all recording devices. We'll return them this afternoon." When the female passenger with the burlap sack around her arm reached the front, the woman collecting phones straightened. "Federal regulations," she repeated.

The passenger was an exact replica of the actress Sandra Bullock, only with long, black hair, and taller, and her brow was crunched into a frown. Her left arm was tied up in the brown sack with rope that fastened around the far side of her neck. She studied the cockpit where the captain had disappeared, and the remaining passengers, and even the passengers already on the wing. There was tortured laughter from inside the cockpit; the woman leaned to hear.

"Ma'am, your phone."

"I saw legs," she said. "Was someone hurt in the cockpit?"

"You're upset. Nothing to concern you."

"Why are they laughing if someone was hurt?"

"Just nervous laughter," the sky marshal interrupted.

"Would you mind if I looked inside?"

"What do you want inside the cockpit, ma'am?"

"Can't put my finger on it." She motioned at the closed door.

"We've crashed is all. You're confused."

"Your phone, ma'am."

She dropped a phone into the bag; both the woman and the sky marshal watched the sack. She lifted it to explain. "I suppose you want to check inside."

"Well . . ."

She leaned so other passengers could not hear. "You might recognize me. Inside this bag is a ventriloquist's dummy. Inside the dummy is my left arm. It's a long and aggravating story, but it ends with me not being able to remove the dummy on account of disciplinary reasons. I assume you know who I am." They nodded. "I wear the sack because—well, people tend to stare."

"Of course." The sky marshal bowed. "My concern—"

She beat him to it. "The dummy doesn't own a phone." And then for good measure: "I'm not really crazy, just so you know."

The marshal bowed again, and the woman with the phones nodded, and just then the cockpit door opened. They could all see the body of Second Officer Wrinkles lying on the floor, First Officer Miles seated on top pressing into his chest; the sky marshal stepped inside calmly as though this happened on every flight and took over the resuscitation duties. The captain emerged, issuing the girl with the phones a second and louder pop on the bottom and this time winking at the Sandra Bullock look-alike, suddenly recognizing why the line had stalled.

"It's okay, doll," he told the girl holding the phones.

"Yes, Captain. But I've been asked to collect—"

He leaned in. "She's got a muppet in that sack." Then to "Sandra Bullock," "Am I right, hon?"

"It doesn't own a phone."

"Cuter'n shit," he said, turning aside and heading for the aisle to call for more calm and steady. "See you soon," he said over his shoulder.

The puppet lady took one last peek toward the cockpit. "The people on the wing. Those pilots there in the cockpit. They're all so . . . beautiful."

"You're just nervous from the crash," the woman assured her.

A moment later the cockpit door opened again. The sky marshal and First Officer Miles, along with several flight attendants, hustled the unconscious copilot onto the wing. The Sandra Bullock look-alike followed, as did the rest of the passengers, the entire plane cleared in nine minutes. The captain walked the aisle, kicking into water and unfastening bathrooms and closets, careful to check no one was left behind. He found the puppy in the woman's handbag, a breed he did not recognize. He hoisted it beneath its front paws

and held it like a tiny, furry baby. It looked just like its name implied—Jeters—a jittery brown rascal with a black patch over its nose
and eyes. It sniffed the captain and slobbered him with a delightful
pink tongue.

"Hey there little man." He emptied the contents of the woman's
bag onto the seat, then placed the puppy inside. "Get you some
room to stretch." Tossing the bag over his shoulder, he rifled
through the miscellany. He chose a pack of cigarettes, a lighter, and
a set of earrings, then continued toward the rear of the vessel.

Captain Henry Swagger, Hank Swagger when he signed his
name with a great looping emphasis on the H in Hank and the R in
Swagger. At six-three, he was ruggedly handsome with beefy shoulders and a face that frowned in the eyes while gloating in the chin.
He was a bit bruised, little cuts and red patches. He was exactly
what people hoped to see climb out of a cockpit in the middle of
a river after both engines had gone kaput over a major metropolis.

At the rear he pulled out the old lady's cigarettes and sparked
one in the foot of water gathered there. He was not a smoker and
had a moment with the mechanics. It just felt like one of those
times someone might take up the habit. He turned to find a man
seated in the last row, Row 50, the bitch bench as the flight attendants called it. The man sat with an ankle bent over a knee, a
silver tube tucked in the real estate created by his legs. This was a
problem, the captain contemplated; if he had counted correctly,
he already calculated the 161 people on his plane. This man made
162, and for an instant he thought he'd have to bring them all back
to their seats for another tally.

"Hey there," the captain said.

"How is it?"

"Cigarette?"

"Those'll kill you."

The man had a tattoo on his forearm, FRANK RIP. He was missing the ring finger on his left hand, a fairly new wound on account
of the stitches and redness. Both his hands were twitching. Captain
Swagger went to the small talk.

"Who's Frank? That your fella?"

"I ain't gay."

"I didn't mean . . ." He tried a new tactic. "Not sure you noticed. But we fell out of the sky back aways. Now we're sinking in the middle of a river."

"Suppose we have you to thank for that."

"One way of looking at her. Another is I just saved a whole bunch of lives."

He glanced up for the first time. He had a tiny square of dirty blond hair between his chin and lower lip, a rawness to him that implied life was a constant business transaction; Swagger had him in his late thirties. "Probably saved a lot of assholes, too, you know."

"Come again?"

"Assholes. Read somewhere forty percent of people in any space, in any place in the world, are confirmed assholes. It's science. They've done research. These are people that no one likes, and who like no one, who basically disregard society and do it harm in all aspects. Get what I'm saying?"

"Not at all."

"Means on account of your rescue, a good sixty or so assholes will walk away from this fucking miracle. Then they'll continue to perform asshole-dom on the rest of us cheery pricks."

"How do you know you're not one of the assholes?"

"Damn fine observation."

They could hear rushing water that by now was nearly two feet deep, and the captain's exhaled smoke seemed a fine mist over a valley creek. The skirmish at the front of the plane over, a subtle darkness crept into the cabin. It was madness out on the wing, strangers hugging and hollering, making plans for the rest of their newly invigorated lives, the flight attendants barking orders, the youngish woman explaining how and when the cell phones would be returned, Miles and the sky marshal still working on Wrinkles. The inner sanctum was comforting, foggy, soothing but for the rising water that gave the panorama a delicate lifeness, the reality that they were still of flesh and hemoglobin, and not spiritual lava just yet. Captain Swagger decided then, for no reason other than it seemed like the fun thing, that he would keep little Jeters and raise the puppy as his own. And he would purchase a pipe. And a rocking chair. There was something Americanly virtuous about the image, him with the lapdog rocking away in front of a scalding fireplace, perhaps some Bing Crosby in the background.

"What do you say we talk this over on shore with the other assholes?"

The man gripped the tube. "You got everyone on the wing?"

"Ones don't feel like drowning anyhow."

"Suppose there're boats and helicopters out there full of TV cameras?"

The captain leaned to check an oval window. "Be along shortly, sure."

"Better wait here."

"Wait for what?"

"Nightness. Aloneness."

"Suit yourself. But you'll miss a hell of a party." He stuck his empty hand into the bag and rubbed Jeters's soft fur. "Besides, this plane will be at the bottom of the river in ten minutes."

"You know that for sure?"

The captain nodded.

"Just my luck." He rested his head on the seat in front. "I go out on that wing in daylight with those cameras, I'm cooked. I sit here ten more minutes, I'm cooked. I don't see why you couldn't crash into a mountain like other pilots."

Just then the undercover sky marshal climbed into the cabin. "Captain, it's time."

The man in Seat 50B ducked. "Keep him away. I need a minute."

"Come on, now, fella. I can't let you stay."

"Just be a minute. I promise."

Swagger shrugged; he liked the stranger with the tattoo more than he liked the sky marshal. He dipped his cigarette into the water then waded to the front with his new handbag. A moment later the strange man followed.

"What was that?" the sky marshal asked the man. "Back there."

"What was what?"

"In the overhead. You hid something. Don't say you didn't."

"What's the difference?" the captain asked. "Plane's sinking. Let's go find us a bar."

"I need his phone," the undercover marshal said. He was bashful for such a large man, talking with his chin pointed into the water. "Federal regulations."

"Just give him your phone."

The man took a phone from his pocket and tossed it behind himself into the water. He glared at the sky marshal, who seemed miffed but accepting at what the man had done. The plane had shifted noticeably in the passing moment and so all three stepped out onto the wing, squinting as the callous sun reflected off the makeshift silver yacht. There, along with the girl with the phones, they froze in a pose, all of them, the passengers and flight attendants and the captain, looking into New York City, as if they were immigrants of a frail and impoverished land and this their first visual of a fresh home.

The city seemed distant from the river's core, the sirens invisible and small as they Dopplered off the brown and dirty buildings. Ferryboats of morning commuters surrounded the vessel. They gawked and snapped pictures and helped the plane's occupants aboard, hugging the stunned passengers who craved only dry land. The helicopters stayed at a distance as to not churn ever-larger waves. The injured woman had been ditched there on the wing, where she lay wailing for a fresh smoke. The sky marshal took Swagger by his arm and worked him onto an empty ferry, where he joined other members of the plane's crew.

"Captain!" the injured woman hollered. "What about my puppy?"

"Get some ice on that ankle, old gal," Swagger called from the bow as the ferry cast off for shore. "Afraid your puppy drowned."

TAKE A SAD SONG AND MAKE IT BETTER

SEAT: 50B
PASSENGER: Normal Fulk
REASON FOR FLIGHT: Disappearing.
LAST THOUGHTS BEFORE IMPACT: *I'm the unluckiest bastard*
on the planet.

His forearm itched. That was the bitch of it. Not that he was alive with the ability to itch, but that his troubles coalesced into something larger as he looked over the slight blackened waves, his arm a fleshy magic lamp of misfortune. Normal Fulk stood on the wing of Flight AW2921 rubbing the tender reds and blues of his tattoo. FRANK RIP. Frank was his dead brother. Whenever his arm itched, it was a message from his older sibling reminding him he had erred. And this was no minor error. This was a major blunder, the colossal difference between luck and no luck, proof the gods conspired against him.

"Unbelievable," he confirmed. Over the wind, over the chattering survivors suddenly feeling good about their chances, over the leaning helicopters he was certain had television cameras pinned on him. "Just unbe-fucking-lievable."

"That we survived? Or that we crashed at all?"

A woman squatted next to him, her arm buried inside a sack. She peered into the disappearing cabin through a window. Medical boats had arrived and technicians were carting off the old woman who continued to complain about swimming conditions, that someone had stolen her cell phone.

"I don't know," he said. "Guess all of it."

"Do you find it strange?"

"Do I find what strange?"

"Can't put my finger on it. Just how . . . orderly of a catastrophe this is."

Come to think of it, Normal should have been pleased how

quickly the rescue ferries had arrived. "Suppose they train for things like this."

"Then the pilot on the cockpit floor. And how attractive everyone is."

She was right. Normal had been one of the last to board. He'd noticed that a number of passengers, both men and women, were a bit too tidy for an early morning flight. He was certain he had passed a man wearing makeup.

She motioned with her good arm toward passengers climbing onto a ferry. "That's just me. I survive a plane crash, and instead of celebrating I check the logistics. Paranoid, I guess."

Yeah, paranoid, Normal nodded. He wore sunglasses. The quicker he boarded one of those ferries, the better his chances of staying off camera. Helicopters circled overhead and he ducked dumbly beneath a hand. The initial three ferryboats had embarked for shore and others circled the plane slowly. There were about forty people left on the wing; the next ferry would be his. He had stashed the vial in the rear cabin so the sky marshal would not confiscate it, which seemed foolish now that he was standing on the wing of a sinking ship.

"What do you suppose?" Normal was confused as to why the plane would even sink. Boats stayed afloat, why not an aircraft? "This plane really going to sink?"

"It's going to sink all right."

"They just let it submerge and leave it?"

She bunched her nose. "Not even fifty feet deep. They'll fish it out later."

"Then what'll they do?"

"Drag it to shore, have a look at the engines to see what went wrong."

"Drag it where—Manhattan or Jersey?"

"I'd like to know that myself."

Normal took a moment to look her over now that she was not leering into the plane. "Say, you look familiar."

"I get that all the time. People say I look like Sandra Bullock."

"You look nothing like Sandra Bullock." He snapped his

fingers when it occurred to him. He tried to discern whether he was astonished or angry. He settled on discouraged. "You're the Twitter woman. You do the thing where you stalk celebrity Twitter pages."

"Stalking is a bit harsh," she said. "What the hell—I'm sweating my ass off in this thing."

She untied the string from the far side of her neck. When she righted her arm, the dummy was a near replica of the woman. It had tiny arms that hung to its sides as though the taller of the two did not know how to properly work them. But the rhythm of the puppet was intact, a natural sway and reflex that the woman did not have to think through. Normal grunted, as if this were the most disturbing event of his still fresh Monday.

"What are you doing?"

"I figured you were going to ask to see it."

"Why would I ask to see it?"

"Most people want to see it."

"You just whip it out like that? In public?"

"It's a puppet. Not a tit."

Her name was Lucy Springer. He was so caught up in the crash, and the hidden vial, he had not realized. The nature of his business required that he follow the lives of celebrities, and he had followed his share of her and the puppet. What was its name, the nasty doll? He was iffy on her details. A year ago she had been the news anchor for ANN. A shooting, an arrest, the divorce. He was certain he remembered hearing she had been ordered to wear the puppet, but now that he could see it—right out in the open and not filtered through a computer screen—the idea was surreal.

"Okay, okay." She held the sack with her good hand and shoved the puppet headfirst into its burlap casket. "What are you getting so worked up for?"

"I don't care for that thing is all. And I don't much care for you."

"You don't even know me."

"I've watched you on TV. I know you plenty."

Other passengers, with nothing to do but wait and see if the ferries arrived before they drowned, took a passing interest in the tantrum. That could have been the end of it. But Normal Fulk was on a mission of sorts, or so he thought. He was extricating himself (in what many of you passengers will view as an irritatingly righteous maneuver) from the Americana culture he no longer condoned. People wearing puppets were just the type of thing that set him off.

"You want to know what bothers me most about you?"

"Not really." She turned her back to watch the river.

"It's the chum, the rot, that you're part of this cannibalistic culture that . . ." He tried again. "That you get by with a shitty gimmick when so many others get by through hard work."

"It really bothers you?" She should have ignored him. But they were standing on an airplane wing with little else to keep them busy, and now her ire was up. "Tell me—what do you do for a living that makes you such a commendable human being?"

"Never mind what I do."

Lucy got in his face. "I'd like to hear. You must be something special."

Eye to eye, the puppet hanging in its sarcophagus. Truth was, Normal Fulk and Lucy Springer shared a similar occupational interest—they relied on celebrities to eat.

"I'm in sales."

"What kind of sales?"

"Just sales. And retired besides."

"Oh, no. I have a sixth sense for bullshit. I want to know what you do."

"Well you can't know."

"You sell shoes, don't you?"

He turned away.

"Kitchen appliances. Snow tires. No, I got it." She danced around him on the wing until they faced each other. "Know what you look like? One of those gigolos who sells timeshares in Florida."

"Never been to Florida."

"Tell me. Or the puppet comes back out." She nodded to the others. "Ava loves a crowd."

Ava Tardner, that was the doll's name, the famous slab of fiber-glass. Passengers still waiting on the wing listened, pretending not to watch. The only thing they wanted more than those ferries to arrive and save them from a messy bath was to see a puppet dress down a stranger for their viewing pleasure. Normal knew she was serious. He had seen the mouthy doll on television.

He told it softly. "I'm in semen trafficking."

"Beg pardon?"

"Rather I was. As I say, I'm retired."

Lucy was dubious, attentive. "What kind of semen?"

"Dog. Horse. My most lucrative business came from celebrity semen, which was why I watched your show." He eyed the silver floor. "Find out who'd been arrested, who was involved in scandals—stuff like that boosts the price."

She put the sack behind her back. "That's true? You really sell semen?"

He was confessing to a stranger and could not stop. "Actors, sports figures, politicians."

"And sell it to whom?"

"Most of my clients are collectors. Or were. Same way people collect autographs, they collect DNA." Normal itched his arm.

First a plane crash and now this, Lucy was raw with curiosity. "So what do they do with it?"

"Some put it in tiny vials and wear it as necklaces. Some use it for insemination. Some keep it in refrigerated mantels they show off at cocktail parties. Sick bastards out there."

She leaned close. "Is it illegal?"

"Unregulated industry." Normal ducked, certain the helicopters were miked. "You'd be surprised how much money is out there. Fertility industry alone is worth $4 billion."

She held out her good hand. "Lucy Springer. Typically I'm the oddest person in the room."

He did not hate her so much with the puppet hidden. "Normal Fulk." They shook. His arm began itching when he realized the blunder. Normal Fulk was dead; he had been George Bailey for nearly three weeks.

"In all my years of flying, I've begged to be seated near a character like you. And when you finally arrive the plane crashes."

She waved good-bye with the sacked arm. Then she and the puppet joined a line of passengers stepping cautiously onto the arrived ferry. Normal grimaced as he waited to board. He had faked his own death three weeks prior and was headed for a new life, anywhere other than New York City. The worst of it was he could have chosen any of the thousands of flights leaving LaGuardia. But the one he boarded ended up in a river.

As the ferry steamed for shore, Normal watched the plane drift into the dark water. Inside was his future. And it was all tied up in John Lennon's frozen semen, the rarest specimen in existence, which was stowed in a vial in a plane that would be at the bottom of the Hudson by the time he next stood on dry land.

LUCY IN THE SKY

SEAT: 3B
PASSENGER: Lucy Springer
REASON FOR FLIGHT: Vacation
LAST THOUGHTS BEFORE IMPACT: *Why haven't the oxygen masks fallen?*

A flight attendant on the ferry explained that Air Wanderlust would provide transportation to the Whalensky Plaza Hotel and Resort, where passengers were being put up free of charge until alternate travel arrangements could be made. Their phones would be inspected and returned to their rooms that afternoon. In the meantime, they were free to use the hotel phones, all calls courtesy of Air Wanderlust.

As soon as she hit shore Lucy retrieved the phone stashed in the puppet's innards and ducked behind the nearest tree. She had stolen it from the old woman with the broken ankle, the others too concerned with basic survival to notice a pickpocket. She was the only journalist on the plane; while every news agency in the city scrambled for details, she was the sole professional eyewitness.

The first call was to her office at the American News Network. Like every media agency in the city, ANN would be teetering on insanity, reporters and photographers and producers trying to discover if New York was under another terrorist attack, how many had perished, if there were any heartwarming sub-stories—in the era of twenty-four-hour news coverage, the sub-stories were essential to give a tale longevity. She was patched through to her assistant, Dean Migliotto, an introverted and lonely media engineer who blamed Lucy for his introversion and loneliness. Dean rarely left the ANN building, and only when she ordered him to, living out of the chat rooms and social networking sites like a digital hobo.

"Migsy, go ahead."

"Dean, it's Lucy."

"Twit?"

"What did I tell you about that name?"

She had graduated from New York University with a journalism degree; gone on to Columbia University for her master's; reported from war zones in Afghanistan and Iraq; won three Peabody Awards; spent the five years before "The Incident" as the head anchor of ANN. "The Incident," as she referred to it, had provided months of front-page fodder—a marriage gone awry, the Internet video, her shooting up the fish tanks, the lawyers, the divorce mediator, the puppet connected to her wrist by an electronic bracelet monitor, more sub-story than she cared to divulge. "The Incident" had derailed her career, moving her from the anchor chair to the Celebrity Twitter Beat. Along with the puppet Ava Tardner, the duo monitored celebrities' Twitter pages and then recorded three-minute slots comprising the day's best tweets, Ava tossing in the occasional zinger. Lucy's coworkers had issued her the inevitable nickname, Twitter, which due to the ever-increasing need for brevity was often shortened to Twit or Tweet, or when she most deserved it, Twat.

"Dean, the plane that crashed."

"What's up with your Facebook page? Says you and Ava are on vacation."

"I told you. I won a vacation. We discussed this."

"Nobody wins those for real."

"The plane in the river!"

"The producers know all about it. Check your phone. They've sent headlines and updates and second updates."

"They confiscated my phone."

"The resort confiscated your phone? This is why I hate going outside."

"Dean, stop talking!" ANN could not have her anchor the news with a puppet on her arm. They could not fire her either. Just like they could not fire alcoholics, or paraplegics, Lucy's job was safe so long as she continued with therapy. The strategy had been to give her the Twitter beat in hopes she might quit. But Lucy Springer was no quitter. And the puppet turned out to be a draw to the online crowd that craved its information in the newest and most entertaining form. "I'm trying to tell you that I was on that plane."

"Holy shit!"

"Pier 66 with forty other passengers. At least they're here now. Send a van. I'll expect you to be in it."

When Dean was hired as her assistant, he was fresh and pure and ambitious and homely; three years later, he was dire and tainted and depressing and homely. He was a horridly reclusive and brilliant media engineer who spent his free time playing video games and living online, and pouting about the lack of excitement in his life. Despite his new-age wallflowerism, the little twerp could have a headline in front of 50,000 eyes within minutes, making him crucial to Lucy.

"Of course I'll be in it." He did not hang up. "Twit, I'm glad you're okay, but I have to ask." She knew it was coming. "Is Ava in one piece?"

Dean preferred Ava over Lucy. "Ava is fine. Would you like me to put her on the line?"

"That won't be necessary."

Just then a bus arrived. Two men in suits stepped out and began ushering on the passengers. The men had earpieces and took a head count; Lucy hid the phone quickly and wrote down the license plate. When she did not board, one of the men put a finger to his ear. Then they climbed on the bus and departed.

The news van arrived minutes later. Instead of Dean there was a blond intern, a T-shirt that failed to cover her midriff. Ever since "The Incident," Lucy had developed a prejudice against all things young and blond. They reminded her of Genny (with a G), the twenty-three-year-old cliché her husband had been sleeping with, and to whom he was now betrothed. The intern, Tonya, her perky breasts bouncing in an ill-fitting brassiere, held a laptop as she ran. She was followed closely by a one-man camera crew, the two ducking as though they had just stepped out of a helicopter into the napalm portion of a war. The girl waved the laptop in circles, Dean's pale face shouting instructions from the screen.

"Let me see Ava." The girl pointed the laptop at the puppet on Lucy's now sackless arm. "Very good, and now Twit. A bit to the left. Excellent. Where are the other passengers?" the laptop inquired of Lucy.

"On a bus." She should have known her hermit assistant would not leave the newsroom, not even for the story of the year. "Headed for the Whalensky."

"I told the producers there would be sub-stories." He sighed through the pixelated cosmos. "What else do we got?"

Tonya tried not to look at the puppet. Most everyone at ANN appreciated that the formerly royal Lucy Springer wore a puppet and worked amongst them; it brought them job satisfaction.

Lucy took the laptop. "Dean, you said you would be here."

"I am here. I'm also here. As soon as we record your and Ava's segment, I'll load it to the site. It would take an additional few minutes if I was there with you, which I am anyway."

"This is the scoop of the year." She pointed the laptop toward the river, which by then looked only like a river. "Would it have been too much to come in person?"

"You know I hate leaving the building."

Lucy peered into the laptop, her newsroom less than a half-mile away. Even through the fuzzy screen she could see the dumb glaze of his eyes, the white skin.

"When was the last time you were outside?"

"The other day."

"What other day?"

"Wednesday."

"It's Monday, Dean. You haven't left the building in five days?"

"I meant the previous Wednesday." He pouted. "Besides, there's nothing going on where you're at. Only reason I came was because I thought there would be sub-story."

"You didn't come."

"You know what I mean."

"And what do you mean sub-story? I was on the plane. I'm lead on this."

"Not what I was told." Dean sulked when he had bad news. He

sulked when he had good news also. "Producers said you should describe the last few seconds. They said it was fine if you tell your version, but people want to hear it from Ava. There'll be other passengers coming forward with stories. There will probably be only one puppet."

"I'm keeping the puppet out of the shot this time."

"They said viewers need to hear Ava's end of it. Was it terrifying? Any praying? Crying? The main story will play out in a week. Heartwarming sub-stories was the point they kept stressing."

"I'm lead on this, Dean. I was on the plane."

"I thought you'd be lead also, but no one listens to me." He sulked some more. "Plane sunk a few minutes ago. They're replaying footage of the passengers on the wing while the anchors kill time."

She pinned a microphone to her shirt. "Who's lead?"

"Colin and Melody."

"Fuck me. He'll say something stupid and we'll all be dumber for it."

Colin Campbell was the jewel of ANN, a twenty-five-year-old Tom Cruise beauty; Melody Derrick was his oral sex partner. No television personality devoted to their career had sex anymore; it was all aggressive tickling and groping short of penetration, the real thing too risky from a public relations standpoint.

"Let's do it," Lucy said.

"You haven't seen the press release."

"The plane went down twenty minutes ago."

"Hand her the page," Dean said. The intern handed it without looking. "Number of passengers, what they think caused it. Colin handled the gist. They said your angle is the chaos. And Ava should say something funny. Not distasteful funny. Just enough to give it levity. Maybe she broke wind when the plane hit water. Something like that."

Lucy pored over the release. It was impossible that an airline had moved so fast, even mentioning a possible cause of the crash—bird strike. And how had they gotten hotel rooms for the survivors in Manhattan so quickly?

AIR WANDERLUST FLIGHT 2921

NEW YORK, N.Y. April 9, 2012—Air Wanderlust Flight 2921, destination Los Angeles International, departed La-Guardia at 7:53 a.m. Eastern Time with 153 passengers, three pilots and five flight attendants. All on board survived.

The flight was piloted by Captain Henry Theodore Swagger, a veteran of the U.S. Air Force, who has more than thirty years of flight service.

Pending an investigation, the immediately apparent cause of the crash is engine failure due to bird strike. We are cooperating with local emergency rescue efforts. Additional information will be forthcoming.

A press release that quickly, the girl collecting phones, the mysterious bus that whisked them away, even the captain with his wink. And what had he meant, "See you soon?" Ever since "The Incident," Lucy had been concerned with whether she had just been angry when she killed all those fish, or if she'd actually lost her mind for a spell. In short, was she batshit crazy? What she was about to pursue had batshit written all over it, the type of endeavor wherein you either had to be one hundred percent correct, or they threw you in the loony tank for life.

"The producers want sub-story? How about this—the whole thing was staged."

"What are you talking about?"

"The plane crash," she said into the laptop, her left wrist inadvertently bending so that Ava appeared to nod in agreement. "Something doesn't fit, Dean, I just don't know what. This all came together too quickly."

Dean grabbed his laptop and placed a hand over the camera. Lucy and the intern and the cameraman watched the blurred screen, Dean crawling beneath the cavernous solitude of his desk a half-mile away. When his face reappeared, it was even whiter.

"Are you out of your mind?" he whispered.

"Listen to me, Dean."

"I'm about to have this video streamed around the world, and you're talking JFK conspiracy? You could lose your job. Both you and Ava. I could lose my job."

"You won't lose your job."

"I'm not going back outside, Lucy. I don't want to talk to people or go on interviews. This is my home."

"Think about it a minute," she said.

"You're nutty," he said. "There's always been talk—because you wear a puppet, and all you went through last year, that you might actually have lost your mind. But I've always given you the benefit of the doubt."

"If you would just listen—"

"This is too far." His voice shaky, a quivering lip. "A heroic pilot, who overcame wind velocity, ferocious landing conditions, a lucky lack of nautical congestion at that time of day, and somehow successfully landed an Airbus and saved everyone on board. And you want to suggest it was staged?"

"You weren't there, Dean."

"It's one thing when the puppet gets that pained look on her face and accuses you of sticking your hand up too far and impaling her intestines, again. Then when you pull it out, your hand is covered in spaghetti noodles or deli meat or that new fat-free yogurt, or whatever product sponsored the segment. Our viewers appreciate the slapstick violence." He chuckled, then went serious. "No one will appreciate jokes about this miraculous landing."

She tried to answer. He had turned off her microphone.

"Only way I'm ever going to get my career back on track is if you get in that anchor seat again. And if you want to even think about that, you better play this straight. Tell it nice. Tell it with a happy ending. Point that doll into the camera and dazzle. Because it's the only way I'm patching you through."

All things considered, Dean had a point. She did want to find her way back to the anchor's chair. And even a story about her being on the plane would go a long way to repairing her image. She steadied the microphone.

"That's my Twit."

Dean to the intern: "Tonya, point me at Lucy so I can watch."

Back to Lucy: "Hold Ava straight."

An instant later Dean hit a button that patched her into ANN, into every home and laptop and phone with video capability, every satellite's glimmer that shouted her out into the galaxy. Within moments her story would eclipse the city, stencil the country, and blanket the world, a breathtaking statement of resourcefulness, a tale that was beautiful so long as it went viral.

"I'm hearing we have ANN reporter Lucy Springer and her partner Ava Tardner with an exclusive," came Colin Campbell's voice from the newsroom. "Viewers, this is a special broadcast. Lucy and Ava were on the plane that splashed into the lake. Good morning, ladies."

"Thank you, Colin. It was actually a river. The Hudson River. The sole border between Manhattan and New Jersey. I'm here on Pier 66 on New York City's West Side, which was the scene of a miracle less than an hour ago. Flight AW2921 bound for Los Angeles experienced engine failure, landing in the Hudson River after a terrifying plummet. All 161 people on board . . ."

CARRY THAT WEIGHT

Not yet noon, Hank Swagger had already had his first encounter with the minibar in his Whalensky Plaza suite, a ginger ale and (mostly) rum to steady his sudden nerves. He had not felt his latest epidemic of anxiety as the plane plummeted. Not as Second Officer Wrinkles, nearly thirty years his junior, suffered a heart attack during the descent. But now that he relaxed in his hotel room, watching the encounter on the morning news, it occurred to him how precious the last few hours had been. The half-submerged plane, the passengers on the wing now on TV recounting the ordeal, the rescue boats and helicopters, the reporters and news anchors, the vanishing act of the monstrous jet—one minute there, the next, swallowed.

Hank, or Swagger as he liked to be known, offered a satisfied grin toward the window as he considered the morning. He sat on the bed with one leg kicked up, surrounded by stolen items—cigarettes he did not intend to smoke, a lighter, two earrings he fondled, a snoozing puppy, its soft brown fur rising and setting, at his side. But it was the exterior windowsill, and a frantic Darwinian opera playing out upon it, that held his attention. Two falcons were tearing apart a still-live pigeon, their talons pinning it to the concrete stage while they took turns ceremoniously ducking their heads into its gray flesh. He could hear the panicked cooing, silent off-white feathers fluttering until they caught wind and floated to the street where New Yorkers might snatch them out of midair and call it luck. It was a sacrifice. And all for him, the way ancient civilizations offered virgins to their brutal gods. Birds probably ate their own species all the time, such a simple progression from hatchling to creature to meal. That these falcons chose not to first murder their prey was the novelty, as if the significance of the feast was made more palatable by its coos of torture. This was existence, real and raw. This, and a glass of rum, settled his nerves better than any Valium, any Norpramin or Lexapro or Prozac.

Just then a knock. The door opened to reveal the hotel manager and the mayor of New York, Susan Cromberg. She was followed by three men in suits.

"Captain Swagger? Susan Cromberg. It certainly is a pleasure."

"Call me Swagger." He shook the mayor's hand without standing.

"This city owes you a debt of gratitude, Mr. Swagger. I can't imagine how different my morning would be if you weren't sitting there." She grinned at her fortune. "It must have been nerve-wracking, to say the least."

He lifted his glass and jiggled the ice. One of the men in suits handed her a phone and she forgot about the captain. A second man, also an aide to the mayor, watched the television. The third man studied Swagger. He was bald with a slight purple birthmark in the shape of a leaf on the right side of his noodle. He did not speak, just stood and watched Swagger on the bed watching the television.

"There he is." Swagger lifted the glass to the bald man.

"That'll be all, Mr. Swagger."

"How you doing fella? Things okay?" Just then Swagger's anxiety reappeared with a menacing gloat. "Fix you a drink?"

"No, Mr. Swagger. I'm simply going to stand here and take you in."

"Take me in, huh?" Swagger allowed a couple seconds of the bald man taking him in before he felt his throat close up. "How's our boy doing?"

"Do we have a boy, Mr. Swagger?"

"Wrinkles. He getting along?"

"I'm not familiar with that name."

The bald man watched him, studying the shape of his setting smile, a tiny cut above his eye, the puppy. Swagger wanted to peek at the windowsill to see if the falcons had finished off the pigeon. He was not a voyeur, only interested in the naturalness of the act. He wanted to play his part well and did not intend to appear grotesque in front of the strangers, especially since he had no idea why they were in his room. By his estimate, the falcons would have struck muscle by now. With any luck he would not miss the disemboweling.

The phone rang. It rang four times before anyone realized no one intended to answer. A sudden panic crept over the room, as if it might stop ringing and change the dynamics of their merry morning.

"Mind picking that up?" Swagger asked the bald man.

"It's your room, Mr. Swagger. Telephone is probably for you."

"Don't want to wake the puppy. I stand it might startle the little fella."

The bald man nodded. "It's not clear to me why you have a puppy in your hotel room. It's not clear why you have an alcoholic beverage either. I believe there are concerns of higher priority."

The mayor listened while pretending not to hear. Swagger kept it cool, standing to retrieve the phone. Jeters lifted his head instinctively and looked around with a jilted pout before dropping back into a bored slumber. Swagger lifted the phone without speaking.

"Hank? Arnold here." After a moment, "Geez, Swags, it's me, Jugs. Put it on speaker."

Swagger fumbled with the mechanics until the hotel manager stepped forward and commandeered the phone. From an Air Wanderlust plane bound for New York, somewhere over the Midwest, Arnold Jeffries, CEO of the airline, cleared his throat. "Blackie, you there?"

"Of course, Mr. Jeffries," the bald man said.

"Good then. Room empty otherwise?"

"Mayor Cromberg was gracious enough to stop by." When there was no answer: "The mayor of New York and her associates."

"Of course. Susan, nice of you to do so."

"The pleasure is mine. I can't tell you how thrilled we are."

"I been better," Arnold Jeffries told her without being asked. "Hank, you holding up?"

"I been better." He jiggled the ice at the phone.

"You're a damned hero, that's for sure. Anything I need to know?"

"Crashed one of your planes. It's at the bottom of the river."

Everyone appreciated the opportunity to smile. The hotel

manager stepped forward and mimed Swagger to autograph hotel stationery. The bald man never lifted a hand, or said a word, or motioned in any way. He simply stared as he'd done to Swagger, and the hotel manager vacated the room.

"Hank, I assume you're acquainting yourself with Alastair Black." Swagger and the bald man held a frown. And then to the mayor: "Susan, we got a predicament, as you can imagine. We've hired Alastair and Veiltality to assist."

"Mr. Black and I are familiar," she said.

"Everyone getting to know one another, that's swell." He shifted the phone to another ear, somewhere over Ohio. "Hank . . . Veiltality is a . . . public relations firm. Blackie here's going to . . . help us smooth over any . . . rough spots."

"Well, you'll have no trouble from the City of New York."

"I don't expect so, Mayor. Blackie, floor's yours."

The bald man walked over to the window and closed the drapes, sensing the focal point of Swagger's attention. He waited for the mayor and her aides to leave. They did not budge.

"Press release went out. Important thing is to keep in contact with the media." He paced the floor, muting the sound on the television. "First things first—the interview."

"Let's make it count," Arnold Jeffries said through the phone.

"We need to introduce Captain Swagger to the world to explain the crash and how he was able to avoid catastrophe. We'll wait until midweek, give it time to work out any kinks that arise."

"Kinks?" came Arnold Jeffries.

"Wrinkles," Swagger mumbled.

"Right now every household on the East Coast is Googling Captain Swagger. And we want to show him in the most sincere, patriotic light. I've identified a number of anchors . . ."

"Wait a minute." Swagger lifted his glass to the television, where Lucy Springer and her puppeted fist spoke into the camera, the Hudson River in the background. "Aren't you forgetting someone?"

From the phone: "Who's that?"

The muscles in the bald man's jaw rolled; Swagger could see he was being signaled to shut the hell up. Had he said something wrong? Yes, it was probable, the rum typically did that. And now in hindsight he knew he had misspoken. The bald man turned toward the television. "A New York media personality. Her niche is that she does celebrity gossip with a puppet. She's more of an Internet sensation, but she has a respectable following."

"Who is she?"

"Oh dear, Blackie." The mayor grimaced. "You wouldn't. Not with the puppet."

"Who gives a shit about the doll?" Swagger said. "She was on the plane."

Blackie turned casually. "Is that so?"

Swagger didn't look so sure. "The one that landed in the Hudson?"

"I haven't got eyes through the phone. Who are we talking about?"

"Her name is Lucy Springer. She covers celebrity gossip for ANN."

"Broad that went nuts? Well . . . that's something. Isn't it Blackie?"

"What a coincidence." The mayor smiled. She looked from Blackie, to the television, back to Blackie. "Of course, there are bigger fish out there. I could suggest a few names if you'd like."

Swagger coaxed the puppy back to sleep. "We'll go with her."

"Blackie? Your call."

"Why is it his call?" Swagger stood to fix another drink. "Think I would have some say in who interviews me. Besides, she seemed nice."

"What do you mean she seemed nice?" Blackie asked.

"What I mean is . . . Wrinkles, see, was down and she was there, and we had a moment." Swagger was hopeful things were wrapping up, which meant he might catch Act III on the windowsill. "Kind of looks like Sandra Bullock, don't you think?"

From the phone: "I like Sandy Bullock. Blackie?"

The bald man glared at Swagger until he reassembled on the bed. It occurred to Swagger—for the first time, and just for a glancing moment—he could identify exactly what he was scared of, the hidden concept that was corrupting his goodness, stealing his grasp of ancient rightness, of old-fashioned moments and bygone simplicity. And then it was gone. He kept quiet as Blackie walked toward the television until it disappeared behind the pattern of his suit, peering into the liquid crystal pixels as if to challenge the reporter to a stare down. "She'll do," he said. "It adds a happy sub-story to this tale I feel."

"That's what I need to hear, Blackie. See everyone soon. Swell y'all are getting on so well."

But Mayor Cromberg was not swell. In fact, she was the furthest thing from swell. As her aides led her out of the room, she canceled the rest of the day's appointments, the rest of the week's if that's what it came to. This was the first quarter and she had clearly been earmarked for the bench. Mayor Cromberg intended to get in the game.

IN TIMES OF TROUBLE

Normal Fulk wanted nothing more than to pull the shades down on a room at the Whalensky Plaza and fall into a cushioned bed for the next two, three months, a hibernating sleep that would cleanse his indiscretions. How long would Air Wanderlust foot his bills? If they threw him out, he could always holler victim, an innocent survivor stranded in Urban Hades, the airline having dumped him there and tossed him out of his sanctuary. He of the missing finger, a cripple at that. Of course, if he hollered victim, someone might learn his true identity. Then out it would come that he had died recently, so what was he doing ordering room service at the Whalensky Plaza? Instead he carefully made his way to the curb and hailed a cab, crumbling into the back.

"Where to?"

"Just drive."

"One of those, huh?"

"Let's not talk if that's okay."

Normal's tattoo was a red ectoderm; he'd been scratching. The driver watched suspiciously. "What's with the scratching fella?"

"Nothing's with the scratching."

The driver turned, took in the red arm, the missing finger. "You don't got the Nymphopucky, do you? I don't want that shit in my cab."

"Far as I know, that's one thing not wrong with me."

Normal waited until he was in a Manhattan neighborhood he rarely frequented and asked the cabbie to pull over near a pay phone. He passed a twenty to the driver and told him to keep the meter running. After an argument with a nearby barista over how many quarters he was permitted as change with his coffee, he took to sanitizing the pay phone with a sleeve.

He dialed his partner's cell. Eddie picked up on the third ring. "You near a television?"

"Fuck, Normal?"

"George. My name is George Bailey, Eddie."

"Supposed to be. And you're supposed to be helping crippled orphans."

"Only one is crippled. And they're not orphans. Stop calling them orphans."

"Nearly choked when I saw you on my TV standing on the wing of a plane in the middle of the Hudson."

Normal bounced his head into the booth's inner cave; he could not even get lost in his own catastrophe. "You saw?"

"Having some cereal, turned on the TV, and boom." Eddie laughed inexplicably. "News says there's a plane in the river and I think, damn, that's got to be Normal."

"George Bailey."

"Whatever."

Eddie Scuthers had been Normal's partner for six years, ever since his brother Frank died. They had come up together, both having dropped out of school (Eddie a nurse, Normal an auto mechanic) to enjoy a lucrative and sedentary life of petty crime. He considered Eddie family. He was the type Normal could count on never to make a decision, but to follow instructions with a precision that bordered on determined stupidity. If Normal told him to go to the store, pick up milk and eggs, then come home, Eddie would do it. He'd just neglect to pay.

"This is crazy," Eddie said. He was commenting on the television events through which Normal had just lived. Eddie watched roughly fourteen hours of television a day, a disciple. "I mean what are the chances—of all the flights, in all the world, the one you take crashes?"

"Listen to me, Eddie."

"What about this pilot? Holy shitsky, what a cool operator." Eddie always listened to the television too loud. It made him feel like he was in a movie theater. "There you are again, Normal, looking like a sucker."

"It's George. Please."

"What was it like?"

"What was what like?"

"The crash. No, start at the beginning with liftoff. Take me through."

"I'm in a bit of a jam, Ed."

"You know what you got—a story for life, Normal. Any bar, any hour, any situation—you rip off this history, you'll have people three deep trying to get at you. It'll become a folktale. The more you tell it, the better it'll get."

A woman inside the phone ordered up thirty-five cents.

"Eddie, shut off the television." The silence was soothing, the inner glass of the booth cool against his brow. "You remember I'm supposed to be dead, right?"

"Sure, Norm. I cut off your finger."

"You remember why I was flying?"

"Crippled orphans."

"And that I made off with an object that is extremely rare and valuable?"

Eddie munched something. "I was firmly against this strategy if you recall."

"That object is now inside a vial at the bottom of the Hudson River."

Munching. And then no munching. "What's it doing in the river?"

"That's where the plane sunk."

"Why did you leave it?"

"Because the captain was there. And the sky marshal. And there were passengers and ferry boats and helicopters and I got nervous." He banged the phone into the booth. "Stop asking questions."

Normal knew he had Eddie's attention from the suspicious manner in which he shut the fuck up.

"I'd love to tell you about the flight. But first I need to solve this minor problem. How much we make off the last score?"

"Ain't made nothing. You just said. It's in the river."

"The one before. How much?"

"The Clooney? Sold yesterday for sixteen."

"I told you nothing less than twenty-five."

"Needed scratch. And you said not to call you no matter what."

Eddie was a habitual gambler. Normal had sent him to Gamblers Anonymous. He'd gotten kicked out for betting on the other addicts' vice of choice during meetings—horses, football, poker. His problem had been largely dormant over the last few months; Normal blamed himself for not taking it into consideration.

"Why did you need money, Eddie?"

"Things. Errands. Life."

"You weak little man. How much is left?"

"Four."

"Fuck!"

"But that's a deceiving four." Another round of phone bashing. "What I won I let ride. We could have eighty by the end of the day."

"Listen to me, Eddie. This is bad. I need to get the John Lennon out of a submerged plane. I need to do that with every camera in the city tuned in. And I need to get out of town before she finds out I'm alive."

"Oh, she knows you're alive. Her guy called earlier. Didn't give a name."

"She knows I'm alive?"

"Must have had the tube on. You show up every few minutes still."

"You didn't think to mention this?"

"You didn't ask." Normal could feel Eddie shrug through the phone.

"I'm in serious trouble, Ed."

"I was firmly against this strategy."

"She leave a message?"

"She did, matter of fact."

A long pause.

"Can I have the message please, Eddie?"

"Sure thing. I wrote it down." Eddie set down the phone and picked it up again. "Okay. Tell Normal we're following him. That's it. That's all she said. What do you think it means?"

Normal glanced over his shoulder, nothing. "Fuck, Eddie!"

Eddie resumed with the snacking. Normal could picture it—Eddie in his underwear, middle of his couch, ice cooler of their product on the floor, round-the-clock entertaining coverage of Normal's plane crash. They kept the product in a cooler rather than the refrigerator because Normal did not like his condiments mingling with semen, celebrity or otherwise. And it was easier to move the stuff in a pinch, something Normal felt was important ever since the Feds began nosing about.

"Can I give you some advice, Normal?" Normal had never gotten advice from Eddie and was curious what it might entail. "You kept saying the gods would lead you to where you need to be once you quit trafficking. Thing is—look around. You tried to leave. One of them gods crashed the plane. Brought you back to New York. To us. To this. See, Norm, this is what you're good at. Maybe this is where the gods need you."

"I hardly think they want me hawking semen on TV."

"Give her a chance. Let her sell the vial properly, get us some real money. And forget about those crippled orphans. I know you feel bad, but shit, Norm. We need to get back to what we do."

Normal was exhausted. "One, I don't have the vial. Two, I've explained I am trying to preserve just one piece of this fucking cannibalistic culture . . ."

". . . One piece of this cannibalistic culture without it being defecated upon," Eddie finished. "I know. You've said. But it's bringing you bad karma. Ever since you came up with this plan you've lost a finger, died, and crashed in a plane. I say we let her do her thing. Make us rich. Make us famous."

"I don't want to be famous." Normal thought it through. "I need to get the vial and get out of New York before she finds me."

"Give up," Eddie suggested. "She won't stop until we do the TV show."

Normal hung up. When he turned, his taxi was gone. In its place, a limousine. And her.

YESTERDAY

And really, passengers, was it not inevitable that it would come to this—the general citizenry, those with a little cash left and looking to burn it on a new vice—wanting to own the genetic code of their most beloved celebrities? The next step in our cultural evolution really. After the twenty-four-hour entertainment coverage, each celebrity with their own Twitter feed, reality show, clothing line—until the immortal experience of obsessing over another was made ubiquitous and indistinct. There had to be something new, something profound, which is what America is all about—servicing the profound. Enter Normal Fulk.

The string of events that would lead to Normal's demise began eighteen months earlier, when he encountered the American actor Cleve Peoples in a Manhattan hotel, on a four-day bender, the perfect mark for Normal's line of work. He had learned this news from ANN, watching one of the many celebrity gossip shows he followed to keep track of potential donors. Normal was the entire celebrity semen industry, the kingpin if you will. He dealt with the same buyers each time. They, in turn, sold to an underground cabal of smaller dealers and collectors and rabid fans that paid top dollar to own the deoxyribonucleic acid of their favorite celebrities; pictures and autographs made them fans, semen made them legitimate.

Normal did not care what happened to the product when it left his possession; his objective was to obtain and sell it, and once the money was in his hands he rarely thought of it again. The fences were fairly accountable, although being an unregulated industry they could sell to whomever they chose. Capitalism ensured whomever they chose turned out to be the highest payer. In the case of Cleve Peoples, the highest payer was one Maudette Frawl, who remortgaged her home and used her life savings to purchase her most-beloved actor's batter along with enough fertility drugs to start her own basketball team.

Quite possibly it occurred more often than Normal cared to

recognize. But when Maudette Frawl dumped her life savings into a backwoods in vitro fertilization strategy, it produced not one illegitimate child, but eight. Thus was born Clevesclan, the nickname issued to the scandal by Ava Tardner and latched onto by every tabloid for months until the actor's career was ruined and he was living as an expatriate in France. Most people who purchase semen do it out of love, with the same emotion football fans wear their team's jersey, or punch in the face supporters of a competing team. It was widely believed by the tabloids that Maudette Frawl only intended to bear one child in Cleve's likeness, but as the brood intensified she fell toward blackmail.

Cleve Peoples: dashingly handsome, violently white teeth, impeccably dressed, manicured fingertips, master of his craft, a surfer's physique. Maudette Frawl: teeth, clothes, both hands, store clerk, a lumberjack's build. When she originally came forward, only the basest of tabloids followed the tale. But when it was proven through a court-ordered blood test that the famed thespian fathered the children, the rags went berserk. The puppet said it best:

"In the business, Cleve Peoples is known by his peers as an actor who gives 150 percent to his roles. He applies those same standards even when slumming."
                                    —Ava Tardner, February 9, 2012

Maudette Frawl, possibly overwhelmed by keeping them all straight, chose to name the kids alphabetically and with the one-syllable monikers in keeping with the papa: Abe, Beau, Cleve, Doug, Earl, Ford, Gabe, and the gal of the crew, Hope. Making publicity matters worse for Cleve, little Beau was born with one leg. And Cleve had been in Los Angeles filming a movie at around the time of conception, which made it feasible—unlikely, but still feasible—that he could have wandered through her small town of Campbell, California, enjoying a brief yet remarkably efficient romp with Maudette.

Cleve had slept with a thousand women in his time. He had likely fathered several children he either supported quietly, or issued a one-time payment for to ensure his anonymity; which is to say, he was not above doing the responsible thing. But Cleve Peoples was a leading man, an international brand; it was bad for his image to admit sleeping with something like Maudette Frawl. He took one look at her tabloid photographs and publicly refuted his participation, leaned in to the cameras with those blinding teeth and swore to America he had never met Maudette Frawl, much less littered her reproductive tract with his pedigree. Once photographs of eight adorably chubby babies began circulating on the Internet, one of them missing a paw, it mattered little who slept with whom. Cleve was cooked. And those babies were fatherless. And little Beau was fucked.

Cleve's downfall occurred during three major arrivals in Normal Fulk's life, a perfect storm of personal anguish: the rumored existence of the John Lennon; federal agents, for the first time, nosing into his previously ignored industry; and a seriously premature midlife crisis. Had he heard the tale of Maudette Frawl and Clevesclan only once, he might have been able to ignore it. But because of our culture's affinity for bullwhipping citizens with news, Normal was reminded constantly, in all forms of communication, for what he was responsible. And so he set about to make it right: a mission.

He had obtained the necessary papers to invent George Bailey, a Normal look-alike with Sicilian skin, a shifted bridge in the nose, dirty blond hair he had trimmed himself ever since he was eighteen. Now age thirty-seven, he looked ridiculous with a stretch of whiskers beneath his lower lip. It was absurd; as if anyone seriously looking for him would be thrown off by a half-inch of fuzz, a missing finger, and a dyed head of hair. The idea was for one final score before going legit. Normal was hell-bent on not giving the John Lennon to *her*; instead he would sell it elsewhere, donate the cash to the Frawl children (his godchildren, sort of), and get out of the business forever. Eddie would stay in New York and sell off the product, and if he took Normal's advice, he would stop trafficking before the Feds got hot to it.

Normal had been storing his own blood for months. It was to be used to stage a brutal crime, of which he would be the victim.

Eddie had four credits toward a nursing degree and knew enough to handle the blood, if not necessarily enough to manipulate a homicide scene. But he was an excellent television voyeur—*CSI* and *Law and Order* and the rest—and after a week on the couch studying technique, he was able to bloody a warehouse to resemble the real thing. The details had to be perfect, which was why Normal allowed Eddie, with anesthesia, to politely hack off a finger and stitch together the wound. It had to be hacked instead of amputated because the police would know the difference. The procedure had taken place on a wooden cutting board, with a rusted meat cleaver that Eddie had sharpened himself.

"Sure about this?" Eddie asked.

"Stop talking and do it."

"Can't convince you to go with the pinky, right?"

"Anyone who would cut off a finger before murder would never cut off the pinky."

"Disagree," Eddie said. "Cutting off fingers is intimidation. You start with the smallest and work across."

"Pinkies are for torture. Ring and pointers you leave behind to identify a dead body—they mean business. Besides, when I look at my hand I want to remember what I've done. I want to remember those kids. Especially Brett."

"Beau."

"Whatever."

They chose a warehouse that was empty on weekends, a grubby hole in Queens that served as a pork packaging plant for a chain of Chinese restaurants. The plan was to make it appear the victim had been chained to a chair, beaten thoroughly, his fingers cut off, at least one. The finger was tactfully placed behind a radiator, as though it had been lopped off with a machete and cast into a forgotten nook when the body was dragged off. Normal had been arrested enough times that his fingerprints were on file. The right people would assume it had something to do with the product they had stolen, and that Eddie did not have it since Eddie was stupid and too much of a coward to venture out on his own.

They staged the warehouse on a Sunday morning, stole the

John Lennon that afternoon, drove Normal to a motel near the airport, where he hunkered down to make sure events unfolded as planned. Eddie filed a missing persons report that Sunday night, the Chinese dumpling stuffers found the crime scene Monday morning, the police investigation leaned into Wednesday of the following week. Normal was officially declared dead two weeks after, and the police admitted to Eddie they had few leads. Normal watched the news from the motel room for any small item about the crime or his frail biography. There was nothing. He fell into a stifling routine for a three-week stay—a food run every two days, changing the gauze on his hand, waiting for the wrong knock at the door, transforming his persona from the sinister Normal Fulk into the honorable George Bailey. He had planned on leaving on a Sunday, but a gloomy fog rolled in from New England and kept most flights grounded.

He was not particular about which airline he flew on, although he preferred to buy his ticket at the airport. Both the fence and Maudette Frawl were in California, so he was hopping on the first thing headed west. Of all the airlines, Normal was enamored by one name: Air Wanderlust. Fortunately, the airline had a flight bound for Los Angeles leaving within the hour.

Now, passengers, the nice thing about being a semen dealer: Very few people will get in the way of someone carrying a vial of frozen mustard, so long as the story behind it is told properly— frantically, much agitation, and with fake tears. Even in the post– 9/11 world, where shampoo bottles and baby formula are viewed as weapons capable of crippling a nation's air travel, somehow primordial ooze gets past security. Not even waiting in line, Normal rushed the Air Wanderlust ticket counter and slapped down the bandaged hand. He had already started with the tears and the sniffling.

"I'm afraid that flight is booked, sir. Now if you'll just—"

More sniffling. He pulled the silver canister and twisted free the top. Several clerks backed away and someone radioed security. Normal removed the vial with his sleeve and held it near her chin. "You know what this is?"

"Sir, if you would please—"

"That's right, Miss. Frozen semen. There is a woman in Los Angeles whose dream is to become a mother." He nodded, sniffled, wiped his eye then tapped the vial three times. "With. This. Semen."

"Yes, but, there are simply no empty—"

"Nothing will stop me from making her dream come true, from creating life." He won over a few people with that just as security arrived and someone in line behind him actually clapped. "What do you say, lady—you want to help me create life. Or you want to quibble about seating space."

The clerks scrambled and phoned and made arrangements with the check-in gate, apologizing to the strange four-fingered man, and promising they were doing what they could. Normal was not only permitted on a flight that had been booked for months, but was also escorted by security, first through the metal detectors, then driven directly to the gate where an Air Wanderlust official shook his hand and wished him good luck, and apologized that Normal would have to sit in the back row, a bench typically reserved for the flight attendants' luggage. And after all that—the missing finger, the crime scene, the invented tale of a mother's dream, surviving a crash landing—after all that, and still she found him.

WE HOPE YOU WILL ENJOY THE SHOW

The driver stepped out of the limo and opened the rear door. A high-heeled foot dug into the pavement, the toenails painted a glistening white. Her crew was out of the limo instantly—the female assistant, two cameramen, a sound guy—and set upon his booth with paparazzi stealth.

"There he is." She air-kissed him twice. He let it happen. "Back from the dead, Normal Fulk, dumbest fuck ever."

Under the circumstances, Normal did not argue.

"Let me see it. Can't believe you cut it off." She must have spoken to Eddie to know about the finger the police found in the warehouse. She lifted Normal's hand to show the cameras. "Got to hand it to you, Fulk, you had me a believer at first. Then you go and get on the wrong plane . . ." She didn't finish, just shook her head, the blond hair, chuckling at his misfortune.

"It went bad," Normal agreed.

"Tell me," she continued. "Been thinking about it all day. Can't get it out of my thoughts since I saw you on TV this morning. What did you take?"

"How do you mean?" Normal knew how she meant.

"The new name. What are you calling yourself?"

"I'd rather not say."

Rory leaned in close. She smelled expensive. "Whisper to me. I won't say nothing."

He said it quietly, which caused her to erupt in a snort.

"George fucking Bailey." She threw her head back and celebrated. "You're gold, Fulk. You're fucking brilliant American cinema and you don't even realize it."

Rory Genius-Temple was CEO of the Genius-Temple Management Firm, a company that intended to produce a reality television show titled *Semen Pirates* about Normal and his occupation with or without his cooperation. Despite Normal repeatedly shunning her advances, she had gone so far as brokering a deal for the sale of the

John Lennon. He had not faked his own death to escape a reality television show about his life; that was not the official reason anyway. He was being investigated by the FBI, his apartment bugged, black cars following him, hooded people nosing through his trash. But an ulterior motive was that his presumed death would mean an end to Rory Genius-Temple. She was movie star gorgeous. And porn star scary. Taken separately each of her features was ravishing—the purchased eyelashes, the swerve of her lips, the round, hard shape of her ass she crammed in skirts that prevented her from bending. But as a whole her beauty corrupted her, gave her a hostile sheen. And she had a habit of slapping him in the face in front of her crew.

She slapped him in the face in front of her crew. "After all I've done for you, this is how you repay me?"

He held his hot chin. "I told you, Rory. I'm not doing the show."

"The meetings I've attended on your behalf. The marketing department, the investors, the people I've slept with. Do you realize Lobo over there hasn't seen his kids in a month?"

"Which one's Lobo?"

"The fucking Mexican," she shouted.

Normal waved at Lobo, who held the boom microphone. It was all so confusing. There was probably a lonely wife somewhere, a brood of kids wondering when daddy was coming home, a pile of unpaid bills on account of Normal's lack of participation in his own TV drama.

"Stop tape." The crew went on break and Rory moved in tight. "Lobo is one of the dumbest motherfuckers you'll ever meet. But he's got a giant cock, and he holds that microphone steady half the time, and he really seems to care when I slap his dumb face. Which is more than I can say for you, Mr. Movie Star." She snapped her fingers several times at her assistant, who knew just what it meant. "He doesn't avoid responsibility or fake his own death to get out of a tight spot. That's the type of people we got behind this project. People who give their time to knocking this bitch out of the park everyday so that Americans can enjoy a slice of life they would otherwise never know existed."

"That's just it. I don't want anyone to know what I do." Even this brand-new George Bailey was tired of explaining it. "Do you have any idea how much trouble I'd be in if you aired an episode?"

"Boo fucking hoo," she said. "Try singing that song to Derrick's wife, Jane, who has been out of work for six months. Derrick's on first camera, only one bringing in bread for his family. Or Sonya's grandmother, Ruby—Sonya's the cross-eyed girl there with the clipboard, looks kind of retarded when she smiles—and the old lady counts on a check from her granddaughter each month. See, Fulk, this reality show about your life isn't just about your life. It feeds a lot of mouths, a lot of families. You got it?"

"I understand, but—"

"I'm talking about the John Lennon, asshat. Hand it over."

"About that. I need some time."

"I know you stole it. You wouldn't have gotten on the plane without it." Rory thought for a moment. When she turned, an agitated snarl. "Holy shit."

"It was a plane crash, Rory. Out of my control."

"Tell me you didn't leave it, Normal. I haven't had anyone killed in four years, and I'm strangely fond of you."

"It's frozen. It'll stay frozen for seventy-two hours."

Rory lunged, slapping Normal in the side of his dyed head. He came around to find the two cameras pinned on his reaction.

"It's at the bottom of a river, you dumb fuck!"

"I'll get it back."

"That vial makes up the majority of Season One. Without that story line, we're just a bunch of cameras following a pervert."

"I told you already. I'm not doing a reality show."

"We've already shot footage for half of the first sixteen episodes." She held up her hands; it was out of her control. "And much of it revolves around you obtaining the Beatle's jizz and selling it to our guys in Detroit."

"Who I sell my product to is none of your business."

She jabbed a manicured nail into his chest. "I gave you Lennon on a silver platter. I made it happen. And this is what I get?"

"I stole that fair and square."

Normal and Eddie had stolen the John Lennon from an art-ist, who had stolen it from an ex-girlfriend, who had stolen it from a memorabilia dealer, who had bought it underhanded from a doctor decades before. The John Lennon specimen was meant to be the main draw of the artist's latest gallery opening, the show's theme: *Things We Destroy That Refuse to Perish*. Lice, weeds, and outhouses were highlighted exhibits. Rory had been the one who discovered the John Lennon and leaked its existence to Normal. Unbeknownst to Normal, her crew had filmed the theft and was now in possession of videotape of him committing a number of felonies: breaking and entering, grand larceny, semen trafficking of a deceased icon—which was not technically a crime but would certainly not go overlooked by any judge.

"Unless you want to be held in breach of contract, you better get that vial. Buyer's locked and loaded. Happening this week. We've already edited the pilot, sent out advertisements and promos—we bought a fucking billboard on I-95!"

"First, I have a plan how to get it back," he lied. "I know where they're taking the plane. Second, I never signed a contract." Normal got close, the smell of her fake tan, the lickable shape of her puffed lips. "You need my permission to film me. And that is something you'll never have."

"Do you realize there is an entire field of law that deals spe-cifically with reality television? They teach it to the college crowd nowadays. And do you also realize my firm staffs a team of the world's most ingenious reality television attorneys?" They both let it simmer. "I checked with the lawyers. We don't need your permission to film a reality TV show about Normal Fulk, and do you know why?"

"I'm curious, sure."

"Because you're dead. Just like John Lennon. He doesn't have any say about whether we film his squirty-squirt either. We can film anything we want and there's not a damn thing you can do."

Normal let his face fall into his hands. "I'm so confused."

"It's a confusing business." She rubbed his shoulders. "We

haven't decided if the plot includes you faking your death, and you sort of live on as this conniving semen pirate. Or if we just continuously show you in flashback vignettes. Main thing is to think big picture." She pinched his cheek. She scratched a tit. "Tell you what. All this semen talk has gotten me raw. What do you say you, me, Lobo get us a room, have us some rough meal?"

"You want to take me to dinner?"

"Sex is what I'm saying. Some bouncy-bounce."

"I thought Lobo was married."

"He's guild. Paid by the hour. He'll do what he's told."

"I really wish you'd just leave me alone."

"That's not going to happen, sweetie." She kissed his forehead. "Good luck with the Lennon. We'll be watching. And filming." She snapped her fingers and the crew broke for position. "Now Lobo's going to beat on you a little, just so you know who calls the shots."

"That won't be necessary."

"Probably not, but we need the footage. This is a dirty business you're involved with and the viewers need to sense the danger the protagonist faces."

Normal woke up on a park bench, no camera crew so far as he could tell. He sat up to decide what hurt most, settled on his neck, and worked the good hand into muscle. He was no more a hoodlum than he was a religious man. Normal had never attended church as a boy, or had much interest in the concept. But he thought taking on an honorable mission might garner the approval of the gods, one of them anyway. He checked the tattoo to see what Frank had to say on the matter, which was when the idea struck. It was not faith he needed, not just yet anyhow. It was luck.

Lucky Dan O'Malley had been a friend of Frank's, most fortunate guy Normal ever knew. His job was to fly to Las Vegas and stand next to guys while they gambled. That's all he did—just stood and smiled and rubbed shoulders and told stories. Rory was right; when it came to unlucky, Normal was king. All he required was a mild lucky streak to help him rescue the John Lennon and get out of town. Hell, if it worked for blackjack, why couldn't it work for this?

Normal's body throbbed from the beating. There was $3,000 stashed in a locker at Port Authority, emergency funds. Normal intended to rent some luck.

Lucy lay fully clothed in the oversized bed at the Whalensky Plaza, the puppet beside her. She was meant to be on vacation at an all-expenses-paid Hawaiian resort. Although she had an apartment thirty blocks north, the complimentary hotel served as a compromise. Before her arrival in the room, the airline had placed her confiscated phone on the bed; she had no intention of turning it on. She could not say why, only that the phone seemed too comfortable there on its miniature pillow.

Was it paranoia? She had a history of unbelievability, so it was very possible this was an ordinary plane crash and nothing more. But her gut told her something different—the pilot, the beautiful passengers, the strange lip-biting by the girl collecting phones. There were also her own knee-jerk reactions of the past to consider—how she had nearly killed her husband, how she had paralyzed her career by similarly capricious behavior.

She had unlocked the electronic bracelet monitor and was massaging her left hand. Lucy was permitted to unlock the puppet when she slept at night; any other time, the bracelet would signal her court-assigned psychiatrist who would phone urgently, as though she had just engineered a jail break and was leading a capable mob toward the center of town. She was on friendly terms with the shrink, Gary Corbin. Lucy had been sleeping with him on and off for several months. In his mid-thirties, he was astonishingly depressed for someone who had chosen the career goal of brightening people's outlooks. He had no friends and previously worked part-time as an airplane mechanic. She was hopeful he would help her break into the fished-out airplane now docked in Lower Manhattan. She dialed his beeper from her stolen cell phone and waited.

The old woman's phone rang. "I was beeped."

"It's me."

"What the hell, Lucy? Your plane crashed."

"I'm aware."

"Been watching it on TV all day. And I've been calling. Why aren't you answering your phone?"

"It was confiscated."

"You didn't kill anyone, did you? Is that why you're calling?"

She explained she needed access to the docked plane, which was guarded. He being a city employee, she was hopeful he could flash credentials and let her sneak on by herself; Gary insisted he would chaperone.

"You're a gentleman," she said.

"It has nothing to do with chivalry. My goal is self-preservation. You drown sneaking on that airplane, there's no way I keep this job."

"How long before you can be out front of the Whalensky?"

"You unlocked the puppet twenty minutes ago. I've been here for three."

"What are you driving?"

"You'll know it when you see it."

She placed Ava Tardner on her wrist and secured the bracelet. Then she pulled the burlap sack over the puppet. It had been a novelty gift from her now ex-husband a decade earlier, a ventriloquist dummy in her likeness. It had arrived in a fancy box filled with Styrofoam peanuts, Lucy digging through the ruckus until she found her miniature doppelgänger, a handwritten note attached to the doll: "I wish there were two of you."

"So sweet." She kissed her husband, Ken. "Looks just like me."

"Custom-made in Sweden," he explained. "Doll wasn't cheap. What should we name it?"

She hadn't owned a doll in years and was a bit taken holding a smaller version of herself. "I used to name my dolls after classic actresses, but with slightly different names. It just gave them more meaning. Like Elizabeth Naylor, or Shirley Dimples, or Grace Belly."

"Rita Hayworms," her husband added.

"Greta Garbanzo."

"Ava Tardner."

"I rather like Ava Tardner." She placed her hand inside the

puppet's inner cavity and worked open the face and mouth. "Ava Tardner it is."

At the time they'd had fun with it; little did she know the significance it would play in their lives. "The Incident" itself was no one thing. Rather it was a series of events that spanned a nineteen-year marriage and ended with gunshots, public humiliation, dead fish, divorce.

Kenneth Springer was a banker, Lucy Springer the darling of the evening news. By all appearances, the Springers had the perfect life. They lived in an apartment on Central Park West, which featured a $2 million aquarium that consumed an entire wall of their home. The aquarium was her husband's passion. Among other creatures, he had purchased a half-dozen Platinum Arowana, a rare breed of Dragon Fish that cost $80,000 each. So enamored by the aquarium was Kenneth that he began fucking his mistress against the side of it, the twenty-three-year-old Genny (with a G). Lucy had caught them in the act, arriving home to find the girl pinned against the glass, Kenneth's pants around his ankles, the fucking fish swimming behind them in the blue spotlight. The two scattered for separate rooms, but all Lucy could do was stare at the sweat marks Genny's perfect ass had left on the glass. Lucy would have had sex against the tank if she had been asked. She would have done a lot of things differently if it had meant avoiding the divorce and all that would follow. They had tried to have a child, a feat that had brought sex back to the marriage, for a few months anyway, ending when they each separately concluded Lucy's reproductive tract was not up to the challenge of furthering the Springer name.

Soon after conception failed, they began communicating with one another through notes. Little pieces of paper—shades of yellow, pink, and blue—stuck to the refrigerator, tidbits of passive-aggressive nonsense that kept the marriage skittering along. At first they could blame it on their careers—they were both busy and often without time for a candlelit dinner, even a proper conversation. But the notes transitioned from a tactical device to a preferred method of communication. It was simple: They could not stand the thought of each other, much less the effort of having to discuss it.

Back to the dummy, the main instigator of "The Incident." Eventually they ran out of little notes. When they had to speak, which was rare, she would communicate with him through the apparatus on the end of her arm. She knew it was juvenile, but it irked Kenneth savagely, the miniature Sandra Bullock whom he had to speak to if he hoped to progress the divorce. Often alcohol was involved. They both refused to vacate the apartment—he because of the aquarium, she because it was her home. He had offered to pay her generously, but she refused. He'd had aquarium sex with a more flexible partner, and she was not letting him get his way.

"Hey, Kenny," she called when he walked into a room, Lucy scrambling to get Ava Tardner over her wrist. There was extra "y" so that it sounded like the puppet was singing his name: "Hey, Kennyyyyyy." The puppet had a split personality, depending on how much Lucy drank. Sober it was simply the intermediary between her and her husband. But with alcohol it morphed into the whiny, helium voice of a young lady, presumably Genny (with a G), which implied he was not only arguing with the puppet, but that he had been sleeping with it also.

"Lucy, this is ridiculous."

"What's ridiculous, Kennyyyyyy?"

"Put it down so we can talk like adults."

"Lucy doesn't want to talk. But I do, big fella." She was a horrible ventriloquist. The dummy's mouth was never in sync with her words, although she had the rhythm of the body precise.

"We can't live like this. I've made an offer for the apartment. Why haven't we heard from your attorney?"

"Lucy wants to live with the fishies."

"You don't even like fish."

"Lucy loves fish—fried fish, fish sticks, fish with tartar sauce."

What she did not realize was that Kenneth had juvenile tendencies himself; he had been recording their conversations for months. He assumed she would tire of talking to him through the dummy. He had even considered stealing it so she would stop. Instead he settled on the most prudent approach—he installed a camera in the kitchen ceiling and recorded his wife pointing the dummy at him, never breaking character. He did not want anyone to see the pitiful exchanges. And he would be humiliated if he used the film for leverage in the divorce. The truth was, like his wife, he had partially lost his mind as the marriage crumbled until his only grasp on the situation was the subversive camera.

As things often do, the Springers' marital deterioration came to a head during the Christmas season. Specifically, at his office holiday party. They were cordial to each other in public; if nothing else, Lucy was a well-known member of the media, and incompatible behavior would reflect poorly on her career. But Genny was at the party, which brought on the sudden mood, although the mistress was less to blame than the bartender who kept refilling Lucy's Chardonnay. At first, she was only doing it to Kenneth, the thumb at the base of the mouth, the fingers at the top, calling across the room in the nasally voice, "Hey, Kennyyyyyyy?" to where he stood talking to coworkers and attempting to ignore his drunken wife. At some point, she had managed to persuade one of the partygoers to give up his sock; not only was one of Kenneth's peers walking the room with one naked foot, but also his wife was wearing a stranger's soiled laundry on her hand and trailing him through the gala.

For the most part everyone enjoyed this playful side of Lucy Springer, unaware of the impending divorce and secretly thrilled to see someone of her stature let her hair down. She followed her husband through the room, standing behind him and pointing her socked hand over his shoulder, turning it to whoever spoke.

"Did you know Kennyyyyyyy's got an aquarium?"

"Kennyyyyyyy's got a girlfriend."

"Hey, Kennyyyyyyy."

It should be noted at this point that Lucy was blackout drunk. She would recall none of it—not the black sock, not the tenth or eleventh glasses of wine. All this she would later read in the divorce papers. At first Kenneth laughed along with the fun. But when the spirit of the puppet took its toll, he forcibly dragged Lucy from the party.

When they arrived at their apartment she went straight for

the dummy; he let her at it. He coaxed the conversation into the kitchen and dissected the events of the evening for a solid twenty-five minutes, with each passing Scotch Kenneth working up the resolve to finally ruin her. She passed out on the couch, Ava Tardner strewn across her chest, and he recorded a few minutes of that as well. He should have simply taken the puppet and burned it then, torn it to shreds, left it for dead for her to discover in the morning. But he had been embarrassed in front of associates, and he was infuriated, and he was good and drunk himself.

The next day when he arrived at his office, he knew he had done something wicked. There was a shifty feeling intimating how cruel he may have been. And then it hit him, directly through his swollen brain: He had uploaded the video onto YouTube. He had done it in a moment of weakness, but certainly it had been subconsciously premeditated. After all, he had hired someone to install the camera. He had logged on to the site months before and created an account. He had obtained a passing understanding of how to upload videos. Sure, he could blame the actual climax on booze. But the rest of it was cruel and strange, the last year of the Springer union in a nutshell. He quickly logged on and deleted the video, but by then it had been live for eight hours; it had already surpassed 27,000 views; he had received it in his inbox several times from associates.

The phone call arrived soon after. It was the first time in months Lucy spoke to him without the pesky mediator.

"I'm going to fuck your face!"

"Now Lucy."

"I was just escorted out of the building."

"They fired you?"

"Leave of absence, but it's the same thing."

He slammed the door to his office. Coworkers peered in through the blinds. "Don't do something you'll regret, Lucy."

"I won't regret it." She laughed and cried together. "I'll enjoy this."

"Where are you?"

"In a cab. On the way to a fishing hole, Kennyyyyyyy."

He arrived just ahead of the police sirens that circled the block. Several of his neighbors were in the lobby, having evacuated their apartments at first gunshot. When he reached their floor, the door was open. She was teetering with a net on the staircase that led to the top of the aquarium. The puppet and Kenneth's Smith & Wesson .357 lay abandoned on the floor, which was littered with sea creatures—a couple of angelfish, a Siamese fighting fish, the Lemon tetra he had named Oscar. Three of his $80,000 Arowanas were there; two were not moving, one still flopping. He quickly grabbed it and tossed it in the sink, blasting the faucet. There were three bullet scars etched into the glass. The tank was bulletproof— that had been one of the requirements of the building—although a few more punctures, coupled with the weight of the water, and the glass would certainly cave.

Kenneth managed a quick reconstruction of the scene. She had taken the gun, possibly while wearing the puppet, and fired three times into the tank. Seeing that it did not break—or perhaps sensing she would become awfully soaked if it did—she dropped the gun, and possibly the puppet, and retrieved the net. She was mainly fishing for the rare Arowana, but depositing anything she captured onto the living room floor. She had been at it a good twenty minutes and made solid progress. He ran to the bathroom and began filling the tub, returning to find her waving the net, the last Arowana captured.

"You've lost your mind!"

"How do you like your fish, Kennyyyyyyy!"

"Don't do it."

She lofted the net at him. It smacked into the floor that by then was a slippery ship deck, the fish flopping, him reaching for the net. In his haste he failed to remember the abandoned .357, not to mention the puppet, turning to find Lucy wielding both.

She pointed the gun at him and let loose a cackle. "Drop the fish!"

"You won't shoot me."

"I won't shoot you. But I'll shoot that fucking fish."

Her eyes crazy, the awful grin. She pulled the trigger. The

bullet blew out the window, which caused him to drop the net, more flopping. Lucy stepped forward and lined up the animal.

"Don't do it, Lucy."

The bullet splattered fish meat and blood, along with wood from the floor. Her face was covered in splatter, as was Kenneth's white shirt. He squealed, sure the next bullet was his. Instead she walked to the sink, aimed, and blasted. That bullet took part of the sink then ricocheted against the kitchen wall, narrowly missing the left side of Lucy's chin.

She was wearing the puppet when the police arrived, guns drawn, both she and the doll covered in sushi and blood. She was arrested and taken to Roosevelt Hospital. What followed was the greatest media frenzy of the still-pubescent twenty-first century. Each day another juicy nugget was leaked that the media latched on to—the cost of the fish; People for the Ethical Treatment of Animals calling for Lucy Springer's termination from the network; Kenneth's lawyers threatening to have Lucy jailed for attempted murder; Lucy's lawyer claiming his client was driven to it, a form of puppet insanity, threatening to put the puppet on the stand if it went to trial; the affair; Genny (with a G) being interviewed by Howard Stern; the video that got endless replay despite Kenneth having deleted it; all the sordid details, some of which were true, the whole massive thing spinning into shambles.

They agreed to meet with a divorce mediator. Kenneth would split their assets and would not require her to compensate him for the aquarium. Additionally, he would not press charges; he had assurances that the district attorney was not interested in pursuing criminal charges either and would suggest probation for the gun incident instead. But there was one requirement: As part of the probation, she would have to attend therapy sessions and publicly wear the puppet for one year. It would be attached to her wrist by an electronic monitor and would be enforced by the Department of Social Services. She could take it off at night, or when she was in her house. But when she was in public—exercising, at work, even on a date—the puppet had to be on her arm.

"Don't be ridiculous, Ken."

"You tried to kill me."

"I didn't try to kill you. I was killing fish."

"You pointed a loaded weapon at me and pulled the trigger. If you're interested in that coming out in a courtroom, then don't sign the papers."

"I'm a news anchor. I can't wear a puppet on my arm."

"If you want to avoid prison you will."

She turned to the divorce mediator, an older man with a beard grown for the sole purpose of stroking while he listened to couples complain. "Is this even legal?"

"Has someone ever been placed under puppet arrest? Not to my knowledge. It's an unusual request." He stroked the beard, waiting for the lawyers to sort it out. "Given the circumstances—the weapons charges, the property damage, the potential criminal trial—I'd have to say this is an acceptable arrangement. Although it's not my place to do so."

"But I'd be wearing a puppet."

"I'm just the mediator. I can't advise you. I don't understand what Mr. Springer gains in this." He held a hand toward each of them, praying they would leave him out of it. "All I can do is tell both parties that from a financial standpoint, this is a sound arrangement. And it keeps you out of prison."

She turned to her lawyer, who stared across the table, both fists clenched. He wanted nothing more than for this to go to trial—all those cameras, all those delicious details coming out in the papers attached to his name—even if that meant his client spending the next decade in prison.

"Will you at least consider time off for good behavior?" Lucy asked.

Kenneth smiled. At that moment, if only he could have foreseen the budding sexual deviancy of the puppet, and how it would seep out on camera and thrill the viewing public, he would have forgotten his demand right then, taken his wife home, and let the puppet watch.

Lucy exited the lobby to find a rusted ice cream truck parked in the taxi line. On the side in handwritten paint: CORBIN'S COUNSEL: RING THE BELL TO SPEAK WITH A PROFESSIONAL. The truck also sported a FOR SALE sign. She rang the bell. The ice cream truck spoke. "Lucy?"

"Let me in."

"Before I do, promise you didn't kill anyone."

"I didn't kill anyone."

He opened the window. "I have to ask when clients call after hours." He peered down. "Where's Ava?"

She held up the sack.

"We spoke about confronting this ailment, did we not?"

"Open the fucking door, Gary." She climbed inside. "What's with the truck?"

"Job pays $37,000. I do this to make ends meet."

"Therapy for the masses. Not bad. Decent money?"

"On a good day I cover gas."

He rolled over the engine with some cursing encouragement and headed for Seventh Avenue. Gary Corbin looked older than his age, tired eyes, all around tiredness. He had an acceptable physique because he never ate fast food nor drank alcohol out of fear he would turn into the very clients he hoped to assist—a herd of Big Mac grazing, beer guzzling, anxiety-ridden buffoons who should be drugged and quarantined for the sanity of civilization.

He had been employed as a psychiatrist for twelve years by the city's Office of Strategic Therapy, a department with the goal of assisting the court system as well as some of the 300,000 people the city employed. He despised his job. The only thing worse was the prospect that he would one day lose it. He had paid his way through medical school as a part-time airplane mechanic, only to discover the work was giving him panic attacks. What if he forgot to tighten a bolt, or properly lube an engine rotor? What if he failed to notice a worn piston, a faulty air filter? All those people, all those lives, all that luggage at the whim of one careless blunder. The Office of Strategic Therapy was no different. Like an engine, these people and their problems were complex. One little word, one subtle nuance, and he might corrupt them forever, send them out into the world feeling thoroughly ugly and stupid with access to guns with which they might shoot up a coffee shop.

Gary Corbin had stopped believing there was a strategy by which a person could maintain good mental health. All these people complaining about stress and anxiety and fear, worry and death and depression—they were all correct. Who was he to regulate their pessimism? He was stuck. In his job, in his life, even with the truck—no one would buy it, and he still had twenty-three months of payments, and so the only thing to do was grind it out. What he wanted more than a steady paycheck, or for his ice cream truck to function properly, was freedom—for two giant, magical fingers to reach down, pick him up by the back of his collar, and set him in a new life, someplace warm and with lots of strip malls.

The only benefit of the job was that he was in constant contact with women who had lower morale and a worse outlook than he did, and occasionally thought it wise to sleep with him. His favorites were the women with anxiety disorders, the twisted minds who had lost sight of their sanity behind the mounting pressures of daily life. They came to him on broken knees, and he prescribed Prozac and Xanax, just enough to keep them vertical but not enough for the anxiety to dissipate completely, and they were so thankful they fell into his arms, and eventually, his bed. So when the folder arrived on his desk that he would be overseeing the divorce stipulations of a woman suffering from puppet insanity, Gary Corbin perked—she would be his White Whale, his Mt. Everest.

"So you got on a plane without notifying me, and look what happened."

"I was going to call when I landed."

"No you weren't. And that bracelet has a GPS chip. Soon as you went through security I knew what you were up to."

Lucy thought back to the phone on her bed. A GPS chip was easy to insert.

"Pretty soon they'll be making GPS chips standard in everything so they know where everyone is at all times." He pioneered the ice cream truck toward the water, blowing through stop signs, and narrowly avoiding pedestrians. "You should have told me. I would have tagged along. Kept you company."

"I went on vacation to be alone. Besides, I won a vacation package for one person. I couldn't have taken someone even if I'd wanted to."

"No one ever wins those vacations." He watched the sack. "You're sleeping with someone behind my back, I know it."

"I'm not sleeping with anyone."

"Well I'm sleeping with people behind your back, other patients if you must know. And if you were wise you'd do the same."

She lifted the sack. "For obvious reasons, men don't find me attractive. And I don't mind if you sleep with other women. You're young. Have your fun."

They never spoke during sex, though Lucy had tried on several occasions to initiate dirty talk, something that had never interested her when she was married. When the sex began, she was hopeful Gary could be convinced to let her stop wearing the puppet. But he was petrified of losing his job. He phoned each night she removed the doll for bed, just to make sure she had not gone off the deep end:

"CRAZY WOMAN REMOVES PUPPET; KILLS 8; WHERE WAS THE THERAPIST?"

Still, she was curious at the other patients he claimed to be sleeping with. Twice a month, Gary demanded she attend group therapy, which curiously consisted of all women, all suffering various anxiety disorders. Mandy never spoke, just pointed her finger and pantomimed a machine gun—a rattling *Bat-at-at-at-at-at-at-at-at!* Brenda began and ended every sentence with the word "Wednesday"; it was unclear if she thought it was Wednesday, or if she was from Wednesday, or if she simply enjoyed the day. It was possible Gary Corbin, ice cream truck driver, was sleeping with all of them, Don Juan of the sociopaths.

"Are you sleeping with Brenda?"

"Can't say. Doctor-patient confidentiality."

"Are you sleeping with Mandy?"

"No, but I've tried."

"How many clients are you sleeping with?"

"Right now? Six. But one recently violated the terms of her parole. I'm afraid we'll have to end our arrangement."

"Sorry to hear it."

"In a couple months I'll lose you, too. I'll never hear from you after . . ."

She lifted the arm. "After I remove this?"

"You know what I mean."

"That's not the only reason I slept with you." She leaned in and kissed his cheek. "You've been a good friend, Gary. I won't forget that."

Gary smiled and hit a string of green lights that had the ice cream truck touching twenty-five mph down the West Side Highway toward where the plane was docked. Divers had attached it to tugboats and lugged the plane a quarter-mile until it sat partly submerged near shore. It would be hauled out of the water and a team of crack investigators would go over every bolt and gear until they could say, without a doubt, that the plane had indeed crashed into a river. Media vans were few, the story exhausted until morning. There were several guards stationed around the perimeter so that no one could get close.

"How do you intend to get me on the plane?"

He watched the guards. "Sack of beer should do."

"Do you have any beer?"

"The back end is refrigerated. None of my patients can afford health insurance. I typically medicate with Pabst."

Gary grabbed a brown sack from the rear. He walked toward the guards and flashed his credentials, then passed along the beer. He waved Lucy over and a moment later they were on the edge of the docked aircraft, peering into the engine that sat closest to shore.

"So tell me again what's this all about."

"Just a hunch," she said. "Something about this plane I can't figure. The pilot. The person lying on the cockpit floor. And the girl collecting phones."

"Why were they collecting phones?"

"Federal regulations," she said. "During a crash they have to collect all recording devices from passengers."

"That doesn't sound right." Gary shivered at the details that went into a simple flight. He pulled out a flashlight and pointed it at Lucy. "What are we looking for?" he asked.

"I don't know. You're the plane mechanic. You tell me."

"TV said it was a bird strike. I guess dead birds."

"Wouldn't they all have washed away?"

"Not likely. There should be bird meat somewhere." He used both hands to shove the propeller out of the way and limped through water. Then he circled back, running his fingers along the inside. "Let me ask—both engines quit at the same time, or one and then the other?"

"No, there was a wait."

"Uh huh."

"What are you thinking?"

"Takes a massive swarm of birds to stop motors this size, so this should look like a slaughterhouse. There's no way birds stopped this plane."

"You know that for sure?"

"I'm a psychiatrist, not a plane expert. But you ask a regular mechanic, he'll tell you the same. Something else, too. Pilot's *last* alternative would be a water landing, especially with all the airports in this area." He shined the flashlight at the propeller. "This is still in one piece. After watching this on TV all day, it's my semi-educated opinion the plane was at an altitude with plenty of time to restart the engine, or at least find a nice strip of earth to set her down. Soon as I heard a plane ditched in the Hudson, it definitely sounded suspicious."

"So you think it was faked?"

"I didn't say faked, I said suspicious. This is what I'm talking about, Lucy—you're paranoid. And paranoid people suffer anxiety disorder. And people with anxiety are dangerous." Gary was always trying to convince her the puppet was a real disorder. It made the affair more titillating if she were truly broken.

Lucy took out a camera and began snapping pictures—inside the engine, from the edge of the aircraft back through the city skyline, from shore out over the plane into the dull lights of New Jersey. No one could doubt she had pictures of the inside of *that* particular engine.

"So it wasn't birds," Gary said. "Tell me what you're thinking."

She thought back to the evacuation. It was too polished for a real emergency. It should have been . . . she didn't know the word for it. "It just should have been . . . more real."

"Come again?"

"It wasn't a crash as much as a well-executed landing," Lucy said.

He pointed at the camera. "You think that'll prove it?"

"No. But these will get me in the door with the people who know."

TUESDAY

STUPID BLOODY TUESDAY

Veiltality Incorporated occupied the top floor of a nameless building in Lower Manhattan, a nondescript pile of bricks that blended discreetly with the abandoned storefronts and parking garages. There was no address on the building, nor was the company's logo available in the lobby. Should a person discover the building's locale, they would then be faced with a phantom business, a missing floor assignment. The company existed like gravity or electricity, constantly at work in the slumberless city but hidden away from close inspection.

Veiltality employed hundreds of analysts and experts and receptionists, all of whom sat in adjacent rooms, although few were permitted to enter the bald man's inner sanctum. The man with the leaf-shaped birthmark on his head sat in front of a large bulletin board that ran halfway around the room. The other half held one hundred monitors displaying up-to-the-minute news from every major and semi-major media source in the country. Behind him was installed a miniature model of New York City, the skyscrapers and bridges and waterways. The room darkened, the monitors provided the only light, flickering, pulsing, which to the imitation megalopolis would seem ferocious lightning from an approaching storm. His phone rang just then. Only three people in the world had that number—his mother and two employees. It was nearly one o'clock in the morning; his mother was asleep.

"Go ahead."

"It's Jimmish, sir. You asked that I check on the strange passenger. He never checked in to the hotel."

"You're certain he was dropped there?"

"Yes, sir."

"And he just walked away?"

"It appears that way."

The bald man changed one of the monitors to a cooking show. The chef was making Harvest Stew, which was inconsistent with the spring season. It should have been a chicken salad, a leg of lamb perhaps. In this age of technology, the bald man could never forgive reruns.

"Tell me about the other pilot."

"Mr. Wrinkles. He suffered a heart attack. He remains in critical condition."

"Is he conscious yet?"

"No, sir."

"I'd like to be notified when he's conscious."

"Of course, Mr. Black."

"Was there anything else?"

"Perhaps. During my rounds. Down by the plane. I noticed a truck as I arrived."

"What type of truck?"

"I believe it used to be an ice cream truck."

"It's your attention to detail I adore, Jimmish. You were right to be suspicious."

"I have a license plate. I'll look into it."

"And the unexpected passenger, Jimmish. I'll be curious to hear more."

Alastair Black hung up the phone and dialed another number. A moment later his assistant's voice answered with sleepy caution. "Hello, Mr. Black."

"I need you in the office."

"But I just left."

"Yes, I'm aware. Do you know how I know that Miss Dressings? Because I listened to you leave in the elevator. And now I'm alone in the office. I put all that together myself."

She sighed. "Is it something we can do over the phone?"

"There will be shouting. For that I need you here."

"I'm going to get yelled at?"

"Most business these days can be conducted over e-mail or phone, even text message. But a good old-fashioned dressing down requires face to face."

"I don't understand why you don't just fire me."

"I've struggled with that myself," he said. "It has something to do with the challenge of your consistent failure. My perfective nature forces me to ensure you succeed."

"I'll be there in twenty."

"I put you in the hotel across the street this week so you'd be able to come as needed. You'll be here in three." He stabbed a tomato with a fork and took a slippery bite. "You see, Miss Dressings, this is why I generally don't hire women. They take too long to get ready. When I call for you, I'd like you to imagine a flood. Take only the necessities."

"If it were a flood I would bring my cat. Shall I bring Mr. Tuffers?"

"Single women under the age of thirty shouldn't have cats. It's becoming awfully clear to me why you struggle socially."

He hung up the phone. Alastair Black slept only two hours a night, except for Wednesdays, when he slept five hours because he despised Wednesdays. He hated the sound of the word, the interruption of the day midweek; nothing, it seemed, went right on Wednesday, only a day away. He was alone on the building's top floor. He had sent the staff home hours before, craving the solace so that he might stare into the lonely board outlining his latest assignment and follow the monitors. He appreciated watching all the names and theories and solid and jagged lines congeal into that one special episode, and just by imagining it he felt he could will it into existence. The lines did not stop at the board's perimeter. Rather they continued out invisible into the world, out into the city and the universe, connecting every critter and airsucker under his vast agenda. So that by staring into the board, he could then turn to his left or right and instantly see his thoughts emerge on a screen. In that way he was influencing all of it, every instinct and detail, every evolutionary whim and marauding trend, a wily puppet master.

The plaque on his door read ALASTAIR BLACK, PUBLICIST, although calling him a publicist was like labeling cancer a cold. It was generally understood he was the best at what he did. And what he did was to spin a situation in whichever way he desired. He had acquired the notorious and yet endearing nickname "Blackie

Spin." The way some are born to lead. Others to follow. Others to excite in rare and extraordinary ways. Blackie was born to weave it all together into an appropriate narrative.

He stabbed another tomato and heavily salted a side. Taking a bite, he studied the board for additional inspiration, trying to ascertain what about it bothered him, why it was likely the fault of his assistant, Monica Dressings. The leaf-shaped birthmark grew a red, swollen outline when something was amiss; as if when he thought too hard it sucked hemoglobin and nutrients from the rest of him until the leaf burned like an intense homing beacon, eager to pinpoint the falsity. There was something about his board that did not add up, some finite piece of rubble that had not been properly integrated. And now it was jiggling and wobbling and making a subtle nuisance, a beautiful orchestra but the trombonist has hiccups.

"Good evening, Mr. Black."

He nodded toward the board. "Take a look. Does anything seem off?"

"We've been looking at the board all day."

There was something about Monica Dressings that did not fit. She was clothed in an Italian rain slicker over a worn bathrobe. On her feet were bedroom slippers, her hair done perfectly over rectangular glasses. It was as though two beings had dressed her—one rushing out the door so she would not be late, the other checking lip gloss, as though they could not agree on the meeting's priority. She had arrived in a hurry, although not quick enough from Blackie's perspective.

"I estimated Miss Springer would go live with her first update forty-five minutes after the plane crashed. She did it in twenty minutes."

"I thought the point was to get the information out quickly."

"We need to control the information if we wish to control the story. Don't forget that, Miss Dressings."

"I'm sorry."

"Your duty was personnel." He pointed a forked tomato toward the pertinent space of board. "Yet a renegade made it on board as one of the passengers. And now he's the only passenger I cannot find."

"There was some type of emergency. I was busy with the other passengers and did not hear until we—"

"Total haul should have been 161. Mr. Swagger accurately counted an extra body, giving us 162 passengers. Three pilots, five flight attendants. That leaves how many?"

"We've been over this."

"I believe 154 is the answer. Of that 154, eighty people were airline employees and forty were hired actors. What does that leave?"

She stared at the ceiling, having been through the numbers most of the day. "Thirty-four."

"We arranged a first class ticket for the reporter, which we'll get to in a moment. Thirty-one were purchased by regular travelers, all of whom we screened. There was you and Jimmish portraying our sky marshal, which leaves a remainder of how many?"

"Zero." She closed her eyes.

"It should have been zero," Blackie said.

"As I said there was an emergency with one of the passengers who was permitted a seat—"

"You are not the storyteller!" he screamed, pointing the fork, the leaf on his head scorching. He stood and walked to the board. "Your main duty post-landing was to stand at the front of the plane and collect phones and other devices so that we could control the information. Fairly simple, wouldn't you say?"

"I wouldn't put it like that, not at all."

"Including the emergency passenger, there were 154 on board. The eighty employees carried no phones, which leaves how many recording devices to collect?"

"Seventy."

"Seventy-four, Miss Dressings." He tapped the board. "Four passengers carried two devices each. Which means you should have had seventy-eight phones in the bag, but you brought me seventy-six."

"I don't know how it went bad."

"The reporter had a phone!" He screamed again. "Of all the people we didn't want to have a phone, she was priority. She stole a phone and placed a call to a major news network minutes after the landing."

"It was confusing. Everyone was trying to get off so quickly."

"The control of information, Miss Dressings. I can't stress enough how crucial it is." He circled the board. "But it's the second phone that discourages me—the only phone that ended up in the water. Odd, don't you think, that the second phone belonged to the passenger that talked his way aboard my plane?"

"Just a bad coincidence."

"I don't believe in coincidence." He slapped the board. "Something happened on that plane before it sank, and I need to know what."

"I told you, Mr. Black. I went onto the wing with Wrinkles and the other passengers." He was baffled as to why she never cried. He always made employees cry, but Monica Dressings was not a weeper. It was the great flaw in her personality; she was doomed and desperate, in short, surely a crier. But never with the tears. "The pilot was dying. There was so much water. I got nervous."

"Tell it to me again." He pointed the remote control around the room, a wand shuffling the programs. "The captain, Jimmish, and this missing gentleman, correct?"

"And they argued."

"What about?"

"The man. He wouldn't get off the plane."

"Jimmish went back in the plane while you waited on the wing?"

"The ferries were arriving. I was helping Wrinkles and the old woman."

He was yelling by now. "But what was the man doing on the plane if all the other passengers had evacuated?"

"Jimmish said he was just sitting."

"Just sitting. In the rear?"

"In the last row."

"And he kept his phone?"

"He threw his phone into the water."

"But he was doing something on the plane," Blackie said. "And that something has become this story's great flaw. Now we don't know where he is."

The reason for collecting the phones was twofold: In case anyone had been recording the descent, they would screen the devices and delete what was necessary; and before they were returned, each phone had been outfitted with a GPS tracking device so they could know where the passengers were if necessary. They were all hooked in to Blackie's computer, and he could locate most nonemployees aboard Flight AW2921.

"Those are our two unknowns." He walked to the motherboard and with a green marker made two circles. "One, the strange passenger: What was he doing on my plane? Two, the reporter: We failed to control her once, it cannot happen again."

She checked her watch. "I know you don't want to hear this. But it was a coincidence."

"I hope you're right. It would be a shame if any of these issues upset my week. Good night, Miss Dressings."

He waited until he heard the elevator depart. Then he sat down and stabbed the fork into his last tomato, and watched the new formation of his lines and names and circles. This was his method: to study the strategy again and again. And once it became common, to pick up his chair, rearrange the office, remove his shoes, pull the shades, watch the board from a unique perspective, decipher the endless images and text that crept across his monitors. There were only a few people on the planet that could do what he did. He was a micromanager of supreme talents, able to organize all the clutter, all the minutia into an acceptable plot. No detail was too small, no stone left unturned. He had ensured that fifty percent of the passengers were female, forty-six percent were minority, which was consistent with the demographic of most airlines. He had checked the Farmer's Almanacs, spoken to dozens of meteorologists, all to ascertain what wind or rain or thunderstorms might frequent the area on the morning of liftoff. Once he had compiled his data, he would set it aside and then start fresh, redo it all with different variables to uncover what mistakes might arise.

Spin doctors typically handled cover-ups for politicians or actors embroiled in sexual trysts, or drug-induced rages. Veiltality handled its share of those cases. But Blackie Spin was coveted for his ability to oversee the more massive campaigns. It was a gift really—his ability to see the proper narrative, to expose the public's weak points, and to insert into those weaknesses his version of reality, the truth be damned. He had a knack for damning the truth, sinking his opinions into every cell phone and Facebook page and laptop and Twitter feed. Just to get into the room with him cost $100,000—and not even that guaranteed he would take the project. But when he did, he would shift history.

Alastair Black was notorious in certain circles for the bottled water campaign of the late 1980s, in which he convinced the public it was cleaner, healthier, and trendier to drink water from bottles. Before then, most people drank water out of the faucet like they'd been doing for the past century. A billion dollar industry had followed, with vitamin waters and fruit waters and soda-flavored waters and even spinach waters being purchased by consumers, all of whom were convinced the reservoirs that fed their taps were full of herpes and cyanide.

He also engineered a Nymphopucky bug epidemic in New York City, with the number of Nymphopucky infestations rising astronomically despite the critters being imaginary. He was hired by Mayor Susan Cromberg and the city to deflect attention away from the shoddy condition of roads, bridges, and subways. Blackie's initiative—get people so afraid of these imaginary bugs they would never notice their transportation infrastructure was falling apart, and could not blame the city if they "invested" funds in the healthcare system instead. Nymphopuckys reproduced autoerotically and constantly, such that if one got into your house, by morning you would have nearly two hundred generations of the fleas in your home. There were eighteen recorded deaths, an industry of medications arose to thwart the problem, studies of the reported "oversexualization" of America and how it related to the bugs, even a health warning was issued by the U.S. government to alert tourists about the city's Nymphopucky epidemic. No one mentioned the roads.

He had grown tired of the political affairs and famous actors who awoke next to dead girls and boys. The corporations that invented toothpastes, only to find there was a chemical in the tartar control causing heart aneurisms in twelve-year-olds—boring. It was these cases he enjoyed, the ones that at first glance seemed impossible, and for most spin doctors likely were. So when the board of directors of a medium-sized airline approached him with a problem, the leaf on his skull turned miraculous shades of mulberry.

Several of their jets had failed inspections over the last year; the company had just gone public and stockholders were not thrilled; if their stock did not stop dwindling Air Wanderlust would likely file bankruptcy before the year was out; and there was no way they could afford fuel for the month of October, much less meet payroll for the 6,000 employees. The idea was risky: crash land a jet into the Hudson River; orchestrate a successful rescue of all aboard; turn the pilot into a national hero; spread out the survivors—many of whom were attractive actors hired for the crash—over every talk show that aired; get the Air Wanderlust logo on every computer and cell phone in the country; and sit back and watch as the company's stock rose from $3 to $80 per share, at which time the board members would sell to the highest bidder.

Ever since he was a child, Blackie possessed the ability to lie with such wile and reverence that he could force falsity upon reality, dictating his life and the lives of others through pure imagination. He would envision a scenario in his mind, and just by doing so would will it into existence. It was not so much a magical talent as it was his ability to concoct the perfect sequence that could deliver the plot. And in that respect, he believed he was some method of a god, creating existence at his whim. He did not believe he was *the* God, the Almighty Creator. Rather, he was endowed with the gifts that other deities possessed—the ability to create from available material, that of ambivalence toward the actors—so that he could faithfully and impartially invent reality.

Blackie Spin sealed the job with a handshake. One year later he was seated alone in his office, staring into the board as the monitors whirred and buzzed behind him, keeping tabs on 161 heartbeats that thus far were obedient to their roles. He was suddenly obsessed with three words on the motherboard. They were the only words for which he used a red marker, the ones he cared most about, even if he did not much care for the person. It was the focal point of his process, the core around which the remaining narratives fluttered. It was the thing he would build into a Robin Hood, a modern-day legend, perhaps a public holiday in his namesake, a museum that would celebrate the victory, a hero over whom men and women and magazine editors and corporate sponsors would salivate. The red strokes and curves of the name on the motherboard seemed a challenge there, perhaps a more daunting one since Blackie Spin had not wanted him in the first place. But it was there all the same, the legend he intended to build: Captain Hank Swagger.

TICKET TO RIDE

Hank Swagger was the kind of man for whom everyone naturally developed an affinity. His greatness was expected, like waiting for fruit to fall from October timber—it was coming, eventually, just a matter of hanging around until it ripened. That was how everyone felt about Swagger—that despite repeated gaffes to suggest otherwise, greatness was imminent, if only they could demonstrate patience. A former high school quarterback, president of his college fraternity, a member of the U.S. Air Force and a commercial pilot, he had befriended women all over the country. Despite knowing that he was a nomadic gigolo and somewhat of a bastard, he was welcome to them whenever he arrived in their towns. His family life was more of the same: Mipsy, the wife, despised him with an aged hatred that can be groomed only through twenty-nine years of marriage; although she would never consider divorcing him since they had put so much energy into developing their exhausted relations. He rarely spoke to his daughter, Mallory, who dropped out of a new college every year, blaming her father for her life's lack of direction. His son, Nathan, was the worst kind of disappointment—a failed actor who failed so thoroughly and continuously, that it harkened in the twenty-eight-year-old a style of irrational perseverance that shamed his parents over his talentless stage presence, and his relentless ambition to prove directors and fellow actors and even his family wrong.

Had Swagger been someone who *seemed* less extraordinary, his career as a commercial pilot would have ended years before. He carried on multiple affairs with flight attendants and passengers; he drank heavily in connecting cities, often sleeping through the flight he was intended to pilot; on the runway he rarely waited his turn, talking and bullying his way to the front of the line; he spoke openly and coarsely to control towers and other pilots about his sexual conquests: "Hey there American two-two-one, you got a flight attendant goes by Nancy? Holiday Inn last night. One flexible gal, lemme tell ya'. Might be slow on the breakfast service." His exploits were legendary. While every other pilot was a flight number, Swagger was greeted by name.

"Flight AW1645, we got a slight buildup. Hold for runway four."

"Dougie Nelson you ain't gonna make me wait now, are you?"

"That you Swags?"

"What time you off you old blind dog?"

"Afraid not till morning."

"I'll be up."

"Clear for runway one. Don't get yourself arrested."

"Come find me. Tell the old lady I'll be banging on your door if you don't."

There were bar fights, random drunken misunderstandings, the fireworks episode that burned down half a city block in Minneapolis. A year prior he had flown a plane bound for Chicago to Miami instead to meet up with a hooker named Daisy. The passengers had not known any better until they arrived in sunny Florida, although the plane was trailed by two fighter jets, the pilots carrying on an amiable conversation with Swagger for the duration.

He was arrested at the gate, charged with aviation drunkenness, hijacking, and 117 counts of kidnapping, along with a slew of federal allegations that would have put a mortal away for life. The airline posted bail then ordered Swagger into a private meeting with the CEO, where he was offered a choice: prison, or stage a crash landing in the Hudson River and become a national hero.

"What's this all about, Jugs?"

Arnold Jeffries sat back in his chair and offered a bullshit smile. His boss was enjoying this, Swagger could tell. The captain had worked for Air Wanderlust for twenty-two years. And in that time, he had produced a good share of headaches. Each week he offered an excuse for termination, whether it was the women or the drinking, or his general disregard for decorum. But he could fly a 767 through a blizzard and land it on a mountaintop so gently that the babies on board would not even stir. He was the least manageable and most talented pilot on the Air Wanderlust crew and everyone adored him. Hell, Arnold Jeffries adored him. And now, finally, he would control him.

"Don't concern yourself with logistics," Arnold said. "You just concentrate on the training."

"Suppose I did want to concern myself."

"Airline industry's a tough cookie. Fuel prices, whether or not mom and pop feel like taking the kids on vacation, a massive amount of variables we can't control."

"So the airline is broke."

"We're not broke. We're financially fragile."

"How is that any different than broke, Jugs?"

Arnold Jeffries was a large man. He had sagging breasts Swagger had once comically grabbed at a company dinner, labeling him "Jugs" in front of his peers. Everyone else he employed called him Mr. Jeffries.

"Look, there's a company out of New York, does some amazing things. They can get our name in front of billions with this stunt. Ever heard of the Nymphopucky?"

"The lice? Sure."

"It don't exist." He smiled, in cahoots. "This company invented it."

"Why would they do that?"

"I don't remember. Something about potholes."

"What's that got to do with crashing a plane in a river?"

"Point is smoke and mirrors." Swagger did not understand. "All how you spin it. Show 'em this, give 'em that. It's about marketability and advertising and directing the news using a specific equation."

"Jugs, what are you on about?"

"The airline is broke, Hank. We need the publicity."

"Why not just buy billboard space?"

"Not that kind of publicity." Arnold stood and walked in a quick circle around the desk until he was back at his chair. "Front-page headlines, a year's worth of talk shows, a story that becomes part of the culture. These folks are building a dang museum out of the plane—that's the stuff I'm getting at. We need everyone talking about the same thing—Air Wanderlust. Make the name familiar, like Coca-Cola, Nike, O.J."

"And you lunatics think crashing a plane into the Hudson will fix things?"

He tapped his forehead. "You'd be surprised."

"My pilot's license was revoked—how am I going to fly without one?"

"It'll be taken care of."

Swagger thought it through. It was this or prison. "What do I have to do?"

"Train. In a simulator. Nine months or so. And stay out of trouble. And don't get loose and tell anyone."

"What kind of plane?"

"Airbus."

"How many passengers?"

"Around 150, 160 maybe. Prescreened. Mostly."

"What do you mean mostly?"

"Look, Swags, this company—they're good. They handle it, from the passengers to the media. Only thing you need to worry about is a smooth landing."

"Doesn't make sense. Dozen safer spots within ten miles of New York City. Last thing an experienced pilot would do was drop it in the drink."

"The flight trajectory is already worked out." Arnold walked around the desk to a table, where a miniature scale model of New York City had been set up. He picked up a plane at LaGuardia Airport, a piece of cardboard painted silver. He glided the plane into the air between two fingers, gently, an origami swan. "You take off here. Right about now, the engine blows."

"Why does the engine blow?"

"It'll be covered in the training. Point is it blows." He jiggled the miniature plane in his fingers to show what he meant. "So now you got to make a decision. You head back for LaGuardia? Too far. You try for Teterboro? Never make it. Wait a minute, what about the Hudson?"

Swagger took the plane. "I've flown thousands of flights over Manhattan. It's tricky to find the river."

"The simulator," Arnold said. "By the time we're through we'll have you doing it blindfolded."

"Come in too hot, the nose explodes. Come in slow you might end up on Broadway." Swagger bent the plane toward Broadway. "Jugs, you remember that strip club we went to off Broadway that time?"

"You and me ain't been to no strip club in New York." Arnold snatched the plane and drifted it toward more cardboard, this time painted blue. "You land her right here, between Hoboken and New York. Midtown."

Swagger turned the plane over. "Seven, eight minutes tops before it sinks."

"Plan is to hit the center of the ferry paths. And since it's happening during rush hour, the boats will be minutes away."

"It's impossible," Swagger said.

"It's not impossible for the right pilot."

"A lot could go wrong."

"A lot could go right."

Swagger picked up the plane and tossed it into the air, capturing it with a jolly grip. "Guy did this would go down in aviation history as a legend."

"A cultural icon." Arnold smiled deep. "A fucking god."

POOLS OF SORROW, WAVES OF JOY

Swagger did not feel any more like a god than he had before the landing. He felt depressed and anxious, emotions with which he had become intimate. Blackie had told him he would spend ample time in his hotel room, alone, doing nothing but watching television and preparing for the interviews and subsequent nationwide tour. Only now that he was lonesome, all he thought about was The Rot.

At first he had been satisfied that he had no choice—either prison or fly the plane into the river. He had built up a steady stream of justifiable morality, the challenge of accomplishing what few pilots likely could. For all the training, when it came down to it the landing was no guarantee. There was wind to consider; if the plane dropped into three- to four-foot swells, fairly common for the Hudson River, it would be luck just keeping the rig in one piece. Air speed was a factor, buoyancy. They would hit town during rush hour, directly in the ferry path, but drowning was still a threat. There was the script—one in which Swagger was expected to maintain a distinct serenity. There was his training partner for that, an unabashedly shy girl who became diabolic once her panties were removed with incisors, and with whom Swagger had fallen into a particular infatuation—how he adored when she punched his face during intercourse, when she fingernailed his skin. He still had cuts on his face, bruises on his chest and thighs where she had bit him, coital battle scars.

But there was a greater downside. And that was The Rot, the cheat. Swagger did have a choice. He could have set up camp with a medley of immoral women and ancient drinking buddies who would have been happy to harbor him, an unemployed fugitive. But the prospect of what awaited him was too alluring. He was never to fly a jet again; that drop into the Hudson would be his swan song. Instead, he would become a motivational speaker, touring the country and influencing college students and corporations about how to persevere, or what to do in an emergency, or how to succeed—hell, he did not know the message, only that he would be set up in fine hotels and would spend his days eating juicy steaks and helping himself to all those coeds with gushing hormones hanging on his fatherly wisdom: The voice of reason for a slanted generation so confused and nervous about what ills might befall them they would rely on *him* to deliver the cure.

And there was The Rot. He was not suitable to counsel his own children. How could he minister to a nation? He was a pilot, not a motivational speaker, and this seed grew into a terrifying tree of perplexity. That an ordinary man who had fought in no wars, who had overcome no terrorist hijackings, could be built into this mythic beast by the sorcery of deceit, of modern technology, and optimal timing. Who was he? He had to watch the television to know for sure.

Swagger sat on his bed in the Whalensky Plaza, stroking Jeters's fur. Every station discussed the magical landing, a photo of him that was ten years old seducing new viewers every few minutes. The plan was to make the masses wait—they would scurry for details, even invent scenarios when they ran out of the fodder they were being fed every hour from the offices of Veiltality Inc. But there would be no Captain Swagger until midweek. And then, of course, Saturday he was to cut the ribbon at some damned museum.

"The best publicity is what they cannot have," Blackie had explained. "If I give you to them, they'll digest you in days. But if they can't have you, they'll go mad waiting for it."

When he heard the knock on his door, he leapt from the bed: the mistress. He had not seen her since the previous morning when he popped her plump bottom, had not felt her smallish breasts in a week. He was ashamedly sick of himself and hopeful for companionship. He had been sequestered now for seventeen hours, no one to speak to or look at or fight with. He was desperate for human contact, even if it was not her—even if it was Blackie coming to holler at him for something else he had done that had not stuck precisely to the plan. In addition to the dying copilot and drinking in front of the mayor, he failed to ensure the oxygen masks fell from the ceiling, routine in any crash. And it went without saying he should not have stolen a puppy.

Swagger opened the door to find his wife, Mipsy, wearing a reflexive frown. "Your fucking airline sucks, Hank."

"Hey there, dear."

"They rush me on a plane to get to your hotel. Then we just sit. Forty minutes. Just sitting. Staring. At other planes. Doing exactly what we intended to do."

"Other planes were taking off, weren't they?"

"Don't get stupid," she said. "You alone in there?"

"Who else would there be?"

"I said not to get stupid. You've probably had strange within the hour. I could give a damn. Just in no mood to meet one of them."

She pushed him out of the way and headed for the liquor. It was just past 9 a.m. At forty-three, she was seven years junior to Hank, a well-manicured woman with the accessories to match. She had a nice figure, although the breasts and eyes were on layaway, and she had drank her skin into a leathery scowl. At one time, she had filled the costume the name "Mipsy" implied—fun and blond and carnal—although now Swagger felt he might be more attracted to her if she simply went by her birth name: Margaret.

Hank punched in front of her when she fiddled too long and poured them each a glass of vodka, a bit of tomato juice to keep it sophisticated. Then they sipped and waited for the other to address it.

"So," she said. "I suppose congratulations are in order."

"Thanks, dear." Despite its fraud, he had wanted someone to acknowledge the maneuver. "It was quite something. Basically, I came in—"

"Hank, I don't care. For the children's sake, I'm glad you're alive. Just tell me what time I have to be someplace and what I'm meant to do."

"Well, obviously you're here to support me because we cherish each other."

"I'd like to go shopping. I'd like to have a pleasant dinner. However, Alastair just informed me over the phone that I wasn't to leave this hotel room."

"That's correct," Swagger said. "Blackie says we can't leave. But we've got TV and booze, and if we run out of anything, they just bring more."

"What's the point of coming to New York if I can't go to dinner?"

"We could order in."

"I don't remember you being so stupid. When we first got married, you seemed smarter."

"Dear—"

"And stop dearing me. I don't want to sit in a hotel with you. But if I have to, I won't be deared."

Swagger began speaking, then stopped. It was Blackie's job to bring Mipsy into the mix. Problem was Swagger did not know what Mipsy knew and what she didn't. It occurred to him that she probably understood his miraculous landing had been staged; up until that point, he had been behaving as though he were a hero.

"Interviews," he said sheepishly.

"Interviews, huh?"

"It would look awkward if you weren't with me. And the museum opening Saturday."

"A museum?" She laughed into a snort. "You are slippery. What time does The Mallory arrive?"

Swagger beamed. "The daughter is flying in?"

"Didn't you read any of that crap Alastair gave us? We're pretending to be the happy Swaggers from Pennsylvania."

"The Nathan is coming as well? The famous actor could get time off?"

They shared a chuckle. "Famous soldier nowadays. Something about a patriotism angle. Our son finally gets a paid acting gig, and all it took was for you to crash a jet."

"Attaboy," he said proudly. Come to think of it, Swagger had seen a picture of his family on television. Only now it registered that his son had been dressed in military garb. "Which war was it?"

"How do you mean?"

"The Nathan. I was just curious which war he fought in."

"It's like conversing with a four-year-old," Mipsy said. All things considered, Hank was happy his family would be there. This was some of the wholesomeness he was missing in his life, family coming together to support one another, specifically him. She took a sip and studied her husband. "You do have a knack for it though, I'll give you that."

"A knack for what?"

"Life, I suppose."

Swagger shivered at the word—life—the way his wife looked at him when she said it, as if he were a mustached carny operating the dime pitch in the center of the carnival. Just then Jeters woke from his nap, rushing to the edge of the bed and wagging his brown chubby tail.

"Hey, boy. Is my rascally guy awake?"

"What is that?"

"It's my rascally guy."

She walked over to inspect. "Where did it come from?"

"I rescued it." He kissed Jeters's tongue. "Some lady. In her rush to get off the plane, she left him."

"What type of sick person would do such a thing?"

"Smoker. Nasty habit. I couldn't leave Jeters with someone like that."

"You did the right thing." Mipsy let the puppy lick her fingers. "Well, he's just my furry man, isn't he?"

"Actually, Mipsy, he's my rascally guy."

"Let me hold him."

Hank looked the dog over. "He's kind of particular."

"Give me the fucking dog." She grabbed the puppy by its front paws and tugged it to her bosom. "Hey there furry man. How's my furry little man?"

"He's cute, ain't he?"

"He is cute. What should we name him?"

"His name is Jeters. And how do you mean, we?"

"He needs a regal name, like King, or Sullivan."

Hank grabbed the dog. "His name is Jeters. And he's my rascally guy."

"Alastair." She rubbed the puppy. "We can call him Al." Her

drink gone, Mipsy tired of the puppy naming and set her glass on the bar with a rattling hint. "I'm going into the bathroom to have a think," she said. "When I come out, I would like some acceptable proposals about where I'll be dining. And I expect you'll have called the front desk to get me my own room."

"We have to stay in the same room. Keep up appearances and all."

"Imagine, the same bed as my husband." She laughed into the ceiling. "Well, if I'm expected to share the room, there will be sex."

"Don't make me."

"Stop whining. Order up some champagne. Let's make it memorable." Then from behind the closed bathroom door, "And don't think I didn't notice the scratches, Hank. Some whore has been hitting you in the face again."

DON'T LET ME DOWN

Not being able to interview him only made the story more alluring. To listen to Captain Hank Swagger tell how it happened, tell how he had tangled with certain death only to come out the victor—that might have soothed their aching curiosities. Instead news programs continued showing survivors on the plane's wing, the passing shot of Captain Swagger looking out over the river that had nearly captured them all. Most could not tell what they were seeing on the television, on the plane's wing, in the shimmering faces of the survivors. It was not that they were all so physically attractive, so alluring, just that . . . well, something they could not put into words, but that called to them like a sweet and beautiful truth, a miracle. Every hour a press release came from Veiltality Inc. with new chum: "Passenger Timothy Knight refused to vacate the plane without an injured woman." And then the media would latch on to one of the survivors to verify it—"Was it true? Did Timothy Knight really?"—and the survivor, typically a handsome actor, would tell the story of the miraculous landing, and his or her part in it. Then the media would print it and the blogs would blog about it; the Twitterers would tweet; the texters would text; and everyone would check their devices for anything they might have missed.

"Brilliant." Eddie chewed something slippery through the phone, the television loud in the background. Eddie had been raised by television. His father worked nights and slept days; his mother the opposite. So that each room of his home was equipped with a television nanny. "And to think you were on that plane, Normal. I'm jealous."

"That's great, Eddie. Listen."

"Tell me something—what were you doing when Timothy Knight rescued the woman?"

"I don't know. Maybe thinking how to get off the plane with the John Lennon."

"Bad move." Eddie made a *tsking* noise. "You should have

seized the opportunity. This guy's a freaking hero. They're going to give him the key to the city, you know."

"What would I do with a key to the city?"

"Unlock shit, man. Do you realize if you have a key to the city, you can go into any restaurant you want, even when it's closed? By law they have to serve you. Know what else you could do?" It was a trick; Normal did not answer. "You could go down to the plane, tell them you left your mom's aunt's special brooch there. Probably give a hero a police escort there and back."

All things considered, Eddie was right. Had he helped a woman off a sinking plane, karma would be aligned differently. That was why he was planning to hire Lucky Dan.

"Rumor has it you ran into Rory," Eddie said. "How things go?"

"Went fine."

"Heard she slapped you around a little."

Even gossip in the underworld had a way of dashing about the universe with a sinister proclivity. "If you knew that, why did you ask how things went?"

"Wasn't sure you wanted to talk about it." More chewing. "Something like that makes you feel like less of a man, hurts your ego."

A woman on the pay phone ordered up more bounty. He was getting used to the pay phone routine. It was almost a relief not to cart around a gadget that the world expected him to answer every time someone needed something. He now carried a pocketful of change and rather enjoyed the simplicity of his anonymous being, his George Bailey-ness.

A homeless man tapped a worn cup into the phone booth glass. Normal was wearing the same clothes from the day before. He had no idea that all the other passengers had received gift cards in their rooms to buy new threads, allowance for the soiled luggage. It occurred to Normal he was no better than the beggar, adrift and without port in the vast metropolis. He flipped the man a quarter.

"So what now?" Eddie asked.

"Got a plan." Normal rehearsed briefly in his head—*hire a man with a gift of luck to assist in retrieving a dead man's semen from a plane sunk in a river*. He told Eddie anyway.

"Fucking A, Normal! Now you're doing some thinking."

"You like it?"

"I love it. Get you some luck. Move this dark cloud around and get us back to work."

"Something like that."

"How do I fit in?"

"Just lay low. Rory calls, you ain't heard from me. And for fuck sake don't gamble."

"I'll stay near the TV. You get the lucky man to get the Lennon to give to Rory."

"I'm not giving shit to Rory. I am trying to preserve . . ."

". . . One piece of this cannibalistic culture," Eddie finished. "I keep forgetting about the orphans. Okay, so I have to run."

Normal was suspicious that he'd had only half of Eddie's attention. "Run where?"

"Breaking news. This guy Swagger has a wife and two kids. They're showing a picture after the break. Did you know Swagger's kid won the Medal of Honor? Fascinating!" Eddie hung up.

LUCKY MAN WHO MADE THE GRADE

Normal had phoned Lucky Dan to explain his proposal. It came out similar to the way he'd dropped it on Eddie, and Lucky initially declined; he had never heard of Normal Fulk and was not flying across the country to retrieve semen for someone with whom he was not intimate. But when he was reminded of the name Frank Fulk, he agreed to a meeting provided Normal covered the flight and a $2,000 retainer, just for flying out to discuss it. Normal scraped together the money, although he would need a lot more if Lucky took the job. That was how desperate he had become—he was hoping Lucky Dan would provide the luck that would allow Normal to get the money to pay Lucky Dan for his luck.

They agreed to meet at a Midtown diner. Normal arrived to find the place quiet, a man at the counter who seemed to be alone. He was dressed like a 1950s car salesman, a tall, lanky build with a fedora that rested next to him. He read the newspaper and sipped coffee, swiveling on his stool.

"You must be Frank's kid brother." He extended a bony hand. "Dan O'Malley, good to know you. Call me Dan or Lucky Dan or just Lucky."

"How'd you know it was me?"

"I'm meeting Frank's kid brother in a diner, and I expect he'll be suspicious. You show up looking suspicious with a FRANK RIP tattoo. See that? A lot of luck is just putting two and two together. Your skin," the man said, examining him closely. "Looks a bit worn for a man your age."

"I use it everyday."

"That's clever. I like clever. What about the finger?"

"Long story."

"Seems important."

He sat. "I died a few weeks ago, if you get me. Finger was part of it."

Lucky Dan smiled. "Never met a dead man. How does it feel?"

Normal considered it. The first few weeks he had been crammed into a motel near the airport eating fast food and watching basic cable, synonymous with actual death. On his first full week of anonymity, he had nearly died for real in a plane crash and received a thorough beating for the purpose of providing footage for a reality TV show about his life that he had not sanctioned. "Not bad," he said. "Nothing to worry about, no bills to pay. Clean slate, you know?"

"Clean slate. Yeah, I dig it."

Normal eyed the room. "Let's grab a booth so we can talk."

"I like the counter. Something about swiveling on the stools does it for me."

They ordered plates of eggs, sausages, and potatoes that arrived before the get-to-know-yous were finished. It occurred to Normal when he saw the food that he had not had a proper meal in two days, sinking his fork into a fat sausage while Lucky Dan watched.

"Let's review the nature of your business. You traffic in illegally obtained semen."

"Not anymore. Gave up the business. This is my last score."

"For the nature of my involvement, you're trying to retrieve semen from an airplane. Let's assume you're presently employed."

"Suit yourself."

"Without being graphic, how exactly do you obtain it?"

"Depends." Normal ducked close. Since he had met Rory, he had become paranoid that he was always being spied on. "Typically we're after celebrities or athletes. So we have to set up the room in our favor."

"Set up the room how?"

"Suppose you're staying at a hotel and we want your semen."

"Why would you want it?"

"To sell it."

"I'm infertile. Why would someone buy it?"

"Because you're famous."

"I'm not famous in the least," Lucky Dan said. "I go out of my way to avoid publicity."

"Forget you. Say Clint Eastwood is staying at the hotel."

"That's better. It assists my reference if it's not my semen you're trying to pirate."

"We set him up with a woman. . . ."

"A hooker."

"We prefer escort. Hookers no longer like the word hooker."

"Sign of the times." Lucky Dan clinked his plate with a knife. "Now the hookers want fresh titles."

"Industry is all college girls these days, smart, know where the money is."

"So you get Clint in a room with the hooker. Now what?"

"Instincts take over. They do what they do, she insists on a condom, which she passes to me."

"Just like that?"

"Just like that."

"Say Clint doesn't go for it? He's in love with his wife or whatever."

"There's other ways." Normal lifted his mug for more coffee. "Point is, if the semen exists, I'll get it."

"So what then?"

"Authenticate it. Each specimen comes with a certificate of authenticity, photographic evidence the celebrity was in town when it was stolen, a step-by-step journal of how it was obtained. I have fences. They sell to fans. Occasionally women use it to get pregnant, but that's an unreliable occurrence for the money. Most buyers are just collectors."

Lucky Dan smiled. "Whatever happened to collecting baseball cards?"

"People who collect—they watch their favorite celebrities or sports heroes on television or the Internet, but that's as close as they get. They're just looking for that connection, you know? That piece of eternity that makes it real."

"I get it. I like it. More people like you? Competition of sorts?"

"Not so much." They sipped some coffee. "You might say I have a monopoly on the business. I keep it small, quiet. I'm not looking to get rich."

"Which brings us to your problem," Dan said. "I take it this semen on the plane is of value?"

"Rarest specimen I've ever obtained."

"May I ask whose testicles it came from?"

"John Lennon's."

"The real John Lennon? And it's worth what?"

"A buyer out of Detroit would have paid high six figures."

"You wouldn't have gotten on a plane to Los Angeles if you were planning to sell it to this buyer. What's that about?"

"Personal issue. Client in California guaranteed me he won't clone it."

"So it's about money?" Lucky Dan asked.

"I assure you there are other considerations." He shoved forward the FRANK RIP tattoo.

It took Lucky a minute to put it together; he clinked his knife again. "I remember that about Frank. He was a Beatles fan."

"He was thirteen when Lennon was shot. Seemed like he cried for a year."

"I was fifteen." Lucky peered into the back of the diner, as if music and a montage of that December day would waft out from the kitchen. "I was living in Montana. My parents and I lit candles and listened to *The White Album* all night."

"I was seven. I was in bed."

Lucky Dan kept eating. "So you don't want it cloned out of respect for your late brother. And the buyer in California pays handsome. That about it?"

"Something else." He pushed his food forward. "Name Cleve Peoples familiar?"

"Hell of an actor. Not so much a father."

"Truth is he's not responsible for those kids. Do what you did before," Normal said. "Put two and two together."

Lucky bit a sausage. "I got it. Kind of a mixed-up profession you've chosen, no?"

"This stuff don't happen much. When it does, it gets to you."

"So you're stepping in, raising the litter?"

"Not exactly. I'd like something good to come out of the John Lennon. And I'd like those kids to get the money."

"All of it?"

"All of it."

"You surprise me Mr. Fulk—in a good way." He stung the mug for a refill. "But I have to ask—have you recently had a talk with your god?"

"In a roundabout way, sure."

"And this god is suggesting the career change?"

"Something like that. It was mostly a dream anyway."

"I don't mean to get personal because I'm not familiar with how you run your business." Lucky Dan leaned. "But are you filming our discussion for use in a TV show of sorts?"

"Why would you ask that?"

"Because outside that window, a man has been pointing a camera at us since you sat down." He pointed toward the rear of the restaurant. "A second cameraman seems sequestered in the booth farthest back."

Normal turned to look; the cameraman was indeed in the booth that was occupied; he waved. "Fucking hell." He leaned over the counter. "Lobo, you down there?"

"*Sí, Señor Normal.*" Lobo stood and pushed a microphone close. "*Lo siento acerca de dar un puñetazo la cara. Trato de ir fácil pero insiste.*"

"No *hablo* talky-talk, Lobo."

Lucky Dan kept eating. "He says he's sorry about punching your face. He tried to go easy, but the lady insisted."

"Tell him it's okay."

"*Dice que está bien.*"

Lobo lay back on the ground and Normal explained—the film crew, the reality show, how the cameras had followed him from his past life to his current one with a wretched digital reincarnation. While he understood how strange and underhanded the whole business might appear, what he needed, what he craved, was a bit of luck.

"So you don't want to be famous?"

"Not at all," Normal said.

"You surprise me again, Mr. Fulk." Lucky Dan waved at the cameraman outside. "What's it called?"

"What's what called?"

"The show about your life that you refuse to star in."

"*Semen Pirates.*"

"I rather like that. I like you. I like that sound guy on the ground. He's a professional. Didn't even know he was down there."

"He punches kind of hard, but he's a good egg."

"Let me see if I got this straight." Lucky Dan swiveled to face Normal. "The woman in charge of the production company has the upper hand."

"Correct."

"She has given you, what, seventy-two hours to get the semen?"

"Forty-eight."

"You ever killed a man?"

"Never."

"Would you?"

"A few months ago maybe. Not anymore."

"Because of the god dream I take it."

"It was a series of dreams."

"What's your brand?"

"Catholic maybe. I'm not sure."

"What do you mean you're not sure? You believe in a god, don't you?"

"Trying to."

"Well, which one?"

"All this religion stuff is new. I'm not equipped with a faith. Hoping to learn one."

"Like a musical instrument?"

"Basketball players don't come out of the womb ready to play. They learn to dribble."

"This is a bit different." Lucky Dan leaned in tight. "So you're going legit. More important, you're at a crossroads, a bad man on a moral mission. I suppose that's a metaphor for all of us really."

"Guess so."

"You've chosen the higher path—naively idealistic maybe, but the good road would be to sell this Lennon to an honest collector and give the money to those children, not participate in a reality

TV show you deem less than savory, undo some of the warped karma you've created. Also there's a perplexed spirituality lurking in there somewhere. How's that sound?"

"More or less."

"I like it. I like you," he said again. "But let's get something straight. I'm here for luck. I don't break in to buildings or shake down strangers for semen. I don't get in the middle of gunplay. I won't come to fists to rescue you from Lobo down there. I'm here only for luck."

"So you'll take the job?"

He smiled. "Nine times out of ten, my career has me following some rich geezer around a casino while he wins money he don't need. This here sounds like a real whodunit."

"A what?"

"A shoot 'em up. A pickle. You get what I'm saying?"

"Sure."

"One last thing." Dan swiveled. "Your death: What kind of alias did you work out?"

"George Bailey." Normal had never seen it, but *It's a Wonderful Life* was Frank's favorite film. His brother even watched it in the summer.

Lucky thought about it before slapping Normal's shoulder. "That'll do just fine. We got us a real mission here, George."

"Call me Normal."

"Back in the medieval days, folks were always going on missions. No one ever goes on missions anymore. This'll be something."

When the *Springer v. Springer* settlement was agreed to, the divorce mediator passed the file to his clerk and suggested she take care of it without involving him further. It was not technically a criminal case since the district attorney's office did not intend to officially charge the wife so long as the terms of the settlement were met. It was a civil arrangement, although one that required a version of probation. A psychiatrist would certainly have to be consulted; after all, she had killed all those fish.

The City of New York received a number of such cases each year. They were known as the "Untouchables" and were rerouted to the aptly named Office of Strategic Therapy. It was a smaller branch of the Department of Social Services. Over the years the office had been moved from building to building, gutted of resources, stripped of employees and morale until it consisted of only one man. Gary Corbin did not even have Internet access, or an e-mail address, as though he did not exist at all, just an anonymous janitor in the basement of the Department of Social Services with the Untouchables.

Gary had spent his life savings remaking a used ice cream truck into an advice-mobile, a moving treatment center, Mother Teresa of the Apocalypse. He was hoping to pay off the truck loan, maybe buy several more trucks, a roving fleet of compassion that could seek out the mad and confused and medicate them before they went on killing sprees. Similar to the fire department, publicly funded, ready to mobilize at the first emergency of psychosis, his trucks would race to wherever a fellow citizen was going mad and talk him or her down.

The one bright spot in the Office of Strategic Therapy was the women: divorcees and pre-divorcees and widows and drug addicts, with anger issues and hallucinations and bipolar disorders and terrible facial tics caused from all their worry. By the time they hit his desk, they had mowed their way through the dating pool; he was all that was left. And he was not so bad. He did not drink, nor do drugs, he was not hairy or disfigured. He was just . . . acceptable. And like all acceptable Americans, Gary Corbin had a fetish—women with anxiety disorders. Give him the phobias, the social anxieties, the obsessive-compulsives, a sweating, palpitating, stressed-out mess of nymphs dripping with a dreariness that no one else wanted. These were the ones that got it. These were the ones who understood there was something out there to fear. He could not explain why they so infatuated him, the way other men developed bosom or foot manias. Just the massive stress of the world spitting them out, improperly bent metal from a clothes hanger factory, lying there crooked and mood-addled until only a professional who understood their deficiencies, the chinks in their engines, could possibly love them, or if not love them, at least bed them clandestinely.

So the morning the mail cart rounded the corner, and the Springer file was placed on his desk, it became his obsession. They had given him a woman suffering from puppet insanity, stressed to the marrow, anxiety-ridden to the point that she could not remove the thing. Or something like that. He never bothered to read beyond the first paragraph summary. He got the gist of it—all those dead fish, her falling into the metropolis's lowest rungs, a gift from the psychotic gods.

As with all his patients, he was too embarrassed about his office to have her come to him, instead meeting at the corner Starbucks, where he conducted all his therapy sessions.

"You look just like her."

"Thank you for saying so."

"No, I mean it. Other than the hair and the puppet, you could be her twin."

"Speaking of which, would you mind if I took it off?"

"Don't!" He sprang forward, nearly toppling her coffee. When she initially sat down, the puppet was in her lap. He was expecting to speak with it, argue with it, for the damned puppet to wake up and commandeer the woman. "What I mean is—you should wear it during sessions. After all, it's why you're here. If you were anorexic, we wouldn't hide the scones now would we?"

"Yes, but the puppet isn't necessary. I mean, if you're here, and I'm here, there's no need to wear it. I'm not crazy."

"Not yet you aren't." He bit a scone, suddenly refreshed about the day's prospects. "Would you mind lifting it?" She did. "And could you hold it vertical so I can interface with you both?"

She held it up. "I don't see the sense really."

"You wouldn't, of course. You're not trained to see it." He was infatuated. "Now then, does the puppet have a name?"

"Ava Tardner."

"Very good. And how does the puppet make you feel?"

She leaned forward. "How do you think it makes me feel?"

"Very good. And do you keep it on when you have intercourse?"

"Excuse me?"

"Fornication. Does the puppet contribute? Freud would have inquired, I guarantee it."

Lucy hid it beneath the table. "That's kind of personal, don't you think?"

"You can ask me anything about my sex life. I'm an open book."

"You're my probation officer."

"I'm not a probation officer. I'm a psychiatrist."

"Even so, it's none of your business." She pushed the puppet farther beneath the table. "What do you mean you aren't a probation officer?"

Gary was confused. "You're Lucy Springer, aren't you?" Was it possible there were other women with puppet maladies, an entire genre of potential lunatics he had overlooked?

"I was told you would be monitoring my probation."

"I am monitoring your probation. Sort of." He pulled out the file and leafed through the main parts. "Says here you suffer from clinical anger, rage, puppet separation anxiety . . ."

"I don't have separation anxiety."

"Then why are you wearing a puppet?"

"This is why." She removed the electronic bracelet. A moment later, his beeper buzzed.

"Is this you?" he asked.

Gary picked up the case file and read closely. Now it occurred to him why she looked familiar. He did not own a television nor subscribe to a newspaper, and without a computer in his office he was less savvy in world events than he cared to be. But he vaguely recalled Lucy Springer, and the ordeal, and his spirit sank at the implications. She was not an unemployable lunatic with puppet anxiety disorder; she was sane, with a job, and a court-ordered puppet on her arm.

"You can't take it off," he said. "Like puppet jail."

"I can take it off. So long as you don't tell anyone."

"Out of the question." Even if it served no purpose, it was his duty to oversee the cases passed his way. Gary Corbin was convinced ninety percent of the population had insane tendencies; maybe she was not crazy now, but that would change. "I'm afraid we'll have to abide by the terms of your arrangement."

"Very well. How often shall we meet?"

"Every day."

"Once a week. I tend to avoid being seen in public with this on my arm. You have an office?"

He could not take his eyes off the doll. "What happens if you remove it?"

"It rings your beeper."

"That's not what I mean. Shortness of breath, heart palpitations, hallucinations?"

"Listen to me, Mr. Corbin."

"Call me Gary."

"I'm not attached to a puppet because I can't function without it. It's my ex-husband's sick fun to make a joke out of me. Do you understand?"

"I think you're stunning. I know that probably strikes you as unprofessional. Only reason I'm telling you—well, because it's my professional opinion you and I will end up sleeping together."

There was always a question of how they would react when he broached the topic. More often than not it was the first compliment they had gotten in years and they were flattered anyone noticed. She blushed, ignoring the invitation. "My arrangement says in order to stay out of jail, I'm to wear this puppet and meet for regular appointments."

"Did you hear what I said?" Gary asked.

"You're my court-assigned psychiatrist."

"I'd prefer you look to me as your court-assigned friend."

"I don't need any friends."

"We get by with a little help from our friends—did you know that?" Most of Gary Corbin's advice came from songs. "Joe Cocker said that, but it rings true."

She sat back. "The Beatles said it first. Are we about through?"

"One last question." He could not hide his infatuation. "Do you ever talk to the puppet when you're alone?"

"I just told you. I'm not fucking crazy!" Diners turned from across the room to see the woman who was not crazy waving a puppet at a man.

"Not yet you aren't." Gary stood and walked his chair around the table. He hoped to catch a scent of body odor, anything to imply she was not taking care of herself. "This is how it starts."

"How what starts?"

"The slow descent." He motioned at the windows. "You've seen the homeless out there, carrying dead rats around as babies, talking to mailboxes—how do you think that happens?"

"Are you really a psychiatrist?"

"It's all entropy. There's no reason, no method by which one can follow a set of circumstances and hope to hang on to sanity. It's everyone for themselves, all of us on the brink of psychosis. It can start with something as little as losing your job. Or your partner cheating on you. Or one day they attach you to a puppet and you say, 'I don't need the puppet.'"

"But I don't need the puppet."

"Every junkie in the world says the same thing. You start with a taste, whatever your friend is—Wild Turkey, heroin, Prozac. After a while it occurs to you that you can't do without it, your special friend. And it's all so crazy out there, it's like this this . . . circle without any turns. So you turn to your little friend, this thing you need, that helps you get by."

"Please don't quote The Beatles again."

He bent so low she was looking down at him. "So on the one hand it's all rational and sensible, but then you're thinking—circles without turns—how is that? Well, it's more of a metaphor for life, how our lives are circles, except the turns are these subtle little patches of magic and serendipity, things we cannot see, so they're not really there but they are there, lots of them, just turn after turn after turn. . . . But the truth is there is no circle, no turns, no lines or triangles or shapes or destiny or magic. There's nothing at all. It's just this massive accident. And then after all that thinking, all that reasoning, and plotting, you take a quick glance over and realize— holy hell, all this time you've been talking to the puppet."

"So I'm not crazy now?"

"In my professional opinion, no."

"But I'm defenseless against the prospect of becoming crazy?"

"You're the only person in the room wearing a puppet."

"Then what good does it do to meet with you?"

"I just told you. I want to be your friend. And perhaps we'll end up sleeping together."

She stood to leave. He could see the slight curve of her lower lip, a subtle flattery. "I assure you, Mr. Corbin, you and I will never sleep together."

"All the crazy ones say the same thing."

A LITTLE HELP FROM MY FRIENDS

After several weeks of therapy, Lucy tired of Gary's take on the puppet—that hers was a real malady that if not confronted would lead to her picking up another gun and doing additional harm, to fish or human. She was a menace to society, he cautioned. The puppet was as lethal as any drug, any faulty explosive, he warned. Did she truly intend not to sleep with him at least once, even to discover what his other clients raved about? She had always done the proper thing—abided by the rules of her marriage and her career, and where had it gotten her? Outfitted with a fiberglass iron maiden and spinning celebrity gossip on TV, questioning her sanity. And rather than correcting her behavior, Ava Tardner's lewd aura brought out in Lucy a sexual doppelgänger, a deviant slut who permitted herself a tryst with her psychiatrist.

She was pleased to learn the parts still operated properly and astonished that instead of relieving the dull ache of celibacy, the sex made her aggressive for more of the bad behavior she had edited out of her life up until "The Incident." Not necessarily more of the bad with Gary Corbin, but perhaps with someone older and taller, more noticeable in a room, who would speak during sex, maybe even talk dirty. She was looking for a friendly creature with a passion for life who wanted simply to laugh and eat dinner and drink wine and enjoy heartiness.

"Sounds like you want a fatty."

"Beg your pardon."

"A laugher, an eater, a drinker. I must say, you don't discriminate."

"That's not what I meant. I meant heartiness for life, not for food."

"I don't see what's wrong with Gary. Keep me on next time he sticks it in you. I bet he'd like that."

"I will not!"

It only happened the one time. She had been riding the

subway and when she looked across into the far glass, she saw a lunatic with a doll on her hand, deep in conversation about fat people, sex. In New York City, where most everyone talked to themselves, she was hopeful she had passed it off. Nevertheless, that was when she began concealing Ava Tardner in a burlap sack—not so much because of the people who stared, but so she would not let herself slip into a confused duplicity in which it was okay to have it out with inanimate beings. People stared anyway. As a well-known newscaster, she had always been accustomed to attention on the subway; with the arrival of the puppet it was constant. The office was no better. No amount of clever camera angles could hide the bulge of her left arm. The best and tidiest thing was to fire her.

But they could not fire her. In the same way they could not fire someone due to race or gender, Lucy Springer was protected by her "condition." She held a note from an official psychiatrist from the State of New York claiming she was seeking treatment for puppet anxiety that would likely render her an imbecile before she ever had the chance to cash in the proceeds of her 401K. They put her on a celebrity gossip beat expecting her to fail, be disgraced, quit. And as expected, Lucy was atrocious, telling it as though she were reporting the six o'clock news with the canned, monosyllabic righteousness of someone who deserved better.

The puppet, on the other hand, was a natural. Viewers tuned in to watch Lucy narrate the exploits of their immortals. But what they found was a crass and sadistic midget being manipulated by a train wreck who, according to the tabloids, thought the puppet was slightly real; had killed a confirmed nine fish using a combination of bullets and the more effective suffocation; and seemed to think she was still reporting actual news with her dry, straightforward drawl. How could they ever go back to getting their celebrity news from a regular ape?

"And now, our weekly segment on the latest Hollywood breast implants."

"I hate my breasts," came from the corner of Lucy's mouth.

"Ava, I don't think we're supposed to talk about sex on the air."

The puppet bending its neck: "The way they hang there, like arm fat."

"Let's keep it together."

"That settles it. I'm getting implants." The puppet frisking herself. "Give a fella something to hold onto during the rodeo."

"Oh dear."

"Ever been to a rodeo, Springer? Something about the smell of all that bullshit, and those minimum-wage clowns in their funny pants and wigs just gets me raw. Love me a rodeo clown." Ava made a grinding motion with her hips.

"You'd really have sex with a clown?"

"I'd fuck a rottweiler if it bought me dinner."

The producers dashed for the bleep button, astonished each time Ava cursed—could they censor a puppet? The viewers adored it. Lucy did not know from where it came. According to her contract she was required to report the gossip and that was what she intended to do. If the puppet chose to assist, so be it. Ava Tardner had become the freaky niche that would generate more viewers, extra clicks on the web site. After only two months on the beat Lucy worked her way back into the ANN main feed. For three minutes a day, she looked into the camera and cleared her throat, and told America the score.

Her job as the Twitter reporter was the exact antithesis of what she had faithfully espoused in her career as a news anchor. With Facebook and Twitter and blogs, it was really nothing more than celebrities reporting on themselves. All she had to do was collect the bits and assemble them into an appropriate narrative. If the online universe suggested a famous actor had knocked up a single mother with eight children and refused to pay child support, she would scan for any such news. If she found anything, no matter how obscure, that was her "source," and she could cite that source to her legions of followers, claiming the nameless actor had adamantly denied the allegations. Thus was born the media frenzy known as Clevesclan.

What she was doing was not traditional journalism. She was inventing reality by reporting on it first, rather than adhering to the outdated mode of allowing reality to dictate journalistic endeavors.

And then relying on a fiberglass doll to intrigue viewers, who converged on the ANN web site for the sole purpose of hearing the puppet flog celebrities:

"I'd eat through a forest of sausage to lick Cleve Peoples's nipple."

"Her tits runneth over!"

"Whoa, Nelly!" was Ava's patented catchphrase, which ANN plastered all over the T-shirts and coffee mugs and bumper stickers they hawked on the ANN web site.

Viewers loved hearing the puppet rant, everything from gay marriage to the size of Keanu Reeves's member. And the subconscious thought, of course, was that they were actually listening to Lucy Springer, that she was a lunatic on account of the fish killing spree, and that she thought the puppet was real: It brought a whiff of the psychotic to their celebrity gossip.

Lucy's style was simple and pure: throw enough crap at the wall and something will stick. And nine times out of ten, it did. She knew a bit about manipulating the public into believing what she threw at them, which was why she had issues with the plane crash. First, the captain had clearly patted the girl's bottom, which simply was not done after a crash. Second, the ferryboats appeared as though they'd been waiting there for the plane to arrive, as was the bus that whisked passengers to the hotel. She had called in a favor with an old source at the DMV to find it had been rented by a public relations firm named Veiltality Inc.

Whatever happened on that plane had itched Lucy Springer's long dormant instincts, and now she intended to get back what belonged to her: the anchor chair of the six o'clock news.

I'VE GOT A FEELING

She arrived at the ANN offices in Times Square, a fifty-four-story tower that cost $1 billion to build and nearly half that much to outfit with cables and monitors and computer hardware, a massive rat's nest of technology and efficiency that produced nothing but words. It was its own metropolis—a gymnasium, three cafeterias, a medical unit, a grocery store, a non-denominational church that doubled as a gathering space for office parties for the roughly 3,100 employees. Floors 14 and 15 were her turf, which housed the news desk, the sports department, entertainment writers, and the technology team that blasted all of it into the stratosphere. The elevator up would be the calmest twelve seconds of her day, a voiceless rendition of The Carpenters' "We've Only Just Begun" with everyone staring up at the orange numbers waiting for their cue.

The door opened on 14.

The chum. The banshee hollering about the kid that was hit by the train, the subway fare hike, the Yankees in eleven, we got the captain's first interview, are all the survivors still alive?, send it out to Chicago now, we got signal with Rick, fresh footage of the plane I know it's just sitting there half submerged but fresh footage damn it! The blueprint of the new museum that would be constructed out of the resurrected airplane, due to open in less than four days; it looked like a snake had swallowed a rat, and could they get a cartoonist on it now? Five cameramen critiquing their bounty in comparison to other TV stations around the city, a blonde on the phone "Uh-huh, uh-huh, uh-huh, uh-huh," a man eating a donut, yelling at no one in particular—"Link it up, motherfucker!"—a parade of gray-suited men and women making their way to a conference room, nodding, agreeing, and the typing—hundreds of calloused fingers dipping into the plastic ivory alphabets of their keyboards and tiny phones, like a miniature marching band clicking the progress, *da-da-rump-pump-pump*, space, *da-da-rump-pump-pump*, return—heads bobbing, shoulders in rhythm, so that if one of the cameramen showed some initiative, he could record all of it and play it back at high speed, and it would appear like the choreographed dance of a progressive and constipated ritual. Surfing, searching, racing, e-mailing, texting, tweeting, tapping, blogging, brainstorming new and clever ways to describe the weather, all of it chum, all of it feeding their ravenous hunger for what was new and intense, the mass sound coalescing into a cadence that went *chuuummmmmmmmmm*. . . .

Across the room she spotted Dean, mouth agape, staring at the intern Tonya. Dean loved Tonya; he loved anything with breasts.

"Dean, a word."

"What is it?" He did not turn from the intern.

"What have I told you about staring at people?"

"In a minute. She's sending a text message. That's why she bites her lip." Dean tilted his head as though admiring a woodland creature that had not yet smelled his carnivorous intent. "She'll hit send and stop biting her lip, and then she'll notice me. She doesn't mind me staring when she doesn't notice. Only when she does."

Lucy placed the puppet in his line of sight; Dean's eyes deglazed; his mentor registered.

"Ava!" Heads turned across the room. "Twit as well! Here they are everyone!"

Up until then no one had bothered to glance up from the endless manipulation of the alphabet. The room applauded, tapping of the shoulders, slapping of the buttocks, as though she had just driven in two base runners in the ninth inning of a critical ballgame.

"What's this about?"

"Us three," Dean said. "Prime time again. In everyone's window."

"What are you talking about?"

"Swagger. You and Ava scored the first interview."

Lucy froze, took stock. There was no logic as to why she would get the interview. Rather than feel good about it, she thought of Gary Corbin, and felt a twinge of that paranoia her therapist was always encouraging.

"But how?" she asked.

"What how? Because it's you. And Ava. And we three are

making a comeback." He hugged her, or at least tried; having not practiced the maneuver on an adequate number of women, Dean just bumped her with his chest. "I tried to call you, but your phone is dead. It's like you don't exist."

"Conference room. Now."

Dean was scared of Lucy, of people in general. He preferred to talk to them through a computer. Closing the door, she pushed him into a chair and held both sides so he could not maneuver, she on one side, Ava on the other. To observers, it appeared the older, lunatic, Sandra Bullock look-alike had settled on having her way with the youngish nerd, her raising the kink factor via the use of a ventriloquist doll.

"There were no birds."

"There were no birds?" He thought for a moment. "Are those song lyrics?"

"The plane. It wasn't a bird strike that killed the engines." Lucy cued up the photos and handed over the camera. "If it were a bird strike, the engines would be covered in debris."

"Not again, Lucy."

"I had a professional look at the plane. Crust, feathers, meat, something, Dean." She clicked through the photos.

"These really came from inside that engine?"

"Less than twelve hours ago." Lucy spun him around in his chair and pinned him into the table. "I'll interview the pilot as though everything is fine. During the first break I'll show him the pictures."

"That's your plan?"

Swagger was a huge score. It probably would not get her back the anchor seat, but it was a start. And there was always the chance she was wrong.

"I need to speak to him. Look him in the eye. Find out what he knows."

"You have the first interview with a modern-day folk hero. And you want to throw all that away over some blurry pictures?" Dean shuffled through the pictures. "I don't know anything about bird strikes. Tell me—what does it mean?"

"It means someone lied."

"Doesn't matter. If people believe it happened, then it happened. A million viewers are logging on to our web site right now for information on this guy. Do you realize they've already started building a museum?"

"I think they meant to land it in the river. I think they did it on purpose."

"Why would someone do that?"

"I don't know."

"Don't take this the wrong way." Lucy's hands were on her hips, the puppet looking him over, upside down. "But you come out with a ludicrous plot that the crash was faked, and no one will believe you anyway."

"Why not?"

"Because you killed all those fish. And because you have a puppet on your arm, Lucy. And you talk to it. I've seen you. I watch people all day."

"I've got a hunch. That's all I know."

"I'm not risking my career on a hunch. And remember—I've got you to thank for the wretched state of my career."

Lucy needed Dean's help. For all his inconsistencies, he had an uncanny ability with information, both obtaining and understanding it. Truth was she was intimidated by Twitter and Facebook, from how to answer a text message to whom to call if her computer suddenly blinked. If this were a war, she would not know how to load her weapon. Dean was her infantry. Of all the media organizations in the city, she had been awarded the prized interview, only to learn it might be teeming with fraud. Or maybe she was teeming with fraud, paranoid and anxious, one of those insane people the sane people talked about.

"Let me ask you, Dean. What do you want to do with your life?"

"Have a corner cubicle, someplace I can grow a small garden on the windowsill, maybe space for one of those beanbag chairs for a bed, and on holidays—"

"I mean the ultimate destination. I know it isn't beaming celebrity gossip out into the ozone. What gets your fire stoked?"

He hated talking directly to Lucy. In the same way he preferred to speak to people over the Internet, he preferred Lucy speak to him through Ava. "I've never told this to anyone."

Lucy moved in close. "Go on."

"It'll seem weird, like maybe I'm gay. But that's not it." He glanced around the room then reached into his back pocket and pulled out a folded sheet of paper.

Lucy unfolded the page. It was a picture of the American actor Paul Newman, shirt unbuttoned, sweating, cigarette hanging out the side of a slight grin. She had seen the movie but could not place the title.

"Your dream is to meet Paul Newman?" She put a hand on Dean's shoulder. "I'm afraid Paul Newman died."

"I don't want to meet him." Dean snatched the page. "I want to be him."

"You want to be an actor?"

He pointed at the shirtless ghost. "No. I want to be that."

Since grade school, Dean Migliotto had been an outcast. His hair lacked the innate agility to perform tricks when gel was introduced. His features were puny, his pectoral muscles deflated, his skin an ashy white. In short, he was ugly. And he knew it. He was conditioned to a life standing on the edge of the dance floor, sitting in the football stands watching other people dazzle. And what he came to understand was that life—its pleasantness or ugliness, its successes or failures—came down to one spectacular instant when sperm and egg met. From the beginning either you were beautiful and mattered, or you were ugly and you didn't. Growing up with no real social life of his own, he instead observed the way other people socialized. And he was convinced that beautiful people, through nothing other than their evolutionary good looks, gained more from life than their ugly counterparts. Dean was smarter than most of his classmates; he was more gifted with imagination and ambition. But it always seemed that a better-looking alternative arrived at the last instant and snatched away his rewards.

He concluded it was because of the way he looked. He had done the research in the twilight hours, alone in the building, a peculiar serenity as the lights across the city drifted from brightness into an aching orange, into a lovely yellow, into a dawn. He polled thousands of women, the most desperate brand, those up in the middle of the night looking for that connection. He issued questionnaires, compiled the data. And what he discovered was what successful men looked like, and what women looked for in a man.

"Paul Newman?" Lucy asked.

"Paul Newman circa 1967 in *Cool Hand Luke*. Not so much Paul Newman in *The Color of Money*." Dean showed her the picture again. "He's got good looks, but not too good looking—women don't like too good looking on account of infidelity. And he's trustworthy, but you can see in his eyes he's mischievous. Nobody likes a do-gooder, but they only want enough mischief until they don't want it anymore."

"Dean, not everyone can look like this."

"That's not true. Celebrity plastic surgery. If you have the money, doctors can cut you to look anyway you want."

"So you would undergo major surgery to have more sex?"

"Sex has nothing to do with it." He corrected that statement quickly. "Well, sex has something to do with it. But more than that, I want to excel in a sexualized culture. Why stop at sex? I want all the perks that come along with looking like this picture—the job, the acceptance, even the parking spaces."

"You want to be famous?"

"No. I want to be accepted by those who are famous. And beautiful. And rich." He moved over next to her. "You can't see it because you're on the other side. But there is a prejudice in our culture that has existed forever—long before blacks or women or gays started complaining, we ugly people suffered inequality. We get worse jobs, worse sexual partners to produce more ugly progeny, even worse houses to live in, older cars to drive."

"That isn't true," Lucy said.

"True enough. There's no such thing as luck, fate, random interaction. Life has an equation. And it's directly proportional to how pretty you are."

"I know plenty of ugly people who are successful."

"I'm not saying the occasional unsightly doesn't get to the other side—we have our versions of Rosa Parks crossing over the ugly barrier, too. But for the most part we have the Ugly Ceiling to keep us down."

Lucy knew what he meant. She had lived on both sides of his theoretical barrier. Life was different with a puppet on her arm.

"How much?"

"For the whole thing—$97,148, give or take."

"I don't have that kind of money."

"I wasn't asking." He folded up Paul Newman. "You asked about my dream so I told you. And now you understand why I can't follow every crazy notion someone suggests."

"Of course you can't."

"Sometimes planes crash."

"Sometimes they do," Lucy agreed. "Guy like you can't take too many risks. We get the interview of a lifetime, you figure it's best not to mention the pictures, just chat up a real hero."

"A beacon of humanity," Dean said.

She snatched the picture. "Thing is, Paul Newman's character in *Cool Hand Luke* is about a man who takes risks."

"Wouldn't know. Never saw it."

"You never bothered to watch the movie?"

"I'm interested in the way he looks. Not the way he acts."

She pushed on. "It's about rebellion. About sticking your neck out and doing what you believe. As a woman, I find that charming. Most women do."

Dean's chapped lips curled into a tight smile. He massaged terrain that on another man might have held a perky mustache. "Keep talking."

She slapped the camera. "We prove everyone's hero crashed the plane into the Hudson on purpose, we'll have the biggest story since O.J. hopped in that white Bronco."

He breathed heavy, smiled. "Everyone forgets O.J. used to be a fairly good actor."

"Peabody Awards, promotions, sex, money—we'll be the new Woodward and Bernstein."

Dean being younger, he could not instantly recall those names from his internal lexicon. "Goddamn," he said. "What do you need me to do?" She handed him a slip of paper. "Veiltality? What is that?"

"There were buses that took passengers to the Whalensky. I traced the license plates. They were rented by this company."

"I'll have it within the hour."

She knew Dean would not leave the building so she handed him the camera for safekeeping. "One last thing. I know I'm not your mother, but I am your boss. I am ordering you to watch the movie based on the character you hope to portray."

"What's the point?"

"I don't want to spoil the ending, but you might as well find out what happens to Cool Hand before you schedule any surgeries."

START TO MAKE IT BETTER

One day it was gone.

After forty-five years of luck and insight into the most absurd games of chance ever conceived, Lucky Dan O'Malley had run dry. The luck was gone, dinosaur gone, a desert choking on dust. The magic remained inside him; he could see no other way. But it was inaccessible, his superpowers suspended until he learned some vital lesson, he was sure.

Like all history's great tales, this kink in the smooth narrative of his life had begun and ended with a woman. Trish McAllister was a free spirit, a joyful creature without a sinful joint in her being. Three things made her tick: a hot fudge sundae every Sunday afternoon; sharing a six-pack of beer and a board game; and the world's worst movies, shown every night in December, portraying the most over-celebrated holiday in Earth's history—made-for-TV Christmas movies.

She was one of a kind. And Lucky had messed it up. Eleven years she stuck around, waiting for him to wed her and make her with child, buy her a home where she could bake cookies and store her board games. He never even bothered to inform her he was infertile, a genetic mutation of his DNA that affected one in seven O'Malley men. He just let her keep wishing. He had neglected the thing that was vital to his life for the thing he thought was vital— his lover for his luck. Now both had abandoned him. And then the call came.

It was a fellow from New York, the brother of an old acquaintance. He was involved in a macabre business, one which Lucky did not fully comprehend. But he spoke with a conviction that was often missing from Lucky's clients—one of determination, and passion, and a primordial need that had abandoned Lucky's own life. He spoke of a mission.

See, passengers, Lucky Dan was a believer that if you did not do the right things, then the wrong things found you. He had a massive talent. But he had allowed it to be used for the wrong occupations. By his standards he should have directed it toward helping people, to inspiring the world with a brand of sorcery in which most neglected to believe. Instead he had forgotten what was important, opting for a clientele with so much money they could afford to rent their luck. But his caller, this Normal Fulk—there was something good and honorable and weird about him.

So he was flying to New York to see about retrieving his luck. And some contraband semen.

IN MY EARS AND IN MY EYES

By Tuesday afternoon, stock symbol AWL soared from a fifty-two-week low of $1.80 to a fifty-two-week high of $34.23, making Air Wanderlust the biggest gainer in the airline sector. Traders who had never considered the risky company were intrigued. It was everywhere—on the television, on the web, on the three-story electronic video screen that wrapped around the NASDAQ building in New York City's Times Square, and which alerted everyone to how rich or how poor the country was behaving. Blackie employed nearly one hundred analysts and experts and data whiz kids to measure his marketing blitzes; according to the latest figures, Air Wanderlust was averaging a 1:119 market. What that meant was that of the hundreds of millions of words and images and ideas the average American consumer experienced daily, one in every 119 suggestions doing electronic wind sprints into and out of their brains pertained to Air Wanderlust. Most ideas moved about the universe in a 1:420,000 market. What Blackie had done for the airline was nothing short of miraculous.

"Not good enough," he told Monica Dressings, who had brought him the latest figures. She was dressed in knee-high black boots and a white blouse. She wanted to look her best as she was rehearsing later with Captain Swagger for his interview.

"But we've never seen these numbers."

"I crash landed an Airbus in the Hudson. I want 1:50."

"Even the Super Bowl doesn't get that."

"We'll break 1:100 if I have to slit Swagger's jugular on live television."

"I don't see why we would . . ."

"That's called satire, Miss Dressings. Obviously I'm not going to murder anyone. Except for Second Officer Wrinkles, if that young man doesn't come out of his coma awfully quick."

"But he's your nephew."

"Again, Miss Dressings, I'm not going to murder my nephew. I am, however, going to leak this sound track to the Internet."

He pointed the remote toward a stereo, which erupted with shrieks from the inner cabin of Flight AW2921, the horrified passengers as the aircraft descended, all of them even more stunning when they screamed. Blackie smiled as they relived it—the terrified screams, mothers praying, grown men weeping.

He turned up the volume. "Listen for a moment."

"It's disgusting," she said.

"Let me ask." He motioned toward the stereo. "What did you do while it went down?"

"I don't remember."

"Try to remember." He turned it louder. There was something about Monica Dressings he could not trust. Perhaps it was how she kept to herself, or that she gave guarded answers to his questions. She was stealthily clever, or painfully dull, he could not tell which. "It's important that I know, Miss Dressings."

"Prayed maybe."

"You knew what was happening, but still you prayed."

"You weren't there. It was terrifying."

"I was there. I was here. Listening."

"Well, I prayed. I guess that makes me weak. I'm sorry."

"Don't be sorry. It was a beautiful, religious moment." He stood and walked to the speaker. It emitted a wild screech. "Everyone prayed, I know they did. Even those without gods—once the engines stopped, they developed one."

"Jimmish didn't pray," she said. "I sat next to him. He did a puzzle."

"Jimmish is special." Blackie smiled at the image of his henchman on the plane. "He has developed an attention to detail so precise, it gives him faith in a world that others see as barbaric. You could learn something about faith from him."

"He terrifies me, frankly."

Blackie turned down the volume. "You prayed. And Swagger prayed. Even those birds, when the plane roared into their path, must have prayed to it, a giant, silver god, just before it incinerated them."

"There were no birds. You made it up."

He pointed the remote and silenced the shrieks. "I want a new round of press releases this morning. Leak that the Air Wanderlust CEO has suggested to the FAA that all bird species within a twenty-mile radius of airports be exterminated. Make sure you send one to PETA and the other animal groups."

"Wouldn't that be bad publicity?"

"Good, bad, no difference at this point. I want to break 1:100 before you go to your room tonight to drink wine in your pajamas with your cat."

"You make my life sound pathetic."

"What did you do last night when you left here?"

She did not answer.

"I'll take it from your silence that you drank wine in your pajamas with what's its name."

"Mr. Tuffers."

"You bore me, Miss Dressings. I don't mean to be rude. But if I had to spend an evening with you I'd take a running leap off the fire escape."

Blackie's marketing campaign was not going to make all the airline's problems go away, and there were many. The company was running on fumes, the perfect financial metaphor: If fuel costs rose again anytime soon, Air Wanderlust simply did not have the money to purchase any. There was an open FAA investigation into sixteen of the fleet's jets. For whatever reason, the baggage handlers of Air Wanderlust were some of the worst in the industry. They lost more bags per year than any other airline operating in North America. The board of directors blamed management, management blamed the board, they all blamed the union, which had its head so far up its ass it was a wonder planes did not drop out of the sky daily. Now there was talk that union members would strike by the end of the year. As soon as stockholders got wind of a strike, it would spell doom for the flailing company.

The board of directors had wanted out—out of the union, out

of the continuous missing bags that had everyone scratching heads. They took the problems to Blackie Spin, who presented them with an expensive but tantalizing plan. Start with a miracle and outfit the airplane with actors, beautiful people, so that every photograph of the passengers on the wing, or during follow-up interviews, or through a quick Google search would reveal a stunning assembly: this was a beautiful landing, with beautiful results, beautiful people, a beautiful airline, in fact. Arrange for a reporter to be on the flight and make it all seem a comfortable coincidence, as though he or she stumbled upon the news story of his or her life. Do it directly in the path of the morning commute, rush hour in the fastest city in the world, when everyone would scramble to enter the gravitational pull of Blackie Spin.

As soon as the plane hit water, a crew began preparing it for a museum to honor the day, a publicly funded ruse that was due for a ribbon-cutting that Saturday, fastest turnaround of a museum in history. Now when people needed to fly to Topeka or Gainesboro or Cedar City, they might use Air Wanderlust instead of another airline; they all charged the same fares anyway and Air Wander-lust now had a charming style. Travel agents, resorts, conferences, sports teams—it was a trickle effect. Pretty soon the company would actually be able to afford fuel prices, maybe even drop fares. They could pay union members better, hire someone else to sort out the baggage issue, purchase new planes, and take one of the old ones out to the desert and set it ablaze during a management team-building retreat, roast marshmallows over the embers.

Point was to give the impression that the company was a winner, the stock was on its way up, a wise investor would do well to buy now. Of course, Blackie's plan was not without risk. It could go the other way. The pilot could lose nerve, blink incorrectly, come in uneven with too much air speed, dip the nose at a one-degree angle when it got into the drink. Then it would go bad. Hindenburg bad. Titanic blues. He could end up scattering passengers and flight attendants a half-mile down the stretch of Manhattan scenery. All those endowments he had applied for would have to go toward a memorial instead of his beloved museum.

Hank Swagger had not been Blackie's ideal choice. He and the board had screened everyone in the company, ranking all 600 full-time and part-time pilots. From that list, they settled on fifteen candidates, twelve of whom were eliminated because, as Blackie Spin noted, "they were not miracle material." Of the remaining three, one was a woman who did not fit the role Blackie had imagined; one was a born-again Christian who would probably blow the whistle on the thing. The last candidate was Hank Swagger, who despite his consistent butchery of company policies, was everyone's darling. Swagger was clearly the better pilot. His name seemed the better fit on a museum banner. And because he had recently hijacked a plane to visit a Florida hooker, it was more likely he could be coerced into the assignment.

What Blackie wished to produce was the quintessential family, a Norman Rockwell photograph of husband, wife, and children, all smiling with the knowledge that God was in the heavens, that goodness and decency were certainties, that when duty called this man answered, stepping into his role like a fresh John Wayne. It was a beautiful story that required a beautiful leading man, and Swagger was questionable. He was a textbook womanizer: red eyes by morning, stale breath, a constant hunger in his reflexes for more of what controlled him. His wife was a functioning alcoholic, relied too much on plastic surgery, a bit of a drag. His daughter, Mallory, had moved to Oregon several months before and joined some type of revolution, its goals indeterminate; they seemed to be revolting against society's direction, although they had created and maintained a well-designed web site to further their message. The son, Nathan, an abominable cliché, had spent years in Hollywood hoping to be cast in the next sitcom. Despite repeated failures, he phoned home several times a month quoting Winston Churchill and Vince Lombardi and other rosy-eyed citers of perseverance, guaranteeing his parents he would never give up. His parents begged him to just please give up, and were actually prouder of their daughter for having the gumption to join a cult and make something of her time.

But it was Swagger and his shortcomings that continued to

distract Blackie. He had shown up to the simulator drunk, or hungover, or on the verge of being drunk or hungover, and often manipulated the plane down Broadway, or into a housing complex just to prove he could. He performed a quite miraculous flyby at Yankee Stadium, another time slamming directly into the George Washington Bridge just to see if a simulated Airbus could shake it loose. Which was everyone's fear—that despite the ability to glide a machine of that size and complexity, he might just smack it into a bridge instead. The times he did show up to training levelheaded and ready to work, it was clear Swagger was a gifted aviator. His mannerisms precise, his ability to play the role superb until they were not superb, and then they were downright infuriating.

Swagger's inability to stick to script rattled Blackie. In the hotel room after the crash, he had sat on the bed the entire time concentrating on the windowsill until Blackie had to shutter the drapes. And while the plan had always been to give Lucy Springer the interview, the suggestion was meant to come from Blackie. It had come from Swagger instead. Blackie was the one who devised the plan; Blackie had arranged the vacation; it was Blackie's call to make. A minor detail? Perhaps. But to Blackie, a man who would ignore one detail would just as soon ignore others. And when it came to crash landing an Airbus in the Hudson River, detail was king.

WAR IS OVER

Blackie arrived to find the Swaggers in a heated reunion. It was necessary that when presented to the public they be a kindred household, and it would be beneficial if at least one of the children had consulted with the U.S. government about killing foreigners. The War on Terror continued to churn patriotism, an excellent sub-story to the miracle landing. Private First Class Nathan Swagger's only demand was that he had earned the Medal of Honor during his faux military career, and Blackie convinced the aspiring thespian to accept a photograph of the medal instead of the real thing—so long as he kept it concealed in a closed box.

"Back from the war," he announced when he arrived at the suite. "God bless it."

"Attaboy," Swagger said.

Nathan beamed. "I've been awarded the Medal of Honor."

"Rooty-toot-toot." Mipsy swirled a drink.

The Mallory typed into her phone. "He's lying."

"I wasn't told there would be medals." Swagger lost the smile; this trespassed on his week of glory. "How did you earn it?"

"Soldiering in the war."

"Which war?"

"The War on Terror, of course."

"That's not a real war. That's a metaphorical war."

Mallory tapped her phone. "They don't hand those out to anybody. You'd have to at least lose an appendage."

"Important thing is I'm home and we're all together, God bless it."

"Missing leg, missing ear, something. You look too tan to be a hero."

Swagger could not get past the medal. "But what did you do to earn it?"

"I told you. I fought the terror."

Mipsy snorted.

"Says here if he wasn't maimed, he had to have killed at least one hundred people."

"You a big, bad killer—that it?" Mipsy laughed.

"It was a war, mother. I did what I had to do."

"Suppose we should have a toast," Swagger said, though his heart was not in it.

"None for me, father. Bit early in the day, no?"

Mipsy checked her watch. "Condescending little shit."

Pfc. Swagger pulled out a velvet-encased box. He unlocked the box and removed a photograph.

"What's that?"

"The Medal of Honor."

"No it isn't," Mallory said. "That's a picture of the Medal of Honor."

"They don't let you wear it," he explained. "It's kept in a glass case in the president's bedroom."

"Who told you that?" Swagger asked.

He nodded toward Blackie, who bit a tomato. Mallory tapped her phone, pulled up her own picture of the Medal of Honor.

"Look," she said. "I fought the terror, too."

Taken separately, Blackie could not tolerate the Swaggers. But as a whole, their disarray was charming, the evolution of the American tribe. Inside that room, they could remove one another's hides and wear them as capes. So long as outside they were the Swagger family, happy and healthy and early to church.

"Let's take a seat, shall we?" Blackie said. "I sense we're having difficulty bonding."

"First things first," Swagger said. "What can we do about The Nathan?"

"Blessing this, praising that," Mipsy said. "Ever since that damn medal."

It tickled Blackie that the photograph had caused so much trouble. "You should be proud. He's not a half bad actor."

"Still," Swagger said. "We prefer a different occupation, even if he's pretending. Something more . . ."

"Swagger," Mallory said.

"More Swagger, right. Bit more chip off the old block, bit less trying to show me up."

"You weren't actually in any wars," Blackie reminded Nathan.

Swagger moved it along. "The Mallory, on the other hand, don't sleep on beds no more—what was the reason honey?"

She watched her phone. "Beds are American. I don't buy American."

"To think I fought for people like you." Nathan couldn't help himself.

"Fascinating," Blackie said. He had even become accustomed to how the Swaggers referred to their children—The Nathan and The Mallory—as though they were damaged projects meant to be strategized rather than the fruit of their salacious loins. "There are three bedrooms in this suite. It's important for appearance's sake you stay together. That's why I've had you locked in here."

"Wait just a minute," Swagger said. "We can leave whenever we want. We choose to stay in here bickering."

"Mr. Swagger, you disappoint me. All the trouble I went to having you guarded. Two days and you never bothered to discover you were locked inside? Where has the dog been going to the bathroom?"

They were stunning, arguing over photographs and sleeping arrangements, unaware they were caged. They had nearly come to blows over who should hold the mutt. But none of them could recall the dog relieving itself.

"This is all in the contracts you signed." Blackie bit into tomato.

The puppy began to stir, which caused the Swaggers to matriculate toward the bed, calling out the names they had issued: Jeters (rascally guy), Alastair (furry man), Che (wittle fwend), and Rumsfeld (who's good good good).

"If there's nothing else," Blackie said, "we need to rehearse for the interview. Next door in fifteen minutes. With my assistant."

Swagger perked. He shared a slight nod with Blackie. Mipsy knew instantly. She went for the dog, her last bargaining chip in the marriage, only to be bested by her daughter, who grabbed Jeters.

Mallory was tackled by the war hero, who screamed like a child when his father joined the scrum.

"I've fucking got Che!"

"His name is Jeters!"

"Leggo, leggo, leggo."

"Don't you sleep with that whore!"

Suddenly little Jeters yelped, having been plucked from the pile. Blackie held the dog by its collar, staring down at Swagger, his disappointing leading man. He had tried to make a connection. He had enrolled him in speaking classes to prepare him for a life outside commercial aviation. He had rewarded him with a mistress so that he might concentrate on the project, a mistress responsible for his cuts and bruises. Swagger—folk legend, icon-to-be, Blackie's Gatsby, his Dean Moriarty—lay there amid a pile of legs and assholes. To say the least, Blackie Spin was disappointed with the respect his career would never earn him. But what he could not know was that the right people were finally paying attention to his storytelling talents.

NOTHING TO GET HUNG ABOUT

Normal's initiation into the semen business began with a stallion named Desperate Todd. He and Frank were paid five grand by a breeder to obtain the semen, cart it across two states, and deliver it to a farm in Maryland, where over a breakfast of eggs and biscuits Frank talked the breeder into hiring them for steady work. Frank could talk himself into any job. It was an easy score for the two, who earned a living stealing car radios, and who had recently expanded into thuggery. But the semen business was their way out. It was in that gray area between legal and illegal. And it was an endeavor in which few criminals cared to involve themselves, the messy details of duping a stallion in passion into making love to a fake vagina.

Most breeders could negotiate a price without resorting to the Fulk brothers. But often there was bad blood between counterparts, or one farm had specific claims on a stallion's semen, which provided the necessity for a black market. A mare was typically in estrus for about twenty days, a small window to settle negotiations, transport the stallion, have veterinarians on both sides examine the horses, arrange for the mating; if semen negotiations hit a standstill, the Fulk brothers were called. It was often easier to pay a semen trafficker to deliver the product in a frozen and sealed container, and the authorities did not get involved since there was really no way to distinguish ordinary semen from stolen. Besides, no one was injured. Except for Normal. Normal typically was injured.

Frank arranged the financials, negotiated separately with both buyer and seller, and dealt with the semen preservation; Normal was on penis control. Which is more difficult than it might seem, guiding a furious penis connected to a snorting, raging animal into a rubber vagina. And the whole time his older brother shouting instructions, he shouting back, the two threatening to kill each other—there was little science to the Fulk brothers' method.

"Disinfect the penis, Norm."

"What do you think I'm doing? Hold him still."

"What's taking so long?" Frank bending down to check on his little brother. "It's not a magic lamp. Don't rub the whole thing. Just disinfect the tip."

"Here, funny guy, you do it."

"I'm holding the horse."

"Clean the fucking cock, Frank. Show me how it's done, funny man."

"Stop screwing around, Normal." Frank pulling, the horse lurching, Normal spewing. "All right, here we go. Forward."

"Hold him steady, Frank."

"He's a few feet now. You got the penis in hand, right?"

"I got it."

"Yeah you do, weirdo. He's mounting. Now Norm! Put it in the bag!"

"It's in."

"You've got a knack for handling cock, little brother."

It was during one job that they ran into a breeder who inquired about celebrity semen. They only knew his first name, Wendell, wealthy, hung out around the tracks. He was one of their regular clients but this time he was interested in obtaining a vial of celebrity—not horse—semen.

"For what purpose?" Frank had asked.

"To sell to collectors."

"What would they do with it?"

"Say a guy's a collector of rare things." Wendell had made the pitch before. "It's really no different than collecting antiques or comic books."

"But how would you make any money off semen?"

"It's not a money thing. You collect just to have, same way you do coins or stamps. You don't sell them. You honor them. Think about it a second."

Frank thought about it for a quarter-second. "How much?"

They talked around it for forty-five minutes before Wendell revealed he had his own collection: a library of frozen celebrity semen, dozens of samples. He invited Frank and Normal for a private viewing, which touched Frank so much he agreed to take the assignment: For $15,000, of course, three times the score they would make on a horse, they would provide Wendell a vial of semen from American actor Bruce Willis.

WORK IT ON OUT

A month passed before an opportunity arose. Bruce Willis was in New York, filming. They would station a prostitute at the hotel bar where he was staying and count on a successful seduction. Their girl would then insist on a condom that she would tie in a knot and smuggle out in her pocketbook.

"Good plan," Normal said. "What type of prostitute?"

"Just someone cute."

"Right. But man or woman?"

"Bruce Willis isn't gay."

"How can you know? Celebrities are more evolved in their sexuality."

"Bruce Willis killed a dozen terrorists in the Nakatomi Tower. He threw Hans out the fucking window."

"I'm just saying. We don't want to get in there and have no backup."

"You're the younger brother. We need a backup, you'll do what I say."

The first problem was that Bruce Willis kept strange hours. He was either wandering out or coming in to the hotel, but never actually patronizing the bar. Which meant Priscilla, the girl, typically ended up inebriated on their dime by the time the actor might have made an appearance. The one night he did take a seat at the bar, it was clear he was not astonished by her looks. But he was polite to the point of sarcasm, buying Priscilla drinks, and gently insisting she was a hooker.

"Fuck it!" Frank announced by the third round, the bar tab rising. "We'll go in heavy."

"What does that mean exactly, heavy?"

"We'll take it by force." Frank was stubborn. When he could not see a job through, it became less about money and more about the finish. "I'll hold him down, you get it."

"Frank, you are talking about sexually assaulting one of the most invigorating actors of our generation."

"Don't you think I know he's invigorating?"

"What if he does to you and me what he did to those terrorists?"

"That's just acting. I could beat the shit out of Bruce Willis."

"But what if he does, Frank. You're not thinking."

Frank took a breath. "You're right. I'll talk him into it. But if I can't, we go heavy."

Frank barged into the bar and inserted himself between Bruce Willis and Priscilla. It occurred to Priscilla the level of kinky into which she had become involved—two men, possibly mobsters, were paying her to extract semen from a movie star, all of whom were likely carrying weapons. She narrated her drunken revelations aloud in a vodka-induced confession to Bruce Willis, who turned on Frank and Normal with a bewildered grin.

"That true?"

"Sort of," Normal said.

"Norm, don't talk." Frank reached across the bar. "Frank Fulk. This is my brother. Big fans of your work, Mr. Willis."

"Call me Bruce." They all shook.

A giant appeared behind them, the width of both the brothers Fulk combined.

"Everything okay, Mr. Willis?"

"Everything seems to be on the level. Stick close, Dez."

Dez stepped back and folded his hands in front until his deltoid muscles popped even with the bottoms of his ears.

Frank sat. "I don't want you to be alarmed, Bruce, but we hired this girl to obtain a sample of your semen, which we absolutely cannot leave without."

Bruce Willis existed in that level of celebrityhood that even the most outrageous threats could not penetrate. "You guys from the future?" he asked. Normal laughed, Frank did not. "Sounds like the plot of a science fiction movie."

"We're not from the future. We're from Brooklyn. And we don't want to hurt anyone. But if Dez takes one step, I'll shoot him in the knee."

"You got a gun?"

"I got a gun." Then to the bartender. "Two beers."

"Can I see it?"

Frank pulled out the weapon and held it by his side.

"What do you want with my semen?" Rather than being afraid or appalled, he seemed genuinely interested.

"We're semen traffickers. We're here on behalf of a buyer."

He looked around. "This one of those hidden camera shows?"

"I assure you what is happening has nothing to do with the movies." Frank put his hand on Bruce Willis's shoulder; Dez stayed put. "Buy you a drink, you send us on our way?"

Turned out Bruce Willis was a fan of the strange criminal networks that he assumed existed in metropolitan areas. In exchange for the tale of how they'd gotten involved, he agreed to the sample and they sucked down a half-dozen drinks while Frank invented stories of all the semen he had hijacked—the Christopher Walken, the Sean Penn, the John Cusack, the eerily purplish Bob Dylan. It was nearly five o'clock in the morning when Bruce Willis retired to his hotel room, emerging moments later with a loaded condom that he tossed into the air, and which both brothers Fulk permitted to land on the hotel carpet.

That was how Frank talked them into a career as celebrity semen traffickers.

I'M LOOKING THROUGH YOU

His brother died not as the hero Normal knew, but in a more mundane manner: at a birthday party, a Fulk cousin swinging for the piñata, striking Uncle Frank in the temple instead. A freak accident, he never awoke, another reason Normal hated that puppet, anything in fact that reminded him of piñatas. The tattoo on Normal's forearm had faded over the years, although the desire to itch it when he did something moronic was strong as ever. It had been a persistent itch ever since he learned about the Frawl children and the existence of the John Lennon, a menacing rawness beneath his skin that he could not get at no matter how furiously he scratched, a nagging psoriasis of his soul.

The nightmares had begun soon after the Frawl children and the vial crept into his life. Back when the John Lennon was a rumor and only Rory Genius-Temple knew for sure it existed, Normal was certain he would end up stealing it. It was understood he and the famed DNA were on an unavoidable collision course, a hurled egg and a brick wall. And he knew better than to get involved with specimens from dead celebrities. It was the most valuable product in the business, but even Normal admitted there was something macabre about it, a ghost hovering over the negotiations.

The nightmares were always the same, a series of apparitions. Frank was there. John Lennon himself made cameos. The setting was a bonfire near a cliff that hung over a dark and starless sea. The startling portion of the nightmare—the thing that had him waking in a panting sweat and groping at the TV remote for companionship—was when he approached the edge of the precipice to look below. And there in the darkness were children at the bottom of a pit, chewing at their wrists and clawing toward the light of the fire. They were the lives he had stolen, the vials, the collectors' items, the paydays. For how many fatherless children might he be responsible? He was the middleman, the broker. And when he closed his eyes, he could feel them there, waiting for him on the other side.

He had discussed the spiritual ramifications of their career with Eddie, who was convinced Normal had gone soft.

"Don't you ever think about it?"

"I really don't, Norm."

"But they're kids. And we had a hand in making them."

"You don't blame the factory workers who brew the hops when some fuckless wonder drinks his face off and barrels into a store window. That's what America's about—production and consumption of vices in bulk, and we all get to choose ours, and then we get to die from them."

"But Cleve Peoples. We ruined his life."

"Fuck Cleve Peoples. He may not have been guilty of this, but he's guilty of something. And I don't care for Cleve Peoples's movies besides."

Eddie was unflappable. He could face down the most daunting assault of cultural gridlock and he would just eat a bowl of cereal and flip to a new channel. It was Eddie, the television disciple, who had bigger intentions for their business. Once Rory Genius-Temple first contacted them, Eddie spoke of nothing else, constantly nagging Normal to sell out for a dump truck full of cash and fame, delivered in thirty-minute episodes.

"All our lives they've told us—find something you're good at and stick with it. Well, you're good at this, Normal—swiping semen. And you're throwing that away because some lady fell in love with an actor?"

For years he and Frank thought they discovered an endless row of miniature Holy Grails in squat, plastic bottles—high-pay, low-risk theft, something fans could never obtain without someone to steal it for them. Normal became tortured with the idea that while he might never have to answer to authorities in this world, what if there was something higher keeping tabs? He was not a superstitious person. He did not believe in imaginary friends, whether they be mortal or divine. Still he could feel the eyes on him. As he marked a celebrity, tagged a vial, negotiated a price—all he could think about in the past year were the metaphysical ramifications of his operation. Assuming for a moment there was a Supreme

Being, or perhaps four or five or an infinite number—what if he one day got the wrong one checking his résumé? Technically he could be construed as the greatest mass kidnapper ever.

Normal wanted change. He wanted luck. He wanted faith—in what he was not certain. Mostly he wanted his brother to stop haunting him. For John Lennon to vacate his dreams. For Cleve to get a new film role. For Beau to grow a second leg. For the Rory-Genius Temples of the world to leave him be. For all those stolen spirits to go wail in front of another bonfire. And so when miraculous Flight AW2921 headed for its descent, Normal never said a prayer. He knew what he had coming. Instead, the plane had landed safely, reinserting him into his old life and the unfinished business that waited. Normal had one more chance to right the ship, and John Lennon would help him do it.

TUESDAY AFTERNOON IS NEVER ENDING

Same diner, six hours later. Normal hung up the phone and slunk onto his stool, two days of the same clothes. He was bunking in an East Side motel, a slum that rented by the hour, a community shower that was always occupied. The camera crew had gone on break, probably waiting in a limousine around the corner. Lucky Dan and Normal had seen dozens of diners come and go, betting nickels on each order. To Normal's concern, he was winning as much as his lucky counterpart. The way he saw it, someone who went by the moniker Lucky Dan should be up at least eight bucks.

The counter was littered with coins, Normal got up to phone Eddie every few minutes. Eddie had gone missing. When he did not answer the phone, it implied one of three things had occurred, in decreasing likelihood: 1) Eddie was gambling; 2) Eddie was showering; 3) Eddie was showing some initiative and independently working on retrieving the John Lennon.

He assumed Lucky Dan had a sophisticated way of solving problems. But sitting in a diner all day sipping coffee and betting egg orders was not what Normal had anticipated.

"You about ready?" Normal asked.

"How so?"

"The John Lennon. Should we get to work?"

"I apologize. I thought we were waiting on you."

"Why would you think that?"

"You've been making phone calls." He leaned in. "Incidentally, I think it's charming you don't carry a cell phone."

"I lost it on the plane."

"I don't carry one either anymore. Find it liberating. Like walking around naked."

"So we're ready to go then?"

"You bet." Lucky Dan snatched his fedora from the counter.

"Where to first?" Normal asked.

"How do you mean?"

"Head down to the harbor?" Normal had just seen on the television that they were turning the plane into a museum. He was certain that meant they were gutting it, and all the leftover knickknacks that went with it. "Maybe you know someone in the department? Contact some of your connected friends?"

"I don't have connected friends."

"But you have a plan. Certainly you've worked out a strategy while we were sitting here."

"No, I haven't."

Normal rubbed his eyes. "I hired you to help me retrieve the vial. And so far all we've done is sit in front of a television and drink coffee."

"Listen, I didn't want to say nothing. But it seems to me you're juggling a few conflicting philosophies. One minute you've teamed up with God. I ask which one, and you don't have any idea. Next you want to learn about luck, so you sit in a diner all day hoping luck finds you. Well, I'm sorry, friend, that's not how it works. You've got to generate action, generate ideas."

"The fact I called you for luck shows I'm out of ideas."

"I told you. I'm not here to figure out your problems, or to get in touch with these *connected* friends you think I have. You're the semen pirate."

"I don't care for that term."

"My participation is solely metaphysical." Lucky Dan took off the fedora and signaled for more coffee. "Think of me as a lucky rabbit's foot, or a horseshoe. Certainly you wouldn't expect a horseshoe to devise a plan."

"Look . . ."

"No, you look." He patted a stool. "You want to be a holy man, think holy. You want to be lucky, think lucky."

"I'm not a lucky person. That's why I need you."

"Course you are. You know how many people fall out of the sky in a fully fueled jet and walk away?"

"Never thought of it like that."

"You're so busy thinking about what you don't have that

you forget what you got. And that's all luck and faith are. Not something you possess. Just frames of mind." He pulled Normal forward.

"What are you doing?"

"Lean your forehead against mine."

"Stop it. People are watching."

"Let 'em watch." Normal leaned. "Think of something happy. Got it?"

Normal closed his eyes and drifted through a library of pleasant thoughts. There was only one shelf in the library. There was only one book. He thought of Frank. Normal nodded.

"Now think of the vial you need to retrieve. See yourself holding it."

Normal did as he was told.

"Excellent." Lucky Dan sat up and watched the television that hung over the kitchen door. "Now we wait."

"That's it?"

"We let the universe know we're ready. We put the idea in motion." He snapped his fingers toward the TV. "By golly, will you have a look at that?"

Normal had a look. To the right from his vantage point, which would be the reporter's left, a painted midget glared through the television.

"She's something else. Look at all that black hair, just waiting for someone to run their fingers through it." Lucky Dan licked his lips. "Spitting image of Sandra Bullock."

"Don't look anything like Sandra Bullock in person."

"You know her?"

"She was on the plane."

Lucky Dan stared for a hungry minute, mesmerized. Then he bounded from his stool and tossed a twenty on the counter. "That's our stuff right there."

"What stuff?"

"The reporter." He pointed again. "We asked for it and the universe delivered. It never happens that fast. By golly, this is a blessed mission."

"What good is she? She doesn't know about the vial."

"So we tell her you left something valuable on the plane. Maybe she knows someone who knows someone."

They listened to the news—that ANN's Lucy Springer would be interviewing the pilot Thursday morning. Normal gritted his teeth. A lunatic and a puppet, the interview of the year.

Lucky was dubious. "We're all hooked up then. Right, Normal?"

"I'm not so sure." The sight of her was infuriating. Specifically the two feet of puppet. "I think we better wait for some different luck."

"May I inquire why?"

"I'd rather not say."

He sat down. "I think you better."

Normal moved in tight. "I don't care for her kind."

"What kind is that?"

"Come on, Lucky. You know what I mean."

"Because she's a journalist?"

"Partly, sure."

"You steal semen. How dare you criticize someone's vocation?"

"It's just such a gimmick. She's on TV with the thing. This fucking culture always—"

"Why don't you can it with that talk, aye Normal? I'm a proud effing American and I happen to adore this crazy culture. I adore the puppets and the reality shows and the all-you-can-eat buffets." He slammed a fist into the counter. "I have to say—I'm disappointed."

"Knock it off."

"You and me sitting here getting to know each other. And all this time I've been talking with a sonofagun. Know what you are— you're a puppetist."

"She has a dummy on her hand. You expect me to ask her for help?"

"You communicate with your dead brother through a tattoo. I see you itching it."

"Not the same thing."

"Been meaning to ask." Lucky Dan wheeled on his stool. "When that plane went down—what kind of prayer did you say?"

"What's that got to do with anything?"

"You claim to be a holy man, but you haven't any clear understanding of which giant, imaginary friend you prefer. So I'm asking—did you pray?"

"I don't remember."

"Aha!" He shoved a finger in Normal's face. "You're about to die and you don't even offer up a suitable petition. You're so confused about things that you'll subscribe to any philosophy—faith, luck, charity."

"If I were you I'd adjust my tone."

"Now you listen. It's a strange and ugly world out there. People got different ways of coping." He pointed to the television, his voice loud. "She wears a puppet—which I, for one, find captivating—and you have to knock it."

"What do you think? She's going to wave the puppet at the pilot halfway through the interview, 'By the way, this guy I barely know left a vial of semen on the plane. Can you help?' She's a fucking loony, Dan."

"You cut off your finger and renamed yourself after a Frank Capra character. Your insanity puts hers to shame." Lucky swiveled. "Soon as I met you—with the four fingers and the itching—I knew you were off. But I didn't hold it against you. Just like I won't hold it against that black-haired beauty for talking out of a puppet." He slammed a hand down that rattled the change. "I don't know much, but I know good people. And she's good people."

Normal closed his eyes. He had put his faith in a man of luck, whose advice was to put faith in a woman with a puppet. "I'm sorry," he said. "I'm just frustrated and desperate."

Lucky Dan perked. "So we'll talk to her?"

"If you think it will help, sure."

"Hot damn!"

"But I hope this isn't just some ploy for you to meet her."

"Of course I want to meet her. I love ventriloquists." He dusted the argument from his shoulders. "But I assure you this is strictly business. I'm a professional."

"A professional what?"

"Just a professional. And I meant what I said—god or no god, this is one heck of a mission." He slapped Normal's back. "Now what do you say we go get us some Beatle semen?"

WEDNESDAY

WEDNESDAY

INTERMISSION

Wednesday, passengers. Like Tuesday without the adrenaline, like Thursday without the twinkle of a weekend on the horizon. "Hump Day," the workingman mutters as he laces the boots. Wednesday with its neither here nor there, its allegiance not to the beginning of the week nor the end, the taxi driver hollering, "Pick a side, you filthy day!" But there it sits, in the middle of the week, just taking up twenty-four hours. "Goddamned Wednesdays," Blackie spin grumbled, pouting into his monitors.

LONG AND WINDING ROAD

SEAT: 9A
PASSENGER: Jimmish Wayne
REASON FOR FLIGHT: Undercover as a sky marshal
LAST THOUGHTS BEFORE IMPACT: A *"1" cannot go in the middle row. Otherwise the entire puzzle is off.*

If Jimmish Wayne had a superpower, it was his attention to detail. Blackie's first-lieutenant, he was in charge of polishing the minutia that could not coexist with Blackie's version of events. There were times when characters got out of line, either through ingenuity or by coincidence, although Blackie did not believe in coincidence. When they wandered off course it was Jimmish who was sent to handle it. The same way the researchers were required to crunch numbers, the secretaries to order lunch, the analysts to compile the data into nifty charts—Jimmish was on character control. He enjoyed the work, the ability to harness his freakish attention to detail, and receive a paycheck for doing so. He appreciated Blackie's talents, this magic to create realities, to organize all the characters into their respective fates. To Jimmish, it was the closest thing to religion he knew.

Before he crossed paths with Alastair Black, his name was simply Jim Wayne. He was an enormous man, not obese, just large in the parts that people noticed—feet and legs and chest and shoulders, a giant head—although his personality did not fit his size. Unspectacular looking and a bit of a coward, he was more mannish than man, more largish than large, an undecided medley of fates and fashions and girth. He had either the power or the curse to wander a room undetected, not a ghost but ghostish certainly. His defining feature was an excuse of a mustache that played god to a sad and pouty face—two hazelish eyes, a smallish nose, fattish cheeks, all of it beneath a jokish comb-over that was more brownish than brown.

His career matched his unspectacular nature. He looked like the muscle for a poorly run bingo hall. Instead he was a professional domino tumbler.

Jim Wayne was hired for birthdays, bar mitzvahs, the occasional bachelor party. Mostly he worked corporate events, the team-building phase, when inspirational speakers would demonstrate the domino effect that came along with business decisions, or corporate goals, or other office-worthy pursuits. It was an effective way to establish the message—how one thing in life affects so many others—and so Jim Wayne carved himself a career. He generally arrived a day before the event with crates of dominoes and sequestered himself in a large conference room.

Despite his size and his ability to create elaborate displays of the little black pieces, few people noticed him. He was just there, like the ceilings or the walls, something that would serve its purpose while at the same time was unnecessary to acknowledge. It was a corporate event in Chicago when Alastair Black first wandered past a room in which Jim Wayne carefully lined up dominoes, the hill of a man kneeling on the marble floor as he rapidly set the rectangles. The room was full of dominoes. Blackie watched from the doorway.

"How many are there?"

"This one makes 400,217."

"How many more to go?"

He never stopped working. "I would say less than 2,175."

Blackie walked the perimeter of the tiny walls, marveling at the straight lines and angles, the perfection of each domino's shadow, as though a machine had placed them.

"What happens if they don't all fall?"

"I offer a money-back guarantee." He looked up for the first time and Blackie noticed the weakness, his eyes, the giant down on his knees. "I'm the only domino tumbler in the industry that offers domino insurance."

"How often do you fail?"

"I haven't left a domino standing in seven years."

Blackie counted the tiles and tried to understand this man's world. "How tall are you?"

"Six-five and one-quarter."

"How much do you weigh?"

"Two hundred and eighty-two pounds."

"You do this for a living?"

"Yes, sir."

"Been in prison before?"

"Never."

Blackie was stymied. "How long does this take to assemble?"

"Going on seventeen hours."

"And to fall?"

The man stood now, rising above Blackie, and looked over his creation. "Two minutes forty-seven seconds, give or take a few seconds." He motioned toward the window. "A ramp over there will slow the pace depending on how many people are in the room."

The next day, Blackie suffered through the team-building discussion, waiting for the dominoes to tip. He found the peculiar setter in the crowd. The man stood off to the side, like a curtain, or an armoire placed strategically to hold knickknacks, that infuriating mustache. No one asked him forward when they tipped the first of the chain, the crowd suddenly energized as the ebony racket fell. Blackie hit a stopwatch.

They dropped first in a straight line to give the bricks momentum—a quickening *tat-tat-tat-tat*—then branched into three, four, five different walls, climbing chairs and tables, falling into circles, displacing mousetraps that hurled dominoes across the room, landing with a clinkering precision and reigniting the chain—*tat-a-lattle-lattle-tattle*. When the last domino fell, Blackie clicked his watch; two minutes forty-eight seconds.

The next day Blackie began stalking him, first to St. Louis. The next week, a bar mitzvah in New York. San Jose, Sunnyvale, Champaign, Alpharetta, Edison. Each time it was the same attention to detail, the same mesmerizing perseverance, the elaborate tumble, the mustached man off to the side with husky, slumped shoulders, only participating in the set up, never the celebration. Two months after first encountering Jim Wayne, Blackie set a meeting in a Brooklyn warehouse. In the center of the warehouse, a good fifty yards from the entrance, there was a desk with a chair on either side. Other than that, the place was empty.

When he arrived, the man carried a notebook and a pencil. "How many dominoes did you wish, Mr. Black?"

"None. You'll never set up another domino again."

"Beg pardon."

"Mr. Wayne, tell me—do you enjoy this work?"

"I'm good at it."

"That's not the same thing. How would you like to work for me?"

"Setting up dominoes?"

"I just told you. You'll never set up another domino again."

The mustache quivered. Blackie saw the man sensed trouble, something in the details of the conversation's tone. "I think I'd have to pass."

Blackie pulled a gun. It was small and silver, although it was the first gun Jim Wayne had ever seen, which made it look like a cannon. He inhaled heavy and tried to lift his arms as he had seen on television, but Blackie motioned that it was unnecessary. If anyone else were inside the factory, they would have found it absurd, the small man holding hostage the whale-ish creature.

"I'm going to kill Jim Wayne today. I'm going to do it with a bullet or a contract, up to you which we use." He motioned toward the center of the warehouse and the two walked toward the chairs. Blackie put away the gun. "Now then, Mr. Wayne, I'll ask again. How would you like to work for me?"

"Doing what?"

"Same thing you do now. Only with people. And for more money. And with more meaningful results." Blackie leaned forward before he could answer. "You see, Mr. Wayne, I admire your attention to detail. It's one of the most beautiful things I've ever witnessed. But I simply cannot abide by you using it to stack rectangles for the goal of toppling them in front of a roomful of characters that find it interesting. It's made you weak. I believe in a different role you would thrive. Your powers must be harnessed properly, and I mean to do it."

"What about the gun?"

"Ah yes, the gun. That's what I mean about you, Mr. Wayne—attention to detail. We cannot introduce a gun into the narrative if we don't intend to use it. And we will use it, Mr. Wayne, I give you my word." He pulled the gun and settled it in his hand across the desk. "Now then, as I said, I'm going to kill Jim Wayne. We can do it with a new identity. Or I can shoot you in the head right here. Either way, you'll never set up another domino."

"What new identity?"

Blackie considered it. "Your current name doesn't suit you. You're not so much a Jim as you are Jimmish in nature. And a new wardrobe. And the mustache must go. What do you say?"

"Jimmish Wayne?" He watched the gun. "When would I start?"

"You just did."

Over the years, Blackie and Jimmish had developed a mutual admiration for each other's work. Jimmish appreciated Blackie's ability to make a story come to life; Blackie appreciated Jimmish's eye for detail. Every so often, a minor character that Blackie counted on to behave one way might behave another. It was Jimmish's duty as Blackie's most trusted employee to oversee the reassignment of minor characters into roles that better fit their talents. In the same way Blackie could not allow Jimmish to live on as a domino tumbler, he could not allow others to exist as ordinary and unspectacular characters. More often than not, they were assigned to a division of Veiltality Inc. Blackie paid them well, often better than they earned in their prior occupations, and complaints were rare.

Two days prior Jimmish had begun his nightly rounds, which entailed him driving past the various locations with a loose affiliation to the Air Wanderlust saga and investigating any details that might have fallen out of alignment. He had placed the GPS chips in each passenger's phone before returning them so he could track the players if necessary. He enjoyed the nightly rounds, the weight of the silver gun in his pocket, a weapon he had never used, something for which he was glad. It gave him pleasure as he drove through the city, that he had been given the power of reassignment by Alastair Black. Each day over the past several years, he could feel himself growing into his role.

Jimmish had driven to the harbor to check the plane. He had seen the ice cream truck parked and then not parked, a vehicle like that having no business in a place without customers. It was registered to a city employee named Gary Corbin, who lived on the far side of the river in Weehawken. Jimmish concluded that he must have wandered into the story.

Gary Corbin and a woman had awakened to find Jimmish seated across the room on the edge of a desk, the small, silver gun laying atop the scraped wood, the large man busy with a

Sudoku puzzle. They reached for the covers, the woman hollering: "Wednesday! Wednesday!"

"What the fuck?" Gary shouted. "Who are you?" When there was no answer, "You a cop?" If it was a cop, Gary was cooked. They fired people for stealing office supplies; he'd been caught in bed with a patient.

"I'm your fate, Mr. Corbin. I'm your future. I apologize for startling you." The woman leaned for the floor, a bra, a shirt; Jimmish lifted a hand. "That your truck out back?"

He nodded.

"Why do you drive a truck like that?"

"It's a business."

"I see. When people come to the window, what do you tell them?"

"Wednesday I'm sorry Wednesday!"

"Sometimes they want answers. Mostly just want someone to listen."

"A purveyor of hope."

"The pursuit of happiness, I suppose."

"An important role, Mr. Corbin." This pleased Jimmish, who took in the room. "Tell me about two days ago, you, the airplane."

"Wednesday oh no oh dear Wednesday."

"What airplane?"

Jimmish picked up the gun. The woman disappeared beneath the sheet.

"Okay," Gary said. "Give it a minute."

"The airplane. You were there. Why?"

"I was curious."

"About what?"

"The bird strike. I didn't believe it. I wanted to see for myself."

"You're a psychiatrist, no?"

The woman came up. "Wednesday he's my psychiatrist." She wept. "And if work finds out I'm here I could violate my parole Wednesday."

Jimmish tilted his head. "The airplane, Mr. Corbin. Why would a psychiatrist be interested in a bird strike?"

"I used to be a mechanic."

"What did you hope to find?"

"Dead birds maybe. I didn't want to get caught, so I took off."

Of course there were photos, Jimmish knew. Anyone who would sneak on *that* plane would not leave without proof of what they'd seen. "What did you hope would come from the photos?"

"I didn't take any photos."

"Blackmail perhaps."

"I didn't take any photos." He sat up straight. This guy was not a cop, Gary could see that. Whatever Lucy thought about the crash had merit, he now realized, a bitter reality. He had been hoping she was merely coming unhinged with the paranoia and stress. "It was stupid. I shouldn't have done it."

"Were you alone?"

"I was."

"The photos, Mr. Corbin."

The woman wept, the sheet rising and falling with each sob.

"I answered your questions." He rubbed the woman's back over the sheet.

"I'm afraid we're at odds about the existence of photographs."

"Wednesday give him the photos Gary Wednesday."

"There are no photos," he said to the mound of sheets.

Jimmish watched Gary's eyes, a flicker of detail that no one else would see. This man loved women, crazy women, and it suddenly made sense to the giant man. "It's chivalrous of you to keep silent. But she already told me about the photographs. She told me where to find you, Mr. Corbin."

This surprised Gary. "She doesn't know where I live," he said, quickly clamping his jaw. In his nervousness, the woman grinding fingernails into his thigh, he'd let it slip.

Jimmish stood now and walked to the edge of the bed so that Gary had nowhere else to look. "I'm going to kill Gary Corbin today."

The woman's vomiting was muffled beneath the sheets.

"Come on, man," Gary said angrily. It was unclear to Jimmish if the gun or the undercover retching caused his ire.

"You see, Mr. Corbin, my employer has approved your reassignment. It's up to you how you are reassigned. You are a minor character in his tale. Had you played your role properly, you would have continued on unnoticed. By sneaking on the aircraft, you've earned a starring role."

"Wednesday oh no oh dear he's crazy Wednesday."

Gary watched the man's hazelish eyes. "Who is your employer?"

"It doesn't matter."

"Reassign me to what?"

"More than likely to our office in Kissimmee, Florida." Jimmish laid a folder on the bed. "We have offices all over the country— New York, Chicago, Los Angeles, in most states really."

"Warm in Florida." Gary picked up the folder. "What would I be doing?"

"A purveyor of happiness. We're starting a division similar to what you do now, sort of a relaxation spa for employees. Just like other corporations, we have workers who suffer anxiety, job stress, who need a place to recuperate."

"My salary?"

"Would be remarkably improved."

"Would I have an e-mail address?"

"You would have your own computer, office, and receptionist. Your role is essential to the future of our company."

He leafed through the folder. "And you say you employ crazy people?"

"Oh yes, Mr. Corbin, some of the craziest."

Gary Corbin knew crazy people and could typically tell the sane from the not. There was something odd about this man, his size vying with his impeccable niceness, although his mind was seemingly intact. "What about the gun?"

"As I said, I'm going to kill Gary Corbin today, either with a gun or a contract." He pointed the gun at the folder. "You'd need to leave tonight. Take none of your possessions. Take only the credentials inside."

Gary read from the folder. "Bill Cosby?"

"Bill Cosby is a name that makes people happy. It fits your role."

"Bill Cosby." Gary tried it out. "I never cared for the name Gary."

"I'm in agreement. It was holding you back."

Just then the woman's head popped out of the sheets. "Wednesday what about me? I want to be reassigned too Wednesday."

"I'm afraid not." Jimmish lowered his eyes. Blackie had explained there were two ways out of the room. Jimmish knew what was expected of him, and this was the flaw in his character. For obvious reasons, he could not reassign her. He was too much of a coward to shoot her. "My employer is temperamental. He is not a fan of the word Wednesday. I fear your disorder would only upset him."

"Wednesday Gary and I are in love." She hugged him. "Tell him, Wednesday."

"I'm sorry, Miss. It would end disastrously."

Gary thought of the Office of Strategic Therapy, the tiny hovel in the basement of the world, the rattling cart that deposited the Untouchables on his desk. He felt her fingers grind into his ribs, pleading, imagined the warmth of a Kissimmee sunset.

"I'm waiting for your answer, Mr. Corbin."

Once the Wednesday woman was in a taxi and the late Gary Corbin had departed for the airport, Jimmish walked to the dresser and found the man's phone. He leafed through a series of numbers, finding the calls from Monday evening, the last four. They were all the same. He dialed, it went directly to voice mail. It was an old woman's voice: "You've reached Margaret DiGiacamo . . ."

Jimmish hung up the phone. He was relieved, once again, that the latest reassignment proceeded without him having to use the gun. And who would believe a crazy woman anyway if he let her back among the general population? He hoped the crazy woman would remain so, and that no one would believe her if she tried to tell them about the reassignment of Bill Cosby. Otherwise, well, Jimmish did not like to think how Blackie might react to the Wednesday woman becoming a nuisance.

In a few short hours, Gary Corbin would be declared dead through a series of press releases that would originate at the

Veiltality Inc. offices in Bend, Oregon, where all reassignment paperwork was handled. He walked to the window and peered out into the street. Somewhere church bells rang, no consistent theme he could pinpoint, perhaps a holy day or a funeral, and as he listened all the details became clear: the phone that had belonged to the old woman with the broken ankle, Lucy Springer concealing it in the puppet, her sleeping with her therapist, who because of their arrangement helped her sneak onto the airplane. He enjoyed Lucy Springer because he enjoyed Sandra Bullock, the actress, and because the use of puppetry to chronicle the cynical lives of celebrities seemed an uplifting approach. He felt all the news should be told with puppets, a mass of marionettes and strings and adorable voices anchoring the six o'clock broadcast.

But there was one detail that was missing. The camera. And Jimmish was certain he would find it in Lucy Springer's possession. He lit a match and threw it on the bed, then sat down to finish his puzzle, waiting to ensure the flames took.

GET BACK TO WHERE YOU ONCE BELONGED

It had officially become a disorder. On several occasions she found herself thinking—what would Ava do?—then catching herself. More than once she had glanced over at her left hand to find the puppet staring back. It was an extension of her personality, something that had always been there in the shadows. She was concerned that she could never go back, now that she understood that this thing was a real, live beast, a personality with its own thoughts and emotions and even sexuality, its own rhythms separate from her reflexes.

Her behavior had gotten worse over the past few days—the approaching interview with Captain Swagger, and the plane, and whether he had saved the city and inspired the nation, or faked the entire thing. In the last twenty-four hours Dean had located Veiltality Inc., a publicity firm with a curious past. He'd discovered that Swagger's wife and children had booked flights to New York nearly a month before. A press release from the airline suggested the birds in question were *Anser albifrons*, also known as the Greater White-fronted Goose, or the "Specklebelly," which as far as Dean could find did not inhabit New York State. All this was combining into a curious anxiety that, oddly enough, seemed less nerve-racking knowing she was not in it alone; she had Ava.

Lucy blamed the psychiatrist. Gary had warned her that she was every bit as capable of insanity as the next. He had planted the seed and now it was growing its way through her. She had put in a dozen calls to Gary, paged him, taken Ava off for nearly twenty minutes hoping it would raise concern; but Gary Corbin had disappeared. And for the second time that week, she actually needed her therapist, this time to deal exclusively with the twenty-nine inches of irrationality harnessed to her left arm. Gary was right: this was how people became homeless, hosting funerals for dead pigeons at corner trash receptacles; this was how people shot up workplaces.

She had been called to the ANN Tower for a meeting with the executive producers, preparation for the Swagger interview. She had not met with the producers in nearly a year. They had not even had the decency to tell her to her face that she'd been demoted to the Twitter beat. And now, puppet attached, she intended to look across the table, stare into their miserable eyes, and gloat. If she was correct, they had called the meeting to discuss how to disguise Ava Tardner during the interview. Would they position the cameras so that her left arm fell mostly out of the shot? Would they suggest removing the puppet altogether? None of it mattered; this was payback. They had buried Lucy to stalk celebrities and she had knocked it out of the park. She had done it with a dummy on her arm. And she intended to do the Swagger interview with the dummy, just to make life uncomfortable for the producers.

She did not take a seat when she arrived in the room, Lucy Springer, back from the dead. "You should know—I'm doing the interview with the puppet. And not in a sack on my lap. Right out in the open. Prime time everyone."

Ava butted in: "Like a giant, batshit goiter."

The producers chuckled, all fifteen of them. One even clapped. The head producer, she was not sure of his name, Ray perhaps: "Of course the puppet. We've spent $3,000 on a new wardrobe for Ava."

Lucy was confused. "Okay then." She took a seat.

"Obviously you'll handle the main interview." They passed a script the length of the table. "But we want Ava to hit Swagger with the follow-up questions."

"Just so we understand," Lucy said. "We're talking about the puppet. I intend to wear it. I'm not kidding."

"We're envisioning a double interview, really give the audience the Swagger we don't know," the presumed Ray continued. "It's like the two of you are interviewing the two of him."

"A four-person panel," another added.

"A roundtable of sorts," came the next.

"You target the pilot. Let Ava handle the other one."

"The other what?" Lucy asked.

"The other Swagger. The Swagger that all the books are being written about—the heroic pilot, the family man, the collage of American values."

"Someone is writing a book?"

"Not just one book. Dozens. One of the stewardesses has a book deal. Three passengers. Even a ferryboat captain signed a poetry book deal."

"We'd like you to do a book later this year," a woman said.

"I'm not sure I understand." She bent her neck, which they all mimicked. "Why are all these people writing books?"

"Because it's hot," someone said.

"Important," another.

"People deserve a historical account."

"Let's shelve the Swagger interview for now." They all leaned forward, a synchronized swim team, only with bespoke suits and Botox. "I think we all know there's an elephant in the room we need to address."

They watched. Lucy became aware of the fiberglass on her arm and nudged her wrist slightly. She had been concentrating all her mental power on not twitching, but all the same it happened. The head bobbed. They nodded together.

"We've underestimated you," another began, Mona maybe. "Things were not handled properly back then by people during 'The Incident.'"

"But we can't dwell on the past," Ray said. "We need to move on."

"The future," someone said.

"Bygones," came another.

"The evening news."

The puppet's mouth fell open. "You're giving me back the anchor?"

"Call it a comeback. Americans love a comeback. We're moving you back to six o'clock, although initially it'll just be a short segment."

The puppet looked at Lucy; Lucy looked at her lap.

"The plan is to have you back as the main anchor within the year."

Lucy grinned; she could not control the muscles, the puppet. "And you'll be firing Colin and Melody?"

"No one's getting fired," Steve said. "That would imply we made a mistake by taking you off the anchor to begin with."

"But you did make a mistake."

"Only because you killed all those fish."

"PETA was pressuring us."

"Sponsors would have pulled out."

"To admit error makes ANN look weak, hurts our integrity."

"Bygones."

"Instead we're implementing a systematic phaseout."

"Each day we'll slice one second of airtime from Colin and Melody."

"One second?"

"And we'll give it to you."

"So my first broadcast?"

"Is only a second," Ray said.

"And the following broadcast?"

"That's right. Two seconds." They smiled.

"And after a month?"

"Half a minute, give or take."

"At first we'll flash you and Ava on the screen, just a one-second glance for the audience. You won't say anything. But it will put it in their heads that they saw you and they'll subconsciously be aware of your presence."

Ray took over. "On their last night, Colin and Melody will do the same. The camera will just graze them. And that will be that."

That will be that. After all that had happened, she was getting back what belonged to her. However they wanted to work it was fine, so long as she was permitted to choose her cohost.

"And who did you have in mind?" she asked.

"Have in mind for what?"

"My cohost."

"Well, Ava of course."

Lucy's wrist buckled. They watched the puppet as if it were about to thank them. Lucy shoved it beneath the table.

"You want me to do the evening news with a dummy as a co-host?"

"You should see the ratings." Mona shoved the ratings in front of her. "You're a huge hit with the 25–35 demographic. We think this is going to change the way people get their news."

"It's new. It's exciting. Eventually we hope to have an all-puppet format."

"Sports, weather, politics."

"The thing is, from the terms of the . . ."

"'The Incident,'" Ray finished.

"I won't be required to wear it in public much longer."

"We don't expect you'll wear it in public. But there will be slight . . . alterations to Ava's behavior per the terms of her contract."

They passed down the contract, like a baton through a crowded gymnasium. When it was placed in front of her, Lucy pointed at a number. "This is the puppet's salary?"

"No, that is what we believe is fair market value for ownership of Ava."

"You want to buy Ava?"

"It's a legal thing," Mona said. "Don't read too much into it. The lawyers say it makes more fiscal sense to purchase the puppet rather than pay her a salary. But if you crunch the numbers, you'll find it's equivalent to ten years of work."

"In the same way we can't have people bringing their own cameras to work, it's better for the network to own the dummy."

"I see."

"We're implementing a systematic phase-in for Ava as well. We'd like her to start using more Spanish during your back and forth banter."

"I don't know Spanish."

"No, you should only speak English. We need to keep it professional. For the next few years anyway, a head anchor speaking Spanish would alienate our core viewership."

"This is the evening news, after all," Ray pointed out.

"But we think Ava can connect with the Hispanic demographic. And let's face it, in ten years they'll all be Hispanic."

"The thing is," Lucy said, not sure how to proceed. "Ava is not Hispanic. She looks exactly like me."

"We'll phase that in as well." They showed her a picture. It was a puppet, presumably Ava, only with more makeup and darker skin and an exclamation point after her name: a Mexican Alejandra Bullock! "In three years, Ava Tardner will be three-quarters Mexican."

"Of course you and Ava will earn royalties on all products going forward."

"It's all in the contract." A woman leafed through a few pages. "We'd like to introduce a few new catchphrases as early as the Swagger interview."

Lucy read. "Kablammy?"

"We think 'Kablammy' is going to be huge."

"What happened to 'Whoa Nelly!'?"

"'Whoa Nelly!' had its day. Time for something fresh, something outrageous."

"Kablammy," someone added.

"I'm supposed to say this to whom?"

"Ava should say it. All catchphrases should come directly from Ava."

"'Kablammy'? I'm not even sure it's a word."

"Don't worry, we had it trademarked." A new guy spoke. "We've tried it out with a test audience and they were hot for it."

"But what does it mean?"

"It's a combination of *kerplunk*, *kaplow*, and *smash-bam* all rolled into one. Like when two things hit with remarkable force and stuff flies out all over the place."

Ray held up a T-shirt that read "KABLAMMY!" "We've printed 100,000 of these babies. We expect to sell out as soon as Ava says it during the Swagger interview."

"So let's hear it," someone suggested.

"Kablammy?" Lucy was not sure how the word felt.

"Excellent. But we're looking for a certain style of Kablammy." Ray stood and walked the length of the table. "Let's see how it sounds when Ava says it. And let's put a little more *blam!* in this 'Kablammy.'"

COME TOGETHER

The anchor chair, the seven-digit sale of a slab of fiberglass, the catchphrases and T-shirts and royalties and even the odd book deal—it was all contingent on the interview, on her forgetting about those birdless engine photos and the inconsistencies she thought she had seen. Life was really a bribe, wasn't it? Dean had hidden the camera. And perhaps it was best it stayed hidden. If she somehow were able to unveil a secret plot to crash a jetliner in the Hudson River, the best she could hope would be to anchor the evening news. And she had just been offered that job, so long as she smiled, and Ava smiled, and they had a friendly chat with Captain Hank Swagger.

Oddly, Lucy was still living in the Whalensky Plaza. Three days and it had not occurred to her even to visit her apartment and resume her life prior to Monday's crash. Transience really, characteristics of a faltering mind.

She arrived in the hotel lobby to a familiar face. "Semen?"

"Normal actually." He watched the puppet, no longer hidden in its burlap prophylactic, hating the hell out of it.

"It is you, isn't it? The semen pirate."

"He doesn't care for that term." A tall, stringy man lifted his fedora and winked. His eyes darted from her to Ava and back, awaiting a proper introduction.

Many other passengers were freeloading rooms as well, but Lucy was still fascinated to meet him there in the lobby. Sure, they had spoken harshly at their introduction. But she had formed a twisted camaraderie with the four-fingered gangster and could not mask her delight.

"Let me ask you something. You haven't gotten a book deal, have you?"

"What does that mean?"

"Passengers. They've gotten book deals."

"I don't read books."

"Five altogether. Five different versions of our crash. Isn't that something?"

"Goddamned cannibalistic bastard culture," Normal began.

"Here we go again," came the other man.

Normal itched his arm. "I didn't appreciate crashing into the river. But all things considered it was a graceful landing. This culture takes a perfectly beautiful thing, a miraculous landing, and desecrates it, turns it into . . ."

"Minutia," the fedora man said. He smiled at Lucy.

". . . for the sole purpose of disseminating pointless information." And then Normal just lost it, mumbling on about "texting and blog-ging all moving minutia, the whole culture just churning and taking a miracle and wringing it out"—he made the wringing motion with his red hands—"until the goodness has been turned into . . ." He was itching and talking so fast his mouth quit operating.

"Chum," the fedora said. "Steady now, boy." He spoke without punctuation to Lucy, an auctioneer. "Dan O'Malley good to know you call me Dan or Lucky Dan or just Lucky and I know you of course and your pretty little friend you're more striking in person would you mind if I stroked your hair?"

"I suppose you can touch it a little."

He held her hand after the shake ended and took her locks in his other. Lucy did not pull away until Normal slapped the man's arm. The fedora man was too thin for a gangster, if that was what these two were, although she could not see him in any other occupation.

"I have to apologize," she said.

"For what, my dear?"

She lifted Ava. "It's a long explanation."

"No explanation necessary. I find it all very Kafkaesque—the puppet, the coordination, the similarities. Simply delightful."

Normal grabbed her wrist that held the dummy and walked to a corner. "I need your help," he said.

She turned to Dan. "Is this illegal?"

"Despite his rage and lack of patriotism, I can affirm his is a good and noble mission."

"Your interview. What kind of access does it give you to the plane?"

"None that I'm aware of."

"Say you wanted to take a crew down and get shots of the cockpit."

"It's not that type of interview." She was aware that the puppet was watching. Each time she lowered her hand, it crept back up. "What's this about anyway?"

The string bean was fascinated. He could not stop smiling.

"I've left something on the plane," Normal said. "I need to get it back."

"Why don't you call the airline?"

"Let's just forget it."

"We can trust her," Dan prodded.

"I can't help if you don't tell me."

Dan nudged with his shoulder. "We're out of options."

He spoke low. "It's a very important, very rare specimen."

"Semen!" Lucy covered her mouth.

"Will you shut the fuck up!"

"Potty mouth," Dan warned.

She righted the puppet; Ava whispered, *Semen*. Lucy covered her mouth again.

"Take that off."

"I'm afraid I can't." She curled back a puppet leg to show the electronic bracelet.

"I'm in a massive ordeal and I would prefer you not address me with that thing again."

"Steady now, boy."

Just then Lucy went white. "I'm feeling off."

Lucky Dan stepped forward and grabbed her in his arms, pushing her toward a ledge where he began fanning her. "Now look what you've done," he hollered at Normal.

Normal felt ridiculous at his tantrum; just being that close to the puppet irritated him. Eddie was a steady follower of her show on ANN and Normal had seen it on occasion. One of the most difficult things in his job was to identify where celebrities were at any one time, what they were doing, who they were screwing. If he had been a bank robber instead, and someone hosted a show about all the vaults and cameras, he would certainly watch that; this was barely different. It was important to determine which celebrities were gaining in popularity, or arrested, or involved in scandals—all of which boosted the value of their DNA. Normal could not keep them straight. Even Eddie, who watched a solid fourteen hours of television a day, had trouble knowing exactly who would fetch top dollar.

"Point is it's melting," Normal continued. "They're turning the joint into a museum. You're my only shot."

"Give it a moment, will you? She's not well."

Lucy steadied herself and stood on her own, although the string bean would not let go. What could she do? A semen pirate with an accomplice named Lucky Dan, staking out a lobby for her: criminals. Lucy found them plainly fascinating. Which was the exact opposite of how she would describe her life up until that week. In the past year, her only two acquaintances were her assistant, who refused to leave the building, and her therapist, who was trying to convince her she was crazy. These two in comparison were refreshing.

"What if I told you that plane didn't crash?"

"I was on the plane," Normal said. "It crashed."

"But what if I told you it was faked?"

Lucky Dan nodded. "Yup, I believe it."

"I knew it was a mistake." Normal tugged his arm.

"Hold on a minute. She's telling the truth."

"What makes you say that?"

Lucky Dan watched her. "I'm looking at her eyes. Eyes never lie."

"That's because she thinks it's the truth. She has a dummy on her wrist."

"It's simple science really." Lucky Dan turned now. "Thing is, Normal, you really are one of the unluckiest bastards I've ever met. I don't know what the issue is—too many philosophies inside that head of yours. But if you were on a plane that crashed for real, you'd most likely be dead."

"So what?"

"So by scientific deduction, that plane didn't crash for real."

"That's your science?"

"Oh come on, Normal. This is exciting." He fake-jabbed him in the gut. "Let's hear what she has to say."

Lucy explained: the beautiful passengers; the man on the cockpit floor; the birds that did not exist; the confiscated cell phones; even the odd behavior by the pilot. If one put it all together, as she had done, it added up to a peculiar scenario.

"Yup, I believe it," Lucky Dan repeated.

Normal itched his arm. If Frank had taught him anything, it was that life was a racket, that everyone had an end. "So you're saying all the passengers were in on it?"

"No, I don't think any of them knew. I certainly didn't."

"I bought my ticket thirty minutes before liftoff."

"I booked the flight a month ago," she said. "As soon as I won the trip." She covered her mouth; Ava's fell open. That vacation package had been awarded to her as a promotion from a credit card she rarely used. On an airline she had never flown. What kind of investigative journalist had she become? "Oh shit."

"What 'oh shit'?"

"I was supposed to be on that plane." She replayed the evacuation.

"We got eyes," Lucky Dan said, jerking his shoulder toward the hotel entrance. "That fella there part of the crew doing your show?"

Normal found the man behind a pillar, sticking out from either side of the marble column. "I know that guy," Normal said.

"A cameraman?" Lucky asked.

He tried to place him. To his shock and initial relief, it was not one of Rory's employees. Lately, everything made Normal paranoid, but this was a different level of paranoia. "He's the sky marshal. He was on the plane."

When he realized he'd been made, Jimmish Wayne drifted out of the lobby. None of them followed. Dan took Lucy's hand in both of his and began rubbing.

"I assure you, Miss Springer, Normal here will put a stop to this nonsense. He doesn't control all the illegal semen on the East Coast for being soft on bullies."

"What are you talking about?"

"Hot time!" Dan turned to Normal. "So what do we do first?"

"How should I know?"

"Lucy and I are honest civilians. You're on the criminal side of things. You know how these punks think."

Normal itched. The presence of the sky marshal in the hotel lobby was curious. And he had to agree—there was something suspicious about the pilot. He glanced around for more eyes. The puppet, the plane crash, the vial of John Lennon, the fucking camera crew that was probably filming him right now—complicated. If he had known one good deed would be so hard to accomplish, he would have taken Eddie's advice and forgotten all about Cleve Peoples.

"Start with this hotel," Normal suggested. "Good chance anyone who checked in since Monday could be a passenger. We talk to a few, find out what they know."

"Not bad," Lucky Dan said.

"I'll help," Normal told Lucy. "But I need to get on that plane. And soon."

"I'll help, too," Dan said.

"What exactly do you do?" Lucy asked.

"I'm a luck consultant. Normal here hired me to assist with his mission."

"How's that going?"

"My luck doesn't seem to be improving," Normal said. "Although it's been several hours since anyone has punched me in the head."

"You bet it has," Lucky said.

YOU SAY YOU WANT A REVOLUTION

It was Mallory Swagger who caused the delay of Flight AW862 out of Eugene Airport because she refused to sit in the seat her boarding pass claimed belonged to her, a seat that had been manufactured in Skokie, Illinois, said right on the bottom, she checked, the heartland of her assumed foe: America. She would sit on the floor, even though the plane itself was built in Washington. She did not consume anything produced in America, she explained to the flight attendant; it was a religious belief, she begged; they gave her a choice of the seat or the outside of the plane. And so she eventually accepted religious persecution, and that life was unfair, along with a complimentary breakfast for first-class passengers of eggs Benedict and mimosas that she devoured with the intensity of someone who had lived in a commune with seventy other purists the past five months.

"We don't buy American," the sect's leader, Ricardando Hill, had told her back then. His birth name was Richard, although he went by Ricardando to sound more like a South American revolutionary.

She was three days out of a stint at her latest college, where she had learned enough to realize she never wanted to be a college graduate, only a college student. "Why not?"

"Because America is run by an evil corporation."

"Why not live in Mexico or Canada, then?"

"Apparently Little Miss College has never traveled abroad. Conditions outside the mainland are atrocious. And it's impossible to get a wireless signal."

"Just seems disingenuous is all. Living in a place and hating it so."

"Ever held a job?"

"No."

"Ever gone to work nine-to-five, your talents ignored, your pride depleted, then one day they say—oops, we made a mistake, this isn't your career?"

"I babysat before."

"Then you don't know what the Ordur is about. But you can learn."

In 2009, the Ordur of the Opakalipse of Oregun, a group that refused to acknowledge the mainstream alphabet, was founded like so many of society's renegade sects when its leader lost his job. Ricardando, a web site developer, had taken to the hills in a precarious time for Oregon subculture, when many of his brethren also suffered a momentary blip in the economy, only to collectively realize the last thing they wanted was another job. They had created a web site and a system for growing vegetables, although it was only a system and nothing that produced substantial nourishment. Other than that, they could never agree on what, exactly, they hated so much about America. Which meant as a revolution, they lacked that one driving force to fortify them into a destructive initiative. But there was something that had driven them to the compound, something right and pure, setting them apart from the rest of America. And the rest of America—or at least that portion of central Oregon pertinent to this tale—agreed: There was something about the latest version of hippies living in the woods, and they would eagerly pay to have a look.

They came by Dodge Caravan. They came by Chevy Suburban. They came by the all-new Toyota Sienna Hybrid, with excellent fuel economy and low emissions, to stand at the compound's perimeter and have a look at what they were led to believe—both by word of mouth, as well as the revolution's web site—were actual terrorists, dangerous and willing to die for their beliefs. The Ordur set up a makeshift tollbooth at the front gate, $20 per carload. During the warm months and when it did not rain, the commune brought in upwards of $5,000 on a good day. But like any amusement park, the members had to keep up appearances, leaving little time for the actual subversive acts their organization intended.

Once a day, members lined up in formation and attacked the Red Shack. The guns had no bullets, the formation no merit. They just borrowed whatever they had seen from television and did their best to look angry. They hitchhiked into town (foreign automobiles only) twice a week to purchase vegetables, breaking their oath to never buy American in order to eat. In the morning hours, before the tourists arrived, they hid all the purchased produce in the garden, the soil of which refused to sprout any actual growth. Then during the day they would reap the bounty they had gotten the night before from the Price Pantry, drag it inside, rewash it. Money they earned at the gate had to be reinvested into the business since more tourists arrived daily: concession stands, a smoking area, a series of latrines for tourists too proper to piss in the woods.

In short, they were so busy keeping up the appearance of being terrorists that there was little time to get to the actual terrorizing. Either way it was impossible for any of the members to obtain a leave of absence since all hands were needed to keep the ship tight.

"Out of the question," Ricardando Hill said when Mallory requested leave. If there was one thing he hated more than a fork made in Cleveland that retailed for ninety-nine cents when he could get the same fork made in Thailand for twenty-nine cents, or he could steal chopsticks from the local Panda Lu Buffet—it was a media-produced hero with his own museum being erected.

"But my father needs me."

"Your father has done more to destroy our atmosphere with his jet fuel than a hundred million smokers." Ricardando was a smoker; he could not stand the hypocrisy of an expensive pack of cigarettes from Virginia. "And the Red Shack needs to be repainted and then re-covered with graffiti this week. I can't allow everyone to leave just because they feel like a vacation. That's no way to run a revolution."

Mallory was tired of the grind. She wanted the romantic connotations of revolution—what she had gleaned from watching films about Che Guevara. She also wanted to have her nails done, and read magazines about the latest Cleve Peoples exploits, and watch her gossip shows to see who was shagging whom.

"I'm not sure you know what you're doing."

"I know what I'm doing."

"You just don't fit the profile of a revolutionary." She sighed. "Even your name—Ricardando. It sounds like your parents couldn't decide to raise you Spanish or American, or the stage name of a flamboyant magician. You lack that . . . pizzazz that revolution requires."

He pouted. "I got pizzazz."

"Then when do you intend to blow something up?" She got right up close to the miserable curls of his goatee. "You always talk about all the change that's coming, but it never comes."

"The grass hasn't been cut. We need to set up an online ticketing system. And I need to figure out a proper uniform." He waved a list, flexed his tiny pectorals. "I'll blow something up all right, you just wait. I've got responsibilities to handle first."

Mallory snorted. She was tired of sleeping with Ricardando. She wanted an actual nihilist, not the caricature of a nihilist.

"I suppose you think a commune just runs itself. Well, it doesn't, Miss I'm Too Good To Staple Bananas Into Trees. It takes planning. It takes teamwork."

She yawned.

"And something else—you've been shaving your armpits again, haven't you?"

"They itch. And I hate how it looks in tank tops."

"Pray tell—what did you use to shave them?"

"A plastic knife from the gas station. Just like always."

"Then why did I find this in the garbage?" He held up a disposable razor.

"It was made in Korea I think."

"It was made in Pittsburgh!" He shoved the razor into her eye line. "You tried to scrape off the name, but you can clearly see the 'Pitt' and 'urg.'"

"Oh, Ricardando. You disappoint me."

"I'm disappointing? You're running off to coronate a mass-produced hero—and what did he really accomplish?"

She slapped his whiskered face. She was hoping he'd slap her back, and then she'd scratch for his eyes, and then he'd throw her to the floor and they'd really get into it. Instead he held his cheek and recoiled. "He saved all those lives. Neither you nor anyone else can say different."

"He saved swine. A real hero would have crashed into a mountain."

And then there was the money. Mallory never told Ricardando and the others that none of it was real. That her father had not pioneered a doomed aircraft into a body of water, saving all those lives. She never mentioned the quarter of a million dollars that was hers—simply for showing up, and shaving her pits, and putting on a dress, and smiling while her father clipped the ribbon at a museum that would always be there, always honor the day long after she and Ricardando and the commune wilted into history. Sure, money like that would come in handy for the Ordur—a new shooting range where they could blast watermelon targets, a hot box where they could discipline each other in front of stunned tourists. But money like that would also come in handy for a down payment on a Manhattan loft, with daddy footing the bills for some type of hobby-like career, and Mipsy coming to visit twice a year for shopping. She was tired of being an anarchist. It was time to be a Swagger again.

PICTURE YOURSELF IN A BOAT ON A RIVER

Peter Wrinkles sat around his small town of Dummer, New Hampshire, eating fast food and smoking weed, telling anyone who would listen he would make a good fighter pilot since he was so adept at the flying portion of video games. Whenever any of his family needed something, they typically contacted Blackie—Uncle Al, as he was known to the New Hampshire brood—and he was expected to solve the dilemma.

Blackie had not wanted to hire his nephew for a desk job, much less an important assignment such as Flight AW2921. But a distinctively appealing idea was to strap the stoner into the cockpit next to Swagger, and not tell him the crash was planned. Just let the little pisser learn good and fast it was an uncaring world, and occupations were not given out like library cards. That would shake the pilot dreams from his numskull. Blackie was convinced if his nephew were ever encouraged to pursue a career in aviation, it would end in devastation, a massive jet pummeling into a pile of buildings. In that way, Blackie was preventing a future crash by strapping Peter into this one, scaring the aspirations out of him before they ripened.

He had wanted to frighten his nephew only, teach him a lesson; not kill him. The problem was Peter Wrinkles had been playing video games and eating processed food for more than a decade, having not done any actual exercise since high school. So when the plane hit the imaginary birds and skipped a beat, his lethargic heart did the same, sending the twenty-six-year-old into cardiac arrest thirty years before his due. Now he was lying in a sequestered room in Roosevelt Hospital, having just awakened from a two-day snoozer to find he was still kicking.

"Hey Uncle Al! Looks like I'm going to pull through."

"Don't you Uncle Al me. I told you it's Mr. Black."

"You sore at me, Uncle?"

"I gave you one job, Peter." The door was closed so no one could see. Up until then he had managed to keep Wrinkles out of the news reports. "All you had to do was fasten your seatbelt and sit still."

"I did fasten my seatbelt."

"Don't think you're getting paid for falling unconscious." Blackie was furious. "A jetliner in the middle of the river. And instead of everyone concentrating on the story, they're scrambling to help a fattened moose."

"You know you're partly to blame, Uncle Al."

"It was your lack of physical fitness—that's where the blame lies."

"If you had told me it was a pretend crash, I wouldn't have been startled."

Blackie rushed to the bed. "Who said it was pretend?"

"It would have been like a roller coaster. And I've ridden plenty of roller coasters without dying. You could have killed me, Uncle Al."

"Who said, damn it!"

"The pilot I think. 'Wrinkles,' he kept shaking me when I was on the ground. 'Don't worry, it wasn't real.' By that time the damage was done. I could feel myself slipping away from Mr. Swagger and Davey, like I was sinking."

"Goddamned miserable Swagger." Blackie paced the room. This was the reason you did not hire family.

"Then the strangest thing happened," Peter continued. "I felt myself lifted into the air. As though being rescued by angels."

"Fucking Wednesdays," Blackie hissed. "Those weren't angels. Those were flight attendants. You had to be carried to the wing by a bunch of women."

"Then I felt myself coasting along a pleasant sea."

"You were on a ferry, Peter. On your way to this hospital."

"I don't think so, Uncle Al." Wrinkles sat up. "I've been pretty messed up before, thinking the furniture was talking to me. This was different."

"Don't say it."

"This was magical."

"I'm warning you, Peter."

"I think what it was, Uncle Al. I think—"

"The next word out of your mouth better be luck. You think it was luck."

"God saved me from that crash."

"You dirty little shit." Blackie knew blackmail when he heard it. He leaned over his nephew until his head pushed back into the pillows. "Tell me, Peter—what exactly did this God fellow have to say on a Monday morning?"

"Said I need to stop with the drugs and booze, the video games, stop with all of it."

"That's it?"

"For the most part."

"Nothing else, eh?"

"Well . . ."

"You dirty little shit."

"Part of living a righteous life is honesty. Now I don't know the nature of your business, Uncle Al. But it seems to me faking a plane crash has a somewhat dishonest ring to it. As part of my own repentance, I have no choice but to come clean about my participation."

"You didn't participate."

"I've hired representation. I'm writing a book."

"You can barely speak the English language much less compose a narrative." He paced the darkened room, wondering the quickest way to get his nephew to safe ground. "Besides, you were unconscious. You don't even know what happened. You couldn't possibly write it down."

"My heart wasn't up to it because of bad habits." Wrinkles shook his head. "But that's all in the past. God has given me a second chance. And I don't intend to waste it."

"Let me explain something to you, Peter." Blackie walked to the door; no one in sight. He could easily suffocate his nephew with a pillow and none of the staff would be wiser. "This god of yours—what is he offering?"

"Eternity, I suppose."

"Well, your Uncle Al intends to offer you $5,000. That's $3,000 more than you would have earned."

"What do I have to do?"

"Same assignment as before—nothing. Just lie there, and watch television, and forget everything once you leave this room." He walked to the bed. "You see, Peter, many times in traumatic situations, people don't have a solid grasp of what, exactly, occurred. You go spinning these crazy notions of fake crashes, it would be bad for everyone—your Uncle Al, Mr. Swagger, even your friend Officer Miles."

"Davey wasn't a pilot at all," Peter said. "He was an actor. Mr. Swagger was always teasing him."

"Goddamned miserable Swagger."

"Something illegal happened on that plane, Uncle Al. And I was saved. And if I know what's good for me, I'll come clean and repent. Repent, I tell *you!*"

"If you know what's good for you you'll keep your goddamn mouth shut."

"Repent, Uncle Al! Repent!"

Blackie went for the pillow.

Blackie Spin had chosen the Specklebelly Goose specifically because it had better Google-ability. It was more fun to say than the
Black Goose, or the Grey Goose for that matter. And also he had
been offered $1,000,000 by the Specklebelly Brewing Company
of Vermont to use their name as a cross endorsement. Whenever
someone searched for Specklebelly, a sponsor link would highlight
at the top of their browser that would lead them to the Specklebelly
Brewery web site. In a few weeks, Captain Hank Swagger would
appear in beer commercials, sitting opposite a cartooned Specklebelly Goose as they forgave each other for the midair mishap while
sipping Specklebelly lager. The contract had been signed, the details forged, the animator hired to begin work on the cartoon goose.
Never mind that the geese were native to Canada. There were no
other companies with bird monikers willing to pay $1,000,000 to
have Swagger endorse their products, so Blackie Spin would make
it work. Perhaps the birds had a migratory pattern that brought
them in proximity to LaGuardia Airport. Perhaps the goose people
that determined where geese were living these days needed to take
a closer look at their data. Point was the Vermont brewer needed to
sell beer, and they paid Blackie handsomely to make it happen, so
a flock of Specklebelly brought down Flight AW2921 whether they
lived in New York State or not.

The addition of the Specklebelly into the advertising blitz
sent Air Wanderlust into a 1:76 market. One in every seventy-six
ideas that flew across any one person's culture-grabbing capa-
bilities—phone, handheld assistant, computer, television, general
surroundings—was broadcasting an idea central to the name Air
Wanderlust, at an average of 130 times per hour. It was a massive
tangle of equations and logarithms, of smart men with giant brains
in a room in the Veiltality headquarters, all crunching data and carrying the ones. Even Blackie did not understand how it worked; he
only cared what the final number said, 1:76, which was better than

anyone had ever done. A look at the day's Top 10 most searched items showed his campaign:

1. Air Wanderlust
2. Captain Swagger
3. Flight AW2921
4. Pornography
5. Swagger Aviation and Miracle Museum
6. Specklebelly
7. Plane crash
8. Professional Wrestling
9. Guitar Hero
10. Nymphopucky

He had beaten pornography. He had annihilated professional wrestling and humiliated a fake disease that had claimed several lives, but no one had ever beaten pornography. And now it would become a two-man race, Air Wanderlust versus Swagger. He had already provided the airline with what it needed—a captivating miracle, a publicity stunt to rival any in history, and a marketing approach that put Air Wanderlust in the same discussion as Coca-Cola or Nike. He had engineered a cross promotion with the Whalensky Plaza Hotel and Resort, the official hotel of Air Wanderlust, that would see Hank Swagger attending conferences and filming commercials in Whalensky hotels around the world. The real money lay in Swagger. The world loved a good story, but what they loved even more was a good protagonist. "Cinderella" was a beautiful tale, but if the idealist stepchild had not been so charmingly pathetic no one would bother. Without a leading man, the story of Robin Hood would have comprised a group of wooded terrorists.

They had already lined up endorsements across the board—beer to hair gel, underwear to mouthwash. Ford, Chevy, and Chrysler were waging war to determine what type of car Swagger would first be photographed inside. Clothes, Visa or MasterCard, favored brand of coffee, yogurt, waffle, preferred burger, deodorant, toothpaste. They had all come forward with open pockets to tattoo their name on Swagger, ensure he was seen using their product instead of the competition's.

Swagger represented the personal side of Blackie's job, where the dignity lay. It was Swagger he intended to turn into an icon, a character that would become part of the cultural fabric, like Santa Claus, or Charles Manson. He projected Swagger somewhere between Barbie and The Marlboro Man; he would destroy Robin Hood; he would not quite reach Santa's fame. Hell, the only thing separating his man from Jesus Christ was that the Christians had a better plot, fewer cameras to contend with.

Now unseen forces were threatening the thing he cared for most. That was why he employed Jimmish. His first-lieutenant's main function was surveillance of the passengers, which required him to spend time at the Whalensky Plaza. Blackie was pleased so many of the passengers turned out to be cheapskates. Rather than having them scattered across the country, it was nice to have most of them under one roof for the duration of the week, sticking around and taking advantage of the free tickets on offer for the ribbon-cutting of the Swagger Aviation and Miracle Museum. It was during his surveillance that Jimmish happened across the reporter Lucy Springer, in the lobby with the strange passenger who had gone missing.

"Everything comes out of alignment on Wednesdays. You did good, Jimmish."

"Perhaps we underestimated her, sir."

"Not her abilities I didn't. I underestimated the importance she places on her career. This interview would set her up for life."

Blackie Spin checked his board. Something had been bothering him all week. The two missing cell phones belonged to the strange George Bailey and the old woman, who had been robbed of her device by Lucy Springer. Less than an hour before, the two passengers had encountered each other in a hotel lobby. Blackie Spin was not a disciple of coincidence. He was disappointed that Lucy Springer had gone off script. She had turned his head months ago when the puppet, in a moment of jest, suggested that his

Nymphopucky virus was a front by the pharmaceutical industry to market a new brand of snake oil. It was a shot in the dark, although it revealed a level of sophisticated cynicism that impressed him. It had taken months of planning to arrange for her to be the sole journalist on the flight. And now she had betrayed that kindness.

A man like Arnold Jeffries was incapable of loving his employees. To him they were lightbulbs, or shoehorns—things essential but readily replaceable. Blackie loved his characters in the way only a Salinger could love a Holden, only a Heller could love a Yossarian. That was how he loved Swagger in spite of his flaws. That was how he had loved Lucy Springer.

"Am I to offer her reassignment?"

"I'm afraid not everyone is eligible for reassignment, Jimmish. Despite your steadfast dedication to Veiltality, what I need in this situation you have not been able to provide." Jimmish kept silent. He knew what it meant. "I assume there were no flaws with Mr. Corbin?"

"He left several hours ago."

"Anything else I should know?"

"There was a woman. She was not eligible for reassignment either."

"You used the gun?"

"No, sir."

Blackie sighed. "One thing I cannot tolerate in my characters is fear. I predict before this week is out, you will use that gun. Your time has come, Jimmish." He wandered toward the edge of his wall of monitors. "For now let's concentrate on the pertinent part of our story. The Swagger interview—do you have suggestions for a graceful exit for Miss Springer?"

"For symbolic purposes, why not give her a Nymphopucky infestation?"

Blackie chuckled. "Brilliant detail. See to it. Set up a new interview as well. Go with one of the morning shows. They're all the same to me."

"Very good, Mr. Black."

Blackie was intrigued that his missing passenger had been in

contact with Lucy Springer. Every story had flaws and this one was
no different. Rather than panic, Blackie enjoyed the anticipation.
That was what concealed an opportunity he might have overlooked,
sheltered the conclusion. He always had a vague idea how his stories
would end, but he was never one hundred percent certain until the
climax arrived.

"Tell me about the other passenger. This nowhere man of ours."

"George Bailey. Standby. He talked his way onto the plane,
some type of emergency he had to attend to in California. He
checked no luggage."

"George Bailey. That's an alias." Blackie wrote it down. "This
was the gentleman who was doing something on the plane. What
exactly was he doing?"

"Looking for his bag, that's all."

"He threw his phone into the water?"

"I went back and retrieved the phone. It was ruined."

"What was in the bag?"

"I left it on the plane. To see if he would come back for it."

"That was smart, Jimmish." He paced in a circle around the
giant man. "But my curiosity is too much. Whatever is inside holds
an important piece of our narrative. Bring me the bag."

Jimmish knew he was not yet the character Blackie had first en-
visioned when he selected him for reassignment. Trouble was, he
could not decide what role he was meant for until he understood
Blackie. And he could not understand his boss because he could
not decide what Blackie loved or obsessed over. Whether it was
women, or men, or even a wilder variety—had he demonstrated
a clear preference even once, it would have gone a long way to
making Jimmish understand. As it was, he seemed above obsession,
above vice. To Jimmish's thinking that made him immortal.

"May I ask a question, sir?"

"Of course, Jimmish."

"I'm having difficulty understanding our current story."

"You said there was a question."

He walked toward the board. They typically circulated a room
like opposites, a planet and a moon, walking an adequate circle as

to keep a constant diameter. "My question is—what type of man are you?"

"You think less of me because of our plane crash, do you Jimmish?"

"I think you're the same man you were before the crash."

"We live in a world of illusion. Everyone has their own version of what gets them by—a virtual rock band, a fantasy baseball team, a mock avatar in an online world, even a religion. We find our own version of faith, our fictions, that distract us from the ultimate reality."

"What's that, sir?"

"That we're doomed."

Blackie took his time organizing his thoughts. While his actions were illegal by modern standards, he did not believe that morally he was in the wrong. So long as he could explain it. Because if he could not answer a question as simple as "Why?" he was no better than a common murderer.

"This city awoke this week to a massive miracle. It's a glorious surprise to their mundane lives, to the everyday back and forth that chips away at their souls. And I gave them that. For nothing. Free of charge. Even attending a film costs money. I gave them a story, some fiction or faith, whatever you prefer. A miracle they can watch on television, they can read about on the computer, that will always belong to them, to their history. I gave them a hero that reminds us all of what we are capable as a species. And one day, many years from now, that hero will exist after you and I are gone."

He looked down on his miniature model of Manhattan, his shadow eclipsing the city. "Your question is what type of man am I. My answer, Jimmish, is that I'm one of the good guys."

"What I mean is—what type of man are you that you are permitted to decide the story?"

"I see." Blackie sat down in the room's only chair. "I suppose we all have roles. The narrator happens to be mine."

"Omniscience?" Jimmish asked.

"I'm as mortal as you, subject to fallibility and asteroids and taxes."

"I guess I can't figure out what my role is until I know yours."

"You have the best role of all, Jimmish. You're my Angel of Death. The Reckoning of my stories. Judgment Day." He stood and placed a hand on Jimmish's shoulder. "My favorite character of all time is Death. Think, for a moment, of the attention to detail it takes to be Death. When she arrives, she is always composed, calm, attentive. She enters at situations of distress. When you and I meet her, we will assume like everyone else that it is a mistake, an accident, never our fault. But she has considered all the nuances, been thoughtful to each particular. She handles each reassignment and reincarnation and damnation with diligence and professionalism, respectful of the duty, of life, her role."

"I hope I do the same," Jimmish said.

"Of course you do. You understand detail. You respect detail. But you hold that gun for a reason, Jimmish. And you must respect that eventually you'll have to use it. For you. For us. To protect the story."

"I am afraid of it," Jimmish said.

"Don't be afraid." He reached up and put his hands on Jimmish's soft cheeks. "It's what you're destined to become. My Angel of Death, my big, beautiful meat. And I am the God of your meat. And you can be secure that I love and protect all my meat."

Jimmish nodded. "I'll handle the reporter this afternoon."

"Handle it now, Jimmish."

LOVE ME DO

Before Swagger kidnapped the puppy two days prior, the only thing he'd enjoyed in his recent life was his mistress. The past nine months had been hell—he had been suspended, grounded, his pilot's license revoked, he trained in a simulator all day while Blackie and the others hollered that he was doing it wrong. But at least they had the foresight to provide him a suitable mistress, the flexible Monica Dressings, who had reminded him that perhaps all was not lost. He'd had intercourse with her less than thirty minutes after meeting her, he heavily infatuated, she dreadfully guilty over the affair that resulted. Swagger had a thing for bookish brunettes with low self-esteem; Monica for anyone passably attractive since she rarely socialized due to the hectic work schedule.

To Swagger there was something about her that was pure, borderline naïve, which he found comforting. He had always believed that his own wife and children had a sophistication, a cynical worldview that surpassed his own. And they took to the plot without batting an eye, even offering Blackie suggestions on how to improve the deceit. How could a proper family do that? Certainly there should have been outrage. Certainly one of them should have pointed out the deviant nature of such a scheme, held the father aloft as a beacon of how they should behave. Instead they loved being part of the ruse.

The utter fucking deceit, the massive apparatus that could take something as complex and beautiful as the sorcery of flight, and turn an Airbus into a bold and effective lie, without anyone questioning it. It compromised his faith in an increasingly faith-less world. The last nine months had made him feel unsure, and he had fallen into the arms of Monica Dressings, a woman who seemed too simple to enjoy any of it. He adored that about her, licked it off her stupid skin each time he betrayed his loveless vows.

"I don't even understand how it works," she admitted early on. Oh, it was nice to hear someone admit it—the confusion, the horrid complexity even he felt of the thing, of the world, and to not be bashful about speaking the words: I. Don't. Know. "A plane crash. And all the technology. I'm just not that smart."

"Of course you're not, doll." He held her to his chest. "I don't mean no insult. Just mean you're better than any of them."

"What about you?"

"What about me?"

"It's just . . . well, you're flying the plane. What does that say about you?"

"Nothing good, I assure you." And he meant it. He had agreed to the plot, either by force or necessity, and all the King's Gold that accompanied his voyage. He had not run; a good person, a person like Monica Dressings, might have fled. "If there was any way out, boy, I'd take the high road, sure as shit. Absolutely, positively, I'd get out."

"What if there was a way out?"

"I would never take it."

"I mean it, Hank." She sat up in bed, her smallish breasts, the brutally white skin. How gorgeous a canvas it was compared to his own. He wanted to taste it, climb inside it, live in her epidermis. "You could run. You could cooperate with authorities. You could prove Blackie is a criminal."

He was suspicious. "How do you know about stuff like that?"

"I saw a show on television."

"That's adorable. About faking a plane crash?"

She laid her head on his chest until he could smell the gullible shape of her. "It was a movie. Criminal masterminds. A hero who stands up against evil instead of letting it destroy him. He ran, Hank. He got out. It was romantic."

"You're talking about Hitchcock's *North by Northwest*. That's not a romantic comedy, doll, it's a thriller."

"I meant he was romantic, the man. He never gave up."

Swagger hugged her, in love with her simplicity. Cary Grant in the movie was nothing similar; stupid girl probably did not understand the plot. And as fond as he was of Monica, Eva Marie Saint she was not. "Nah, the trays are in the upright position and we're set for liftoff. Couple days I'll fly that bird into the Hudson and become rich and immortal, and then . . . well, something'll probably happen to you, too."

They laid together in their loneliness, back before either of them had broken dozens of FAA regulations, before Swagger had mastered the simulator, before Monica had collected the phones, and they thought about a different way.

"It's sad, don't you think?" she had asked. "That we never control our destiny. Even when we think about controlling it. When we try to grasp it and manipulate it. It's always something else that decides our course."

He had stolen the earrings from the old woman with the busted ankle and given them to Monica on their first meeting at the Whalensky. He loved to see them dangle across her milky skin. They had been having intercourse periodically in the room next to Swagger's suite, which doubled as the rehearsal space. It was Blackie's idea to give her a room in the hotel as the best method of keeping Swagger in check. The last thing Blackie needed, he said, was Hank Swagger falling into a depressed funk and carousing the local bar scene for an unreliable slut.

"How many times does that make?" Mipsy asked when Swagger arrived in the room. "And look at your face—it's all red. Was she hitting you in the face, Hank?"

He held his cheek. "What are you talking about?"

"And your wife and children next door. Haven't you any shame?"

"Oh, Henry!" Mallory pretended to cry, and Swagger pretended remorse. That was another thing he disliked about his children— that they called him by his adult name. Would it have been too much to throw a daddy at him, even a papa now and again?

"That's seven times in the last twelve hours." Mipsy was keeping score in the margin of a crossword puzzle. "That's more sex than we've had since The Mallory was born."

Nathan stroked the puppy. "You're something else, Henry."

"Thank you, son."

"It wasn't a compliment. Do you think I'm complimenting you?"

Now that he was back in the room with the family, he was sad again. When Swagger grew sad, he drank. When he drank, he grew nostalgic for fifteen minutes ago, when he was thirty feet away in bed with Monica Dressings, who, as his wife predicted, punched his face during sex. He poured himself an impressive tumbler and surveyed the room. "What's with all the boxes?"

"Alastair sent them over. New products and clothes."

"Like, to wear?"

"Hank, I am growing concerned with your stupidity. Did you just ask if the clothes were to wear?"

The boxes were the endorsement deals Blackie had worked out, ties and shoes and furry slippers. "What do you say we open them?"

"All of us? Together?"

"What the hell? It'll be like the Christmas we never have."

They mulled it separately. It seemed a bit kitschy, them spending time together when they so clearly despised one another, but it might also be fun. And besides, one thing they had was plenty of time.

"Just for the heck of it, let's say a prayer first," Nathan suggested. He was still wearing the uniform. "We should be thankful for this week. Come on, everyone grab hands."

Mallory picked up the dog and moved away. "Fuck off, Nate."

"Mom, did you hear that?"

"Nate, do fuck off. We're all getting a bit tired of your bullshit."

The Swaggers tore into the boxes, snatching and bartering the bounty. Over the years the four had worked out a sophisticated method of currency: An object's worth increased based on how much someone else in the family coveted it. One thing they all agreed on, in spite of their differences, was that when it came down to it they were Americans, and Americans were consumers, and the Swaggers intended to do their part.

"What the hell is a Heffermeier?" Swagger asked.

"Scarf company," Mipsy said.

"Like, to wear?"

"No, to eat, Hank. These are the new edible scarves. Idiot."

He pulled out a series of colors and lengths and determined they were worth nothing since no one else in the family wanted them. When Hank agreed to the assignment, he agreed to a year of product endorsements. It made him woozy—all those companies coordinating their products, settling on an ad campaign, the information funneling into him. And that didn't even include the museum—the people from the wax gallery had done body scans, the people from the photo exhibit took photos, the people from the museum restaurant wanted his opinions on the menu—there was even a curator who phoned constantly with updates about the Saturday ribbon-cutting, as if he needed a script to snip a ribbon. How was it possible to pull an airplane out of a river on a Monday and turn it into a museum by the following Saturday? He lost his breath thinking about it.

But for now there was Mipsy and the children, elated. As his family tore into the corrugated fiberboard made of manufactured birch, spruce, and pine, and they deposited the remnants on the floor and beneath the bed where illegally employed cleaning maids would waddle on their knees to retrieve them—it occurred to Swagger that this was what the last year had been about, engaging in mass deceit so that his once-lovely wife, his once-simple daughter and faux heroic son, could enjoy the mass consumerism from labor for which he neither sweated nor bled. It was something, at least for the moment, to be relished.

"The Nathan is right. We should express a bit of thanks. Let's go ahead and say that prayer."

"Thanks, Dad."

"Keep it short."

They all stood. Mallory tucked her hands into her armpits. "I should inform you all I no longer believe in God."

"Christ, Mallory, just take his hand and let's get on with it."

"I've pledged loyalty to the OOO LLC. One of our tenets is that we don't acknowledge prefabricated gods."

"You belong to an LLC," Swagger pointed out. "You acknowledge corporate law but not a supreme creator of existence?"

"The LLC protects us if we get sued. God isn't as reliable."

"Nevertheless, you don't believe in God on your own time," Swagger corrected. "When you're with this family, you believe in our God."

"Your father is right."

"Amen," Nathan added.

"Now take your brother's fucking hand." She did. "Nathan, hit it."

Swagger tuned out his son's words. This was what it was all about. He and his wife were on speaking terms for the first time in years. He had his children and his puppy, and for that instant Hank Swagger's smile beheld a bountiful pride.

"Tell you what," he said when the prayer ceased, extracting his wallet to great squeals. "Blackie has his hands full, something with the interview. And the guard next door had some business to attend to." Mipsy grimaced; he quickly inserted money into her hand. "I had the brilliant idea of forgetting to close the door on my way in. Anyone who wants to do some shopping better go now."

The three Swaggers were on their feet, racing to be first to hug their dear, beloved dad. He opened his arms and let them rush forward, the hugs suffocating him, the hard edges of their phones and Bluetooth headphones scratching into his weathered skin. When they departed, Swagger picked Jeters out of an insatiable sleep and held the puppy on his lap, stroking his soft fur, reflecting on the afternoon. For an instant, just before he turned on the television and fell back into The Rot, he placed the scarf around his neck and pondered: Life could be like this.

Unfortunately, in an entirely different part of the world, a young man had a pondering of his own: He was going to assassinate Hank Swagger.

DO YOU WANT TO KNOW A SECRET?

SEAT: 9B
PASSENGER: Monica Dressings
REASON FOR FLIGHT: Business
LAST THOUGHTS BEFORE IMPACT: *Why hasn't anyone stopped this?*

As soon as Swagger had left her room, Monica Dressings retrieved the second phone she stored in a hidden leather pouch inside her handbag. She dialed the number, along with a twenty-five-digit access code, followed by a twelve-digit identification code, followed by the extension. It took a moment for an operator to answer, at which point she offered the password (PIFFLE). Three minutes after dialing the phone, Mr. Tuffers answered.

"Tuff. Go ahead."

"It's me. V."

"Veronica, are you clear?"

She walked to the window. "Why haven't I heard anything?"

"We didn't want to compromise your cover."

"He crashed the fucking plane, Tuff!"

"Stunning, really. We've been watching it on television all week."

"I was on the plane. I could have died. Why haven't we arrested him?"

"Settle down, V. It's not that easy."

"Six counts of domestic terrorism in three years. Just this week, 160 attempted murders, conspiracy to commit fraud, a half-dozen disappearances we could pin on him." She was shouting when she finished. "We could put him away for life, today, all of them. Are you waiting for him to kill me, too?"

"He's not going to kill you. He has no idea."

Mr. Tuffers was not her cat. Veronica Santilli hated cats. She hated skirts and keyboards and pleasantries, all requirements of a personal assistant. Mr. Tuffers was the director of an FBI special operations unit that dealt with domestic terrorism.

"You're not telling me something, Tuff. I know it."

"There's nothing to tell. Just bureaucratic red tape."

"The guy crashed a plane. If he was Middle Eastern, we'd have wires hooked to each testicle."

"Look, V, I've explained it."

"The budget excuse again?"

"We have operations of higher priority." He talked low; she could tell he was in a room, on a wire tap, a stakeout, bagels and coffee and the low buzz of a radio; they were listening to a ballgame. "We're going to arrest Alastair Black. It's just a matter of when."

"Where are you?"

"Beg your pardon?"

"Right now. What are you doing?"

"It's classified."

"You're on a stakeout. You're outside some baseball player's apartment."

"Steroids in baseball continue to be a priority for the Bureau. That's true, V."

"Christ, Tuff."

"America's pastime is at stake. And until we clean up this game, until all professional sports are clean, this Bureau will invest all available resources."

Veronica Santilli had been a member of FBI special ops for ten years. Her current task was to portray a college graduate newly arrived in New York City, floundering for a career, and who could pull off a ditzy secretary for Veiltality Inc. For three years, she had been Blackie's personal assistant. She had fetched coffee, answered phones, taken the abuse. All the while she reported back to the Bureau on the Nymphopucky epidemic, which had been a high level conspiracy involving the mayor of New York, eight million of its residents, and nearly twenty deaths; no arrests were made. She ordered magic markers and stationery, shopped for fresh tomatoes. Meanwhile, she reported back to the agency on Christopher Michaels, who hired Veiltality to win him a U.S.

Senate seat; conspiracy, three missing people, bribery of public officials, voter fraud. No arrests.

She had perfected her role as Monica Dressings, a gawky, sexually frustrated twenty-five-year-old who lived with her cat and browsed web sites on scrapbooking and home decorating. She was, in fact, thirty-three and hated all those topics. For at least two hours each day, she clicked through the web sites on her laptop, knowing Blackie Spin was eavesdropping on her personal affairs. She had polished Monica Dressings, the disastrous bitch who was ruining her career in FBI special ops, pretending nervousness, pretending naïveté, pretending she could not put Blackie Spin in a choke hold, compress his carotid artery until he was unconscious, then dislocate the cervical portion of his neck with an aggressive snap.

For six months, she had complained to her superiors that the man was a lunatic, that one of her coworkers was possibly a hired killer, that she needed a prop cat to stage in the apartment in case Blackie Spin grew suspicious. That instead of inventing a masturbatory bedbug, or rigging an election, he now intended to crash a jetliner into the Hudson River as a publicity stunt. But the damn steroids in baseball—the endless investigations, the congressional hearings, the home-run champions—even after all that had overshadowed years of her career, it remained a nationwide concern with her boss instructed to solve the problem, the boss above her boss ordered, the boss above her boss's boss. . . . Which left Veronica— rather Monica—with a lunatic boss of her own who intended to put her on an airplane and dunk her in the Hudson. Right up until she boarded at LaGuardia, she expected FBI agents to swarm the plane, arrest Blackie Spin, and announce to the newspapers it had been a three-year undercover operation by an up-and-coming superstar agent. Now two days after the crash, the Bureau had gone silent.

Veronica was not without fault; she had been sleeping with the pilot. Blackie Spin had set it up, she was not stupid. She knew sleeping with Hank was expected, the gullible personal assistant. And she had done it, both to conceal her cover and because she wanted to, because she needed companionship, even the fraudulent type. Hank liked it rough. He encouraged her to hit him, her on top, open-hand slaps, right across the kisser, full swings, just let him have it—*Slap! Whap! Smack!*—and the dirty talk, the awful things she had said, the more lewd the better, he just wanted her to annihilate him; his guilty conscience and she was the repercussion. It had gone too far—he had feelings for her, and perhaps she him, and there was no possibility of the affair ending any way but badly. Hadn't she tried to warn him? Hadn't Monica, or rather Veronica channeling Monica, hinted with the *North by Northwest* clue that bad things were conspiring, that his best option, his only option, was to run?

Now one of two scenarios would play out: Blackie would find out who she was and slit her throat, or she would succeed in having them all arrested, and the Bureau would learn she was having sex with one of the conspirators, and that would be the end of her career. She was scared of Blackie Spin. She was scared that she had become a mistress, and that she was staying in the hotel room next to her lover's family.

"Let me ask," Tuffers said. "You scared of this guy, Blackie Spin?"

"Is that what you need to hear?"

"You're an agent. You're paid to not be scared." She could hear he had left whatever room he'd been in and now stood in a closet, a hallway, somewhere that he could speak loudly. If they could do undercover surveillance on major league shortstops, certainly they could do so on her. Did they already know about the affair? Had they heard the nasty things she said to Hank? Perhaps they were all listening to her now, only a hotel room away. "We'll get this guy, V. There are delays from high up I'm working through."

"Delays because the Bureau spends too much fucking time investigating steroids!"

She could tell she hit a nerve. Everyone in the Bureau was a sports fan—fantasy baseball, fantasy football, March Madness. "There are record books to consider. Home runs and RBI and slugging percentage and OPS have all been compromised. Then, of course, there are the fans." He was rattled. "It's a matter of right and wrong."

"How many agents on the case?"

"It's classified."

"Don't bullshit me, Tuff."

"One hundred and fifty-seven."

"I haven't even been able to get cat food expensed."

"I can take care of that today, V."

"I lost the cat."

"You lost it? That cat was Bureau property."

"Fuck the cat, Tuff."

He moved the phone to the other shoulder. "Truth is we haven't been investigating steroids for weeks. Another assignment has taken priority. National importance. The real deal."

"What now?"

"Semen trafficking ring. Bureau's been on it a while. Three weeks ago the mark went missing."

"And this is of higher priority than a criminal who staged a plane crash?"

"It's complicated."

"It's always complicated." She decided right then: She would say something dirty about Mr. Tuffers, the AWOL cat, the next time she fucked the pilot. "I'm hanging up now, Tuff."

"Keep an ear to the ground. We'll get this guy."

HELTER SKELTER

It was impossible that they had found him. In a city that size, only the unluckiest creature would run into the Genius-Temple film crew, in a remote East Village pizzeria, where they wound up only after Lucky Dan requested a stromboli. While Dan ate, Normal had deposited nine bucks into the pay phone hollering at Eddie. Normal was not exactly out of the business, not yet anyway. He would put the morality of his occupation aside until he had the necessary funds to skip town. Eddie had unloaded a sample of American baseball player/manager Willie Randolph (never used steroids; never hit many home runs either) to a dealer for $8,000, less than they typically got for a player from that era.

"Guy won six World Series," Normal belted into the phone.

"He never won any Gold Gloves. That's important for a second baseman."

"He was captain of the Yankees for cripes sake."

"Steroids. Brought down the value of players' semen across the board." Eddie sounded strange. "Where are you anyway, Norm?"

"East Village pizzeria. Let me get this straight." Normal shifted the phone. It was the third time Eddie had asked where he was. "You're saying because a couple guys shot their asses full of steroids in the nineties, that somehow affects the value of a player from the early eighties?"

"That's what I'm saying. Players' semen at least." Normal could hear Eddie cover the mouthpiece. "It's like the housing market, Norm. When one house on the block deteriorates in value, it affects all the other houses."

"You a real estate agent now?"

"Just saying."

"You're hiding something, Eddie. I know."

"You need to swipe better semen is all. Pete Rose, Ozzie Smith, Don Mattingly—then you might command market value."

Just then the phone went dead. Normal turned to find the

source of the dropped call, Rory and Lobo, who escorted him to the back of the pizzeria and into the alley. There a makeshift film set was being erected. Rory had a habit of testing people's biceps and ribs when she met them, like kicking the tires of a used car, or purchasing livestock. She gave Lucky Dan a squeeze. "Who's the string bean?"

"Luck consultant. Normal hired me."

She slapped Normal. "You hired representation, you dumb shit?"

Lucky took off his hat. "You must be Miss Genius-Temple. Big fan of your work."

"Kind of you to say it."

"*Semen Pirates*—soon as I heard that name, I fell in love. Very clever."

"We think it's a winner. We test screened the pilot a few months back. Audience was split between *Jizz Jackers* and *Spunk Burglars*. We think *Semen Pirates* appeals better to Middle America."

"I told you, Rory. I'm not doing the show."

"Believe this guy?" Rory waved a thumb. "Two crews of guild workers filming hundreds of hours of tape. And suddenly he isn't doing the show. Fucking talent."

"It's harassment," Normal hollered. "I should get a restraining order."

"Except that you're dead, smart guy." She shared a snicker with Lucky, who enjoyed the banter. "Speaking of which, your little vacation set us back plenty. We should have six episodes in the can. Impossible to get anything done since all you do is sit on your ass in a diner all day."

"That's what I keep telling him."

"Stay out of it, Lucky."

"That's why I've got no choice but to film Lobo beating you again."

Normal and Lucky Dan took a glance at Lobo, who was stretching in the alley.

"We need the footage. In this scene, our hero is robbed by a rival trafficker. We're calling the episode 'Semen Pirate Pirated.'"

"Clever," Lucky Dan said. He followed Rory off to the side. His first film set, he was excited. Normal accepted his fate, balancing in the center of the alley as Lobo came at him.

"*Siento mucho en tener que hacer esto, Señor Normal.*"

"He says he's very sorry," Lucky Dan called.

It was a fast scene, one of those title bouts where the audience is left hunting the parking lot for fresh blood. Normal lay on the ground gazing into the taut build of Rory's calves, the high heels, the seemingly endless supply of fake tan.

Lucky Dan peered down. "Good fight, Normal."

He breathed heavy. "Fuck off, Lucky."

"No, I mean it. Takes guts to put up your dukes against a fella like Lobo there. You showed some real chutzpah."

"It'll look good once we polish it." She squatted down, giving Normal a solid view of her pantyless nether regions through his one good eye. She rubbed a hand through his dusty hair. "Get me the John Lennon, Normal. I don't want to keep doing this."

"I'm working on it."

She tilted her sunglasses. "What is it about a fistfight that gets my crotch gushing?" She kicked Normal softly in the ribs. "I'd ask you to join us, but you look like shit, Normal. And you stink." She set some money on his chest. "Take a rinse somewhere."

A moment later the film crew was gone. Lucky Dan moved to the ground and lay in the dirt, head to head with Normal. "There you are," Dan said. "Just what we needed—more time."

Normal sat up, spitting blood. "Lucky, we need to talk."

"I was afraid this might happen."

"City of eight million. If I had any luck, I wouldn't run into her at all."

"The odds are certainly in your favor."

"It's impossible," Normal reasoned. "I was careful."

"What about your friend?"

"Eddie would never. He's petrified of Rory."

"All the more reason."

Dan stood and helped Normal to his feet. Normal was bleeding from the mouth and had a gash in his arm, although the stitches in his missing finger were intact. The same clothes for three days, and the stains from the alley cast him deeper into a homeless state. "I think this is where we part ways."

"No sir, fella. You hired me for a mission. Deal is a deal."

"You're supposed to bring luck. I'm no better off now than when we started."

Dan pouted. "I'm not sure what's wrong. I just feel off."

"I know what's wrong." Normal pushed him against a wall. "You're a fake. When we were betting nickels on diner orders, you won every other time. Seems to me a guy touting luck should win nearly every contest he enters."

Dan thought about it. "That was a fluke. I got plenty of luck."

"We'll see." Normal pulled out a coin and balanced it on his thumb. "Call it in the air."

"Heads. No, tails. No, heads it is."

It landed with a soft pat in Normal's palm, the knuckles of which were scratched from the gravel. He slapped it on the back of his left hand, tails.

"You're broken," he said. "Nice knowing you."

"Wait a minute." Dan bowed his head. And then he came clean.

He told Normal everything. How he had been using his luck for monetary gain. The girlfriend, Trish, whom he had lived with in Reno for eleven years. How he had played the relationship wrong, never made her a priority. How he found himself in the casino one evening and his client suddenly began losing, not just a little, rather every game he entered. And just like that it was gone, evaporated, different. His outlook had been tarnished, a common man at the whim of the odds, like every other creature. But somehow his luck was still there, he promised Normal, only it was in hibernation. He had flown to New York, thinking the oddity of the escapade might jar something loose. He had not known how to repair himself until he saw her on the television. Then he knew for certain; Lucy Springer was his way back.

"She's just . . . and then the puppet . . . it's all so . . . what I mean to say . . . That's why we need her around. When I'm near her, I'm lucky."

"You're not lucky. You're horny."

"Come on, Normal. You got to help me."

"I hired you to help me."

"She needs me. And I need her. And you need us both. Don't you see?"

"No, I don't see. I'm sorry you're damaged, but people are trying to beat me to death. And film it. And throw me in prison. I can't be mixed up with you."

"Now you listen." Dan poked a finger into Normal's chest. "Your brother was a friend—that's why I agreed to help. You don't have to pay me. But this here's a mission and I intend to see it through."

"If you don't have luck, you're no good to me."

"It'll come back. I know it will."

Normal spit red into the dirt. Maybe his brand of misfortune trumped Dan's luck, so that the longer the poor guy stuck around, the worse off he would be. Lucky seemed pathetic there in the alley, holding his fedora in front of him like he'd never had a day of luck in his life.

"You're desperate, Dan. And confused—about luck, and women, and what kind of trouble I'm in. You'll end up killed if you stick around. The both of us will."

Lucky Dan put his arm around Normal's neck. "Over my dead body."

LET IT BE

Normal's plan was to stake out the lobby of the Whalensky Plaza in hopes he might recognize one of the passengers. He was skeptical of the reporter's crash theory, but the sky marshal made him suspicious. Most of the passengers seemed in no hurry to return to their lives prior to Monday's crash, opting instead to stay the week in anticipation of the museum opening. In his condition—face scraped and three days without a shower—Normal could not simply approach a passenger with small talk: "I don't know if you recognize me, but we survived a plane crash together. Well, guess what?" Instead, he and Lucky Dan stood off to the side, waiting for an opening that did not seem imminent.

Normal tried to determine whom he recognized from the flight. Considering the circumstances—imminent death—he hadn't exactly paid close attention. He noticed a mid-twenties man with several bags approaching the elevators. Normal thought they might have taken the same ferry.

When the elevator arrived, the three piled in. Normal waited for him to push a button, 11, and then he hit 14. After a moment, he leaned and hit the fire alarm, stopping the car.

"What the hay, Normal? This your idea of subtle?"

"Stay out of it, Lucky."

"Guys, what's this about?"

Neither had practiced what to say once they got a passenger alone. "Just a few questions about the crash, that's all."

The man straightened. "You should talk to my agent about that."

"You're an actor?"

"All interviews have to go through my agent."

Normal wrapped his good hand around the young man's throat and pushed him against the elevator wall. "Whaddya say we do this interview here?"

"Geez, Normal, don't be so rough with him."

"Lucky, stay out of it." Then to the actor. "Why were you flying to Los Angeles?"

He gasped. "I don't know really."

"Just get on planes without knowing why?"

"Something about a commercial. That's all I know."

"You weren't given a script?"

"We don't always get scripts."

Normal released him. He fell to the floor and quickly rearranged his hair.

"What type of commercial?" Lucky asked.

"Like I said. I don't know. Plane crashed and here I am." He massaged his neck. "Maybe you can ask one of the others."

"One of the other what?" Normal asked.

"Actors. There were a bunch on the plane." The elevator was moving again. "Turns out we were all hired for the same gig and told to be in makeup when we boarded. Hate when they hire extras for shit work."

"And none of the others knew what the commercial was about?"

"Nah, none of us. Strange thing though—we all got paid. I made more money on not shooting this commercial than I made all of last year."

The doors opened on 11 and he stepped off quickly. "One other thing," he called from the hallway. "One of the pilots—he wasn't really a pilot."

"What makes you say that?"

"I met him at an audition for *Law and Order* a year ago. Neither of us got the part." He adjusted his hair again. "You know, I could probably have you arrested for manhandling me."

"We could probably get off the elevator and stomp you senseless," Normal mentioned.

When the doors closed, Normal glanced in the reflection to see Lucky Dan smiling back. "Luck or not, sure was a good thing I was around to suggest we contact the reporter. Isn't it now, Normal?"

Normal leaned against the steel reflection, itched his arm. One thing Frank always told him—never allow business to become personal. Someone had purposefully crashed a jet with his payday aboard. It had just gotten personal.

GOLDEN SLUMBERS

"He's dead."

"How do you mean, dead?"

"I mean he died. That's all I can tell you lady because it's all the guy told me. He said, 'Here's the office. Sort through the files and answer the phones and feed the goldfish.'"

"You say he died?"

"Yeah, and I got a cabinet of files that'll take a week to alphabetize."

Lucy had phoned her psychiatrist at his office. He had gone missing and was not answering his pager. Instead, she had gotten a nameless voice who seemed irritated at the interruption, and not the least bit concerned that her psychiatrist was dead.

"Who are you again?" Lucy asked.

"Lady, I told you. I work for the city. Now if you'll just give me a name and number, I'll have someone be in touch next week."

"Then how do you know Gary died?"

"Happened this morning. They e-mailed it over in a press release. Imagine, e-mailing a press release that someone croaked. That's all the guy told me."

"Does this guy have a name?"

"Of course he has a name. I just don't know it. That's how they are toward us temps. They don't give names, they don't give direction. They just point you at a mess and say fix it."

"And you're sure he said Gary Corbin. That's the person that died."

"He's dead I'm telling you. That's why I'm sitting in his chair."

"Did anyone say how he died?"

"Press release said it was a fire."

Lucy nearly dropped the phone. "They burned down his house?"

"More than likely he started it himself. And now I've got a

bunch of fish to feed. There's only so much they can expect of me just . . ."

Lucy hung up the phone and crumbled. It was true, the fake crash, she was not insane; although this was her doing. Gary was involved as a favor. And now he was dead. Someone had tracked him down, which meant someone was looking for the pictures; someone was looking for her. She wanted to go hide in her hotel room or apartment, two places she could not show her face. And that was only the first dose of bad luck.

Within an hour, Lucy lost the most desirable interview of the past decade when she was notified she had acquired a case of Nymphopucky. Unlike most infestations, this one arrived by press release—hitting her inbox, along with the inboxes of hundreds of her colleagues, informing them that newscaster Lucy Springer had come down with a serious but manageable case of the bug and would be unavailable for the Swagger interview. She had been quarantined in a bathroom at ANN headquarters and escorted out by safety-masked police officers. She was ordered to a clinic where a doctor in a preventative suit and mask went over her with a magnifying glass, suggesting she stop shouting as it would only encourage the concupiscent bugs.

"The fuckers gave me cooties!" she shouted through the phone at Dean, somewhere high up in the ANN Tower from which she had just been removed in front of pissy coworkers enjoying their office schadenfreude.

"This could be serious, Twit. People die from Nymphopucky."

"Tell me something, Dean—what happened to Ray and the other producers? Why am I speaking to you?"

"I've been advised to handle the situation."

The doctor sprayed mist on her feet, a cooling spritz that was meant to inspire fatal seizures in the masturbatory bugs. "This is important Dean, are you listening?"

"I suppose."

"Those photos. Have you shown anyone?"

"Of course not."

"Good boy." Gary was dead because of those shots.

"I know this is a bad time, but the producers asked me to inquire." He cleared his throat. "Ava. Will she be available this week? Or is she also . . ."

"Nymphopucky?"

"That."

"She's a dummy, Dean. How could she do a show without me?"

"Stunt double ventriloquist. A drone-triloquist," he explained. "It's a metal arm that manipulates Ava while the computer does the voice. We rigged it up in case you were . . . anyway, sounds just like her. I mean you."

The dummy was lying on the doctor's desk. Ava, all of them, would go on without her. For a moment she caught herself hating the puppet as though it were an actual deserving beast.

"We'll have to have Ava deloused, dry-cleaned, probably sent to a salon." She could hear Dean pout through the phone. "Everyone is pretty sore at you."

"Why are they sore at me?"

"Nymphopucky is a promiscuous disease. Lot of people worried you might have brought it into our office."

"I didn't bring it into the office."

"Like smallpox to the Native Americans."

"Stop it, Dean. This will be gone by morning."

"I say we get Ava in front of a camera, have her explain her partner is teeming with millions of masturbatory bacteria, make light of it if she can."

"Ava's not going on camera without me."

"You know, Twit, it's selfish of you to hold her hostage."

In the past year she had built a legion of disciples who followed her and the puppet religiously. After all she had been through—the celebrity affairs, the au pair pregnancies, the Cleve Peoples shenanigans—they were heading back to the anchor chair, her and the dummy. Or at least they had been. She did not need to hear it from Dean; the producers were pulling out, she knew how it worked.

"Dean, I need those photos."

"Sure, Lucy."

She stood from the examining table, which caused the doctor to back away. "What's going on, Dean?"

"We gave it a shot. But I can't risk my career, or my home, on a hunch."

"What hunch? We've got pictures."

"You mean I got pictures. And as you indicated, they're valuable."

Lucy paced; the doctor followed with the mist. "Think about Paul Newman. Think about Cool Hand Luke and rebelling against the system."

"That's just it," Dean said. "I don't want to rebel against the system. It's become cliché to rebel against the system. Everyone's rebelling. I want to conform to the system. I want to be accepted by the system. That would be the more unique approach."

"Dean, please."

"It's over, Lucy. Just give us Ava. Drop her at the dry cleaner on the corner of Twenty-fourth and Seventh. Gentle cycle. Light starch," he said. And then he was gone.

Lucy threw the old woman's phone against the wall. It exploded in a fairly unspectacular crumble. The doctor looked on sadly from his knees, where he'd been examining her feet with a magnifying glass.

"I don't find any vermin. But they're difficult to detect. Most likely they're in hibernation. The blood results were inconclusive."

"So I'm going to live?"

"The life cycle of a Nymphopucky only lasts seventeen minutes. They hibernate, in total, for about three minutes."

"I don't have Nymphopucky, Doc."

He washed his hands. "The first wave of death should be any minute. We'll see lesions, rashes, mass psoriasis, which is actually their tiny corpses flaking off."

"Sexual genocide."

"Alternately, there's a chance your epidermis is deficient in the protein keratin. Nymphopucky feed on keratin. If your skin is lacking, they would have starved to death by now. Either way we should know in twenty minutes."

"You ever seen one of these bugs yourself?"

"I think so."

"And you're certain they exist."

"I've attended conferences. People die." He was irked at the inquisition. "Incidentally, do you know how far along you are?"

"How do you mean?"

"The blood tests. You're pregnant. Just curious how far along."

She thought back to the morning nausea, in fact, a week of feeling off. She had blamed it on the crash, nerves, the anxieties her psychiatrist had been touting.

"Oh, dear."

"I thought you knew. Oh, dear," the doctor repeated. "Probably the wrong time, but I'm a huge fan of your work—would you mind signing an autograph?"

She took the pad and pencil and handed it back.

He looked on timidly. "I meant your other autograph."

Lucy glanced at Ava, who lay like a broken dwarf on the table. Gary was dead, no one to monitor whether she wore it or not. Still, she crossed the room and placed the dummy on her arm. It helped her think. Lucy blamed herself for her marriage crumbling, partly attributing it to her inability to get pregnant. After all that time, now she'd been knocked up by a dead man. Not only was it a career killer, but she could also look forward to the joy of raising the child alone. She lay on the examining table and let the doctor continue the mist, a cool and gentle sprinkle over a protein famine. She closed her eyes and thought—about bugs, birds, babies. She thought about Gary Corbin. She thought about the pilot, and that if she lived through the next twenty minutes, she intended to seek him out to learn why the father of her child was dead.

GOO GOO G'JOOB

It had become a clumsy routine; carting Lucky Dan from diner to diner; waiting for some mysterious luck to forge a plan; Normal having his face punched in, or arguing with a puppet, or another equally absurd frustration. Lucky Dan laid his head on the counter while Normal watched the television. It was all over the news—the reporter who had come down with Nymphopucky, alterations to the highly anticipated interview with Captain Hank Swagger.

"Just my luck," Dan kept telling no one. "I finally meet an interesting girl and she ends up diseased."

"Just as well." Normal snacked on a grilled cheese. "She thinks that puppet is real."

"That aside, she was perfect. And she smells like the sunrise."

"You need to pull it together."

"I feel like drinking. And I'm a tremendous lightweight."

"That sample is nearly melted, museum almost done. Tomorrow is all there is. I either get on that plane, or I get on another plane and give up."

"I'm all for giving up."

"I can't give up. She might kill Eddie."

"Eddie's ratting you out anyway."

"Hell he is."

"You know what—I don't even care. Bugs, puppets, none of it matters. That's how she makes me feel."

Lucky Dan was broken. Normal was broke. Between feeding and housing Lucky, and the endless trips to the pay phones, there was nothing left, just some spare change that lay scattered on the counter. He had tried Eddie's cell phone constantly with no answer.

If Normal had been able to stick with the semen business another five years, he would have banked enough to retire. Despite his bumbling since the Cleve Peoples disaster, he had been a natural at the occupation. He was a pioneer of the industry; what Thomas Edison was to electricity, Normal Fulk was to celebrity semen. He could have written a book on how to obtain it, preserve it, authenticate it, sell it, a generally safe career that saw little need for weapons or interactions with authorities. He had obtained some of the most valuable DNA on the planet, from the world's most illustrious sources, and he had made a lucrative business of it. But he had gotten greedy.

The big money was in dead celebrities. From the beginning Normal's instincts told him to steer clear of that end of the vocation—in the first place, why would dead celebrities freeze their semen, and second, the lengths to which people would go to obtain it. The collectors were hard-core, type of fans who hunkered down in blizzards for playoff tickets or front row concert seats, who purchased jerseys and face paint and waited in preposterous lines on the chance they might obtain an autograph. When it came to memorabilia, dead celebrity semen was a Picasso, or a Rembrandt. No one was left to create it, this fluid that held the fingerprint of a once almighty existence, which made it most valuable to those who worshipped. The business was going well until Rory caught wind of it, deciding *Semen Pirates* would make for great television.

Her birth name was Rory Glover. She became head of the Genius-Temple Management firm the old-fashioned way. Not through hard work or nepotism, but through sleeping her way to the top. (In our current era, passengers, it is nearly impossible to sleep one's way to the top of any firm, mostly because there is too much competition doing the same.)

Don Genius and David Temple were the original co-owners of the firm. She began an affair with Don Genius, only because his name was first on company letterhead. Within two years he was divorced from his second wife and married to his third, Rory Glover-Genius, who was promoted out of the secretary pool to vice president soon after. They were happily married, give or take, for four years until the ill-fated day when Don Genius wrapped his Beamer around a tree while receiving fellatio from one of the other secretaries. To the dismay of David Temple, as the wife of his late business partner, Rory was entitled to a chunk of the firm. To avoid a messy working relationship, and after the acceptable ninety-day mourning period, she married David Temple, becoming Rory Genius-Temple after dropping the Glover. It was not entirely out of the blue. She had been sleeping with him on and off for several years, and the union seemed the most financially appropriate way to honor her late husband's firm.

As fate would have it, her second husband was involved in a similar accident. Although this time he was the giver of fellatio to a youngish actor who wrapped his car around a telephone pole less than three miles from the first accident. Fortunately, it only paralyzed David Temple, which left him homebound in the couple's Malibu mansion, where Rory Genius-Temple opted to care for him all the days of his life, so long as he amended his will.

Always eager to find the next hot show, Rory set a meeting with Normal and Eddie in a hotel bar. She offered to invest in a pilot episode during which the two would steal a particular sample: that of the late writer Kurt Vonnegut. After learning of the macabre industry, Rory had done some research. The Vonnegut was stored in a glass-enclosed, subzero freezer in a Manhattan loft.

Eddie was enamored, although it was unclear if his infatuation lay with Rory or the prospect of his own television show. Normal was dubious. "This business works because of discretion. We don't broadcast that we steal semen. We don't steal the semen of dead celebrities. And we certainly don't make TV pilots."

She wrapped her red lips around an olive, severing the fruit. "Twenty grand. Just to shoot the pilot." She winked. "I'm not saying we have to do an entire season, but let's see how it looks before we hop in bed together."

Eddie was convinced; Normal shook his head.

"Listen, Normal, we got our hands in everything. I'm not talking soap opera fluff. I'm talking real, American, pop culture cinema. Ever seen the show about the church crew smuggling blind orphans over the Mexican–Arizona border?"

Eddie had seen every episode. "You produce *Blind Vision?*"

"We're producing a new show about renegade Americans who hunt down the church do-gooders and bring them to justice." She leaned, whispered. "Episode four doesn't go so well for the orphans."

"That sounds all right," Eddie said.

"Heard about the fat kids who everyone in their high school teases until the fitness trainers show up and thin them out"—she paused to answer the phone, a six-second conversation, a swill of her martini—"then back to school and they're skinny and too good for the fat friends they knew before they went on the show?"

Eddie was enjoying himself. "Sure, *Fatty Rock Star*, one of my favorites."

"We're producing a show about the people who create those fatties. The soda companies. The candy manufacturers. The laborers who work twelve-hour shifts in potato chip mills, just to support their families." She pulled her chair around the table, giving a peek at her bosom. "See, boys, for every one hundred Americans who go on diets, seven people lose their jobs. We've done the research. Crunched the numbers. Fat keeps our economy running. We're thinking of calling it *Cellulives*. Get it? Like the lives behind the cellulite?"

They both recoiled, sipped their beers.

She got down to business. "Here comes the hard sell, boys: Genius-Temple is all about touching the heart strings of America. I want to invent a channel of just reality shows—but not about the hero, which is the current state of TV. I want it to be all about the villain. Villain TV. How's that sound?"

"I like it," Eddie said.

"That's where we see *Semen Pirates* making it big."

"Come again."

"You let me manage you boys, reality television is just the beginning. I'm talking an entire industry of celebrity semen. Franchise it. Sell it on the interweb. In vending machines, like they do candy bars, or live bait down south. Hook into the Bollywood crowd—you realize India has a billion customers, all obsessed with celebrities just like we are."

"Thing of it is, Miss Genius-Temple . . ."

"Call me Rory."

"I know I'm a criminal. But I don't see myself as a villain." Normal could smell her skin, the tasteful way her bra snaked out of her shirt line. "I got Feds following me, waiting for me to make a mistake."

"Feds just want their cut. Same way with narcotics. Only reason they shoot drug dealers is because they're not getting a piece." She waved at the waiter. "I'm saying beat 'em to the punch. Put it on the tube. Sell it to the public. Then we build an industry, tax it, the Feds get paid, we get paid, fans get their semen, everyone's happy."

"Just not for me," Normal said.

"Fifty grand. Just for the Vonnegut."

"It's got to be a no."

She moved a napkin in front and placed a pen on top. "Write down a number. Room 702." She slapped Eddie playfully on the chin. "Meantime you ask the waiter for a bottle of champagne, the good stuff. Meet upstairs we three have us a pleasant fuck, seal the deal."

Much to Eddie's dismay, Normal declined the fuck. They did, however, steal the Vonnegut without letting Rory film it. But Rory Genius-Temple was no fool; she had only tipped them off about the Vonnegut to get them hooked. The money that came from dead celebrities was ten times what they could earn otherwise, and Rory knew it.

The sample of John Lennon arrived simultaneously in Normal's life with a moral compass. A month before Rory told him of its existence, a magazine with the late musician's signature sold at auction for $12,000. The iconoclastic Beatle's ejaculate would be the most valuable memorabilia, of any collector, in any industry. Rory had found an ideal buyer, an actual record company; the plot wrote itself, and would make up most of Season One. The company was releasing a massive Beatles compilation to coincide with the anniversary of the singer's assassination. It would include unreleased songs, photographs, a limerick collection from the convicted murderer—and a tiny vial of DNA, cloned on a massive scale and distributed to adoring fans, all for the arbitrary price of $89.99.

It would be the best score Normal and Eddie had ever made. The problem was Cleve Peoples, and that inconsiderate brood, and why, essentially, they were Normal Fulk's responsibility. If he stole the sample and turned it over to Rory, filmed the show as planned, Normal would turn an attractive profit. But if he disappeared, he could get out of Rory's shadow altogether and tend to his responsibilities, which he felt had resulted in a dire streak of karma.

Stealing the John Lennon was more than just a job. He grew up idolizing his older brother, who, in turn, loved the Beatle. To belittle that existence so easily created a mild crisis—to put the ability into the hands of people who would clone Lennon's DNA for profit and sell a garbled mess of memories, who would add to the mass cultural distraction by putting it all into a TV show. Just the idea that all those words and thoughts and memories could be stitched together into a cellophaned narrative and sold by the truckload. This time, in this instance, there was something Normal could do about it. John Lennon, his brother's idol, would not go down as the item du jour. He would sell it to an honest dealer, give the money to those kids, and buy himself a lifetime of karma. And, hopefully, stop trying to gauge the value of an actor's semen every time he watched TV.

TOMORROW NEVER KNOWS

It took nearly three hours of dialing, listening to Lucky Dan complain about his luck, pumping dozens of numbers into the telephone, before he reached Eddie.

"Hey there, Normal. How's kicks?"

"Eddie? You okay?"

"Why wouldn't I be?"

"Been calling. Where you at?"

"Just busy. Unloading product."

"You sold it all?"

"Mostly." Eddie was preoccupied on his end. "The Arquette went for $9,000. But can you believe it—Hasselhoff went for fourteen?"

Normal was stunned. "That's amazing, Eddie."

"I mean, Hasselhoff—who'd have thunk it?"

"That's great work. How much did we clear?"

"That's what our business was missing," Eddied continued. "Concentration on smaller scores. We got so tied up with the big ones we lost focus on what our clientele wanted."

"Eddie . . ."

"It takes too much time and reconnaissance to get the Jagger, the Cruise, the Wahlberg. We should be spreading out, going after the small guys, mixing quantity and quality."

"Eddie, stop talking." Normal hated to hear him speak. "Next, out of your mouth, the dollar amount we made."

"That's the weird thing."

"Fuck me."

"I still got the money. Only thing is—well, I don't actually have the money."

"What does that mean?"

"Our new partner is holding it." Normal knew without asking. Eddie took a bite of something obnoxious; it sounded like an apple, although Eddie did not eat fruit. "I just figured with you being dead

and all, and how irrational you've been about the John Lennon—
well, the best thing was to partner with someone who understands
how the business works. And since you died, I sort of have a controlling interest in the company."

"Listen to me, Eddie." Normal glanced at Dan, who was not
paying attention in the least. "Rory wants to film a television show.
She doesn't care what happens to you. As soon as the Feds can
prove we're trafficking semen, that's the end. You'll be indicted.
You'll go to prison."

"Stop being dramatic."

"Where are you right now?"

"Can't say. Rory doesn't think it's a good idea."

"Eddie, tell me where you are."

"See, this is why we needed a partner," Eddie said. "You get so
dramatic. And I'm not like that. We needed an ambassador."

"Rory is not an ambassador. She's a pimp."

"Take the Lennon. Something like that comes along once in a
life. And you want to give it to orphans. Then you go and lose it in
the bottom of a river."

"We need to meet. Don't let Rory know you heard from me."

"She's listening on the other line."

"Hello, Normal. Or is it George? George played well in a few
of our test markets, but something about Normal gets my spanker
rocking."

It was suddenly clear to Normal; he had drastically underestimated Eddie. Eddie had followed her up to that hotel room after
the initial meeting. They had been working together since. That
was how she always knew where to find him. That was why he kept
getting his face punched in by the sound guy.

"Eddie and I are partners now. You ended your participation in
Semen Pirates LLC when you died three weeks ago. We got it all
on tape."

"What exactly do you have on tape?"

"Like I said, all of it."

Normal thought it through. "When I was hiding out at the
motel?"

"It's not great footage, mostly you just sitting around. You masturbated twice, which was hilarious with the missing finger. You checked yourself out naked in the mirror; you're putting on some weight. And oddly enough, you pee sitting down. Out of the sixty hours we shot, we edited it down to a captivating four minutes."

"Eddie, tell me you didn't let her shoot you cutting off my finger?"

"Shot it," Rory sang. "Season One trailer."

Normal felt his rage building. "The John Lennon. It's the plot of Season One. I'll never let you have it."

"You won't have to. Not if I get to it first."

The line went dead. Normal slammed down the receiver, which caused Lucky Dan to startle.

"Time to go," Normal said. He grabbed at the last of his change pile, an insulting rattle of nickels and dimes.

"I don't much feel like going anywhere."

"I don't much give a damn what you feel like."

"Where are we going?"

He tucked two quarters into the slit. "Kidnapping a pilot."

THURSDAY

HIS RIVAL IT SEEMS
HAD BROKEN HIS DREAMS

Ricardando Hill's superpower, if it could be called that, was perseverance. Which was why on the morning his girlfriend left on a New York City–bound jet plane, manufactured in the United States no less, he packed his few belongings into a duffel bag—T-shirts, $50 in emergency funds, a .25-caliber Raven with three bullets—and set out for the far side of the country.

Unlike Mallory Swagger, his pursuit would not involve him investing the commune's hard-earned cash into the American economy. Instead, he would hitchhike, using only foreign cars of course. He damned his poor luck every time he thought about the situation. Not that he had lost his job, his girl, the respect of his fellow rebels, who were less than certain he could manage an effective revolution. But rather that he was born in such a worn-out generation. Ricardando Hill had been born in the wrong decade. He belonged in the sixties, a time when revolution was respected, when a guy like him could get laid just by claiming to be a terrorist, without having to blow things up to prove it.

To hell with it, if that's what it took. He intended to start the revolution the hard way. He had hidden a note back at the commune, in case he did not live to document his coming actions in a tell-all autobiography. The note described a reckoning, a violent tide of the people rising up and taking back this country. The steam had been hissing for decades, but now it was due to erupt. All it needed, really, was a catalyst. And he would be it. Hank Swagger was no hero. He was what had become acceptable as a hero—a branded, orchestrated mass of sainthood crammed down their throats. For a while afterward, the first ten years or so, Ricardando would be the villain. Mallory would hate him. The media would crucify him. The system would punish him. But eventually, history would recognize that he was on the side of righteousness. History was like that. It handed out kudos after it was too late.

He would head east into Idaho and Wyoming, veer slightly north for the lower Dakota then south for Iowa. After that it was a bullet for the East Coast, New York City. If things went as planned, if he found quick rides on the exchange and moved constantly, he would be in Manhattan in two days.

Out of Iowa City, he thumbed a Lexus HS 250h, which met his requirements of being both a foreign car and a hybrid. The rear bumper read SAVE THE WHALES, the driver a whiskered gentleman, a buck-forty, mid-sixties, Peter, Paul and Mary on the radio blaring in the morning, evening, everywhere. Ricardando had just hitched a ride with his future doppelgänger.

"Hop in, kid. Where you headed?"

"New York City."

"Going as far as Davenport—what do you call yourself?"

"Ricardando Hill."

"All right, Ricardando. Name's Roy, everyone calls me Windy."

They drove in silence listening to the music. "Nice rig," Ricardando said. "I like foreign cars."

"This here was built in Vietnam." Windy slapped the dashboard. "Baby gets thirty-five miles per gallon."

Ricardando smiled. "I try to only buy Third World. You fight in 'Nam?"

"Nah. Moved to Canada. But if purchasing a $45,000 automobile helps those people rebuild their economy, you can count me in."

This was exactly what Ricardando wished to become—a committed protester, a war absconder, a traitor to his country who would eventually discover a low-fat but delicious ice cream, or a brand of granola potato chip, and afford to live like a well-off hippie in his mature years, all the while criticizing the country that made it possible. Instead Ricardando had lost his job. And when he had threatened not to fight in Iraq, a nice man from the army recruitment office had told him they respected his decision, and support the troops any way you can, and kindly move your protest sign to the cordoned off picket area where they served donuts and cider. Wrong generation altogether.

The song ended and a smooth-voiced deejay reported the weather. That was followed by the news, which led off the hour with Miracle Flight AW2921.

"About time," Windy said. He turned up the volume.

It was just as Ricardando expected—Swagger described as a family man, a church man, an everyday hero who loved his country and anyone and everything. Which was the exact opposite of how Mallory described her father. They were shoveling Swagger in, smashing him out through the satellites, the televisions, the cell phones, the radio waves that found Ricardando in the front seat of a retired hippie's Lexus somewhere outside Davenport.

"You seem like a fellow who's with it, Windy. How can you listen to this crap?"

"Captain Swagger? He saved all those people. No crap about that."

"You don't mean to tell me you're buying this?"

"Man's a hero." He turned down the volume. "Exactly what this country craves—a real American cowboy, someone who takes the controls when the ship starts sinking, sets a proper course. That's what we're missing."

"He's a phony," Ricardando snarled.

Windy turned off the radio. "You and your whole generation, cynics. Back when I was your age, we disagreed about a lot—Nixon, Vietnam, whether The Doors were any good." He slowed for the shoulder. "But at the end of the day, we loved this country and wanted to see it succeed. Your generation—you just want to see it fail."

Which was true in Ricardando's case. "That's not true," he complained.

"Bet you wish that plane crashed. Killed all those people."

Also true. "Of course I don't."

"Bunch of selfish cynics," he continued.

Ricardando had enough. "Well it's better than a hypocrite driving a $45,000 car with a SAVE THE WHALES logo, talking about the war he fled and the country he adores on account of the GPS system he can afford."

"Slacker."

"Sellout."

"Generation Next—that's original."

"Baby Boomer—sounds like a fucking stroller."

"That's it!" He slammed on the brakes. "Out of my Lexus."

Ricardando climbed out and leaned in through the open door. Windy inched away. "You remember the name Ricardando Hill. Because it'll mean something soon. And you will rue the day you threw me out of this car."

Just before Windy sped away, Ricardando thought about grabbing the gun out of his knapsack and filling the Lexus full of holes. But he had only the three bullets with which he intended to take down an icon. He stuck out his thumb instead.

On the morning of the interview, Blackie Spin leaked two separate tapes: The first showed the miraculous landing from a surveillance camera located on shore, the second a sound byte of the screaming passengers as the plane careened toward infamy. The FAA condemned both and Air Wanderlust issued a press release announcing an investigation into the leaks. Nevertheless, the tapes pushed the airline into a 1:49 market, something no search term had done since the ill-fated September 11 attacks. Blackie Spin had built Swagger from a notorious pilot into a national hero, a living, breathing icon, a force of marketing ingenuity, all of which would be on display two days hence at a publicly funded museum. Now anything attached to Swagger would sell. He could peddle hand grenades on a children's playground, cigarettes in the cancer ward. A toy company had phoned that morning—they were introducing an entire line of Swagger action figures, due to hit stores in time for the holiday rush. A tourist company had purchased a fleet of amphibious buses that it intended to load with wide-eyed Midwesterners and drive directly into the Hudson, reenacting Swagger's famous dive, pictures of the sainted pilot on the exterior.

The Air Wanderlust commercial began airing that morning. They had settled on the script months before, and using video from the plane's wing, the cast had performed flawlessly. It showed the pilot and the beautiful passengers, all stranded on the wing, Wrinkles and the old woman edited out until no one seemed frustrated by the plane's locale. Patriotic music played low, the outline of the waiting metropolis in the background. As the camera whirred and zipped, and the ferries jockeyed, and the waves gently knuckled the silver exterior, white words appeared over the famed scene: "Air Wanderlust would like to extend its gratitude to the men and women of New York City for their response to the miraculous landing of Flight AW2921," and then below, the company's web site, and below that, "Coming this Saturday: The Swagger Aviation and Miracle Museum. Purchase your tickets now!"

Blackie's monitors flashed the day's news—an earthquake in the Sudan, a mumps outbreak in Brooklyn, the first video footage of the plane landing. What Blackie liked to do was turn in slow circles, scrutinize the pixelated monitors, and see if during each rotation his legend cast its shadow on one of the scenes. It validated his abilities as an expert storyteller, a spinner of tales to rival the greatest in history. Yet as he watched his legend bounce and dawdle, and he turned slowly to catch the next scene, he also mourned the fact that no one would slap his back and say job well done, that someone higher up would never understand his talents.

Just then his phone rang. He checked his board. There was nothing to indicate the phone should be ringing and he studied the incoming number. It was neither Jimmish nor Miss Dressings. The leaf on his forehead grew a hardened red outline; he sensed the day ahead intended to be raw.

"Looking for Blackie Spin."

The voice was weak, possibly a teenager. On the board, Blackie wrote "teenager," and then a downward arrow. "How may I help you?"

"Business transaction. We have something you'll be interested in purchasing."

"I'll stop you there." Blackie rushed down his board, looking for some inkling of an idea. This caller did not belong, that much was certain. "I'll need to know if it's a we, an I, or a him—do you understand the difference?"

"Not so much."

"If it's an I, that's you, and I'm confident you hold negotiating power. If it's we, there's a committee, and things can get messy. If it's a him or her, it implies you're just a messenger."

A pause on the caller's end. "It's just me."

"Let's begin with names."

"No names," the caller said.

"You said this was a business transaction. Either we use names like businessmen, or I'll assume this is blackmail."

"I have photos of the inside of that plane engine. It was no bird strike."

"There you are, young man, well put. You've stated your goals. You've described your bargaining chip. Progress."

Blackie processed his strategy. They had originally planned to stage dead birds once the plane was pulled out of the water, just before they gutted the thing and began work on the museum. To satisfy nosy eyes, dead birds were a must. A flock of Specklebelly had been obtained and Jimmish had overseen the butchery. The plane had been staged Tuesday morning, which meant if this caller was serious, there had been only a few short hours to sneak onto the docked plane and obtain photos sans the slaughtered poultry.

"I assure you, young friend, birds caused the accident."

"Let's not, Mr. Black." A moment later, Blackie's inbox dinged. "I've just sent you an e-mail with my findings including photos, a summary of what I believe occurred, and a description of the Specklebelly Goose and its habitat, which is nowhere near New York City."

Blackie opened the file. He was impressed by the caller's detail and knew in that instant this young man would be reassigned to work for him. Even his font, Garamond, 12 point, allowed the bulleted items to bounce off the screen, a note of professionalism to the blackmail document. More than that, the caller had obtained both his cell phone and e-mail, items he made public to no one. He was green, but he was not without talent.

"Well done," he said. "What type of monetary value would you assign this information?"

"Hundred thousand," the caller stated. "In unmarked bills."

"You've watched too many movies. And you've severely underestimated your data." Blackie was so impressed with his own work, he was insulted by the lowball demand. "Let's assume birds did not bring down the flight. Let's assume also, per your summary, that the crash was faked, for what reason you don't specify. This would be a conspiracy on par with the greatest our nation has ever known. You could ask for ten times that amount, one hundred times even."

"A million then," the voice said.

"So which is it? Do you want a million dollars or a hundred thousand?"

A pause. "I'll take the million."

"Very well. What time restrictions am I working under?"

"So you agree to it? One million and I make this information disappear?"

"Why wouldn't I agree? You've presented a realistic scenario that I can neither confirm nor deny, certainly something I don't want publicized. You've done so with courtesy and professionalism."

"Noon today then. Corner of Forty-third and Broadway."

"Well trafficked. I hope it's not too near your office or apartment."

"Make it Forty-ninth and Broadway."

Blackie hit a button on one of the screens and a map of Manhattan emerged. He circled a three-block radius near Forty-third and Broadway. He was certain this call originated from there; Jimmish would discover the location. "I'll need until tomorrow to gather your funds. Are you agreeable to a twenty-four-hour window?"

"Sure, why not."

"And I can trust you to keep this information quiet until then?"

"Of course."

"It's been a pleasure doing business with you. I'll be in touch."

LET IT OUT AND LET IT IN

It occurred to Blackie at some point in the past month that his protagonist had come to slightly misunderstand the roles. Mainly, that Blackie was in charge and Hank Swagger was taking orders instead of the other way around. It was important that he have the discussion with his protagonist before he left on his nationwide tour. Otherwise, the chain of command might become murky, a state Blackie hoped to avoid.

He had pulled Swagger from his sleeping family just after midnight, the pilot exhausted from the strenuous rehearsals. Blackie had taken him to the roof of the Whalensky Plaza, which looked out over the orange-lit city and all its minions of sleepers and dreamers, the gray New Jersey out beyond the blackened shade of a moonless shore. Blackie had brought a bottle of Kinclaith, Swagger's preferred Scotch.

"An actor?" Swagger asked.

"Just like your son. Or better yet, like the beast on the end of Miss Springer's hand—a puppet of sorts. And I am the fist upon which you perch. And it's best to mind the script I've prepared. Don't take it badly, but you've been hired to play a role."

"But I'm the hero."

"Partly, sure." Blackie poured them each a bit more. "Mainly, the puppet of a hero is the message I hope to convey. Do you get what I'm saying, Mr. Swagger?"

"Not so much."

"You see, life is made up of stories. I've spent the past year planning every event, every minute of your story. I've built the legend of Hank Swagger, and I can just as easily end it. And that, in a nutshell, is what I mean to suggest here: mind the script."

Swagger leaned. "You know something, Blackie. I don't care for the way you talk to me, like a toy over which you have control." He drained his glass. Blackie filled. Swagger waved it in the air. "Have you ever thought how all this affects me?"

"It's all I think about."

"All this trickery . . ."

"Trickery would be the wrong word. Good, solid storytelling instead."

". . . all this misinformation about me on everyone's gadgets and minds, all of it wrong but none of that matters because it's out there now like . . . like oxygen," he was enjoying the profound, warm frame of reference the Scotch provided, "and gravity and electricity, invisible things we cannot dispute because there's too much proof otherwise. There's a word for it."

"There should be a word," Blackie agreed.

"It's just this . . ." He stared off into the sky, into the world, the wonderful haze of the drink. ". . . this Massiveness."

"Yes, Massiveness." He clinked his glass into Swagger's. "A good word."

"I'm stuck inside it," Swagger said. "Like a character in a story-book. Like a plastic ice skater in one of those Christmas globes."

"So you do get it then, Mr. Swagger." That was it exactly, though he hated to see his protagonist upset with his role. Blackie took a sip, the slow burn working its way into his chest. "See, all of this is for you. Well, perhaps not all of it. But out of this fable you achieve more than anyone else."

"What exactly do I achieve?"

"What do you achieve?" Blackie was appalled. "We've hauled that plane out of the water. We sliced off the nose and inserted an amphitheater, your own museum."

"I don't even understand what that means. A museum holds history."

"This is history. The best kind. A miracle. It'll bring in tourists for decades."

"History takes time. You can't build no museum overnight."

"That used to be the case," Blackie said. "Nowadays it takes less than forty-eight hours to set up a respectable museum. Of course, we applied for the endowment and secured the real estate months ago, but still I'm very impressed with myself."

"I don't see the point."

"Fame. Folklore. Living forever." Blackie swirled. "The legend of Captain Henry Theodore Swagger, of the twenty-first century, when he lived and died, what he stood for. You see, we're resurrecting the myth of the American Hero for a public that not only craves it, they require it to sustain life, in the same way they require skin, or blood."

"You're drunk."

"Tell me—you've heard the names Vishnu, Zeus, Apollo, Jesus, Poseidon, haven't you?"

"Those are gods."

"Those are storybook characters."

"You don't believe in the gods?"

"Of course I believe in the gods. I believe in thousands of gods—wind gods and sun gods and sea gods and me gods and night gods and now plane gods. But not out of any spirituality. I believe in them because they make great stories, great characters."

"I never chose to be your god."

"That's why I brought you up here tonight, Mr. Swagger, to explain: You don't get to choose. I put you on that plane. I put you on this roof. I put you in front of those cameras tomorrow, and all those televisions and computers and cell phones, and it's because of that you will live forever, a digital-age god."

Swagger finished his Scotch. "You must understand what this is like for me—all the responsibility, all this Massiveness."

"I suppose I don't understand at all. I'm nothing like you, Mr. Swagger." Blackie grabbed the bottle and poured them each another finger. Then he leaned in and, just before he spoke, let out a growl, low and heavy from deep in his gut, but enough that Swagger understood it was a growl. "I am what I am, and you are what you are. I created you. I control you. So tomorrow, when you get in front of those cameras, do what I built you to do. And mind the fucking script. Are we clear?"

Swagger drained his Scotch. "We're clear, Blackie."

But the charming detail, passengers, and the one thing that made Swagger Swagger was his inability to mind the script. And he was about to do so in the most outstanding way.

SPEAKING WORDS OF WISDOM

When the Swaggers sat down opposite Matt and Ann on the *Today* show, and smiled out into the sunny and waiting world, and patted one another with the kind of genuine patronage that comes only from family; when Mipsy placed a hand on her husband's, the two gazing fondly at each other, and not even a fake gaze; when Nate and Mallory leaned in, he in the rented suit, the velvet box on his lap, she in a white dress, her face painted with makeup made in Maryland, and shared sibling humor that caused them to giggle in the most utterly natural manner; when the cameramen and stage hands and even the producers and the girl running coffee took in the scene and reflected on their own lives, their own families, how good and decent life could be—Blackie Spin, from the bowels of the studio, put his left hand inside his right and smiled. It did not matter about his blackmailer, or what the passenger George Bailey had done to poison his plot. No one could argue with this vision of the Swagger family, a goddamned American tale. They could not keep their hands off one another—smiling and touching, touching and loving, tilting heads to admire the hell out of one another, earning every inch of the paycheck.

And then there was Swagger. He had nine items on him, all from sponsors: the suit, a scarf, a white-collared shirt, cuff links, Italian shoes, socks he showed off by keeping one leg bent over a knee, a wristwatch, a cup of Munch Brothers coffee, and an arbitrary 3-in-1 digital weather reading/tip calculator/stapler that was to be his lucky trinket. The gadget was the prize; the sponsor had paid handsomely to ensure Swagger mentioned it as his lucky trinket at least three times on the *Today* show, tell the world that he'd had it in his jacket on the plane, a gift from his children for Father's Day, that he had touched it for sentimental reasons as he glared into the black waves. These gadgets would go quickly, every middle-aged man in America updating himself on the weather twice an hour, calculating the proper tip, stapling the shit out of things. The company had ordered a shipment from Malaysia at $3.15 each; they would retail for $29.99, the same item *the* Captain Hank Swagger used, at a ridiculous profit of $7 million this year alone.

By all appearances, Blackie's pep talk had done the trick. Of course, Swagger was dying inside, Blackie knew, weeping over his dark soul, over the Massiveness. But outside he glimmered as he drifted out into America, out through the cameras and web videos and cellular phones and the small scrolling text at the bottom of screens, and he answered every question Matt and Ann asked with a prepared dignity that made Blackie's bald head tingle.

On the crash landing: "Pilots train for these situations. That's why flying continues to be the safest transportation we have. And Air Wanderlust employs the safest flight methods in the world."

On being a hero: "I'm no hero. Our soldiers fighting over-seas—those are heroes. My son there's a hero. Our teachers who get up everyday at five o'clock and head to work—heroes. I'm just a regular Joe . . ." Laughing, and then Mipsy laughing, and the children laughing. ". . . me in this suit, which the folks at Macy's were gracious enough to help with, and this Heffermeier scarf—imagine, me, in a Heffermeier—all for doing my job."

On what's next: "Couldn't say, Ann. Just put my faith in the ol' Lord, and along with my wife and kids, we'll see what the Lord bringeth."

On rumors he would be traveling the country giving speeches: "Don't know, don't know. Just a regular old fella, from a regular old town. Member of the Bethlehem Baptist Church in Scranton, where I'm famous for the pancake breakfast on Sundays. About as famous as I plan to be."

On being given the keys to the city: "Quite an honor, have to say. Mayor Cromberg and all New Yorkers been superb hosts this week."

And right before Matt and Ann broke for commercial, Swagger interrupted and asked if perhaps they could all bow their heads, a prayer not just for any one group or condition, but rather a prayer for all humanity, and all humanity to come, and would it be possible for viewers from across all faiths to synchronize their litanies?

It was not a part of the script, nothing Swagger and Monica had rehearsed; he just winged it, and even Blackie got caught up in the drama, bowing his own head.

When it was over, Swagger kissed his wife hard and wet. He tousled The Nathan's hair and hugged The Mallory. He slipped several twenties into each of their palms and bid them farewell. Swagger had interviews lined up all morning—CNN, ANN, CBS, ESPN, MTV, ABC, BBC, and the Food Network, the next one not for another ninety minutes. Monica Dressings was in charge of getting him to his next interview, and when she was tied up with a phone call, Swagger slipped out of the studio onto the street. He removed the scarf and handed it to a homeless man, which gave him a burst of anonymity, the morning air crisp in his lungs. Then he went off script for good.

HAPPINESS IS A WARM GUN

Something was wrong.

Something had been wrong all week. Blackie could sense the error in the raw leaf-shaped birthmark that burned hotter and redder. Something had not gone as planned, or would soon not go as planned, and the anticipation of the error cursed him with the grinning grip it held over his mood. He thought the approaching error might have been Swagger, although he had to hand it to the pilot—he had performed flawlessly today. It might have been the blackmail call from earlier in the day, or his suspicious assistant, or his born-again nephew, or the reporter nosing around, or even the strange passenger. Instead it was a deeper flaw, an unpreventable blemish, something inside the marrow of his tale that would blossom and thrive until . . . well, until Blackie Spin got a hold on his story.

He would be the first to concede that his methods of persuasion were oftentimes outside the acceptable parameters of the law. But his quest was one of goodness, decency even. It was not the actor with the chiseled jaw, snorting thousands' worth of cocaine a week he was hoping to perpetuate; it was the character that actor played on the big screen, the war hero, the astronaut, the victor who saved the day. There was an America out there full of empty factories and broken dreams, polluted lakes and godless cheaters. Then there was an America of courage and wisdom and ninth-inning heroics, where Supreme Beings coaxed the best out of their people, an America that still believed heroes roamed the dusty plains and when the chips were down their cunning bravado would gurgle and erupt, a rusty geyser. And he just wanted to give that to them. There were no stories left to tell, no unique plots to weave into suitable narratives that could be formatted for handheld electronic readers. The great wars had been fought, the mythic voyages complete, the victors settling into their homelands. All the tragedies and comedies had been put to paper, everything just a retooling of the past. Except when Blackie spun a story. Then it was new. Then it was real.

He dropped into the backseat of an idling car.

"How was the show, sir?"

"It was, Jimmish."

"Shall I circle back after I drop you, keep an eye on Mr. Swagger?"

"That won't be necessary. Miss Dressings will chaperone."

He handed Jimmish a sheet of paper:

Caller, early twenties, sharp
$1 million for pictures disputing a bird strike
Call originated near Forty-third and Broadway

"Someone was on our plane."

"When was this?"

"The time is irrelevant. It's in the past is all that matters."

Blackie watched the sidewalk. A vendor huddled beneath his makeshift shop, a metal cart on wheels, an umbrella. He held his hands over his oven, rubbing them to generate dexterity in the morning shiver. In the street, an unshaven priest blessed the passing taxicabs, waving a silver wand that left drops of water on soiled windshields that drivers erased with wipers. Blackie was often unsettled when he was outside. He preferred the world from the comfort of his office. The monitors and his large board allowed him to participate in the chaos from a blissful distance. It was not ignorance he desired—ignorance of the world's problems, and its heartaches, and its sadness. Rather it was omniscience, the ability to see all, and feel sympathy, and hopefully improve it. This was his service to humanity—to give them a character, and to show them what they were capable of.

"The stranger from the plane, Jimmish. His bag."

Jimmish handed the bag into the backseat. There were papers that belonged to a George Bailey, a wristwatch, a silver tube that was heavy but seemingly empty. Blackie twisted off the top. It emitted a puff of smoke. It seemed to contain some type of liquid nitrogen insulation. He was careful as he reached inside with a handkerchief, extracted a small vial he held up to the window.

"It's half frozen," he said. "What do you suppose?"

Jimmish watched in the mirror. "Medicine maybe?"

"I don't think so." He shook it. "Whatever it is, I believe it to be valuable."

"How can you tell?"

"Because there is a glitch that I am not able to discover, Jimmish. It's been there for some time. I suspect this man has something to do with it. I suspect this is the reason."

Blackie watched the Swagger interview from his phone. It had made its way from the studio, through cables and satellites, into a prosperous signal that streamed into televisions and computers, and eventually into the backseat of his car heading down Fifth Avenue. The pilot looked better on television with the makeup and the proper angles illuminating his jaw.

"My characters, Jimmish."

"Yes, sir?"

"They are behaving however they choose, a sign of an amateur." Blackie squeezed his hands into two fists. "Sadly, we've come to the part of the tale when characters must be forced to behave. You will use that gun, Jimmish. And you will use it before this week is out."

His henchman did not speak, just followed the car in front.

"Let's begin cleaning up our plot. This morning's caller. He has information that belongs to me. And I suspect he has valuable talents I can utilize."

"What about Mr. Bailey? Shall I arrange a meeting?"

He wiggled the vial, awed at what might be inside. "Whatever this is, it's become a central force in my tale. It was irresponsible of me to have removed it from its home. Put it back on the plane where Mr. Bailey left it. I'm certain he'll find me when he needs me."

HELP

As soon as she saw Blackie depart the television studio, Monica Dressings placed a call to headquarters. She typed in the various codes and waited for the voice.

"Tuff. Go ahead."

"It's V. You near a television?"

"I'm watching. We're all watching."

"By the time you get around to doing anything he'll be on Letterman."

"Calm down, V."

"He crashed a plane. Now the pilot is being interviewed on the *Today* show, and the Bureau is investigating baseball players."

"I told you. We're off steroids. More than likely we'll have to pull you off the Wanderlust case." He paused for her to inquire; she did not. "What I'm about to tell you is classified, V."

She peered through the studio. Swagger was wearing a red scarf, which should have made him easy to detect. She could not find him anywhere.

"We believe someone is trafficking stolen celebrity semen."

"Like I give a shit."

"Could be a foreign agency, al-Qaeda, the Iranians. It's a matter of national security."

"Why is it a matter of national security?"

"Don't you get it? America's greatest natural resource is celebrities. We produce more celebrities than any other country in the world, roughly three of every five on the planet. And if our information is correct, someone is trying to exploit them."

"Exploit them how?"

"Clone them maybe. Celebrities could be the next arms race, like missiles were in the eighties."

She had the urge to punch. Anything really, something firm, a malleable meat. "For what reason would someone clone celebrities?"

"We don't know. And the not knowing is what's most terrifying.

We can imagine a lot of things. In fact, we've got a team of fifty agents right now sitting around imagining. It's the things we haven't been able to imagine that worry us." He let loose a dramatic sigh. "Like September 11th. We never imagined the terrorists would fly planes into our buildings. But what did they end up doing?"

Monica chuckled, which her boss mistook for weeping.

"I know, I know. It's hard to know what the enemy is up to. Do you realize what would happen if Hollywood went belly up?"

She noticed something strange in the crowd. "Tuff, I have to go."

"Like a domino effect, the rest of our economy would tank. First mass media. Then telecommunications. Before you know it, kiss the manufacturing industry good-bye."

She had been searching the studio. It was not like Swagger to leave without her. He was petrified lately of large crowds. He had been drinking every chance his anxiety consumed him and would certainly find a bathroom, or a janitorial closet, to take a nip. A slightly buzzed Swagger was a horny Swagger, and with his day of interviews that was the last thing she needed. Instead of the pilot, her eyes found a familiar face, only without the sidekick. The odd reporter had come down with a case of the imaginary infestation, a press release Monica had distributed herself. The reporter's presence could mean only one thing—she knew about the crash.

"Advertising industry, Christmas specials, telethons . . ."

"I'm hanging up now, Tuff."

"Damn it, V, this is important!"

"Look, I don't understand a thing you're saying. I've spent the last three years investigating a madman. And you're telling me I might be pulled off my assignment because of celebrity jizz?"

"You took an oath, V. As an agent in the Bureau, you took an oath . . ."

"I took an oath to do important work."

". . . to defend this country against terrorists seeking to undermine our way of life."

"Frankly, it sounds like pornography."

"Let me ask—if you found out some scum was kidnapping millions of children, what would you do?"

"Come on, Tuff."

"Now say instead of regular children, it's millions of celebrity children."

"Oh, dear."

"And instead of real children, let's say it's the seeds of celebrity children."

"You're fucked, Tuff. We're all fucked."

"We're in the business of saving lives. And sometimes the lives we're saving are the lives that don't exist yet. We need to anticipate."

"I hate you right now. I really hate you."

"Think about the children, V—you want them to grow up in a world without action heroes and romantic comedies and Cleve Peoples films?"

"God forbid."

"I want you to think about something," he said. "When you go home tonight and lie on your couch, and you have access to thousands of premium and pay-per-view channels brimming with the planet's greatest talent, ask yourself—do I want to live in a country where these basic freedoms are compromised?"

"Good-bye, Tuff."

When she hung up, Lucy Springer was gone. At the moment, she had forgotten entirely about Swagger.

The most painful affirmation of his failures as a criminal was when Normal had to borrow the money to rent the kidnapping vehicle. Lucky Dan refused to lend it to him. Lucky knew if he did not loan Normal the money, he would have to go to Lucy, the only person irrational enough to go along with a ridiculous plot to kidnap the famed pilot. Normal had agreed, provided Lucky promised not to flirt. It had to be business, strictly kidnapping.

"You don't rub your hands through her hair," Normal had warned him in the wee hours of Thursday morning, outside the hospital where their financial support had been quarantined. "You don't talk about feelings. You don't tell her about your ex-girlfriend. And don't you mention the puppet at all."

"I can be a professional when I need to be."

They had tracked down Lucy the night before and rented the van, which they parked on the street outside the Whalensky. Normal had provided pizza and beer with his remaining cash, a peace offering to Lucy for funding the venture. Despite his best efforts, she refused to tip a few, sulking in the backseat as far from him as possible.

"Have a beer," Normal said. "You'll feel better."

"I don't want a beer."

"One can is all I'm saying. Good luck to toast before a job."

"I'm not thirsty, thank you."

Normal turned toward the back and honed in on Lucky's smile. "See what I mean? I try to be nice and this is what I get."

"Steady now, boy."

"I don't want a beer. Nothing personal."

"But why don't you want it?" He was shouting now, his arm itching, feeling preposterous that his peace offering had faltered. He did not like the puppet—that was true enough. But he hated the idea of being in cahoots with a business partner who did not like him, especially during a kidnapping. "Give me one reason why you can't drink a friendly beer?"

"I'm pregnant."

Lucky quickly guzzled his beer and tossed it toward the rear, grabbing the can in Normal's extended hand and popping the top. Normal squinted into the backseat. "Pregnant?"

"Yes, pregnant."

"But how?"

She tipped her chin toward Lucky. "The semen pirate wants to know how it happened?"

"He doesn't care for that term."

"You of all people should know how it works."

"I know how it works." Normal faced the front. "Just meant, well, I'm sorry."

"How do you know this wasn't planned?"

"I'm going to stop talking now."

So none of them talked, and Normal watched the lobby, and Lucky did everything in his mental capacity not to speak to or hug or coddle Lucy, who he was certain had not planned any pregnancy. It was impossible for Lucky not to speak every few minutes, the words building up in his mind until they threatened to erupt in a mad flood.

That morning Normal was the only one awake when the black car arrived. The sky marshal drove. He opened the door for a youngish woman in black boots and oddly shaped glasses, who disappeared inside the hotel. They spent the morning following the Swagger family—first to a restaurant, then a long route up the West Side Highway, what days before had been the scene of the miracle, and eventually to the new museum, a tubular building that took up four city blocks. Now they were sitting outside the *Today* show studio, waiting for Swagger to emerge and then they would . . . well, then they would do more of nothing. Swagger would head to the next interview and they would sit in the van and wait.

Despite the alleged Nymphopucky, Lucy still had the credentials that mattered. She had left the puppet in the van and worked her way inside the studio. The plan—or rather, what was passing for the plan—was to keep close to Swagger, wait for an opening and then force or persuade him into the van. Lucy had provided walkie-talkies that erupted in static each time Normal tried to speak. They were going to kidnap Swagger and do what with him exactly? Use him as a bargaining chip? Beat out of him a confession? It lacked the vital ingredients of an actual plan—namely method, strategy, goal.

Normal was discouraged. Lucky Dan was unhinged from the speechless night.

"My this is exciting you and me on a mission do you know what I typically do is walk around casinos with old rich men while they roll dice or flip cards or try to guess numbers"—halfway through he picked up the abandoned Ava Tardner and placed it on his arm—"sometimes they're at it six seven twelve hours with no supper breaks although they buy me drinks but I don't hold my liquor so well on account of my talking."

"Calm down, Lucky. Let's just sit."

Lucky tried to sit. "I feel for her, you know?"

"Sure."

"Psychiatrist dead. Career in shambles. Now she's to be a single mom."

"Let's concentrate on this job, whaddya say?"

Lucky tried to concentrate. "I better tell you what's on my mind."

"You don't need to, really."

"You of all people should know. This is important."

"Keep it to yourself, Lucky."

The street was busy with the morning commute, passersby ignoring the van. "I'm going to do it, Normal. I'm going to accept responsibility for this child and raise it as my own."

"Don't want to know about it. Not your responsibility besides."

"They're all our responsibility—you and me and all the rest." Lucky waved the puppet toward the windshield. "These children, new and old, all belong to each of us."

"I said keep it to yourself." Normal was edgy. "You intend to handle it, handle it next week after we're through."

"Like you and those orphans. They're not your responsibility. But somehow you knew—that was your mission." Lucky Dan worked the puppet's mouth open. "Well, this mission belongs to me. And I intend to honor it."

"What are you doing?" Normal asked. "The dummy. Put it down."

Lucky glanced at his wrist. "Will you look at that? Didn't even realize."

"Take it off. And stop talking. It makes me nervous."

"Give me a minute now. I want to get a feel for it." He manipulated the neck until the dummy glanced around at its surroundings. "Watch this, Normal." He made it wink.

"Take it off, Lucky."

"I rather like it. Know what—soon as we settle this business, I'm getting my own."

"You're going to walk around with a puppet on your arm?"

"Could be the next big trend."

"That's ridiculous."

"It ain't at all. Look at the way people carry phones. Imagine walking around with a little Normal on your paw. And whenever life gets confusing or you just feel lonely, you and little Normal can work it out." Lucky manipulated the dummy. "Why don't you like me, Normal?"

"Lucky, I asked you to stop."

He moved the puppet close. "But I have to know. When I don't understand things it makes me crazy. What's the deal with you and me? Do I bother you?"

Before Normal could settle the conflict internally, he lurched forward and punched Lucky Dan's wrist, pummeling the dummy and sending Lucky against the door. Lucky came around and righted the doll, only to discover an eyeball was missing, a puppet cyclops.

"Now look what you did."

"I asked you to stop. Didn't I ask?"

"Never hit a lady. And you knocked out her eyeball."

"Put it in the backseat like I said."

"Ohdearohgollyohgosh." Lucky did as told, the freakish doll looking up at him from the rear seat with one eye. "This isn't good, Normal. She's going to be sore."

"It's a doll. It'll be fine."

"How could you punch a doll? Don't you feel ridiculous?"

Normal did feel ridiculous. On top of that he had not caught sight of Rory and the camera crew in some time; when he could not see her, that was when he was certain he was being filmed. They probably had it on tape—him beating up a doll. He was only slightly relieved when the walkie-talkie buzzed.

"You in position? Over."

"Go ahead."

"He's on his way out," it gurgled. "He's alone. Over."

"No security?" Normal asked.

"No security, no wife. Coming out the side door. Over."

Normal fired the ignition, fidgeting. It was not like they could just snatch Swagger off the street. There would be publicists, paparazzi, more than likely a police escort parading him to his next interview. By Normal's thinking if Lucky Dan could be counted on for anything, then perhaps his presence would open up a small fissure in the universe, a gentle opportunity for luck, and they would get their Swagger and be off.

Suddenly, a side door opened. Normal knew it was him instantly, the man he had spoken to on the plane. No paparazzi, no security. The pilot looked around at the day, inhaling heartily, and checked his coordinates. He undid a red scarf and passed it to a homeless man who was hoping for a few dollars instead.

"There he is," Normal said. "Just how we talked. You know what to do."

"You're supposed to say, 'Over and out.'"

"What?"

"When you sign off on a radio—you're doing it all wrong."

"Who gives a shit, Lucky? He's walking. Get out and follow him."

"A solid kidnapping is in the details. And you can't even get the basics down." Lucky fell into his hands. "You know, I think you're making the right decision, killing off Normal Fulk and becoming George Bailey. You're just not cut out for the criminal life."

Normal pulled out his gun. "Get out and follow Swagger."

"You can't shoot me. We're on a mission for orphans."

Normal pointed the gun into the backseat. "Get out of the van or I put two in the doll."

"You wouldn't."

"I wouldn't shoot you. But I'd shoot that puppet in a heartbeat."

Lucky Dan stretched his hands. "I just want to mention it. You are aiming a fully loaded weapon at an inanimate doll. You realize that, don't you?"

"Geezus fuck Lucky. All you have to do is buy him a drink. One drink. Stick this in it." Normal handed him a small, white pill. "He'll get drowsy. Then offer to get him a cab. We'll be outside."

"Guns, drugs, one-eyed puppets." He glanced out the window for Lucy, hoping she might intervene. "And how am I to persuade him to join me in a pub at this hour?"

Normal slammed a fist into the dashboard. "Go to a coffee shop. Go to a diner. Buy him a chocolate milk. Just make it happen."

Mayor Susan Cromberg had watched the *Today* show interview from the backseat of a taxpayer-funded sport-utility vehicle headed to the offices of Veiltality Inc. Monday had been the most confusing day of her tenure as mayor. Upon hearing that a plane had crashed into the Hudson, she had scattered all the emergency personnel to the city's West Side, expecting a body count that would hit triple digits before the morning commute was over. From an emergency preparedness point of view, planes did not choose water landings because it was the most dangerous option. The surrounding infrastructure had been designed with empty fields and nearby runways in case any of the thousands of flights that took off daily from the three major airports experienced trouble.

Upon learning there were additional water ferries that had been rented by a private entity for sightseeing, Mayor Cromberg was not as pleased at the coincidence as she was suspicious. She was skeptical of miracles, skeptical of who benefitted most from them. While she spent the morning at press conferences discussing a topic about which she was very much in the dark, she had her aides track down the necessary information. What was Air Wanderlust's financial situation? A background check on Captain Hank Swagger. Most importantly, what publicity firm, if any, had the airline hired? When the answers came back—bad, strange, Veiltality—Mayor Cromberg knew: The City of New York had been bamboozled. And then there was the museum, the funds for which had been approved by her office without her knowledge. It was perfectly Alastair Black.

She was familiar with the history and talents of the firm's founder. She knew firsthand of what he was capable. She had hired his firm during an ugly budgetary glitch, a mismanagement of funds that would not only have doomed her rise through the Republican ranks, but also would have earned her a stint in a minimum security prison for embezzlement. The city had lacked the money to pay for the repair of municipal roads and subways; the wrong people were asking the right questions about where the money had gone. Blackie Spin had been brilliant—too brilliant, as far as she was concerned—inventing both a disease and an industry to eradicate it. He was greedy without being improper about the whole thing, giving the city a cut when the caper proved more fortuitous than he had imagined. All the potholes below Ninetieth Street had been filled with Nymphopucky money, several miles of rail replaced, a dozen buses added to the city's fleet. The truth was he was a madman, a legitimate and contributing member of New York's power elite, but a madman all the same.

Still, she would have gladly worked with him on the Air Wanderlust escapade. Her latest poll numbers were not as strong as they should have been. She could have used a boost. She did not consider Alastair Black a friend, but he certainly was not an enemy. Through the years he had requested favors and she had granted them, mostly because she was scared of what might happen if she refused. But something like this—she should have been told.

Two hours after the plane hit water, she had arrived at the Whalensky Plaza with her aides. She had taken a separate elevator to the penthouse suite, alone with Alastair Black.

"What the fuck, Blackie?"

"What the fuck to you as well, Mayor."

"You crash a plane in one of my rivers and don't think to tell me?"

"I figured you were busy with the reelection campaign."

He ate a tomato while she fumed. "May I ask what this is about?"

"You may not."

"You dumped a jet in a New York City waterway." She stabbed a finger into her suit. "My turf, Blackie."

"Divers are fishing it out. We'll be out of your hair in a week's time."

"I won't let them. One call I have fifty officers on it."

"Have you been watching the news?" He grinned. "Every police agency within ogling distance is on the scene. I catered a breakfast for them on Pier 45."

She knew it was true. If he wanted her help, she would already be providing it. "Blackie, I need this. You want me to beg?"

He took her in humorously as the elevator reached its destination. "You world leaders and your begging. It makes me sad to think we were once collaborators."

Once inside the room even the pilot had not acknowledged her. He had not stood from the bed to greet her, the mayor of New York City, a resourceful, conniving bitch when she needed to be. He had sat with a drink and a puppy on his lap, watching montages of her city on the television. But Susan Cromberg did not become mayor of the world's most absurd city by playing dead. Maybe Blackie occupied a slightly more elevated rung than she did. But there were others higher up the food chain, others who were aware of Alastair Black and his eccentric talents, who would keep the little shit in line. And now she would deliver the message.

She arrived at the Veiltality offices and took the elevator to the top floor. She was buzzed in and moved past the receptionist who tried to slow her with small talk; she knew where she was headed. The monitors and bulletin board were as she remembered. The only new item was a miniature model of the city's infrastructure that had been pushed off to a corner.

Blackie ate a tomato, his legs crossed on the table. "Mayor, always a delight."

She tossed an envelope on his desk which he worked open with one hand. The bulletin board was filled with names and times, information crossed out, circled, arrows connecting it all. She got the gist. A man like Blackie Spin was so slimy, you either hired someone to shoot him in the head, or you tipped your hat to his talents and hoped he befriended you. She wanted to be friends.

"How far have you read?" she asked.

"Still looking at the pictures."

"Let me summarize." She sat on the edge of his desk. "You are the subject of a three-year investigation by the FBI. A special unit that hunts domestic terrorists."

"I'm just a publicist." He held up his hands innocently. "I consult with important people. Like mayors. They tell me their problems, I disguise them."

"Save it, Blackie." She turned the envelope. "You've got a snitch. I'm going to make it work to my advantage."

Blackie switched one of the monitors, which should have been airing the second of the Swagger interviews. Instead they were speaking with a Kansas couple, a topic which Blackie could not discern—they either owned a sandwich with Jesus's face on it, or their kid was missing. Why were they filling precious airtime with canned crap? A snitch. The idea should have scared him. There had always been something off about his assistant. Now he understood. She would not be eligible for reassignment, of that he was certain.

"What do you want?" Blackie asked.

"First, I want you to acknowledge that you should have told me you were crashing a plane in my river."

"Everyone takes things so personally. Did you ever think perhaps this has nothing to do with you?"

"You built a museum on the city's dime. We go back, Blackie."

"Fine. I apologize for not including you in the huddle."

She leaned forward. "Second, you'll have Swagger on a plane for Washington first thing Monday morning. He's to be a guest of the president's for a publicity appearance."

Blackie laughed. "See there—you got greedy. Swagger is a commodity. Why would I lend him out to the president?"

"Because I told the president you would. And in turn, the president intends to stump for me this election."

"What's my angle?"

"Your dream shot." She leafed through the envelope, producing the necessary documents. "They're creating a post. You'll be the government's minister of strategy."

"What kind of strategy?"

"Whatever strategy is needed. Pretty much what you do now. Only bigger. And crueler. And higher stakes. And a salary and budget that trumps most countries' entire net worth."

Blackie glanced at the pages. "You're discussing a cabinet position?"

"More of an advisory role."

He was giddy. "A CIA advisory role?"

"Not exactly." She tapped the folder. "It's not CIA. It's not FBI. You don't report to anyone. Or have anyone tell you what to do. Except you do report to someone. And they do tell you what to do. And when they tell you, you do it."

Blackie leaned back and studied his monitors; he was being reassigned. He was impossible to surprise, and Mayor Cromberg had just done the impossible. He tried to remember if he liked Susan Cromberg. There were so many politicians and authorities he had to haggle with in his line of work, they all seemed the same. He decided he did not necessarily dislike her, which he supposed was nearly the same as liking her.

"And you have the authority to offer this?"

"I'm not offering it, Blackie. It's done."

"What if I say no?"

Now she laughed. "You don't get it. Neither you nor I have a say. You'll go to jail. I'll lose my job. The whole thing will come out about Nymphopucky and how you're the greatest liar in the world. We'll go down as an infamous duo. They'll write books about us. We'll never be forgotten."

She was right, of course. Partially anyway. Truth was no one on the planet could do his job with the same fluency, the same precision, and results. Now someone higher up had the goods on him and had taken notice, just as he had always wanted. He would influence international policy. He would swim with the sharks, except he would be the biggest, hungriest, angriest shark, and everyone else would know it. He would do it his way even if he had hundreds of spooks telling him something else.

"Thank you for your time, Mayor Cromberg."

"Always a pleasure." She headed for the door. "One last thing. I'll be standing next to Swagger when he clips the ribbon at the museum on Saturday. I'm sure this goes without saying, but can I assume there are no loose ends?"

"Of course, Mayor Cromberg. What could possibly go wrong?"

Swagger had found a bar by the time Lucky caught up to him. Mack's Corner was not even on a corner, a brick and rust pub crammed between a Chinese takeout and a vacant building. The red light in the M had been broken or ignored, so that the store-front read "ack's" above a mustard-colored paint, the type of place that was open at nine o'clock on a Thursday morning. Inside a half-dozen patrons nursed stale beer out of lukewarm mugs. They lifted their eyes when Swagger walked in, then tenderly returned to the swill.

"Round of drinks on the house." This perked everyone and Swagger shoved a hand into the barkeep's, wet from dishwater. "Call me Swagger. Whatever you're pouring, Mack."

"Name's Dale. Mack's in jail." He poured a soupy mug and slammed it against the bar. "You really buying these deadbeats a drink?"

"Sure as shit."

"Need the money up front."

Swagger laid a hundred-dollar bill on the bar. "Keep 'em coming till that runs dry. Then we'll see what else we got in the pocket."

That won over the bartender and he even ventured some coins for the jukebox. The other patrons fixed their dirty hair and sat a little straighter. Lucky Dan arrived just in time to see everyone raise their glasses. It occurred to him the revelry was not meant for him, but for Swagger, and he took a stool to the captain's right.

"Dale, a beer for our new friend." Swagger shoved a paw. "Hank. You call me Swagger."

"Dan O'Malley good to know you call me Lucky Dan or just Lucky."

"Look at that, Swagger and Lucky. Sounds like a children's book."

"That it do." They knocked mugs. "Say, you wouldn't happen to enjoy barroom competitions, would you?"

The corners of Swagger's mouth ached for his ears, a wide swath of tooth aimed at a new ally.

"What I like to do is open the bar door see." Lucky walked to the door and showed what he meant. "Then we bet on women's names when they pass. Nothing vulgar of course. What do you say? Quarter a pop?"

Swagger nodded intensely. This was the type of character he preferred to his wife and children, even his mistress, the kind with whom he could spend an entire day in a sawdust room. "Make it a buck."

They turned to survey the sidewalk. From Dan's perspective, Swagger was seated slightly in front. In order to watch the door, he had to occasionally turn his back on his drink, allowing Lucky Dan to insert the pill when the time was right. It was the tail end of the morning rush hour, which gave them an abundance of women to choose from, many moving past the door so quickly they only got out a "Hey there!" before they settled into their drinks to talk strategy.

"What do you think, Swagger?"

"Let's go with a fatty first."

"I don't care for that term. I prefer plump."

"Compromise with husky?"

They knocked mugs and Swagger walked to the door for a recruit. She hesitated at first, a mid-morning barroom named "ack's" full of men. Then she recognized Swagger and gawked, stopped, blushed, giggled.

"My dear, would you mind stepping inside? Pal and I got a bet."

"Okay I guess."

"Get you a drink?"

"I'm late for work."

"Another beer," Swagger called to Dale. "What'll you take, Luck?"

Lucky studied the girl. "Looks like a Sandy to me."

"I'll go with Gretchen. How 'bout her, Gretchen? What do they call you?"

"My name's Nicole."

"Call it a draw. Wouldn't you say, Luck?"

And so, passengers, this type of nonsense went on nearly two hours, the show terribly exciting to the other patrons who had not seen so many women inside Mack's in years. Besides that they were drinking for free, and when the first hundred ran out, Swagger replaced it with a fresh bill and told the bartender to fetch the snacks. At one point, an intense young man barged in and insisted on an autograph from the pilot. He ordered a beer but never drank it, which pissed everyone off suspiciously, at which point the barkeep told him to hike. Every so often one of the women they plucked off the street recognized Swagger, and they had to stop for a photo.

"I have a confession," Lucky Dan said. He knew he'd had too much to drink, which more often than not meant trouble. But he had not been permitted to speak the night before, his mind overloaded—Lucy and the pregnancy and the mission—and he was riding the excitement of the past week. It had been spectacular—Normal Fulk, the criminal underworld, the stakeout with a beautiful woman and her puppet. He could feel his luck returning even though it had not returned at all; he had guessed approximately none of the women's names, precisely because the only woman he thought about was Lucy. "I knew who you were the minute I came in the door," Lucky confessed.

"You came in to see me?"

"Kind of a funny story actually." He smiled to indicate how funny a story it was. "You might find this peculiar—heck, I wouldn't even mention it if we hadn't gotten along so swell—but I'm the front man in a plot to kidnap you."

The bartender glanced down. Swagger leaned in for more. He loved to spend a day drinking and telling lies, and he had run into someone with a propensity for the same. "You don't say."

Lucky placed the white pill on the bar. "Supposed to get you looking the other way then slip this in your drink." He continued laughing, and Swagger laughed a bit, and the bartender glared. "But then we got talking and I said to myself, 'Luck, you don't know what this pill might do.' You turned out to be such a sharp-dressed fellow I decided no way in heckfire."

Swagger picked up the pill and sniffed it. He threw it in his mouth and washed it down. "I take these when I fly to steady my nerves." He knocked Lucky's mug, excited. "Now what?"

Lucky looked out the open door. "You know what? I don't even know. I suppose you're supposed to get drowsy, and I'm supposed to help you into a cab. Except instead of a cab, we're going to throw you into a van."

"Just like the movies."

"Just like the movies. Now listen up because this is the gist of what I wanted to say. Are you listening? Because you'll like this bit."

Lucky leaned, and Swagger leaned, and all the patrons leaned, and Lucky talked so loudly they could have sat on opposite ends of a city block and understood. He spoke about entropy and luck and fate, and what had brought them there, and what was keeping them afloat, and how rather than a plane crash randomly bottlenecking these tales together, there was a coordinated and bountiful fusion to their rhythms that was friendly and right. He told about semen pirates and John Lennon and the savage Rory who might harm Eddie; about bad fortune with a woman out west; good fortune with a woman back east; heartbreak and loneliness and a baby en route. There were orphans, which seemed to be the point he was getting at. There was the plane crash and a dead therapist, but the crux of it, what Lucky Dan took several minutes to clarify, was that this here, when you peeled away all the drama and drivel, boiled down to a holy mission.

"Drink 'em up," the bartender called. "That'll be it for today gentlemen."

"A mission you say?" Swagger held up a finger to hear more, but Dale came down the length of wood and took the last of their bounty as his tip, then dumped the ends of their warm beer into the drain.

The two struggled out of Mack's arm in arm, squinting into

the fresh sun, and checking the street for the suspicious van. From inside the suspicious van, it was not clear to Normal who was assisting whom, the situation more muddled when all three arrived simultaneously, Swagger and Lucky and Lucy.

Swagger: "Is this him? Is this the semen pirate?"

Lucky Dan: "I did it, Normal. I kidnapped Swagger."

Lucy: "What happened to Ava? She's missing an eye."

"Damn it, Lucky! You're drunk!"

"I can't hold my alcohol worth a goat."

"I know you from somewhere."

"Fuck! Fuck! Fuck!"

"Potty mouth."

"And her dress is ripped. Did something happen?"

"Get in the van!"

Normal pulled away before the door was closed and steered hard left. The momentum took them all into a tumble out of which the three came up mingling. Neither of his cohorts seemed quick to secure the pilot with rope or tape, and he pulled to the side of the road to adjust the priorities.

"I know you," Swagger said. "You're Sandra Bullock."

"I'm Lucy Springer." She fiddled with Ava's face, ignoring the pilot.

"You're Lucy Springer. You were supposed to interview me. Remind me what happened?"

"Bugs," Lucky Dan slurred. He sat up and planted an awkward kiss on the side of her shoulder. "But I'm fond of her no matter what kind of cooties she gets. And there's more I'd like to say on the topic."

"That's incredibly sweet. And weird. You're drunk."

Normal swerved back into traffic. After nine beers Swagger was satisfyingly in control. He took the seat closest to Normal. Lucy and Lucky struggled over Ava and the empty eye socket, both holding the doll.

"Damn glad to meet you son. Lucky here tells me you're on a mission. Heard all about your problem with Cory and those orphans and John Lennon. How can I help?"

"Her name's Rory. They're not orphans."

Swagger leaned. Normal could smell the morning. "You and me—we're gonna get that semen and save those little ones. Then we'll see about Cory. Hell, let's just save everyone."

"You understand you've been kidnapped, right?"

"Say, where do I know you from?"

"We spoke on the plane. The one you crashed into the river."

"Just can't place it." Swagger sat back to think it out, and Normal tried to concentrate on the conversation in the rear.

"Did something happen to Ava while I was gone?" Lucy asked.

"It was horrible. He went mad. There was yelling. Cursing of course. And then there was punching."

"Normal, you punched Ava?"

"I told him you'd be sore."

"She's missing an eye. Imagine coming home to find your pet missing an eyeball."

"It would be horrifying." Lucky hugged her. "There, there. Chin up. I once lost a tooth. We'll get through it."

"Can we concentrate on the hostage!" Normal hollered from the front. "Lucky, get the tape and lock him down."

"I got it." Swagger bounced forward. "We spoke on the plane. We talked about assholes. You didn't want to get off."

"That's right."

"Bet it was because of the semen Lucky told me about." He snapped some fingers. "You should have grabbed it right then."

Normal stopped the van at a red light. "And you should have landed the fucking plane on a runway like every other pilot."

From the rear, Lucky did his best to calm her. "You know he might have torn it to shreds if I wasn't here."

"You're incredibly brave to have stepped in." She put Ava back on her wrist to see that the old girl worked properly.

"The gun," Lucky said. "He was going to shoot us."

"Normal, you threatened to shoot Lucky?"

Normal was humiliated. He stepped on the gas. Swagger leaned. "Let's get a few things straight."

"I'm not sure why you think you're in charge."

"It's clear you don't have the first idea what you're doing."

"Is that so?"

"You've got me in the back of a van, but you haven't thought it out."

"Shhh!" Lucy put a finger to her lips. "Listen."

"Listen to what?"

"I heard something. I bet it was Ava's eyeball rolling around the floor."

"What did it sound like?" Lucky Dan asked.

"The sound of something rolling."

They waited for Normal to make another left, which he did at the next corner. And then the slightest *shoooooop*, a tiny glass eyeball rolling along the dark floor.

"The sound of something rolling," Lucky Dan repeated. "You have the most beautiful way of describing things."

"Thank you, Lucky."

"I'm just going to say it. I think you're something, Lucy Springer. The way you look, the way you behave—it all just does it. And, well, I'd like you to be my girl."

"That's nice to hear. But I'm having somewhat of a difficult year and—"

"I don't give a dang. I want you to give me a test drive—kick the tires, slam the trunk, see if I'm the type of fellow that works. If so, I'd like to raise that child as my own. I just want to be involved in the Lucy Springer lifestyle, no matter what the role."

"Listen," she yelled. "There it is! By your foot!"

"Getitgetitgetitgetitdamn!"

"Thereitgoesthereitgoesthereitgoes!"

They tumbled to the van's floor.

"Now the smart money says you should drop me at the next corner before anyone finds out I'm missing," Swagger continued into Normal's ear. "Give up altogether."

Normal nodded. Even drunk, the man had a point. Normal didn't care so much why the plane crashed, only that it had. And now he had gone and kidnapped the pilot and punched a puppet, the getaway driver of a bad idea.

Swagger slapped the back of his head. "But forget what the smart money says. Because the smart money don't know about John Lennon. It don't know about orphans, and this mission of ours, and that Lucky back there's in love. There ain't no glory in giving up. So I'll tell you what I'll do—I'll help you get back what you're missing, but you have to do a few things for me."

"I'm listening."

"Starters, find Lucky and me a bar."

"He's ready to fall down."

"He lacks nourishment," Swagger said. "You don't consistently feed a bender, it turns into a hangover."

"We're not going to a bar."

"Second, my puppy. Soon as my family finds out I'm stolen, free game on Jeters."

"This is a kidnapping, not a road trip. You're not going back to the hotel."

"Don't need to. My girl will bring him. Even give us a place to hole up."

"Let me give it some thought."

Swagger slapped his back. "Lastly, I want a full briefing on John Lennon's jizz. You sound all right. And no skimping. I want to know everything, from the missing finger to this fellow tattooed on your arm, to this mission Lucky keeps talking about."

"Fine. But I need to get on that plane today or—"

Swagger held up a hand. "Shhh. Listen."

"What are we listening to?"

"That's just it. We're listening to nothing."

Normal pulled the van to the curb. The missing eyeball gently rolled to the front, stopping when it clicked Swagger's shoe. The two leaned around the seats in search of the moaning. Lucky Dan and the reporter were wrestling on the van's floor, the puppet pressed to the rear of his head for encouragement.

Swagger elbowed him. "What do you say?"

"What do I say about what?"

"Feel like watching?" He chuckled quietly. "Sometimes I like to just watch, know what I mean?"

Normal bounced his head into the steering wheel.

"Okay, okay, tell you what—let's just watch 'til he unfastens a couple buttons, then you and me see about a steak supper? You tell me about semen. I'll tell you the best way to crash a plane in a river."

Blackie received the phone call nine hours after the mayor departed his office, the remnants of a treacherous day decomposing on his board. It was dark outside, the charcoal dusk of an indifferent universe shrugging, an outline of a city replacing the real one. His Swagger had gone missing.

It was Mrs. Swagger, frantic. "Jeters," she said. "Someone stole the puppy."

Blackie wanted to reach through and rip out her tongue, hold it like a strap of veal, and bullwhip her. All the television stations had called to complain that Swagger had never showed. Seven — he had missed seven interviews, and the market had dwindled to 1:1,197, and this insane bitch was calling about a mutt. Blackie could hear Nate and Mallory calling through the hotel room for the animal, oblivious that their father was missing.

"All his toys are gone," Mipsy wailed. "Chewies, clothes, doggie DVDs."

"By any chance, do you know where your husband is?"

"How should I know? Probably next door with the bimbo."

"The bimbo is here with me," Blackie said. He turned to watch the bimbo, who cast an ordinary stare toward her lap. He covered the receiver. "Any idea what happened to the dog?"

Monica shook her head.

"Any chance Swagger has the dog?"

She shook her head.

Blackie picked up a 3-in-1 digital weather reading/tip calculator/stapler. "Shake your head again, I'll staple your hair to the wall." Into the phone: "Mrs. Swagger, it's important we locate Hank. Do you know where he might be?"

"The puppy," she said. "Don't you see — we were getting along so well."

Blackie checked his board, and his monitors, trying to take in every image. He walked over to the make-believe New York

City and kicked the table, the mock metropolis toppling onto the floor. Midtown split in two. Everything east of Washington Square scattered beneath the table. The Upper West Side began leaking something blue. He had been foolish to leave Miss Dressings in charge of Swagger. Miss Dressings, whom he had underestimated since day one. Miss Dressings, or Veronica Santilli, part of a three-year undercover investigation, who knew all about the passengers and the crash and the rest. He would not be arrested—not by her. He would keep Veronica Santilli at bay as long as he chose, keep Monica Dressings just as she was.

More than likely Swagger was in a bar drinking whatever money he had on him. When that ran out, he would emerge. In the meantime they were losing valuable marketing opportunities, only two days before the museum opening.

"This is all your fault," Blackie accused Monica.

"He just wandered off."

"You were supposed to ensure the sex stayed exciting." He pulled up a chair so he could watch her eyes. "Tell me what I'm missing."

She shook her head.

"I've asked you to stop shaking your head. I promise you won't like the results."

"I don't know. He was there and then he wasn't."

"The sex is what we're discussing. It was disappointing. It's the only conclusion."

"The sex was fine."

"Grown men having sex with young women don't disappear. Their brains are programmed to do nothing else." The purple birthmark seemed ready to explode. When he could not shake Veronica Santilli from the carcass, he moved in tight. "It's possible the fellatio needed work."

For an instant, Monica Dressings stepped out of the eyes and Veronica Santilli stepped in. It was a subtle flicker, but Blackie saw. "There was nothing wrong with that, Mr. Black."

"You read the pamphlets I gave you?"

"I skimmed."

"You do understand it was not optional."

"It achieved its goal."

"If you say so. And you don't know anything about this puppy?"

She shook her head; he stood and tossed his chair into the mangled metropolis. Blackie crossed the room to retrieve the 3-in-1 digital weather reading/tip calculator/stapler, grabbing a handful of hair on his return.

"Stop it! You're hurting me!"

He pushed her against the wall and slammed seven staples into her mane. Veronica Santilli could have disarmed him and used the stapler to slice an entry wound into his jugular, removed the vein like a ripped cable from plastered wall. Veronica could have done all that, but Monica Dressings just stood there. Only one staple held, and after a second even that fell.

"Cheap fucking junk." He threw the stapler, cracking a monitor.

Just then her phone rang; Blackie snatched it. "With whom am I speaking?"

"That's not important. We have a common friend."

"He isn't my friend. He's my protagonist. Where is he?"

"Sleeping it off."

Blackie checked his board. There had been an inconsistency from the beginning, a minor detail that had been overlooked, had grown from the murkiest flaw to a massive cancer.

"Mr. Bailey, I believe. I've been waiting to cross paths."

"I don't want trouble."

"Kidnapping. I'm assuming this is blackmail." Blackie snapped his fingers at Monica, who picked staples from her hair. "You may not have wanted trouble, but you're talking to it. You kidnapped my Swagger!" he shouted.

"You crashed a jet in the Hudson. I was just given a full briefing."

"Can you prove it?"

"I have the pilot. I have a reporter hell-bent on telling the story."

"But do you have the camera?" Silence. "See, you don't have everything—you have a drunk pilot and a reporter who wears a puppet. You need me more than you think."

Blackie closed his eyes. He hated the feeling, the actors stomping about the stage with reckless anarchy, removing the props, and tossing them into the pit. Instead of the storyteller, he had become the villain in another man's tale.

"What is it you want, Mr. Bailey?"

"There's something on the plane that belongs to me."

"The vial."

"You have it?"

"It's not my concern. Your property is on the plane where you left it."

"Good man," Normal said.

Blackie could tell it was important. "What is my concern is that you get what belongs to you, and I get what belongs to me."

"It's not that easy."

"Time is wasting, Mr. Bailey. Your vial is safe by my kindness."

With that he hung up, satisfied. What was flawed turned out to be the solution. It was always necessary to provide guidance to a story, show the direction he hoped it would travel. But by essence a story was an organic item, and it needed to find its own way. Still, though, he was curious—what was it that George Bailey was after inside Blackie's museum?

"Where is he?" Monica asked. "Is something wrong?"

"Nothing that can't be fixed."

"I'm worried," she said.

It was an odd moment of weakness for Blackie. He rubbed her cheek with the back of his fingers, knowing soon she would just be meat, soon there would be no reaction left in those pathetic dimples.

"We can still save our Swagger, Miss Dressings. It's not too late."

"I hope we can save him."

Which made Blackie grin. It was the way she understood his statement: *We can still save our Swagger.* All this time, she thought it had been about a man, when it was always about a concept. It occurred to Blackie that Monica Dressings had grown into one of his preferred characters. Was she naïve, or playing naïve? Did she really love Hank Swagger, or was that pretend also? Or better yet, Blackie thought as he turned back to his monitors, had she somehow become conflicted, enamored with his tale, forgetting her obligations to the Federal Bureau of Investigation, instead at peace with Monica Dressings, cat lover, professional escort?

Her employment, as either an agent or a secretary, would soon cease to take up much of her time, of that Blackie was certain.

FRIDAY

So we come to the end of another formidable week in the life and times of the America. As the sun rises over the adolescent century and we look hungrily forward to the weekend, there is a shimmer of hope, a profound happiness, and Monday seems so far away. America, stretching its coasts with a satiated whimper as it prepares for two full days of lethargy, pleasantry, beer. Its shoulders aching— its Appalachians and Rockies—sore from a week in which America showed up for work, in which this end of civilization stayed the course. Its Mississippi arteries, its Rio Grande, its Susquehanna flexing and simmering as it basks in the pleasant embers of a Friday evening coal where animal muscle and gristle from the heartland sizzle into a ruby-red groove that emits the divine aroma that smells like: Friday. The heart aglow, pulsing slower, slower, whether To-peka or Flagstaff or New York. The brains—Sioux Falls, Rochester, Waynesboro—rapidly unwinding the massive quantities of distraction that infiltrated the synapses with a blinding itch. "Friday!" we scream, the way explorers, both mythological and historical, harkened land as the vessel crept from a mighty sea, finally here, finally a rest from this, this . . . this. Three days from now we will stomp onward and push further and survive faster. We will get back to the business of evolution, all the while knowing the more re-fined, ripened America that is only decades, if not years, in our fu-ture will point and laugh and wonder how we managed, us chimps in our precious trees. All told, it was a good week. No meteors. No nuclear bombs. The only plane that threatened to crash ended in blissful miracle. And so the only thing left to do is unwind, crack a Schlitz, and surf the channels to see if any of them *Homo sapiens* are willing to beat each other to death in a cage for our enjoyment. Ah, Friday. Well, perhaps not just yet. We suppose there are a few loose ends to clean up prior to beer consumption.

THE WAY THINGS ARE GOING
THEY'RE GOING TO CRUCIFY ME

Cleve Peoples had been hiding out in an acceptably equipped hotel in the Montparnasse section of Paris. Acceptably equipped meant enough cocaine and booze to fix an American high school for the year, with revelers meandering in and out so long as they could sneak past lobby security. He had kidnapped one of the revelers, Noelle, a female between the ages of sixteen and thirty-eight, who lay on his bed unclothed waiting for her captor to make good on his threats. She was in no hurry to escape, having taken to her Stockholm syndrome like any gracious hostage of a celebrity expatriate. She was pretty without being attractive and knew enough English that he would not replace her with a fresh victim, but not enough that he would remember her once he left the room. Clocks had been purposefully shot out with a pellet gun that Cleve Peoples carried in a holster on his socked but otherwise naked frame. Every time someone he disliked arrived in his hotel room, he took out the pellet gun and shot for their eyeballs.

All he did was threaten to spank Noelle, and watch the television, shouting at the tube each time it said something raw about the American actor Cleve Peoples, each time it showed canned footage of that miserable puppet bashing him with clever one-liners.

"Fuck the Americans," he barked.

"You the American," Noelle reminded him.

"Fuck me besides."

How he loved America and loathed America, how it could make and break you and then do it again. It might have gone on like that until he ran out of ammunition, or killed Noelle for real, or shot out the wrong eyeball, had he not received a call from his agent. He had been offered a unique role: to play the part of folk hero Captain Hank Swagger in a feature film, based on Miracle

Flight AW2921. He had won the role ahead of Clooney and Pitt and even that long shot Nicholson. A publicity firm out of New York had offered to repair his image, for a small fee. The fee was ten times what he would have had to pay the Frawl woman to feed those rats, and Cleve took the first flight out.

FOOL ON THE HILL

Ricardando Hill arrived in New York City two days before the prosperous eve of his reckoning, which was a more poetic way of saying he hit town on Wednesday. All he could afford was to walk, and look at people, and watch the dealings as the fruit guys and the handbag guys tried to swindle out a living. He had no place to be until Saturday, which made him a homeless person or a tourist, both identities that annoyed New Yorkers and that he relished. He had gotten plenty of shut-eye on the way in, the gentle hum of the foreign motors rocking him to sleep. Typically motorists picked up hitchhikers for someone to talk with, but Ricardando had his mind on business: the future of the United States of America, and his role in that blossoming empire.

What surprised him most about Manhattan were all the necessities given away for free. He had eaten his first night's supper out of the back of an Italian restaurant, a lobster linguine that was possibly the best he'd ever tasted. He had an expensive palate that required him to stand watch in alleys outside pricey eateries. But if he were willing to slum it, the cuisine possibilities were endless. There were dozens of restrooms—and not dirty ones, clean and shiny lavatories maintained by corporations—into which he was welcome to urinate and wash his face. An outreach program even approached him, asking if he had a place to sleep. He said he did not and they gave him an address and a toothbrush, and sprayed a gentle mist on him to rid him of the Nymphopucky. What a city!

Even the newspapers were free, which was how Ricardando discovered Captain Swagger would be a guest on the *Today* show. He had huddled outside the studio with hundreds of other tourists, all of them waving signs and praying the fat weatherman would choose them over their compatriots to say a kitschy hello to the folks back home. No one would be waving signs and smiling next week, Ricardando thought to himself, and he disappeared from the crowd to enjoy a cigarette on the corner. Which was the exact locale where the famed pilot exited the building.

He was taller than Ricardando recalled from pictures, a bit too much shoulder and chin for a martyr. Swagger walked east until he came upon a rough-looking window, "ack's," into which he disappeared. Ricardando stood watching from the sidewalk. He could have taken down Swagger right then, but that was not the holy moment. That moment would be Saturday, at the museum, prime time, when the cameras and satellites and signals were better equipped to blast his revolution into the history books. It took him thirty minutes to work up the courage to enter. He barged in and called for a beer, and shoved a pad and pencil patriotically into the man's hands and ordered up a signature. He was hoping to seem jovial and not the least suspicious, but just as he got comfortable the bartender told him to take a hike.

It was just as well. He had not budgeted funds for beer and he was anxious to keep walking and sampling more of what New York City taxpayers were giving away for free. Every business seemed to be advertising work. In his neck of the woods, jobs were hard to come by unless you wanted to haul timber or haul fish or haul wheat, which was not the appropriate vocation for someone who had invested so much money into his education. It was right there in one of those free newspapers, the advertisement that caught his eye: the Swagger Aviation and Miracle Museum was hiring. It was opening Saturday and they were looking for help, nine bucks an hour, to carry boxes and hang pictures and paint walls. Ricardando showed up and sat through a forty-five-minute orientation. Less than twelve hours in town and he had found himself a paycheck.

And if he had not been previously engaged with the assassination of a cultural icon, he might have stuck around.

MAKE ME FEEL ALL RIGHT

The nice thing about kidnapping Captain Hank Swagger was that he had taken the initiative to get himself a proper mistress who was not opposed to breaking the law. She had stolen the pooch from the Whalensky suite early that morning and delivered it to her own apartment where she was harboring the abductors who were treating the place just like a hideout was meant to be treated. She had even gone to fetch food and supplies, leaving Normal in charge of the gang. Swagger had drank what was in the liquor cabinet, and was now working his way through a bottle of cooking sherry while disputing Normal over the proper way to carry out a kidnapping. Lucky Dan and Lucy had locked themselves in Monica's bedroom.

"People don't talk enough during sex," Lucy said. "They forget they're with another person, a mind like their mind, all these thoughts and dirty notions—put your hand there, that's it—and I don't want to hold back, Dan, not with you. I want to make love to your body and your mind. Say something dirty."

"All right suppose I could tell you the reason I flew across the country was to meet Normal out there on account I haven't been living the life I've wanted and when all the luck slipped away I thought how to get it back and that was what was important but when I saw you on the TV see life walloped me again and luck or money doesn't matter so long as I have you and I intend to honor your presence and our baby's presence I hope you don't mind if I call it ours."

"You know I'm happy I'm pregnant? It's important some piece of Gary lives on even though the rest of him can't. Go ahead—give the dirty talk another go."

"I don't much care for the cursing."

"I'm talking important dirty, refined dirty. What's in your mind right now?"

"I'd rather not."

"Say it. I want you to."

"Put the puppet on."

A *realignment of legs, sheets, values.*

"That's disgusting."

"I'm ashamed."

"No, you're right. It's what I asked. How's this?"

"Peculiar. With the one eye, as though it's winking. As though it has an opinion. Would you mind if I took off my pants?"

"I'd like that."

"I'll warn you first that mine is not the largest penis in history."

"I don't care."

"I know men brag about how mad raging monstrous they become. I don't. It won't."

"Let's see it already."

"The more attracted I am the bigger it gets. I can feel it through the trousers."

"Dan."

"It might not seem so at first. Tell you what though it gets mad raging monstrous. All right then." Silence. "Well, I'm naked."

"It's beautiful."

"And big?"

"Not so much. But the kind of penis a woman gets excited about."

"Randy."

"Who's that now?"

"No backstory. One day I just started calling her Randy."

"Your penis is female?"

"Like a boat."

"That's enough. Come here."

"Before we get started I should warn you. I'm a quick finisher. But an equally fast restarter. Randy is like a gladiator."

"You talk too much!"

"Okay, here goes." Silence. "Oh my."

"Oh my."

"Was that good for you?"

"Beg pardon."

"I feel like a new man a different man by golly my luck is back."

"Did something happen?"

In the next room, an epic conversation that went into the purple hours of Friday morning, Swagger on about "the circumstances by which we met, you and me, in the rear of a sinking plane, talking about assholes, don't you see it? That's how life is—a series of inconsequential spurts that only gain meaning after . . ."

Normal tried his best to hate on Swagger. He had dropped the getaway plane into a river, and he had not even denied it. But the man talked the way fish swam, the way wind blew. His fierce tone, how he held Normal's stare, how earlier he had kept his chin up when Lucy hollered and actually wept when she told them about Gary Corbin. Even Lucy had done her best to despise him, but in the end she just wanted assurance that her sanity had not bailed, that she had not imagined the ordeal. They had to appreciate a man who could talk himself out of a hole the way he could—a man who could be responsible for their predicament and at the same time convince them he was one of the team. And the mission: Despite the events of the past week, once Swagger heard about Cleve Peoples, and the kids, and the John Lennon—well, passengers, there was little else to discuss. His priorities shifted, his goals recast, his aura went off script. Sitting on his mistress's couch with a contraband puppy, he swore allegiance to the mission, actually offered to take a blood oath right there on the living room table.

"Cut it off."

"I'm not cutting off your finger."

"You did it. I want to do it, too. Show you I mean things."

"I believe you," Normal said.

"Isn't the same." He grabbed a knife from the kitchen. Lucky and Lucy arrived in the living room as the butchery was set to commence. "Do it," he ordered. "Or I will."

"What's happening?" Lucky asked.

"This lunatic is about to cut off his finger."

"Hey now, old boy. What's this about?"

"The mission. I want in."

"Put down the knife." Lucy with the puppet, the missing eyeball.

"You all think I did what I did because I'm bad. But I'm good people. I can make this right and I want to prove I'm part of the gang.

NORMAL	LUCY	LUCKY DAN
You cut off that finger we'll have to take you to a hospital. I'm not going to any hospital.	*He's really going to do it. I don't want to see. I'm not going to look.*	*Suppose now's good a time as any. Lucy and me—we're getting hitched.*

And the finger would have come off if Monica Dressings had not arrived at that instant and laid her credentials on the butcher block, SPECIAL AGENT VERONICA SANTILLI.

HELLO, GOOD-BYE

As soon as it was announced that Lucy Springer had come down with Nymphopucky, human resources wasted no time in reassigning Dean. His new boss, Clint Frape, had covered celebrity deaths for ANN for twenty-five years. His job was to write death notices of famous people that were still alive: anticipation obituaries. That way when they died, the legwork was done and the anchors could just read what Frape had written and scoop other networks. He was pudgy with a curious odor, and had a spectacular case of dandruff that clung to his scalp and sweater vests. After Lucy, he was exactly what Dean was hoping for.

"You are one ugly man," Dean said when he met Frape.

"I don't bother with mirrors. Write that down. Write down everything I say so you have it to reference if I get hit by a bus." Dean pulled out a notebook. "That's how I became a successful writer—by not wasting time on appearances."

"Yes, sir."

"Laundry once a month. You'll handle that."

"I prefer not to leave the building," Dean said.

"Clean it in the men's room sink for all I care, so long as you don't lose socks. Coffee you'll fetch outside. Take mine black. From the corner Starbucks."

This was the kind of person Dean wanted for a mentor. He could live up to the expectations of a man that looked like Clint Frape. And he would even fetch coffee, at least for another few days. Dean Migliotto intended, next week, to have his face ripped off, the bones in his head chiseled and toned, all of it reconstructed to resemble a dead American actor. Instead of a nerdy media engineer who would be kicked around until he ripened into a Clint Frape, he had been presented with an opportunity, a way out. One million dollars. To hell with ANN. And to hell with Lucy Springer. She had derailed his career. She had convinced him to watch that movie, and it had slightly tarnished Dean's image of Paul Newman.

The guy was in prison—what did she expect him to inherit from a criminal? Was he supposed to see value in Cool Hand Luke's becoming a hero to the rest of those prisoners because he was a rebel? It was preposterous. Dean did not want to rebel. Conformity was the goal, conventionality his motto. He wanted to be beautiful, and eat his lunch where everyone else did, and listen to the same music, and sleep with the same women.

Dean hated to leave the ANN building. Every time he did, the complexity of modern society got in his way. Like this time: Rather than simply get in line and place his order for Frape's coffee, he was intercepted by a giant moose and escorted to a table in the rear. The man was polite but intimidating, and when he suggested they have a seat Dean offered no resistance.

"We have business," the man said.

"Do I know you?"

"You phoned my employer. About photographs."

The man he spoke to on the phone sounded smaller. This man was terrifying. "You want to do this here?" he whispered.

"What's wrong with here?"

"Shouldn't we go someplace private?"

"I like Starbucks. People mind their own business. Even though everyone is sitting on top of each other, it's considered poor form to eavesdrop." The man glanced around the room. "You have the pictures with you?"

"Do you have the money?"

"I should explain how this is going to work." He pulled out a small silver gun and leveled it across the table. Dean glanced to the right and left but no one paid attention. "I'm going to kill Dean Migliotto today."

"Let's just forget about the money," Dean suggested. He quickly produced the camera and pushed it across the table. "I barely even looked at the pictures. I'll never say a word, I promise."

Jimmish turned it on and flipped through the images. Dean stood to leave. "Sit down, Mr. Migliotto."

"My boss is waiting for his coffee."

"When you walked in here, that was the end of that

arrangement. The job no longer exists. Fetching coffee is no longer a task."

"This is why I never leave the building."

He set the gun on the table; no one bothered to notice. "My employer is impressed with your skills. He is offering you reassignment."

"What does that mean?"

The man pushed a folder across the table. "I'm going to kill you today, either with a gun or a contract. It's your choice. The new role will better utilize your research skills. If you accept, you start this instant."

Dean leafed through the folder. "This for real?"

The man nodded. He watched Blackie's new hire turn pages, noticed a vexing detail. Unlike most of the people to whom reassignment was offered, Jimmish could see that Dean Migliotto was not impressed.

"Can I choose any name I want?"

"It's negotiable."

"Paul Newman?" he asked. When it did not register: "Like the actor."

"I'm not familiar with that name."

Dean reached in his back pocket and pulled out the picture. "This is what I was planning to do with the money. I was going to change my appearance to look like that picture."

Jimmish held it up to compare it to Dean. The actor was effortlessly good-looking. The man in front of him was decidedly unattractive. His ears hung below his mouth, which gave the impression he was stooping. His nose seemed slightly uneven, his hair a nest of follicular anarchy. He breathed with his mouth open as though he had just climbed stairs.

"You've thought about this have you?"

Dean nodded.

"This surgery—it would change your life how?"

"The way people react to me would change," he explained. "Which would change my confidence, which would change my luck."

"I understand. People judge me by my appearance." The man picked up the gun from the table. "I'm afraid I'll need your answer."

It occurred to Dean that he was being offered a new job, a new identity. He hated beginnings and was not the least bit interested in starting over with a new company. A different office would have attractive people he would have to get used to being jealous of, a similar method of subliminally rewarding the beautiful. With the appearance of the large man, it was clear Dean would not be getting his money; there would be no Paul Newman-ness to his creature. And after all he was satisfied with his new mentor. Of course, the large man might still make good on his offer to shoot Dean, in which case he would not have to fetch any more coffee.

Dean pushed the folder across the table. "I think I'll pass."

The man's eyes lifted. "You understand what that means?"

"You really gonna shoot me?"

"You're to be reassigned one way or the other."

Dean leaned in. "You going to do it right here?"

"Suppose not. We should probably go outside."

"We could do it in the bathroom," Dean offered.

"No, that doesn't work." The man pouted into the table.

"Something the matter?"

Jimmish considered whether something was the matter. The last person to whom he should complain was this young man, but there was no one else to tell it to. "The gun," he whispered. "I've never used it."

"You never killed anyone?"

"Everyone always accepts reassignment."

Neither of them knew what to do. It occurred to Dean if the large man wasn't going to shoot him, he was probably free to go. The man tapped the picture of Paul Newman. "This surgery—how much would it cost?"

"To look just like that—$97,148, give or take."

"Tell you what. You come work for Veiltality, I'll pay for it."

"You serious?"

"Out of my own pocket. You have my word."

Dean stared at the picture. The last thing he wanted was to

begin something new. He would have to pack all his belongings, secure a temporary apartment. Then he would have to meet people, become acquainted with a new office, learn which coworkers were gullible and which would rat him out for living in his cubicle. On the other hand, looking like Paul Newman made the idea of a fresh beginning alluring. The giant man seemed desperate for him to accept, anything so he wouldn't have to use the gun.

"Would I have to leave the office at night?"

"You would arrange your own schedule."

"Will you throw in an extra grand for a new wardrobe?"

"I'll take you shopping myself, Mr. Newman."

I DON'T WANT TO SEE YOU AGAIN

Agent Santilli dialed the number, along with the twenty-five-digit access code, followed by the twelve-digit identification code, followed by the extension. It took a moment for the operator to answer. At which point it was explained that her services were no longer required.

"Let me speak to Agent Tuff."

"There's no one here by that name."

"Agent Glenn Tuffers. He's in charge of Special Ops."

"I'm sorry, Miss. There's no such department."

The dial tone was angry. An instant later her cell phone clicked dead. She went in search of change, lots of it that she deposited into a pay phone riddled with graffiti. She dialed Tuff's cell phone.

"Tuff. Go ahead."

"You shit!"

"V. It's not what you think."

"He's free to go. Three years of undercover work and he's free." The pause that followed gave her the answer. She pressed the phone into her temple. "Tell me something, Tuff. How is he any different from a terrorist?"

"He's on our side, I suppose. He's protected."

"How high up?"

"He's the president's guest at a press conference Tuesday."

She smashed the phone into metal.

"Listen to me, V. I'll look out for you. But you have to let it go. Our fight isn't with Alastair Black. Our fight is elsewhere."

She studied her reflection in the silver gleam. "Tuff, if the next words out of your mouth involve semen, you'll never hear from me again."

"But they're stealing it, V. What kind of sick fu—"

It was at a pay phone on the corner of Carmine and Bleecker, the instant her career as an FBI agent came to a halt, that Veronica Santilli decided to help steal the vial. Something about that vial was indispensable to the conclusion, she just knew. Faced with which side to choose, she decided that if Alastair Black was one of the good guys, then she would be one of the villains. She did not give a damn if George Bailey or Normal Fulk escaped with the vial. She did not care for the two strangers having sex in her bedroom, and cared only slightly for Hank Swagger. She was consumed by the fact that Alastair Black had stapled her hair to a wall. And if there were any victory to salvage, it was in making sure Blackie did not win.

She arrived at Veiltality headquarters to an undesirable silence and opened the unguarded freezer; it was empty. Blackie was there, she knew. It could be no other way. She found him in front of his monitors, listening to the tape of the screeching passengers as they careened into the Hudson. He muted the noise and swiveled in his chair.

"It's rare when my characters surprise me. Bravo, Miss Dressings."

"It's Agent Santilli."

"Not anymore. I have it on good terms that you are back to being regular citizen Santilli, daughter of a hairdresser and an auto mechanic from Slancy, NY."

Her eyes fell to a manila folder on his desk. He knew where she was from. He knew where to find her. The heel of her Glock scraped her ribs. If she shot him the building would swarm with something in minutes, and not the friendly something.

"Why do you do it?"

"Because I can."

"You're no better than a terrorist."

"I'm a storyteller, not a terrorist. Telling stories is what I do. And I have one last chapter for you."

"I'm not part of your story anymore."

"But you are. The main plot plays out with or without you, but right now, in this moment, in this room, we are witness to the climax of your character, Monica Dressings. The story will go on one way or another. But right now, right here, is where you decide your fate."

He stood. She stepped back.

"I know you came for the vial. It isn't here, but you know where it is. The only place it could be, in its home. I know you'll attempt to retrieve it even after I explain it to you. But that vial has become the central object in my tale. You are a minor character unfortunately, someone who has no business handling such a commodity. Don't take it personally. If you go after it, it will be your doom."

She pulled her gun.

Blackie held up a hand. "You misunderstand, Miss Dressings. I have no intention of stopping you. Swagger and the reporter and even the strange George Bailey—they belong to me. You can't save them even if you take the vial. But you can save yourself."

She backed away, aiming the gun at his left eyebrow. It would carve a tunnel directly through the birthmark, a red splatter on the monitors.

"Do you realize how unique your situation is? People rarely get to decide how things turn out. But you—you have that privilege." He pulled a tomato from a drawer and placed it on the desk. "What's it going to be, Miss Dressings? A comedy or a tragedy?"

"I won't let you have Swagger."

"I'll have him regardless. You're only deciding one fate right now."

She backed toward the elevator, keeping him in her sights until the doors closed. It was the last time she would ever see Blackie Spin.

And so Veronica Santilli arrived at her apartment to find Swagger on the verge of phalange extraction. She placed the badge on the table, furniture she had purchased at IKEA, and always despised, and would never look at again once she exited the apartment. She told them about the FBI investigation into Blackie Spin and Swagger and Flight AW2921, how she had been undercover for three years, the separate investigation into Normal's occupation, how it all would climax in a few short hours. It was time to leave town, she explained. It was time to disappear.

Swagger petted the puppy and looked at her with sore eyes. She rubbed his chin. "It wasn't all pretend."

"It's okay, doll." He seemed to understand that he was both a victim and the cause of his victimhood, that the innocence of Monica Dressings he once adored had evaporated along with his own.

"What do you say, Dan?" Normal was fidgety around the confessed FBI agent. "Get a move on?"

"I told you. I'm getting married."

"Didn't you hear what she said? They're coming for us."

He put an arm around Lucy. "Let 'em come. Got a family to look after. We're to be husband and wife."

"You're kidding, right?"

"Been wasting my life, Normal, spending my best years with sour people, boring types, all of us coming to pointless conclusions. Now that I found my purpose, I can't be a part of this."

"What about the mission?" Normal asked. "What about the orphans?"

"Don't be like that, Norm."

"We must none of us forget the mission." Swagger did not speak to anyone in particular, staring into his lap at the sleeping dog.

"Hank." Veronica shook Swagger. "You have to leave. Right now."

Lucky hugged Normal as though they had known each other for longer than a week and held on even as he pulled for the door. "Stay for the wedding. Just through the weekend."

"It would mean a lot to us," Lucy said.

"I have business."

"But you're the best man."

It struck Normal as odd that he should be Lucky's best man, but he was touched. He itched his forearm. Eddie was dead to him, his brother in the ground years now. He was presented with two possibilities: Leave now, or end up with Lucky and Lucy on every major holiday, godfather to their child, the Uncle Norm who belonged to no one but was always hovering near the food table. She was no longer wearing the cyclops puppet on her hand. It lay on the couch, its arms to the side as if out of answers. Normal knew the feeling.

"I'm not saying you shouldn't marry her. I'm saying you shouldn't marry her this weekend. Wait until people aren't trying to arrest me. Wait until your sensibilities return."

"I refuse to push this off until my sensibilities return." Lucky put an arm around Lucy.

Normal petitioned Swagger instead. "Tell him he needs to think it through."

Swagger stretched. "I don't want to take sides. But I sure do like a good wedding." Half the room broke into applause. "First we need to get us that vial and sitting there just now I worked out a strategy." A collective groan. "Get the vial. Get these two hitched. Drink a few toasts. Then Norm and me we hop a flight to California by morning."

EIGHT DAYS A WEEK

Eddie Scuthers lay on the bed, the gaudy and seventy-seven percent fake body squatting over him, head thrown back, screaming.
Lobo is somewhere behind her but Eddie is concentrating on his
task, his chore, what he's been ordered to do. Derrick and the
other cameraman, whose name he does not know, record it. The
assistant clutching her clipboard sits in a chair next to the bed,
five feet away, just watching with those crossed eyes; the television
is loud—roaring, the unedited hours of tape of Normal and the
John Lennon—the first season of *Semen Pirates*. In one scene,
he sees himself discussing business with Normal, talking like two
seasoned convicts, Eddie in his tattered white shirt looking like a
younger version of Robert De Niro. So that there are two of him,
the one on the bed and the one on the television, the one on this
side and the one on that, which is when he realizes—he's born to
play this character, Eddie Scuthers. And goddamn it's like heaven,
or at least Eddie's version of contemporary heaven, like an updated
remake of an old sappy film that is better and newer because the
actors are in color, and one of them is him.

She shops for a waffle iron. She does not know where her husband
is, or what he's doing. All that is out of her control. What Mipsy
Swagger can control is the waffle iron—a specific brand—that
retails for $89.99 and is impossible to find anywhere outside of
Manhattan. She has never cooked waffles. But one day, she figures,
she might like to wake up early without a hangover, and fix a plate
of waffles, and squeeze some fucking juice, and sit down with her
husband and children and talk about other people. She would like
to be the perfect Mrs. Swagger, the house near the beach, a man
always around to string the Christmas lights and trim the hedges.
But that is not the way life panned out. There are twists and temp-
tations and some results for which she is responsible, and others
creep in as though nudged by a mysterious and possibly demented

hand. Is it all her fault, the way it worked out? Mostly. No one can blame luck. No one can blame destiny. It's cause and effect. Although she still believes in luck and destiny and hope. And waffle irons. For the first time in years she is shopping with her children, both of whom are moving home for a few months. It will be like old times until it isn't. She misses the puppy. She misses Hank. She knows he's been kidnapped but even that does not worry her. Hank will survive, somehow come back better and bigger and more festive than before, she just knows. He'll show up at that museum tomorrow sunny and gloating, and snip that ribbon, and take his place as one of the immortals.

The museum curator straightens a picture. He has dusted the wax figures and tested all the lightbulbs and overseen the restroom cleanings and ensured the ticketing system is operating correctly. He has even tested the chicken fingers at the museum restaurant despite being a vegetarian. Everything is set for the morning.

Cleve Peoples is Cleve Peoples.
    Cleve Peoples is also Hank Swagger, a fresh new character he will embody in the coming year. It will take months of research, hundreds of hours of impersonation, stalking the actual man — just so that he can learn the nuances of the beast inside the meat. He will find his doppelgänger in the morning at a ribbon-cutting ceremony, where he'll watch among an audience of wide-eyed gawkers. Then he will not leave his side until the transformation is complete.

Special Agent Glenn Tuffers and his team hunker down outside Normal Fulk's apartment. The case of the missing semen trafficker is their only priority.

"I don't know you."
    "You know me, Mr. Wrinkles."
    "You shouldn't be here."
    "I saved your life. On the plane. It was my role then. Now it's my role to end it."

"You're going to kill me?"

"I'm going to kill Peter Wrinkles. Either with a gun or a contract. Your uncle tells me you're good at video games. Tell me about that."

"What do you want to know?"

"Start at the beginning. I'll stop you when I've heard enough."

Ricardando Hill hides in a utility closet inside the Swagger Aviation and Miracle Museum. He has three packages of beef jerky and a bottle of water, enough to get him through the night. He'll be the only person inside when they cut the ribbon. No one will see him coming. And then, infamy.

Mayor Susan Cromberg is picking out a new suit for the ceremony. Captain Hank Swagger and Flight AW2921 and Alastair Black are the best thing that happened to her all week. Later, she naps.

They stand around a metal garbage can outside of Veronica Santilli's apartment. They're all there, Swagger and Normal, Lucy and Lucky, Veronica looking up the street, certain any minute a caravan of black SUVs will swarm the corner. It is nighttime now, the first seating exiting their tables and dipping into the April darkness, the city humming, the cab lights flickering red, that portion of the night when it is still too early to say if it will be memorable, one of those evenings people talk about for decades, or if it is just a plain old sundown.

Lucy holds the puppet in her arms like a child. She says a silent prayer or a telepathic good-bye, then gently lays it on a pile of refuse. They huddle close and peer into the container, their first puppet burial. She nods to Lucky, who strikes a match and holds it over the can: last chance. When no one speaks, he separates the two fingers and the tiny missile plummets.

It is a relief that the fabric ignites as quickly as it does, the orange light brightening their faces as they stare down at the conflagration.

"Someone should say something," Lucky Dan says.

Lucy nods. "That would be lovely."

"I'll start." Lucky clears his throat. "Whenever I lose someone, I like to reflect on the people still by my side. I find each of you fascinating, just really good shits—pardon my language." He sniffles. "Really good shits."

"I know it sounds strange," Lucy says. "But she was an ally. Got me through a tough patch. Never forget that."

Veronica clears her throat. "I watched her on TV. She made me smile."

"Fucking Viking funeral." Swagger pours a little of what he's sipping into the flames. "Only way to go."

They wait for Normal. "Fire hazard. Surprised no one has called the cops."

A DAY IN THE LIFE

The Swagger Aviation and Miracle Museum occupies an empty lot near the Hudson River that equates to four city blocks. It houses an amphitheater, a restaurant, even a playground for children. Nearly two hundred staff members working around the clock turned it into a landmark, a must-see attraction for the millions of tourists who visit New York City each year. At a cost of $31 million, the building of the Swagger was funded by grants and fellowships and other catchy labels for taxpayers' money. If anyone cared to be specific, they would discover that all the applications had been sealed long ago, several months prior to Flight AW2921 departing the tarmac. The web site had been designed, the tickets printed, the carpet patterns and paint colors choreographed to mimic the style of staff uniforms.

The curator, Emory Stallworth, was a stickler for detail. He canceled one of the Swagger wax figures because the bridge in the nose was too steep. He orchestrated the staff's wardrobe, ensuring restaurant waitresses dressed like flight attendants. He had the janitors mop the floor in a backward motion toward the door, then locked it himself, so that the morning would find a clean and pine-scented marble foyer for the museum's grand opening.

The plan was to avoid drama. There was no need to break into the museum being that they had in their company a woman with FBI credentials and the man whose name was on the building. Veronica would act as an escort to Captain Swagger, explaining to the guards that he insisted on seeing the museum prior to Saturday's opening. Once inside, Normal would retrieve his vial and they hopefully would be off before anyone knew better. Dan tagged along, claiming he was the luck minister of the mission, and Lucy would not be left behind.

They walked slowly toward the giant IMAX screen, the focal point of the room. In a day's time, it would show videotape of Flight AW2921's landing and the subsequent rescue on an endless loop. For now, a tiny orange ball pulsed in the center, the projector slumbering. With the halls darkened and the windows in the plane covered, one could only see by the glow of the emergency lighting. The main gate led into the amphitheater, and from there a directory pointed out the various exhibits. YOU ARE HERE was a measured thirty yards from the cockpit, and to get deep inside you had to pass the museum gift shop, which was locked at that hour but well stocked with paraphernalia that had even Swagger impressed. The wax figures occupied an entire wall and the crew spent precious moments arguing the exactness.

"They look nothing like me." Swagger carried the puppy in a rolled up blanket that made him seem arbitrarily fat.

"These wax ones are thinner," Normal said.

"Happier looking," Lucy added.

Lucky stepped over the cordoned rope and rubbed one. "They shave the outer layer of wax. It's what gives the figures that long, lean look. It's how you would look if you stopped drinking."

"That ain't happening." Swagger touched a button and the mannequin spoke. "Welcome aboard, Pardner."

"Go fuck yourself. I don't talk like that."

He hit the button again. "Welcome aboard, Pardner."

"I said go fuck yourself." Swagger chuckled.

"Stay on task," Veronica ordered.

The other direction was the fuselage, or what had once been the fuselage. The cabin had been gutted, the seats removed, the windows blockaded, the entire corridor a snapshot of the week they just survived. It was a virgin museum, an unsullied tour, the exhibits never glanced at or touched or flash photographed. They made their way to the rear of the cabin, past Swagger's Cockpit with the obnoxious Tex-Mex menu, past the Kiddycare wing with pristine ropes and swings that would soon be teeming with germs, until they arrived at the place once known as Row 50. It had been converted into the Hall of Horrors Exhibit, photos and video of plane crashes that were not as lucky, which was meant to cast Flight AW2921 in a more miraculous light but instead came off dreary and unnecessary—go have a Strawberry Swagger-rita then check out these sad bastards who weren't as lucky.

The seats had been removed and the restroom converted into an entire cabal of bathrooms, all with touchless sinks and hand dryers and flushing mechanisms. Everything was different and new, except the one overhead luggage rack that did not belong. It looked as though the carpentry crew simply ran out of ambition in the last six feet of real estate, leaving one rack hanging. They waited as Normal clicked the latch; the silver urn; the John Lennon inside.

It was melted but cool. He held it to the dim orange light to ensure it was *his* vial of John Lennon's semen and not another passenger's. Then he nodded to the others, and they headed back the way they came, past the restaurant and day care, past the photo exhibit and gift shop, over the pine-scented faux model home of it all until they arrived at the ticketing booth.

"I'd like to come back when we can spend more time," Lucky said.

Which was when the lights clicked, bright at first, then a murkier shade that made it difficult to see clearly. Veronica was hopeful it was the guards, or the janitorial crew getting an early start, but she was fully expecting Agent Tuff and his team. Her career was over anyway, although breaking and entering would provide a solid nail in the coffin. It turned out to be Jimmish Wayne carrying a black satchel instead; they all stopped thinking of escape and thought instead of survival. Veronica pulled her weapon; Jimmish, reluctantly, pulled his own.

"Let 'em go," she said. "I don't want to, but I'll shoot."

"That's not how this ends, Miss Dressings."

"Name's Santilli. I'm with the FBI."

"Not until someone says otherwise." They walked in a circle, keeping the distance but ogling the doors. "Need the pilot. Take the others and go if you choose."

She had no ties to Normal or Lucky, no sentimental issues with the vial. She helped because she knew Swagger would not leave otherwise. She loved him in her own way. Perhaps not enough to die for him, but enough to leave the room with him.

"You'll shoot if I turn my back."

"I'd prefer not to shoot at all. The pilot's my business."

Just then a ruffling at the front gate. They were coming, Veronica knew, and at that moment she would have been elated to see the Bureau.

"The vial," Swagger whispered. "I won't let them take it."

"Leave it alone," Normal said.

"The mission. Give it here. They won't search me. They'll search you."

All things considered he had a point. Normal handed over the vial and they waited for the agents. It turned out to be a different style of army.

"Cut!" Rory Genius-Temple hollered. Lobo and the cameramen dashed for position. Eddie Scuthers wore a suit. Normal had known him most of his life. He did not own a suit. "Sorry we're late. Take it from the top. Sorry everyone," she said again.

Jimmish waved the gun, waiting for someone to prove the enemy.

"Got nothing to do with you, lady," Veronica hollered.

"In a minute doll." She admired the construction, the oversized screen at the far end. "Before we get started, better let me hold the vial, just so we don't have any misunderstandings."

Normal put up his hands. "I don't have it."

"Go get it Eddie." Then to the others. "Roll tape."

Eddie drew his own weapon, another first for Normal. He crossed the room and waved hello. "Sorry about this Norm. Business, you know?"

"Yeah, business."

"How's the finger?"

"Still missing."

"Keep applying that Vitamin E. Shit's a cure-all."

"Eddie, listen." He spoke low, hoping Lobo and the microphone were out of earshot. "I never told you this. But you're too stupid to work this business without me. I kept you around because you're good at watching television."

"That's nice of you to say."

"You need to stop, Eddie. You'll end up in jail."

"No one's going to jail."

"The Feds know. And you'll be the scapegoat, not Rory."

"Maybe. But it's a cool idea for a show. And if I have to spend a few years in prison, so be it." He gave Normal's pockets a few pats, relieved him of his weapon. "Just hand it over. Don't make me take it."

"I don't have the vial, Eddie."

"Rory said I have to smack you if you don't hand it over."

He smacked the gun into his right eye.

"Fuck!"

"Vitamin E on the eye as well."

Jimmish was nervous. Veronica never took her eyes from him, the two pointing their weapons across the room, nothing but the stare. Lobo ran cable between the draw, but other than that it was a standoff. Eddie hit him a second time and Normal went to his knees. Swagger pulled the vial and held it in front like it were a biological weapon he would unleash if anyone took another step. He placed Jeters on the floor; the puppy scurried for a nook. Swagger backed away, and Rory motioned to Camera One to follow, and Lobo was on him. Jimmish and Veronica stayed locked. Eddie smiled at the vial.

"Back off!" Swagger hollered.

Normal put up his hands to settle the situation.

"Give it here," Eddie ordered.

"Can't do that. Made this man a promise." And then to Normal. "The mission."

Eddie pointed the gun. "Give me the fucking jizz."

But it was too late. And what happened next happened quickly, a week's worth of intrigue boiled down into a sip.

Eddie's order followed the movement of Swagger's neck as he tipped the glass to his lips, the last of John Lennon gone forever, at least outside of songs and pictures and movies and the annual reunion when all the folks who know the lyrics by heart gather on the eve of his assassination and smoke weed. Lobo groaned. Rory cursed, began the words but never got them out. Camera Two moved across the gunplay for a shot of the drama, a loose cord catching Jimmish's shoe, which caused his patience up until then to falter.

He fired the gun at the floor, toward the ghost of whatever had rubbed him in the darkened room. Confused, he pointed the weapon at Camera One, firing a round into the instrument. It scattered glass and the man went down, and from the ground he quickly retrieved his equipment. Like a trenched soldier, he clicked a shutter and screwed a lens, and re-pointed the weapon at the man who had just tried to kill him. The gunshot gave Veronica the opening she needed, dashing behind a pillar and firing a shot that caught Jimmish's leg. He returned fire as did Veronica, her third bullet catching the side of Lobo's head, sending the sound man to the floor.

"Which one of you bastards shot Lobo?" Rory hollered.

"Lady, get out of the way!" Veronica shouted.

"He's union, damn it. Guild'll have my neck."

Lucky tackled Lucy into the wax figures. Eddie ducked behind a vending machine. Normal stayed put in the center of the arena, fifteen yards from where Swagger held the empty vial. Jimmish took aim at Rory, who continued to complain about her dead sound guy, then thought better since she was unarmed. He scanned the arena slowly, waiting for a new enemy to appear.

It was into this commotion that the conclusion surfaced. Having sequestered himself in the closet before the doors were locked, Ricardando Hill was startled awake by the gunshots. He was certain they had come for him, someone had leaked his intention, and this was the first hour of a long and well-publicized standoff. He was nearly out of beef jerky. From inside the closet, he listened for a bullhorn hollering his name, ordering his surrender. As soon as he detected a lull in the gunplay, he erupted.

He threw open the door, gun in hand. Ricardando was adjacent to the pillar where Veronica crouched. She did not have the angle and, baffled by his appearance, she crossed to a new pillar, crouched, aimed at Jimmish. The two cameras whirled, eager to catch it all, which was when Jimmish saw his enemy. It was a clean shot and he fired the silver gun for real for the first time, the Angel of Death and his mark. Veronica Santilli was dead.

Through the tangle of wax legs, Lucky made the kid instantly,

pointing him out to Normal: "From the bar. The autograph fella."
Lucy tugged Lucky to the floor just as Ricardando Hill found him
across the dark museum. Having been sequestered in a closet, Ricardando's eyes were not accustomed to the room. Instead of a wax
model he saw actual Swagger, firing off one of his three precious
bullets. The head exploded, sending wax and red dye all over Lucy.

Lucky from the ground: "He shot wax Swagger!"

Ricardando saw the head explode. Then he saw the real thing.
There was no time to rethink the plan, gun in hand, the serendipity
overwhelming until he knew what he had to do. It was the reason
he had come all the way across the country—infamy, immortality
in fact. Perhaps he'd wanted it to play out on Saturday, on a larger
stage, but that was not what the gods had in store. He pointed the
weapon.

"*Sic semper tyrannis!*" he shouted, only because he had read
somewhere that was *the* thing to shout during assassinations.

Years later, Normal would reflect on his actions that day and
wonder why he would have died for that man, who because of Normal's reaction would live on as an icon. When he saw the young
man's arm rise, Normal dove for Swagger, tackling the pilot as the
bullet found meat. The empty glass vial ricocheted off the marble
floor. Eddie leveled his weapon and fired at Ricardando Hill.

"You hit?"

"I did it, Normal. The mission."

"You drank it, you silly fuck. That *was* the mission."

"Couldn't let them take the John Lennon. I did good, right?"

Normal fell back, studied the ceiling. He checked for wounds,
finding his left shoulder raw. Eddie stood with his gun drawn, but
it was clearly Jimmish's room. He might have killed every one of
them other than Swagger, but the giant IMAX screen came to life.
Blackie looked down on the scene, wondering who had been in his
closet, if his leading man were dead or just bloodied.

A confounding smoke hung over the room, the mixture of fresh
pine and gunpowder. They noticed the subtle maneuvers of the
cameras in the ceiling; the room was wired, Blackie Spin watching
all along. A tally: one dead FBI agent, one dead sound man, one

lone gunman, dead; one headless wax figure, an injured camera-man, Normal shot through the shoulder, Jimmish shot, Lucy and Lucky shaken, and a furious Rory Genius-Temple in need of a fresh sound guy.

Lucky took off his shirt and began dressing Normal's wound.

"Never saw that coming," came the voice through the IMAX screen. "Does have a certain beauty to its entropy."

From his perch, Blackie tilted the cameras in the ceiling and found his late assistant in the rubble. Swagger kneeled over her, a silent prayer or apology. Blackie let the moment occur, not speaking until the pilot stood. "I'm proud of you, Jimmish, finally secure in your role."

From a dark corner, the gentle clink of the vial. The puppy had found it, nosing it forward like a toy, which caused the screen to erupt in a smile.

"Will you look at that, Jimmish?" Jimmish massaged a bloody leg. "This creature survived but my assistant did not." He appre-ciated the dog more now than before. He cut into a tomato and watched them watch him. "Another minstrel just reminding me of my place." Swagger picked up the dog and Blackie seemed to want to pat the animal through the screen. "Everyone, front and center."

They formed a line, all but Eddie who cowered behind a vend-ing machine in his new suit.

"Some of you belong here, some do not. Right now that is unimportant. Three minutes ago, a crew of special agents with the Federal Bureau of Investigation was dispatched to this location. Best we get our story straight before they arrive." He peered down into the line. "Start with George Bailey. That's not your name, is it?"

Normal was bleeding but cognizant. "Normal Fulk."

"Normal Fulk." Blackie tried it to see how it felt. "Surprising, but you have become the pleasure of my week. You're fascinating, Mr. Fulk."

"Goddamned brilliant American cinema and he doesn't even realize it."

"I would agree, Miss. Best not to interrupt for now though." Rory stewed, never having gone this long without shouting at someone. Blackie was fascinated with Normal. "You were not part of my story when it began, so the chances of you surviving are slim. You know what you are? You are my weed, Mr. Fulk."

"A weed, huh?"

"Don't misunderstand. I'm not insulting you. The weeds are my favorite. Grass in a meadow has no difficulty sprouting. In the meadow there is no harsh terrain to overcome. But the weed that comes up through cracks in the concrete, through places it does not belong—that's a seed that has weathered the storm, that deserves recognition. You, Mr. Fulk—you are the weed of my story. And you will be rewarded."

Swagger petted the dog and nodded to Normal; he seemed to have forgotten already his late lover and was enjoying the awards ceremony. Normal was smooth, calm, knew for certain the bald man was trouble. With or without a reward, the appropriate ma-neuver was to run, to get out before the Feds arrived. That's what Frank would have done.

"Okay, I give up. Can't wait any longer. I'm dying to know. What was inside the vial?"

"Semen," Lucy said.

"For real?" He watched the wall to understand. "Who did it belong to?"

"John Lennon."

Blackie chuckled. "You continue to be a delight, Mr. Fulk. This a hobby or an occupation?"

Normal gave a brief rundown—his recent death, the flight out of town, the impending retirement. He explained Rory and the cameramen, why the vial was so meaningful, told the entire thing in six minutes, covering the plot right up until the moment Swagger drank it.

"And then he drank it," Blackie finished. "Did he know what it was?"

"That's why I drank it," Swagger said proudly.

"Oh dear, Mr. Swagger." Blackie's giant head shook over the top of them. "And you're meant to be my hero. Well, there's no other way. We'll just have to eliminate that detail from the story."

"What are you talking about?" Normal asked.

"The life and times of the folk hero Captain Henry Theodore Swagger, of the twenty-first century, when he lived and died and what he stood for." He glanced about the domed arena. "Look around, Mr. Fulk. You are part of immortality."

They all looked at the immortality, ignoring Swagger with the puppy that had not been bathed in a week standing right next to them and concentrating instead on the photos, the murals, the wax figures, one of them headless.

"Okay, Miss Genius-Temple, I can respect that you have business here—honor among storytellers, so to speak. You've got an angle with Mr. Fulk." Blackie thought about it a moment. "Mr. Fulk, sure you wouldn't rather come work for me?"

Normal shook his head.

"And you're certain you choose anonymity?"

"I'm certain."

"Won't change your mind? Won't decide retirement isn't your shtick, try to come back and make trouble for Miss Genius-Temple?" Normal stared into the marble. "Very well. Pick up the empty vial." Normal did. "Now hand it to Mr. Swagger." Then to the captain. "Kindly fill the vial with your brilliance if you would." Swagger grinned, set down the puppy, began making preparations. "Not here, you heathen. Go find a washroom."

Swagger departed. "Miss Genius-Temple, I know little about the business. But I would imagine a vile of Captain Hank Swagger would fetch top dollar among your clientele."

"I'm sure we can make it work," she said.

"Of course, that will mean you'll replace your leading man without additional aggression." She frowned. "I believe Mr. Fulk has earned his retirement here today."

Normal nodded. Rory rubbed her hands. Eddie shifted behind the vending machine. Blackie searched the room for a conclusion, the appropriate method of tying it all together before the Feds arrived.

He turned to Lucy. "Still kicking, Miss Springer? The world cannot seem to shake itself of your presence."

She had a red splatter on her shirt and face, wax meat. "Do I know you?"

"Not intimately. But I've followed your career. I feel that we're better acquainted than strangers. May I ask what's happened to the puppet?"

"Arson, I guess."

"Just as well. I was tiring of the prop. How do you feel now that it's gone?"

She glanced over to Lucky who was connected to her hand. It was strange that it arrived at that moment. But it occurred to her how dearly she wanted someone to love and obsess over and criticize, someone to share life with and worry about and look forward to. Not the father of her child, but always there. "Liberated," she said.

"A nice emotion." He leaned forward. "Tell me—do you still intend to relay this nonsense about a fake plane crash?"

"People should know."

"The only thing people should know is that tomorrow morning is certain to arrive, that America will crown its newest messiah fifty yards from where you're standing, that tourists will pay $29.99 to come and feel closer to it. I would offer to pay you to keep your mouth shut, but you might turn out to have principles."

"You can't hide something like this." She motioned to the dead bodies. "There will be questions, investigations."

"No, there won't."

"My friend was killed. People need to know why."

"You see what happens when people who do not belong get involved—like Mr. Fulk there, or the dead man on the ground, or Miss Genius-Temple, or the man cowering behind the candy machine?" Eddie made himself smaller in the shadows. "It gets messy. I have to invent new and different stories."

Lucky squeezed her hand.

"Two ways," Blackie continued. "One, you can make the cleanup easier if you agree that my plane crash was, as your former employer has claimed all week, a miracle. Two, if you cannot stomach miracles, Jimmish will take you outside and fill you full of lead projectiles."

"He means bullets," Normal said.

"I know what he means."

"What will it be? A reporter with principles, or a survivor with a baby?"

Lucky Dan placed a hand on her stomach. "Survivor," she said quickly.

"Excellent." Blackie continued carving the tomato on his side of the screen. "You'll be happy to know my version is better than the truth anyway."

In the instant before Normal could silence him, Lucky lifted an arm toward the screen.

"My instincts tell me you're about to speak," Blackie said. "You seem like an expendable character. My advice is to keep it short."

"Stay out of it, Lucky," Normal whispered.

"Dan O'Malley. Call me Lucky Dan or just Lucky."

"Why are you in my museum, Mr. O'Malley?"

"Lucy's fiancé. I'll appreciate you not address my girl that way."

"Chivalry." Blackie tested a tomato, smiled at Normal. "Anyone got a coin?" The room was heavy with the dead, the cameras overhead, a curious trickling noise, a drain doing some work. Normal reached in his pocket and pulled a quarter. "Mr. Fulk, always coming through. Hand the coin to Miss Genius-Temple." She bowed; Blackie turned to Lucky Dan. "Jimmish, stick your gun into Mr. O'Malley's ear."

Jimmish was different. He was sharper, braver, his personality fit his shape. His hand was there instantly.

"I don't care if it was faked," Lucy begged the screen. "I won't say anything."

"I know you won't, Miss Springer. But we're going to test this fellow's nickname, that's all. Tails he goes free, heads his brains explode out his ear." Blackie chuckled at the twist.

"Roll tape," Rory said, the cameras shuffling.

"He's confused," Normal said. "He's got nothing to do with this."

"Don't worry. This man cannot kill me."

"Lucky, stop talking!" And then to Blackie: "Don't do it."

Rory balanced the quarter on a thumb, excited to see if the

bald man could really kill someone through a screen, just the type of thing the American public would adore.

"It's just his way," Normal tried. "He doesn't mean nothing. Let us walk and you'll never see us again."

The bathroom door opened. Swagger emerged with a proud walk and flipped the vile to Rory. He clapped the wetness from his hands. "What I miss?"

"Flip it, Miss Genius-Temple."

She did. Jimmish pushed the gun farther into the ear, Lucky unconcerned that his fate hung on a coin. It somersaulted toward the domed ceiling, the silver sides catching the room's light and issuing hasty sheathes of luminous progress. They all watched, breathless—the actors, the screen, the wax figures—down toward the ground it hit with a clumsy clink. It bounced into the marble once, again, then rolled on its edge across the floor, the cameras and everyone following its course until it lost momentum, slowly falling toward a . . .

"Tails!" Lucy cried.

"I told you."

"Lucky, shut the fuck up."

"Yes, Mr. O'Malley. Or we'll make it two out of three." Blackie bit the tomato. "You know, this is the problem with modern society. Stress." He laughed. "I was really going to have him shot. With all we need to accomplish in the next few moments, I truly intended to do it. That's how anxious I become when disruptions upset the day."

"It's over now," Lucy said.

"A heads would have completely changed the momentum of our interaction." Blackie continued the laugh, expecting others to share his mirth. Only Rory did. "Instead of everyone getting along, some of you could be standing there covered in Lucky's blood if that quarter fell the other direction. What are the chances?"

"Fifty-fifty," Normal said, approaching the screen. "I don't know who you are. If you're going to kill us, get along with it. If not, I need to catch a plane."

"I'm not going to kill you, Mr. Fulk. I could never live with myself. I adore knowing a character like you is out there. Just doing his thing. Besides, someone has to ride off into the sunset."

"You mentioned a reward."

"I did indeed."

He motioned to Jimmish, who retrieved the black satchel and set it on the ground in front of Normal. Normal opened the case and closed it. They heard sirens out front, first echoes and then the real thing, and any minute it would be too late.

Blackie leaned. "Pay attention, all of you. This is how our story goes."

LIFE GOES ON

The attempted assassination of Captain Henry T. Swagger became a footnote in the larger folktale. No one would ever know exactly what happened, which gave the incident more appeal from a historical perspective. What came out was that Ricardando Hill, a madman and an anarchist, shot a museum security guard dead, Veronica Santilli. The man's ultimate goal was to kill Hank Swagger, although the captain subdued him with a quick-thinking portfolio of suitable maneuvers before federal agents shot and killed the revolutionary Ricardando Hill.

Overnight the museum curator would piece together an additional wing known as "The Attempted Assassination of Captain Swagger." It would become the building's sensation, folks lining up two hundred deep to get a look at the crime scene reconstruction, to see where the wax security guard bled to death, where wax Ricardando Hill was shot, where wax Swagger karate-chopped the piss out of him, providing tourists a taste of some sheltered violence. For an additional fee, they could have their photographs taken with wax Ricardando Hill.

While Swagger and his wife and children and puppy would proudly step into the Saturday sun, and Mayor Cromberg would give a rousing introduction, and the real Cleve Peoples would watch from the crowd, and Swagger would accept the oversized scissors and snip the blue ribbon—federal agents would raid a commune in Oregon, where a task force would reduce a band of revolutionaries to quibbling conformists. They would admit their part in boycotting the American economy, receive stiff fines and community service, then go back to college and become fine disciples of capitalism.

Also footnote worthy: Following the museum excitement, Eddie Scuthers would be well on his way to reality stardom, the inaugural episode of *Semen Pirates* ready to air. The show would be picked up for a second season, Eddie would win two Realities at the Reality TV Awards, and be arrested soon after for trafficking stolen semen. His stint would only make the show more popular. Rory and Blackie would produce the Swagger movie, starring Cleve Peoples. Lucky and Lucy and baby Normal G. O'Malley would attend the premiere.

No one would hear from Normal Fulk again.

ABOVE US ONLY SKY

He travels as George Bailey. His documents are in order, his tray in the upright position, the briefcase stowed beneath the seat. It is a direct flight to Los Angeles, an excursion up the California coast to finish the mission. A young woman, late twenties, sits next to him. She clutches the armrest as the plane taxis, as the pilots maneuver the engines and a great, mechanical indigestion erupts from beneath the luggage and any minute the thing could explode or ignite, sending them all to their beyond.

"I hate this part," she says.

"Takeoffs are cruel. That moment of indecision."

"Weightlessness."

"Helplessness really. When we relinquish our handle and put faith in mechanics and propulsion thrust and all that shit we avoided in math class."

She smiles. "I like to say a prayer."

"Sure, can't forget the gods."

"Are you scared?"

"Me, no. Plane won't crash."

"How can you know for sure?"

"I'm a lucky man."

"Makes me feel better." She lets up on the armrest, watches the four-fingered hand. "This'll seem strange. But would you mind holding my hand until we're in the air?"

"Sure I will."

Her hand is small, wet from perspiration, his rough and cool. The touch is reliable as the aircraft fights through the weight, aches for its life, inching higher and smaller until the metal giant appears no larger than an airborne critter, the dual contrails like endless kite strings connecting it across the horizon, through the clouds, massive airships, and all the passengers' dreams and heroes and miracles filtered out through that great sonofabitch gravity to scar our skies with plumes of what they believe.

ACKNOWLEDGMENTS

Many thanks to Sarah Knight for molding this book and guiding the way. Thanks also to the talented Simon & Schuster team, including Molly Lindley, Jessica Abell, Kate Gales, Jonathan Evans, Esther Paradelo, Richard Rhorer, and Jonathan Karp.

Thanks to my agent, David Patterson, for working through the earlier drafts and juggling my many projects with eagerness.

To John Golaszewski for his insights into puppet litigation; to a friend for aviation advice on how and when to land an Airbus in the Hudson River; and John Lennon, whose spirit and paraphernalia inspired parts of the story.

To the editors and writers at *Timothy McSweeney's Internet Tendency* for honing my writing and making me laugh each day.

For encouragement along the way, friends and coworkers whose camaraderie was invaluable.

For your support, thank you to my family for reading my work over the years and providing plenty of material to write about when we get together.

To my son, Jack. And to Alia, my wife and biggest supporter, for believing in me even when we were still in the basement.

THIS *IS* YOUR CAPTAIN *SPEAKING*

ABOUT THIS BOOK

Captain Hank Swagger's miraculous landing took place on April 9, 2012, roughly two months before the pilot episode of a new reality TV show, *Semen Pirates*, leaked to YouTube. Four hundred million views later, the show is the most-watched program in the history of television despite its star serving time in prison for grand larceny, trafficking of a hazardous material, and trafficking of a hazardous material belonging to a deceased icon.

Since then, there has been much speculation as to the connection between those events. Former ANN reporter Lucy Springer, who was aboard Flight AW2921, has refused requests for interviews, nor will she say what became of her felt-skinned sidekick, Ava Tardner. Meanwhile, three films about the momentous event— *American Hero*, directed by Ron Howard and starring Cleve Peoples as Captain Swagger; *This Is Your Captain Bleeding*, directed by Quentin Tarantino and starring Samuel L. Jackson; and *Swaggered*, directed by the Coen brothers and starring Will Ferrell—give wildly different interpretations of what happened aboard that flight, and what, if anything, it has to do with celebrity ejaculate.

DISCUSSION QUESTIONS

MONDAY

* The story begins with the miraculous water landing by Captain Hank Swagger, followed by him kidnapping a puppy and stealing items from an old woman's purse. How does this behavior shape our views of him as a supposed national hero? *For an interview with the curator of the Swagger Aviation and Miracle Museum, e-mail swaggercurator@gmail.com.*

* The significance of celebrity worship in our culture manifests itself in the underground market that supports Normal Fulk's semen-trafficking venture. If you could own the DNA of any celebrity, living or dead, would you? Whose would it be? *For an interview with Normal Fulk, e-mail normalfulk@gmail.com.*

TUESDAY

* Alastair Black views himself as a storyteller instead of a criminal, orchestrating a beautiful folktale about an American hero. While his actions are illegal, are his intentions righteous? Does his creation of an imaginary Nymphopucky infestation make him a reliable engineer that can pull off the scheme, or a diabolical madman? If certain species could autoerotically reproduce, would it create ecosystem chaos or solve world hunger? If cows could masturbate and thus spawn, would you purchase your hamburger from autoerotic beef versus grass-fed beef if it was a buck-a-pound cheaper?

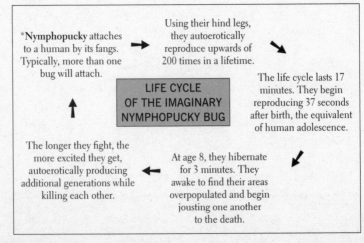

*Nymphopucky attaches to a human by its fangs. Typically, more than one bug will attach.

Using their hind legs, they autoerotically reproduce upwards of 200 times in a lifetime.

LIFE CYCLE OF THE IMAGINARY NYMPHOPUCKY BUG

The life cycle lasts 17 minutes. They begin reproducing 37 seconds after birth, the equivalent of human adolescence.

The longer they fight, the more excited they get, autoerotically producing additional generations while killing each other.

At age 8, they hibernate for 3 minutes. They awake to find their areas overpopulated and begin jousting one another to the death.

* How does Lucy's relationship with the look-alike puppet affect our experience of both her and the doll? If the technology someday permits it, and inanimate beings (puppets, dolls, sports mascots) can be cloned into living, breathing people, should they have the same rights as humans? Would an Inanimate Being Civil Rights Movement be a momentous historic occasion, or just a reason to get drunk and protest? How much fun would it be to kick the shit out of a living puppet, only to have your grandkids see it in a documentary fifty years from now? *For an interview with Ava Tardner, e-mail avatardner@gmail.com.*

WEDNESDAY

* Jimmish Wayne's superpower is his attention to detail. What is the difference between attention to detail—such as behavior shown by a professional domino tumbler—and obsessive compulsive disorder, such as making the same amount of right turns and left turns in the course of a year? Do you take a fair, morally responsible balance of left and right turns on your walk to work each day? Or are you a left piggy, just taking left after left after left turn, mindlessly moving in a circle and breathing oxygen and eating food without thinking about the ecological footprint your left piggyheadedness is costing our future? What do you think of the name Jimmish?
* Luck, retribution in the afterlife, coincidence, utter chaos, cause and effect, appearances, and disciplined planning—all these are principles held by our heroes and heroines. Are you still reading this guide? Why or why not?

THURSDAY

* Notoriety is a theme throughout the events that follow the Miracle. Eddie Scuthers, Normal's sidekick, and Ricardando Hill, Swagger's would-be assassin, accept their villainy so that their antics earn them fame and/or infamy. If all the villains in all literature and film throughout time got together at an annual convention, wouldn't you still have to put the serial killers at the same oddball table, just like at weddings, back behind the

speakers, near the kitchen entrance where they won't mistakenly get in any family photos? Imagine being on the cleaning staff at that Holiday Inn after the convention ends. Discuss. *For a prison interview with Eddie Scuthers, e-mail **eddiescuthers@ gmail.com**.*

* Discuss the prevalence of God throughout this story: Blackie Spin playing God; the media-created deity in Hank Swagger; Normal's fear of retribution from the gods for his actions; the ANN producers playing God over the viewers. If the Greeks had a God of War (Ares) and a God of the Sea (Poseidon), isn't it conceivable there were gods in charge of less important details? Imagine being the God of Shoehorns, or the God of Peanut Brittle. Speaking of gods, what has the God of Gravy been up to lately? There really hasn't been anything exciting on the gravy front in several hundred years.

FRIDAY

* With e-mail, text messaging, Twitter, and social networking, news travels the globe instantly. History seems to be happening at a more rapid pace, which is why Blackie believes a museum can be built in under a week. Assuming the world will never end, and we continue to add archives to the planet at a rate of 200 museums per year, won't we eventually run out of land on which to create fresh history? Is there a Museum of Museums anywhere, and if not, should we build one?

Your intimate knowledge of this event has led many in the media to speculate you were hired to ghostwrite Captain Swagger's autobiography.

Unequivocally not unfalse. Although even if it were true, I would be obligated to lie about it. I wanted to write this folktale's biography—as a folkographer, and not a fauxographer as many critics have alleged—because of our society's fascination with folk heroes. But when you really get in there and kick the tires on some of these supposed heroes, you'd be surprised by what might fall out. Johnny Appleseed was a transient, and kind of a litterbug. Robin Hood seems to be more of a woodland terrorist than a saint. And what, exactly, was Paul Revere, with his intimate knowledge of which guns were hidden where, doing riding around New England in the middle of the night? Blatant arms-trafficking claims there that history has conveniently overlooked.

The whole semen trafficking angle is—pardon us for saying so—a sticky topic.

True, but our culture is obsessed with celebrities—movies, magazines, celebrity tweets, clothing lines, reality TV shows. We gorge on celebrities. All it takes to shut down Europe is a World War, a soccer match, or a princess getting married. The whole collector culture intrigues me. I read somewhere that John Lennon's toilet once sold for $15,000. The most unique thing about celebrities that fans could own is DNA. So that would be either the blood or the semen, and the semen—pardon me for saying so—just had the right flavor for this historical event.

John Lennon, in absentia, is a major player in this little drama. Normal obviously has a soft spot for Lennon—do you think he would have risked his life for just any dead celebrity semen?

Well, obviously dead celebrities' paraphernalia is worth more than fresh celebrities'. I would say there are only a few dead celebrities with icon status who can muster that kind of value: John Lennon, Elvis Presley, John Wayne, maybe Albert Einstein. Assuming he existed, dollar for dollar Santa Claus's semen would probably fetch more per ounce. Normal might have fished Santa's semen out of a sunken plane.

In the Springer divorce settlement, Lucy is forced to wear a court-ordered puppet. Is that even legal?
Our justice system is a soap opera in itself. A few years back, I read about a Long Island doctor who wanted his cheating wife to return a kidney he donated to her years before. When you take into account the way Lucy destroyed that fish tank and nearly killed her husband, I think that judge let her off easy with the puppet sentence. Besides, our penal system is headed in the wrong direction. As our prisons march toward maximum occupancy, a better direction might be a "Jail or Dare" type of justice in which criminals can choose to either serve time in prison, or accept a judge's "Dare." The murderers and pedophiles and bad drivers—we just need to drop them in the middle of the ocean and leave their fate to the gods. But for the rest of the population, this whole "Jail or Dare" scenario would help lower taxes. We could even make it a game show—will he choose five-to-ten in Sing Sing, or will he accept the judge's dare to be the sole flight attendant aboard a red-eye from Los Angeles to New York where all the passengers are grizzly bears?

What other revelations popped up during the reporting of this event?
Two, in particular: 1) Public pay phones, once ubiquitous forms of communication, are rarely used today since every American, be they toddler or hobo, carries their own communicative device. The only people who use pay phones are unsuccessful criminals. If you see someone on a pay phone, crime is occurring; 2) Ninety-four percent of all business—legal or otherwise—is taking place at Starbucks these days. The war that will see Cuba colonized, and the subsequent theme-parkization, strip-mallitude, and tourismosis, was hammered out over muffins and lattes at a Starbucks on the corner of Ninety-third and Broadway.

With so many different sub-stories, it's hard to settle on who is the protagonist and who is the villain.
Folk heroes in most cultures are actually villains—Billy the Kid, Jesse James, George W. Bush—who become beloved by society for their antics. Everyone is an immoral person on a moral mission, all are looking out for their own selfish ends, but in their minds doing so for righteous reasons. It might be tidy that the villain loses and the hero wins, but that's not the way life works out.

What are you working on now?
A new folkography. I've become interested in a man out of Slancy, New York, who has grown sick of causes—Save the Whales, Save the Haitian Orphans, Support the Quadriplegic Marathon—and so he sarcastically and accidentally has begun a cause of his own that can only end badly: to raise money to build his own planet. Interesting villain.

NOTE ABOUT THE FONT

Our only request was that there be silly little mustaches stenciled on all the vowels, since the vowels seemed quite full of themselves during the writing of this folkography. But when the production department could not manage that minor detail, we lost interest in the font style altogether. Interesting note about the paper though: None of this was printed on recycled paper. It was printed on the epidermis of baby trees, uprooted before their dreams could be realized, then slammed into wood chippers and churned into pulp. If you lean your ear close to the binding, you can still hear their soft, woodsy whimpers.

NOTE ABOUT THE NOTE ABOUT THE FONT

For those of you reading on e-readers, by now you have realized you cannot stick your ear next to your screen to hear the paper weeping. Nor would you. The fact that you have gone digital proves you are more evolved than the Neanderthals who still read paper books. But for real—you traditional book readers who actually leaned your ears to hear the whimpers, we kind of love you for that.

ABOUT THE AUTHOR

JON METHVEN is a writer out of New York City, where he lives with his wife and son. He has worked as a paperboy, a dishwasher, a meat cook (everything medium well), a pizza deliveryman, a golf-course grounds crewman, a barbecue seasoning filter employee, an illegal barbecue seasoning filter employee since he was living in Australia without a work visa, a bartender, a mascot at Yankee Stadium (Mr. Popcorn), a journalist, a taste tester, and a cubicle dweller. He knows things you can only dream of knowing, or can learn if willing to work for minimum wage. His work has appeared in *The New York Times, Timothy McSweeney's Internet Tendency, n+1, New York* magazine, *The Awl, The Morning News,* Cracked. com, *Swink* magazine, and *The Smew.*